A CORNISH CHRISTMAS AT THE FARMHOUSE BAKERY

Linn B. Halton

HEAD *ZEUS*

An Aria Book

First published in the UK in 2023 by Head of Zeus,
part of Bloomsbury Publishing Plc

975312468

A catalogue record for this book is available from the British Library.

ISBN (PB): 9781804546437
ISBN (E): 9781804546413

Cover design: Head of Zeus

Typeset by Siliconchips Services Ltd UK

Printed and bound in Great Britain by
CPI Group (UK) Ltd, Croydon CR0 4YY

Head of Zeus
First Floor East
5–8 Hardwick Street
London EC1R 4RG

WWW.HEADOFZEUS.COM

To my dear friend Nicholas,
whose take on life is truly inspirational.

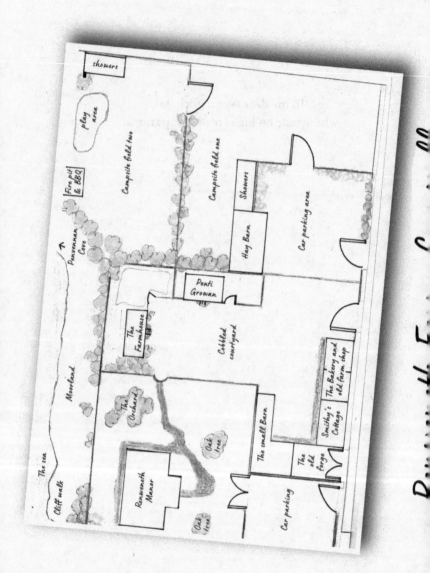

showers

play area

Campsite field two

Fire pit & BBQ

Penvennan Cove

Campsite field one

Showers

Hay Barn

Car parking area

Moorland

The sea

Cliff walk

Penti Growan

The Farmhouse

Cobbled courtyard

The Orchard

Oak tree

The small Barn

The old Forge

Smithy's Cottage

The Bakery and old farm shop

Renweneth Manor

Oak tree

Car parking

Prologue

Gabe Newman (Cappy)

Saturday, Twenty-Fourth September – Renweneth Farm's End of Summer Celebration

'Cappy, I had no idea Jess was going to...'

'Surprise us all by announcing that the two of you are a couple?' I chuckle, noting the pallor on Riley's face.

'Well, yes... I... um... meant to have a word with you about it before—'

He's a serious young man but if I was going to entrust anyone with my wonderful granddaughter's – and great-granddaughter's – future happiness, it would be Riley Warren. The poor chap looks a little shell-shocked but Jess obviously felt the timing tonight was right and I totally agree.

Celebrating how far Renweneth Farm has come since I handed over the running of it to Jess, is also a tribute to how hard Riley has worked as our resident builder. Following her divorce I feared she'd never find a man she would be willing to entrust her heart to again, and yet, against all the odds, I've been proven wrong. And my great-granddaughter, Lola, already regards Riley as a friend, which is a wonderful way to ease himself into her life on a permanent basis.

'It's obvious that neither of you were expecting this turn of events,' I admit, placing a hand firmly on his shoulder to reassure him. 'But I've seen the changes in you both and I couldn't be happier. Now, take a deep breath and get back to the party. Renweneth Farm is in good hands with the two of you at the helm. I know you have a few problems still to iron out before your new life falls into place, but together you'll get there. Of that I have no doubt at all.' And with that, I thrust out my hand to him; his handshake is firm and unwavering.

For me it's a blessing, but also the end of an era as I doubt Jess will be needing my input once Riley is living here. What am I going to do with myself now? I wonder.

OCTOBER

IVY

Stroud, Gloucestershire

I

It Never Rains but it Pours!

'Morning, Jess. What a way to kick off October. This is the greyest, murkiest start we've had to a Saturday in Stroud for a while. There's a threateningly dark band of clouds gathering on the horizon that doesn't bode well. Rain would just about cap it off,' I say with a sigh. 'Our customers will be wanting to scurry back home, not stop for coffee and cake. What's it like looking out over the beautiful Cornish coastline?'

'It's a little breezy here, Ivy, but the sky is blue, and the sun is out.'

I make a little moan. 'Oh… rub it in, why don't you?' I laugh. But it is good to hear my best friend's voice.

'The sea will be freezing, of course,' she concedes, 'but it looks so inviting as I gaze out the bedroom window. I've literally just grabbed my phone and was about to give you a call. I'm not long back from dropping Lola off at her friend Daisy's house. Erica has been rushed off her feet this week and I've been doing the school runs, so she's repaying the favour.'

In the sixteen months since my childhood friend, and her daughter Lola, left Gloucestershire to take over her granddad Cappy's farm, Jess and Erica have become firm friends. I have a lot of admiration for Daisy's mum Erica; she's trying to set up a small business from home on a shoestring budget.

'Oh… how I wish I was there with you. Give Erica my best regards, won't you,' I ask.

'I will. It's hard to believe that this time last week you and Adam were here in the garden of Renweneth Manor joining in with the celebrations for our first end-of-summer party,' Jess remarks, wistfully.

'We had an amazing time! And announcing that you and Riley are planning a future together put a big smile on a lot of faces,' I exclaim.

'I think it raised a few eyebrows, too.'

That included my husband, Adam. Even I only recently discovered that what began as a simple friendship, formed by working together as employer and employee, had secretly turned into quite a passionate affair. It's always the quiet ones who surprise you the most, I smile to myself. 'Lola was jumping around, she was so excited and the way Cappy embraced Riley, made me a little tearful.'

'It's true to say that a lot has happened in a short space of time but I've never been more sure of anything, Ivy. Ironically, it's Riley who is still adjusting to being treated like one of the family and not just the hired help. I don't think that will change until he's sorted out the problems with his ex and decided what to do with his beautiful cottage.'

'That's understandable, Jess.' Without realising it I let out a sigh. 'Life is seldom straightforward, is it?'

'You sound like you're flagging, Ivy. That's not like you.'

'I am a little.' My determination to stay upbeat didn't last long and now Jess is wondering what's up.

'Vyvyan was under the impression you were due to sign your new lease a few days ago.'

'Me, too,' I admit. Vyvyan is Jess's marketing manager at Renweneth Farm. Jess has already refurbished The Farmhouse and completed phase one in repurposing a series of old stone cottages set around a cobbled courtyard. She also runs an extensive campsite. Being set in the middle of moorland, and a stone's throw from the sea, it's the perfect place to reconnect with nature. Vyvyan has been helping me with my lease renewal negotiations on the shop I rent, as her career began in property management.

'Fingers crossed my landlord, Mr Williams, will be dropping the papers in today for me to sign. When I opened up this morning there was a trail of muddy footprints from the hallway to the back door. Which means he was obviously in last night and has finally cleared out the two rooms on the first floor that he's been using as storage space. I've just finished mopping the floor and I'm seething. I left it spotless when I locked up yesterday. Still, it's a positive sign and a bit of a relief although I'd have felt even better to see an A4 envelope waiting for me to open as he promised.'

'He caved in and is going to rent you the whole building, then? You'll be able to double the number of tables, which is wonderful news, Ivy!'

It is, but my nerves are now beginning to get the better of me. Mr Williams is a difficult man when it comes to communication. We've always received post here for him and once a week his assistant calls in to collect what is often quite a little pile. The man himself is notoriously hard to contact. His phone always goes straight to voicemail, and he seldom replies if you leave a message.

'I can't relax until I've signed on the dotted line, Jess. Honestly, that man is so disorganised and my patience is wearing thin.'

'At least things are moving in the right direction, Ivy,' Jess points out. 'Although it's cutting it fine, which isn't fair on you. Doesn't the old lease run out at the end of the month?'

'Yes. To be honest, if he hadn't agreed to letting me have the first-floor space too, I would have been forced to look elsewhere. As you know, it's a prime spot but it's a small building wedged between two bigger retail outlets. While The Cake and Coffee Emporium is making a profit, I desperately need to expand the business, or Adam and I will never be able to afford to buy our own home. When the weather is good, having the tables outside can double my daily take, but when the weather is inclement, some days I'm only just covering the bills.'

'That was going to be my next question. How's Adam doing?'

A wave of sadness hits me full-on as my mind begins to wander. I instantly picture Adam's face as he leant in to kiss me goodbye this morning. He was trying so hard to appear upbeat as he headed out for the day.

'Adam got a phone call late yesterday afternoon to say that the job he was due to start on Monday has been postponed. Money problems, apparently. Honestly, Jess, it's totally out of order for someone to pull out at the last moment. Either the funds are in place or they're not, and what's the likelihood of an unexpected change of circumstances happening so close to the start date? It's mean, that's what it is. Adam had already purchased a lot of the materials he needed to make a start.'

'Heck! It was a big job, too, wasn't it? How did Adam take it?'

'He put on a brave face but he's out doing the rounds today, desperately trying to find some work for the next three weeks.' I can't help feeling both gutted and angry on his behalf.

'Oh, Ivy. I'm terribly sorry to hear that. It was the last thing you needed right now. Adam just can't seem to catch a break, can he?'

I let out a soft groan. Jess thinks the world of Adam, and she knows this is yet another setback when he's trying to go it alone. Having walked off a job when the building company he was contracted to decided they were only going to pay him for four days' work, on a job that was already in its fifth day, I was proud of him. And rightly so. The company were doing the same thing to his mates, too, and someone had to make a stand. At least we don't have children yet, and we're not tied into a hefty mortgage, so I guess we're lucky in that respect.

'It doesn't seem like it, Jess. Once I've signed the lease that'll lift his spirits. I'll get four, four-seater tables in each of the two new rooms and one of them looks out over the main thoroughfare. It's going to make a huge difference to our income and, hopefully, will take the pressure off Adam for the time being.'

'Adam said that starting out on his own again was going to be tough, but it's been brutal, Ivy, hasn't it?'

'Yes. It reminded him why he got into contract work in the first place. But they're always putting pressure on the guys to speed up and that means cutting corners. It's wrong and we all know it. Often, it's simply to boost their bottom line so both the customer and the contractors lose out, just in different ways, and yet the profit margin increases.'

Jess tuts. 'I'll keep my fingers crossed he finds some work to tide him over, quickly. And, Ivy, text me when you're holding that lease in your hands, won't you?'

I laugh, picturing myself doing just that and, if I'm lucky, within the next hour or so now that Mr Williams has officially vacated the property.

'I will. I'm leant against the windowsill in the now-empty first-floor room at the front, waiting for the floor to dry but from the sound of it there's a queue downstairs. That'll teach me to work backwards from the door!'

Jess gives a little half-hearted laugh at my attempt to lighten the moment. 'Don't worry, Ivy, I think you're due for some good luck, so let's hope today is the start of it. Speak soon, my dear friend!'

Adam never works late on a Saturday, but it's almost five o'clock when the sound of the front door opening makes me rush out into the hallway. I watch as Adam hangs up his jacket.

'What's up?' He looks at me askance.

My frown relaxes a little, but not the tension in my neck and shoulders. 'Your phone has been going straight to voicemail,' I chide him.

'Oh. I expect it's out of charge. It's been a rather depressing day chasing my tail and getting nowhere. Sorry, Ivy.'

Adam pulls me into his arms, and we stand there hugging each other, trying to shake off the troubles of the day. He places his hand under my chin, tilting my head back a little so he can gaze down into my eyes.

'You look weary, honey.'

Suddenly, I can feel the tears begin to well up and his look intensifies. 'What's wrong?'

I swallow hard, forcing myself to regain control. 'Mr Williams has decided to sell the shop, rather than lease it.'

I didn't think I had any tears left in me, but it seems I could be wrong about that. When I got the call late afternoon, I'd locked myself in the cloakroom at work and literally sobbed my heart out for about twenty minutes. Poor Rach didn't know what was going on. Tears won't solve my problems though, and I promised myself I wouldn't add to Adam's worries.

He looks understandably shaken for a moment, then I can see his mind frantically ticking over. 'I know that's not what we planned, Ivy, but if we use our nest egg... with your increased earnings maybe we can—'

'Not to me.'

He shakes his head, looking confused. 'What do you mean?'

'Mr Williams already has a buyer. His assistant called to inform me that contracts were exchanged yesterday and I need to vacate the premises at the end of October.'

'What?' The word erupts from Adam's mouth like a pistol shot.

I grab his hand, leading him into the kitchen.

'Come on, the kettle is boiled. I've been well and truly played, Adam. Mr Williams cleared his stuff out last night because he's too cowardly to face me.'

'Can he back out of your negotiations just like that?'

Adam slumps down onto a chair, undoing the laces on his work boots as I shovel coffee granules into two mugs. I so wanted to be able to give him some good news and I don't have the heart to turn around to see his expression. Keeping my back to him, I continue talking.

'Negotiations are just that and it's not a done deal until both parties have signed on the dotted line. If he was renting it to someone else maybe I could have... I don't know... offered to up the rent. In all honesty, he's been utterly useless from day one. He didn't want to tell me until he had the deposit in his account; I was the backup plan if anything went wrong. It's immoral but not illegal. However, I feel like a complete and utter fool.'

Our eyes meet as I carry the coffee mugs over to join Adam at the table.

'It should be you sitting here, Ivy, and me making that for you,' he mutters, softly. 'I'm sorry about my phone, I really mean it. It was selfish of me. My charging lead wasn't in the pickup, but I knew it was a big day for you and I let my own problems block out everything else.'

'Hey, I understand. Everything happens for a reason. You know I truly believe that, but right now it's hard to see the *why* of it.'

Adam looks just as devastated as I feel. 'Me neither, Ivy. It's one knock-back after another. So what's the plan?'

'I spent over an hour this afternoon phoning around various rental agencies but there's nothing at all on the market in my price range in the centre of Stroud. My budget for the fitting-out costs just wouldn't stretch to a full-size retail unit. I did get a call-back about some available space in a garden centre, though. It's the other side of Stonehouse, so further to drive, but it's an interesting one because all that's required is a couple of days' notice to take up occupancy.'

'Hmm... that might be a bit of a red flag. Even so, it's worth taking a look at it.'

I shrug my shoulders. 'In truth, it's that or – come the last day of October – working from our impossibly tiny kitchen here to honour the hamper and party food orders I have booked in via the website.'

He puts his hand up to stop me. 'Hang on a second, you're not shutting the business down, are you?'

It's horrible to watch as Adam begins to realise what this means. Suddenly, my business is worth nothing.

'Wherever I work from, if it's not in the centre of town I've lost eighty per cent of my income overnight. It's all gone, just like that!' I click my fingers in the air. 'I have no choice in the matter, Adam. What I desperately need is access to a commercial kitchen and quickly, to fulfil the click-and-collect orders already in the system for November. If I start letting customers down, there'll be no point setting up somewhere new, even if I can find the right property at the right price.'

Adam raises his eyebrows, letting out a huge sigh. 'Strewth, Ivy, no wonder you're reeling. I'm having trouble taking this in.'

Sitting back in my chair, I lift the coffee mug to my lips and gaze at him over the top of it. That impossibly curly blond hair of his that he constantly sweeps away from his eyes always melts my heart. He is my gentle giant, my rock. Solid muscle from the hours he spends in the gym, but inside he's a softie with a heart of gold.

I'm immediately transported back eighteen months to the day of our wedding. It was the lavish affair that our parents and, at the time, both Adam and I wanted. Now I wonder whether it was an extravagance for which we're about to pay the price. Back then, our future was looking rosy.

'Have you… do you have any plans for this coming Monday?' I ask, hesitantly. If he'd had good news, Adam wouldn't have greeted me wearing such a dispirited look.

'No. A couple of my contacts said they'd keep my number handy in case they need any extra help, or someone lets them down, but it's a waiting game. I'm all yours.' The depth of his smile is enough to make my heart skip a beat. He'd do anything for me.

'If you could step in for me at the café for a couple of hours after lunch, while I drive over to scope out the garden centre, that would be amazing. I'll ring the agent first thing Monday morning to confirm the time of my appointment. I'm sure some of our customers will appreciate having a hunky builder serving them coffee and cake for a change,' I quip – anything to brighten this dire conversation.

Adam grins back at me. 'Really?'

'You'd be surprised.' I wink at him. 'If it's dry, in between, do a little sweeping up outside while you're there. Who knows, you might entice a few first-timers through the door.' The moment I say that it hits me square in the gut that whatever I do between now and the end of the month is wasted, because after that the café is going to be turned into a shoe repair shop.

Increasingly this world we live in makes less and less sense to me. I don't deserve this any more than Adam deserves what he's been put through. All we've ever done is work hard and yet unscrupulous people like my landlord, and his former boss, trample over us for the sake of making an even bigger profit. Maybe we're just naïve and it's time to wise up.

'Ivy, it's only me. Sorry it's late… you aren't in bed, are you?'

'No, but not far from it, Jess.' I stifle a yawn. 'I did mean to text you but, uh… hang on a sec.' I pull the phone away from my ear to shout up to Adam. 'I'm just on a call, babe. I'll be up in a few minutes.'

'Okay,' his voice filters back to me. 'I'm going to read for a bit.'

I saunter out to the kitchen and shut the door behind me. 'Sorry, Jess. It's been a fraught day all round.'

'Oh no…'

'Yep. Mr Williams has sold the shop. The snake – he never even breathed a word of that to me and I'm fuming. I was obviously his backup option if the sale didn't go through. Unfortunately for me they exchanged contracts yesterday, which is why he cleared his things out overnight. His assistant made the call to inform me and I could tell he was really embarrassed about the way I've been treated.'

'What on earth will you do? Time isn't on your side,' Jess blurts out, sounding scandalised on my behalf.

'There's only one option on the table and it's a long shot. It's not even a shop, it's in a garden centre several miles away.

It used to be a small in-house café, but they shut it down. The thing is, I have a stack of online click-and-collect party catering and bespoke hamper orders booked through until the end of November. I wish now I hadn't started the new initiative. All that advertising and effort wasted; come Monday, I'm going to have to turn people away. I can't cope with a delivery service but unless I have an outlet up and running, I can't even honour the bookings I have in the pipeline. As for The Cake and Coffee Emporium, without a town-centre location it's dead in the water.'

Jess's sharp intake of breath fills my heart with dread. She immediately understands the full impact of what I'm telling her.

'Assuming you can set up some sort of kitchen at this garden centre, there's bound to be some passing trade. Maybe you'll be able to continue to run the click-and-collect service via the website and kick-start the café at the same time?' Jess suggests, hopefully.

'Most of the leads came from the flyers I put in the café directing people to the website. It's too new; there's not enough traffic to begin with. I have a fitting-out budget I'd set aside for the two rooms I thought I was gaining at the old premises, and some capital expenditure earmarked for additional equipment for the kitchen, but online advertising is costly. My budget would probably be spent before I'm able to see enough of a return to pay the bills and keep out of debt. That's assuming I have a proper commercial kitchen to work from, of course. I have no idea what the set-up is like at the garden centre.'

'You can't give up on your dream, Ivy. There must be a way around it. Can you rent kitchen space from a bigger concern, or find some shared space until something else comes on the market?'

'There's no point in kidding myself, Jess. Every agent I've talked to has been straight with me. They all said that small units are few and far between and I should double my budget, which isn't an option.'

My mind hasn't switched off and I think I've considered every idea, no matter how crazy, and ended up back at the same place. 'The hard truth of it is that unless I can remain in the centre of Stroud, I no longer have a viable business. I'm going to check out the garden centre on Monday as a short-term solution and I have agents promising they'll call me the minute they take on a new rental. But there's no point if I can't afford it anyway.'

'Oh, Ivy…'

'Maybe I'm not meant to run a business, Jess. I should imagine it's a bit like having a baby – until you go through the process you have no idea what you're taking on. I'm not sure I want to do it again.'

'Don't say that. It wasn't your fault.'

'I believed what I wanted to believe, Jess, even though I knew I was dealing with a person I couldn't trust. It was probably more hopium than stupidity, but the fault was mine. Anyway, this will put a smile on your face. Adam is going to cover for me at the café on Monday. It will certainly make the day of my regular eleven o'clock ladies – the *coffee before lunch brigade*, they call themselves. They've doubled in numbers in the last year. Not one of them is a day under seventy-five and they're all darlings! It's funny that we get the widows, but not the widowers, for some reason.'

Jess gives a chuckle. 'Men don't really do coffee mornings, not when they're on their own – do they? How many lonely men would benefit from a bit of friendly banter, a cup of excellent coffee and a homemade slice of cake in good company?'

'If a miracle happens, I might try to tap into that market, Jess.'

'Hang out for *coffee, cake and conversation at eleven*,' she muses. 'It sounds like it has potential.'

My best buddy is still the only one who can cheer me up when I'm feeling down; even though she ended up escaping to Cornwall to nurse her broken heart. When you've been married for nine years and your other half suddenly discovers they're no longer in love with you, it's devastating. I've seen that first-hand, with Jess. But my, she's certainly bounced back. Jess and her daughter, Lola, are now living a dream life. Even though that, like everything else, has its highs and lows their future looks bright.

'Actually, Ivy, I was calling to run something past you.'

'Sorry, I didn't mean to bombard you with my doom and gloom! How is everything going at your end?'

'Great. Riley is struggling a bit, as we begin the next phase of the renovation work. Until he's fixed the roof on the small barn, we're at a standstill and none of his contacts are available at short notice. I mentioned to him that Adam is looking for work, but I don't know how you'd feel about Riley reaching out to him?'

I wasn't expecting that. After her divorce from Ben, Jess arrived at the farm in need of a good builder. They came and went, as often happens until Mr Fix-It – Riley Warren – turned up. He, too, has a child from his previous relationship, so both he and Jess are taking it slowly. But if ever there was a perfect match, they embody it. He lives on the other side of the moor, in what was formerly a derelict cottage that he renovated himself. They live apart for now, but together they're the force behind Renweneth Farm.

'That's so thoughtful of you, Jess. I mean, suddenly we've gone from two fairly consistent incomes, down to one, and whatever work Adam can get is a bonus.' As things stand, my income isn't going to continue for much longer and every penny counts.

Jess tuts to herself, sadly. 'Look, I know the thought of Adam working away from home isn't ideal, particularly when you're going through a traumatic time yourself. That's why I thought I'd sound you out first, Ivy. At a time like this you need to be together – I get that. But Adam wouldn't have to pay out for accommodation or meals and Riley would be very grateful, because I don't do heights. Insulation I can turn my hand to, but plasterboard is heavy and even though I call it the small barn, you've seen the size of it. It'll mean working Monday to Friday, so Adam would be back with you for weekends. Just think about it and let me know either way. If I don't employ Adam, then it'll be a case of waiting until someone local can lend a hand, but he gets on so well with Riley, I had to ask.'

Ever so discreetly, Jess is trying to help me and Adam. Now that's what a true friend does and it's because of things like that, Jess will always be a second sister to me. On the other hand, my biological sister, Ursula, is a law unto herself and if we speak three times a year, that's a lot. She's the only divorcee I know who still has date nights with her ex-husband. Why, I have no idea, as he's sadly lacking when it comes to common sense, which means he causes a lot of his own problems and I made the mistake of telling her that. However, my gorgeous niece, Tillie, at eighteen months old is a real joy, and when she's with Mum I get to spend time with her. I'm conscious that my dear friend is waiting for my response.

'You're the best friend ever, Jess. I always knew that, of course. I think it might be nice if Riley approaches Adam direct. I'm sure that after one stint working at the café, Adam will be only too delighted to get hands-on, replacing that roof on the barn and hauling plasterboard around!'

'Stay positive, Ivy. You never know what's around the next corner. Just look at my situation. At one point I felt so lost that I didn't think I'd recover. Now I have Renweneth Farm and Riley. No one saw that coming, including me.'

'I know and I will. Promise. Enjoy the rest of your weekend, Jess, and thank you!'

2

A Chink of Light on the Horizon

You know that feeling when you have a decision to make, and you know you're going to live to regret it? Well, that's me now on a chilly, grey Monday morning. I'm standing inside a series of buildings, some of which are interconnecting greenhouses, which make up Riverside Garden Centre.

'Hi, my name is Ivy and I'm here to see Delia.' The woman standing the other side of the counter, using a handheld machine to price up a box of fat balls, gives me a pleasant smile.

'That's me!'

I thrust out my hand and we shake. 'It's very kind of you to show me around, Delia.'

She turns her head. 'Tom, Ivy's here,' she calls out and a much older man with a slight limp, comes hurrying over.

'Nice to meet you, Ivy,' he says, as he takes over from Delia.

'Now, Dad, I want the labels to go on the bottom of the tags so the customers can still read the instructions.'

'Got it!' he replies, giving me a charming grin.

'Follow me, Ivy. The kitchen is in the far corner, next to the gift shop.'

As we walk through, I only see two other staff and yet it's a sprawling site. Admittedly, there are no more than a dozen customers at most browsing; the place feels deserted.

'For the past two years we've opened the café in the spring and summer months and there's enough trade to keep two members of staff busy. It's quieter outside of that period, naturally, and as our focus now is more on supplying plants to the trade, my father and I decided to shut it down.'

Oh dear. Delia and her father are lovely people but even before I see the kitchen, I know this isn't for me. As we walk, I ask the usual questions: what the opening times are, do they have any access restrictions to the site and what the internet connection is like. Delia's answers are honest and there's nothing to really put me off. But if their focus is now on the wholesale side it means they aren't getting enough footfall to make it viable on a retail basis.

'And this is the kitchen. The appliances are all less than three years old. Obviously, it needs a bit of a spring clean as it's been shut since mid-September.'

I'm pleasantly surprised. The kitchen facilities are much better than I'd expected. Everything is commercial grade, with stainless steel workbenches and good quality fixtures and fittings. No wonder they're eager to rent it out, as this represents quite an investment. I wander around and there are probably twenty tables in a light and airy space. It's chilly, but none of the overhead heaters are turned on. The big problem for me is how to get people here. Advertising is costly and the only access road is a very narrow, winding lane that goes on for several miles.

'What do you think?' Delia asks, a lift in her voice.

I imagine her crossing her fingers on the hand that she has tucked away out of sight.

This is tough. 'You've clearly spent a lot of money to set this up, Delia. And the kitchen is perfect for my needs. My only problem is that because it's not up and running as a going concern, I simply don't have the time, or the budget, to get the café re-established. Some of my regulars would probably follow me here, but the truth is that I'd need a constant flow of new customers just to make a living.'

She looks crestfallen. 'I understand, Ivy. Dad and I thought it was a bit of a long shot. You're the second person to consider it and they said the exact same thing.'

'I'm sorry I can't make it work. It's a lovely setting and all the plants look so well-tended.'

Delia gives me a knowing smile. 'Dad has green fingers and I doubt there was a single day when I was growing up that I wasn't at his side helping him take cuttings, or deadheading. It's time for us to focus on what we do best.' As she walks me back to the entrance, she continues to chatter away. 'We'll probably end up using this area to expand our range of exotic plants. There's quite a market for that right now.'

'Well, thank you so much for the tour. I'll be pointing my mother in your direction as she loves houseplants and you have some wonderful aloe vera, I noticed.'

We shake hands cordially and I give her a grateful smile. I've lived in Stroud all my life, but never once have I seen an ad for this garden centre. It's not even marked up on the turnoff and after that it's probably a good two miles down a one-track lane with infrequent passing places.

I guess it's a case of waiting to see where fate steers me next, but I'm not holding my breath as what I need is little short of a miracle.

'How did Adam get on?' I ask my full-time assistant, Rach. She gives me a mirthful grin as she pulls a tray of sponge cake out of the oven.

'He was great. The customers were all whispering about him, Ivy. You know… he's a hunk and he's so polite. I'm sorry to break the news that being a waiter isn't really his forte, though. It's the little things… like remembering the napkins and forks.' She gives a derisory little laugh. 'Did you tell him to sweep up outside? He disappeared for a while and suddenly, we had a rush on!'

I give her a knowing wink and she shakes her head at me. 'Really?'

'It sounds like it worked. I hope he didn't get under your feet.'

'Adam did his best, bless him. You have a real treasure of a man there, Ivy – you do know that?'

'I do.'

'Oh, Ivy. I can tell from your face that the garden centre isn't an option?' She grimaces.

'No. The lane leading down to it is really narrow and with hardly any lay-bys. It seemed to go on forever. In all honesty, it's more suited to wholesale than retail, as no one could expect a hulking big lorry to reverse up if you meet one head-on. It would be a nightmare for a nervous driver. I think that's partly why they couldn't make a real go of the café in the first place.' It's hard not to look dejected.

'This is so unfair, Ivy. Mr Williams isn't fit to be a landlord.'

I can't dispute that.

'Look, Rach, there's no way to put a good spin on this. When we close the doors and hand back the keys, that's it.'

This doesn't just impact me and Rach, who has a young family, but my two part-timers and a lady who helps on Saturdays if any of us are on holiday.

'I love working with you, Ivy, you've taught me so much. I have some savings but I need a regular income coming in.'

'I know. We're a good duo, Rach. You're definitely the queen when it comes to icing a cake, whereas I'm just the humble baker,' I stress. 'Obviously, if anything new comes on the market the agents will contact me immediately, but they've already warned me to think about doubling my budget. My only other option is to look for space within another outlet. It's a long shot, but I thought I'd wander around the town centre to see if I can spot anywhere with potential.'

'Several of the shops have stockrooms above them rather than flats, Ivy. You could be onto something there, as long as there's a separate entrance. Depending on where a property is situated, some of them have spectacular views out over the hills, which would make for a great tearoom.'

My mind was going off in that direction, too.

'With overheads rising all the time, I was thinking about Kit and Craft Galore, in particular. It's a massive premises and they only use the ground floor. I figure anything is worth a shot.' Rach's face brightens as I turn to greet a customer.

'Hello, Mrs Stuart. The usual for you and your sister?'

'Of course! What's the cake of the day, Ivy?'

I point to the glass-covered cake stand next to the display of muffins. 'Lemon pound cake with a lemon and ginger drizzle.'

'Perfect!'

'Take a seat and we'll pop that over to you. Can I ask you a quick question?'

Mrs Stuart looks at me, raising an eyebrow. 'Of course.'

'Have you ever heard of the Riverside Garden Centre?'

She pauses, then shakes her head. 'Can't say I have.' She does a half-turn, waving her sister over to the counter. 'Martha, you love plants. Have you been to the Riverside Garden Centre?'

'No, where is it?' Martha looks puzzled.

'It's a twenty-minute drive away,' I interrupt. 'Near Stonehouse. We're having to vacate this premises at the end of the month and I'm searching for a new location.'

Both ladies look at me as if I've just dropped a bombshell.

'You're moving, Ivy? Why?'

'This place is going to be turned into a shoe repair shop.'

'I can't believe what we're hearing! Where will we go for our afternoon chat over coffee and cake?' Martha turns to face her sister and I realise it's time to put a notice in the window. But first I need to contact the rest of my staff and let them know the garden centre isn't a contender. It's heart-breaking to deliver the unwelcome news that I don't have a solution, but they need to know before word gets out.

Rachel hurries off to make two cappuccinos as I assure both ladies that I'm going to do my utmost to find a new spot somewhere close by. However, the chance of that is slim to impossible, and I know it.

Arriving home feeling decidedly downbeat and drained, Adam, on the other hand, seems quite perky as I walk into the kitchen. He has a pot of water bubbling away on the hob and pops in a dish of shop-bought fresh pasta.

'The sauce is simmering, and this will only take a few minutes to cook.'

'That's a big smile you're wearing. And thanks for stepping in to do a couple of hours helping Rach today. It meant a lot.'

Adam hurries forward to wrap his arms around me. 'I did my best, Ivy, but I'm not sure Rach would be in a hurry to have me back. I'm a bit ham-fisted at times.' He places a kiss on the tip of my nose, anxious to get back to stirring the saucepans. 'Take a seat. You deserve a little spoiling after the day you've had. I was so sorry to read your text about the garden centre. The fact that the café wasn't up and running was a bit of a giveaway, wasn't it?'

I shrug my shoulders. 'I guess so. I called each of the girls this afternoon and put a sign up in the window at the end of the day. It's only fair to let our customers know what's happening as word is going to get out pretty quickly. I'm dreading tomorrow as everyone is going to be asking the same thing – where are we moving to – and the answer is we're shutting down.'

He turns to pull out a chair for me. 'Sit and relax; I'll get you a glass of wine. One door shuts, another opens. Something will turn up.'

'I know.' I sigh dejectedly as I slump down into the chair.

Adam is already popping the cork on a bottle and he turns, glancing at me empathetically over his shoulder. He looks so darned cute standing there. And he's cooking his signature tomato and basil sauce, which smells divine.

'I do have some news but I'm not sure how you're going to feel about it.' I can tell from his stance how edgy he's feeling. And the fact that he's turned away from me.

'I contacted Greystoke and Sons Building Limited; they've

asked to see my CV. In the meantime, I've been offered a couple of weeks' general building work.'

I'm stunned. 'The temporary work is good news but you're applying for a permanent position with one of the big firms?'

'Don't sound so disappointed, Ivy, please hear me out. We're not in a good position right now and with some temporary work to fill the gap, this will allow you some breathing space. After speaking to the HR manager at Greystoke, who also happens to be one of the sons, I'm in with a real chance of snagging an interview. We're not talking about being taken on as a carpenter, or a plumber, but a foreman's job. He said they're looking for people with all-round experience to train in-house and it's a generous package.'

'But they cover the whole of the south-west, don't they?' There's an awkward pause as Adam hurries over to the sink to strain the pasta.

'That's the only drawback. I'm not selling out, Ivy, if that's what you think. This is a solid opportunity for me.' He sounds upbeat, but I don't see this as a cause to celebrate. It means his dream of being in total control of his working life is slipping away and he'll be back on the treadmill.

When he's finally ready to join me, he gives me a sheepish look. 'Obviously, going back into employment wasn't a part of the plan, Ivy, but this is different. It's not contracting, it's a good job with an established company. It's a big jump up for me in terms of responsibility, in a role I know I can do justice. It comes with a hefty hike in salary, which will ease things for us financially.'

With no solution of my own in sight, I can't argue with his reasoning.

'Just don't go jumping into anything too quickly, Adam. Think about what it's going to mean going forward. We can live off our savings for a while if necessary.'

I twirl some pasta around my fork, avoiding eye contact.

'No, Ivy, our savings are for a deposit on our dream house.

I have no intention of letting it dwindle, it represents eighteen months of us both watching every penny we spend.'

Adam is my rock, and I knew he was the man I was supposed to be with from the moment I first set eyes on him. Having wasted five years being engaged to someone who wanted a relationship of convenience, where we lived separate lives most of the time, finding true love with Adam turned my world upside down. I'm turning thirty next year and the life I'd envisaged from a young age still feels like a distant dream. I have the perfect man, but will we ever get on that mortgage ladder and put down roots? And as for the two children, a dog, and a cat... I find myself sighing, wistfully. Maybe I watch too many romantic films where the happy-ever-after just falls into place.

'You've gone very quiet,' Adam prompts me.

'If you're doing this for you, then I'm perfectly fine with it. But if you're settling because of my situation, that would weigh heavily on my heart, Adam.'

'I am truly excited about it, Ivy. Now, let's talk about your day.'

It's hard to know where to begin.

'I'm worried about Rach and what she'll do. And that stack of orders we have to fill in November. I've put word out among the other retailers that I'm looking for space, even if it's temporary. But if someone does come forward, it'll take time to get everything set up.'

He's studying my face. 'You have a lead?'

'Maybe. I spoke to the owner of Kit and Craft Galore. He runs the shop with his wife. I often wondered how they make ends meet, as it's a massive shop and it's not as if people are queuing out the door. Apparently, they run a thriving online business from there, too. I should have guessed. He showed me around the first floor. It was a flat at one time and it has a small kitchen, a bathroom and two large bedrooms. Then there's a staircase to a second floor, which is open plan. It's used purely as a stockroom and office. They have two people packing up online orders from there ready for dispatch.'

Adam puts down his fork, sitting back in his chair as he processes the information. 'If the kitchen is small, you'd have to do your baking offsite, and would you get enough income from two rooms?'

I stare down at my plate, still toying with the pasta on the end of my fork. 'No, but he's about to move his upstairs operation. The intention is to renovate the top two floors and turn it into a spacious flat to rent out. I very subtly pointed out that every one of my customers would walk through his sales floor on their way to get their coffee and cake.'

Adam beams at me. 'You sure have a good business head on you, Ivy.'

'They're going to think about it. It might not come to anything, and the fitting-out costs would be at my expense, but it's a stone's throw away from our current location. It could be the perfect answer, although I'd still have a short-term problem. It could take several months to seal the deal and get everything kitted out.'

'Look, even if this doesn't work out, it just goes to show that there are options out there. You simply need to keep looking. In the meantime…' He pauses to glance at me a little bashfully. 'Anyway, the temporary work is with Riley. He's been in touch and he's desperate for someone to give him a hand.'

I plaster on a fake smile, knowing it's a lifeline we desperately need, but the thought of Adam being down in Cornwall while I'm here all alone is unsettling. *It's time to suck it up, Ivy,* I tell myself. *Nothing worth having comes easy and it's time to get real.*

'That's wonderful, babe,' I exclaim, feeling that any good news at this point is welcome.

His face changes from deadpan to sporting a wayward little smile in seconds. 'It's not ideal, I appreciate that, Ivy. I'll be back at weekends and it'll be better than wasting fuel looking for work and coming up with nothing. Let's not worry about Greystoke. If I don't get an interview, something else will turn up, trust me. I feel the same way about you, Ivy.'

We both push back on our chairs and as soon as Adam's arms are wrapped around me, I know we'll get through this. That's not to say it's going to be easy, but this time next year who knows where we'll be? A new café, a new job for Adam, and maybe… just maybe… the keys to our own home? Every cloud has a silver lining and from now on that's what I'm focusing on.

ADAM
Renweneth Farm, Cornwall

3

A Bird's Eye View

Riley and I are sitting astride the ridge on the roof of the small barn at the farm. It's a week to the day since Ivy and I sat around our kitchen table and realised our lives were about to change forever in ways we couldn't have anticipated. It's still sinking in and there are no guarantees, but at least I'm working.

In the gap between the abandoned Renweneth Manor and the recently renovated farmhouse, the sea is a vista of blue. The sky is cloudless and the water sparkles. There's a bit of a breeze and the tip of my nose is cold, but it's refreshing.

'Wow – the view from up here is unbelievable, Riley! This is just the tonic I needed.'

He starts laughing. 'That leaves me scratching my head, mate, as a pint does it for me, but you're welcome, buddy. Having you here until the end of the month means the worst of this part of the project will be out the way. Jess isn't happy when I assign her to smaller jobs but to be honest an inexperienced pair of hands would have slowed me down.' He passes me a couple of ridge tiles and I place them in the bucket ready to lower it down to the scaffolding platform when it's full.

'On a day like this who wants to work inside?' I reflect. A part of me is trying hard to push away the image of Ivy's eyes, glistening with tears, when I kissed her goodbye at four-thirty this morning. It was tough, but if I get a job with Greystoke, spending periods of time away from home could become the norm for us. 'It's great to see The Farmhouse Bakery doing well. Once the barn is open for business with a variety of smaller retailers, Renweneth will be quite an asset to this small community.'

'That's the general idea, but—'

'I'm coming up!' a voice calls out and moments later Jess's head appears. 'Ooh, my legs feel a bit shaky up here,' she confesses, both hands grasping on to the metalwork so hard they start to turn white. Give the woman her due, she takes a moment to get her bearings then pulls two insulated mugs from her bulging coat pockets.

'Here you go, guys. Wish I'd brought one for myself so I could join you.' Her eyes light up as she grins at us. 'This is an exciting day for me, and you brought the sun with you, Adam. We had a storm over the weekend but the forecast for the next few days is that it's going to be a bit nippy, but dry.'

'Rain wouldn't have stopped us, eh, Riley?' I pass him one of the mugs and then take a grateful sip. 'Thanks, Jess, much appreciated.'

Jess's smile fades. 'How was the drive down?'

What she really wants to know is how Ivy was when I left her. 'Fine. Not much traffic at that time of the morning and it's a straight run. If you get a chance to give Ivy a call, let me know how she's doing. She made me promise I wouldn't be on the phone every five minutes.' I roll my eyes.

'I will, Adam. Just take it one day at a time. It's an art I've had to master and look who turned up? Riley, my Mr Fix-It.'

Riley eases his beanie hat further down over his ears with one hand, while he drinks his coffee from the other. 'Hey, I'm good for more than fixing things!'

The banter between them is flirtatious and it's good to see Jess finally finding the personal happiness she deserves. As for taking over the farm, it's a huge responsibility and a potential money pit. But she has a good head for business, plus a lot of common sense. Now Riley is in her life, I think that between the two of them they'll put Renweneth Farm firmly on the map.

'Is Cappy around?' I enquire, but she shakes her head.

'No. He's back in Gloucestershire for the next couple of days. He's moving some of his personal stuff into storage as he's going to rent the house out for six months.'

That's a surprise. When Ivy and I were here for the end-of-summer party a couple of weeks back, I was under the impression that Jess was hoping to talk her granddad into returning to the farm for good.

'He changed his mind about taking on the role of general manager?' I glance at Jess, who looks across at Riley.

'No,' he replies. 'Initially he'll be back for six months to organise and then manage the work on the campsite, so that we can add extra market days. We see it as a stepping stone to easing him back into returning to the farm for good.'

I can tell that Jess isn't happy. 'We wanted him to move into Smithy's Cottage, but he insists I should be making money from it.' She sighs, dejectedly. 'However, I'm not giving up. Vyvyan keeps asking when I'm going to let her advertise it on the website but I'm holding off in case he changes his mind after he's been here a few weeks. When Cappy gets back he'll be staying in my guest room at The Farmhouse. The upside to having the cottage standing empty is at least we can offer you some nice accommodation. I wondered whether you could entice Ivy down for the weekend? Just to have a little break. What do you think?'

'It would probably help to lift her spirits and I'm sure the girls will cover for her. Rach is really worried about Ivy. They're all reeling still. Ivy feels she's let them down, which is utter nonsense, but she can't see that. Even her mum has offered to help if Ivy needs a little time off to catch her breath.'

'In which case, perhaps a change of scenery would help.' The look of empathy in Jess's eyes is touching.

'I'll try my best.'

'Right, I'll leave you to it. Riley has tasked me with clearing out the old forge while you're working on the barn. If you hear a scream it'll be me, discovering something small with a long tail. Luckily, my protector will be on hand.'

Riley pulls a face. 'It might take me a few minutes to come to your aid, Jess.'

'I wasn't referring to *you*, I meant the intrepid Misty! See you later.'

That makes me chuckle to myself. Misty is the cutest little grey and white short-haired cat imaginable, but she considers anything that moves as fair game. And I do need to convince Ivy to drive down for the weekend, as this is precisely what she needs. Clean country air, a cathartic walk along the cliff path and a little downtime among friends.

We sit in silence for a few minutes, watching the bakery's customers come and go. What was a tired-looking courtyard with some beautiful cottages overrun with vines and creepers is gradually being brought back to life. Riley hands me his empty mug and I pop them both in the bucket so we can get back to work. Painstakingly recycling tiles takes longer than just throwing them down a plastic chute directly into a skip. The end result, once we've replaced all the timbers and got them back in situ, is that no one will ever guess that the roof has been replaced.

Doing a job like this is a real pleasure and, if I could, I'd cheerfully do it for free. Maybe one day I'll be in a position to help when they start work on Renweneth Manor. I can't think of a better way to spend a weekend than breathing in that fresh Cornish air.

I pop the phone on speaker and gaze out the sitting room window of Smithy's Cottage, feeling refreshed after a much-needed shower. 'Hey, how're you doing, honey?'

'Okay. Missing you, obviously, but looking forward to having the TV remote to myself this evening. How was your first day on the job?' Even trying to inject a little humour, Ivy can't fool me. There's a hollowness to her voice that is crushing to hear.

'Riley and I had a real laugh as we stripped off the old tiles. Not least because of all the shrieks coming from Jess. She was hauling rubbish out of the old forge next to the small barn. It didn't deter her, though. You know what she's like.'

At least that elicits a little laugh. 'I do. Why d'you think I chose her as my best friend at school? My mother always drilled into me how important it was to surround yourself with friends who inspire you. Jess certainly did that and she brought me out of my shell. Rach is another and she's been an angel today.'

'That's good to hear, Ivy – I mean, about Rach. So, your unflinching determination is down to Jess?' I'm only joking around, but it's good to banter. I'm just trying to keep this call upbeat.

'Yep.'

'You're still standing and that's what counts.' I know for a fact that Ivy's had a bad day. Jess wouldn't share the conversation she had with her at lunchtime, but she warned me to tread warily when we spoke.

'For the most part but, rightly or wrongly, I've made a decision.'

My heart misses a beat; I can tell it's not good news.

'Kit and Craft Galore aren't going to rush into making a decision, Adam, so I rang Delia at Riverside Garden Centre.'

'You did?' Oh, that came out sounding a tad less enthusiastic than I'd hoped.

'It's the only option on the table and time isn't on my side. We've agreed that I can rent the kitchen space on a month-by-month basis, on the understanding that if they do get someone interested in leasing the café, I vacate when my monthly lease is up.'

No wonder she's not happy. This isn't a solution, it's a stopgap going nowhere. 'At least you can honour the orders you've already taken, Ivy, which is a smart move.'

There's a telling pause before she responds. 'Rach thinks I should just go for it; sign a six-month lease and have faith the customers will come. In Stroud, our regular clientele pop in while they're shopping and I'm sure some of them would, occasionally, take a car ride to visit us at the garden centre. But imagine turning up day after day, baking our hearts out, only to get a handful of customers who just happen to drop in to buy a plant and discover they can get a coffee and a slice of cake? Rach says word will get out, but how do we pay the bills in the meantime?'

'I wish I was there to give you a hug, Ivy, but what if Rach has a point? If you invest in Riverside, maybe the owners will consider sharing the advertising costs. It would benefit them, too.'

The sigh I hear echoing down the line is distressing. 'Rach is five years younger than me, Adam, and optimism alone isn't going to solve the problem. While she's a great baker, she has no idea about the financial side of running a business. Rach is grasping at straws because she can't believe this is happening. What she needs is a job with a guaranteed future and I can't offer her, or my part-timers, that beyond the end of November.'

The decision is made and I respect Ivy for standing back and looking at the bigger picture. I guess that's exactly what I've done, pinning my hopes on getting a job and she supported me, so now it's my turn to support her decision.

'So this is an exit strategy for them?'

'Exactly. We'll fill the online orders and it gives everyone an extra month to find alternative employment. I doubt we'll break even taking everything into account but that's the best I can do. They're my posse, my crew, and I love them for the way they're concerned for me as much as they are for themselves. I owe them this extra time to get something sorted.'

I try hard to swallow the huge lump that has risen up in my throat. I've never heard Ivy sounding this despondent before. I feel I haven't done enough; we should be at a stage where I'm at her side supporting her, instead of scrabbling around for what work I can get. She deserves better and I'm going to do whatever it takes to convince Greystoke they'd be fools not to take me on.

'I think you're doing the right thing, Ivy. Really I do. How I wish our savings pot was bigger to give you more flexibility, but if you can't make it work there's no point throwing money away, is there? Look, I know this is a little out of the blue, but how about driving down to the farm for the weekend? We'll have Smithy's Cottage all to ourselves.'

The seconds tick by ominously. 'Running away from my problems for forty-eight hours won't change a thing, Adam.'

A sharp pain in my chest causes me to take a few shallow breaths in quick succession before I launch into it. 'No, but what we're both going through isn't because we did anything wrong, Ivy. It's a setback, but it's also an opportunity to rethink our future.'

She's silently shedding a few tears while bravely trying to mask it, but I know my wife.

'Okay. You're right and it's time to stop feeling sorry for myself. I'll drive down on Friday evening after I close up. It's just that... sometimes doing the right thing can feel so very wrong, Adam. It's an impossible situation to be in.'

'Ivy, you've done everything you can. Now go cook yourself an omelette, then grab a tub of ice cream and watch your favourite film. Imagine I'm sitting next to you.'

This time that tinkling little laugh comes from the heart. 'And I'll be speaking the actors' lines as they say them and you won't be there to give me that eye-rolling stare. But I am missing you, Adam, and what that tells me is that it's time to plan a new future for *us*, because when things fall apart it usually means something isn't working right.'

'Together we'll fathom it out, I promise, Ivy.'

'Hmm... whatever it is you have cooking, it smells amazing,' I declare, as I saunter into the kitchen at The Farmhouse. 'Hi, Lola, how was your day at school?'

'Good. We're learning all about rainforests. My class is going to make a big poster for the hall and my job is to draw some flowers.'

Riley is standing in front of the range, cooking, and Jess is busy getting out plates and cutlery, but they both turn to grin at me. 'That sounds like it's going to be an explosion of colour, Lola.'

'I have some awesome highlighter pens in bright pink, yellow and orange. Mum's going to look online as I want to get the flowers just right.'

'And you will,' Jess jumps into the conversation. 'Don't you have a blue one, too?'

'Oh.' Lola begins to chew on her lower lip. 'I think I do. It's probably at the back of my drawer. Can I go and check, Mum?'

'Yes. Dinner will be another twenty minutes yet,' Jess confirms and two seconds later Lola is off her seat and running up the stairs as if she's being chased.

Jess winces. 'How can someone so little be so heavy-footed? Imagine what it must be like with several children running around – total bedlam I should imagine!' Riley does a half-turn to look at her and Jess bursts out laughing. 'What?'

Her words have amused him. 'You don't intend to stop at just the one, do you?'

Jess's eyes widen. 'I haven't given it any thought.'

I let out a spluttering sound and they both turn to look at me. 'Sorry, guys. I feel like I'm intruding. Maybe I should go and see what Lola's up to. And where's Misty?'

'Misty's probably curled up in her tepee, in Lola's bedroom. While we have you to ourselves, did you manage to talk to Ivy?' Jess enquires, her mood instantly changing.

'Yes, I did. She'll drive down on Friday night after she locks up.'

Jess looks triumphant. 'Oh, Adam. It broke my heart talking to her today. Did she mention what her mum said?'

'Yes. It was good of her to offer to help if Ivy needs an extra pair of hands.' Jess's reaction tells me we're not talking about the same thing and now I'm feeling a little confused but I don't want to say the wrong thing and put my foot in it.

'Oh, um…' Jess pauses for a moment. 'Obviously, her mum is concerned for you both.'

She's holding something back and I catch Riley shooting her a warning glance before he starts speaking. 'I'm glad Ivy said "yes". We'll fall in line with whatever suits you guys this weekend, won't we, Jess?'

'How about on Saturday night the four of us go to The Trawlerman's Catch?' Jess suggests. 'I'll speak to Erica about Lola doing a sleepover with Daisy.'

'That sounds like a good plan to me. Ivy will be tired when she arrives on Friday evening, so I'll plan a quiet meal for two. Perhaps Saturday morning we'll do the cliff walk. There are a few things we need to talk through.'

Riley and Jess exchange another nervous glance.

'She's made a decision,' I explain. 'Unless something unexpected turns up, Ivy is going to move everything into storage at the end of the month. The idea is to rent the kitchen at the garden centre to fulfil outstanding orders from the website during November. By then, fingers crossed, I'll have a job that'll support us both while she considers her next step.'

There's a stunned silence until Riley clears his throat and Jess strides across the kitchen. 'In which case, I think it's time to uncork the wine. Once Ivy knows what the next step is going to be, Adam, she'll be off and running. Believe me, I've been there and I know that it turns disaster into… not a triumph, exactly, but an exciting new direction. And that *is* something worth celebrating!'

IVY

Stroud, Gloucestershire

4

An Achievable Dream or an Impossibility?

'This is beyond belief,' Rach says, swiping the back of her hand across her forehead. 'We've never had a Tuesday as busy as this and those who can't get a table are content to take out. Ivy, I really do think you're missing a trick here. With people flooding in to find out what's going on, we could be spreading the word about Riverside Garden Centre.'

Mum stops cutting sandwiches into little triangles, to look at me.

'I was thinking the same thing, Ivy.'

I feel like I'm being attacked from all sides as the next customer in the queue steps up to the counter. 'I can't believe you're shutting down, Ivy! It's only temporary – you're redecorating, right?'

I glance up at the woman and her friend standing there looking hopeful.

'I'm afraid it's permanent, Betty. Sorry for the wait. Did you want to sit in?'

They glance at each other, dumbstruck. 'Oh... yes. Our usual, please. We'll hover until a table is free but this is very disappointing news, isn't it, Ethel? We're going to miss you, that's for sure.'

The only way I'm going to be able to cope with this is to zone out. How on earth am I going to get through the week, I wonder, as I pass another order to Mum. Never did I dream of the day when it needed three of us to cope on what has always been one of our quietest days of the week. Poor Mum might regret her generous offer to help and if I'm going to have any chance at all of organising the move, I'm going to have to ask the girls if they're willing to do a few extra hours mid-week.

Am I the only one who can see that this flurry of activity was to be expected? People are simply curious about why we're closing down. Yes, some of our regulars are going to miss us, in the same way that we'll miss them, but our spot here in the centre of the town is convenient. Riverside Garden Centre isn't. As the day progresses both Rach and Mum keep their thoughts to themselves, but it's obvious they think I'm making a huge mistake.

Lying back on the sofa I'm feeling totally drained. I'm glad Adam isn't here as he'd be pressing me to eat something, even though I don't have an appetite. When the doorbell sounds I groan out loud as I get up, hoping it isn't Mum and shocked when I open the door to see Rach standing there.

'This is a surprise. Come on in.'

She gives me an apologetic smile. 'I know I should have called first, Ivy, but I need to talk to you.'

My heart plummets as I usher her inside.

'Let me take your coat; I'll go hang it up. Take a seat, Rach.'

'It's been quite an emotional day, hasn't it?' she says, the moment I walk back into the room.

'Yes, but that's to be expected. Mum can't make it tomorrow, so the girls are going to do a half-day each in addition to Saturday. I think we're more or less covered, so we can relax.'

Rach is nervously twisting her hands in her lap. 'I didn't come to talk about the work schedules, Ivy. I want to talk about Riverside.'

I ease myself down heavily into the armchair facing her.

'Look, Ivy, I'm more than happy to jump on the computer

and print off a simple handout saying we're going to be working temporarily from the garden centre. Just until something else comes up. What harm can it do?'

'That's not the arrangement we have, Rach. We're only renting the kitchen to complete the orders we have in the pipeline. After that our doors are closed.'

'But we're turning away lucrative orders for December, which is utterly ridiculous. And what better time to attract people to a garden centre, if not in the run-up to Christmas?' There's a fiery passion in her voice and I understand why. Acceptance is a wonderful thing, but she's not there yet.

'In my opinion running the café isn't a viable option. I wish it were, Rach, really I do. But what happens after Christmas in the quiet months when the weather's bad? If there's ice, or snow, that narrow lane is going to put customers off. Would two months' trade be enough to cover overheads through until the spring? The location doesn't work. If it did, Delia would have the café up and running again.'

To my dismay, her eyes fill with tears. 'But what if—'

'You don't make business decisions based on wishful thinking, Rach. That's how people end up going bust and losing everything.'

'Could we just try it? I'll get my other half to print off some handouts if you can talk Delia into letting us use the whole of the café throughout November as a trial.'

'Why? I can't see the point. We all need to be looking to secure our futures. In fact…' I reach out to open the drawer in the coffee table in front of me. 'Read this; it might be an option.'

I hand an A4 sheet of paper to her and Rach's jaw drops as she starts reading. 'Mawsley House? The conference centre?'

'Yes, the owner heard we were shutting down and emailed this across to me this afternoon. After a huge revamp, they're going to be reopening their rather posh café in the new year. It's virtually on our doorstep.'

'They're offering you a contract?'

'No. They want to run it in-house, but they've heard good things about us and are looking to staff up.'

'They're offering you a job?' Instead of delight, she looks appalled.

'Not just me. A job is better than nothing, Rach. Adam's hopes are now firmly pinned on following a career path. You know how hard it's been since we first opened up. The location is great but having a landlord who made promises and took forever to fix even the basic things has been a nightmare. It took him five months to get the burglar alarm fixed. Some of our customers spent as much time outside as they did inside – no matter what the weather was doing. And, in hindsight, the rewiring work to give us extra sockets in the kitchen was to make the property more attractive to his buyer. Working for someone else means all those worries fade away and we get to enjoy doing what we love best – baking cakes and serving customers.'

The look of disappointment on her face is hard to bear.

'Ivy, is this seriously what you want for you, let alone the rest of us? I'm talking as your friend here, not just an employee who loves working for you.'

'I don't have a choice. There are no guarantees that Adam will get an interview and at least one of us needs a fixed income. Setting up somewhere new will use up every penny I've saved since starting the business. If I get a job, not only do I get a salary, but that modest lump sum can be added to our savings and we could start looking to buy a house.'

'You really are giving up?'

'No. I made the decision based on what my head, and not my heart, is telling me. That's why I struck up the deal with Delia to see us all through November.'

Rach looks crushed. 'What if I was prepared to take on the risk?'

'What do you mean?'

'My parents have offered to draw down some of their retirement fund if I decide to set up on my own.'

Oh no... 'Please, Rach, don't go down that road. You have

no idea what you're facing. If I really thought it was possible to build something profitable at the garden centre, I'd grab the opportunity to keep us going.'

'Hear me out, Ivy. It's enough to get me through until the end of spring, at the very least. If I took a six-month lease—'

I can't stand by and watch her risking everything. My mind is in free fall as I stop her. 'Okay. Print off some leaflets and we'll hand them out. I'll talk to Delia. Please don't commit to anything until we see how November goes. I'll bear the costs up until then and if you still feel the same way, you can negotiate your own lease with Delia at that point. Agreed?'

'Oh, Ivy, thank you!'

'There's nothing to thank me for, Rach. My advice to you is not to do it.'

The eye contact between us tells me I'm wasting my breath and she immediately changes the subject. 'What's happening with all the equipment and the furniture at the shop?'

I let out a sigh. 'I'm going to put it all into storage at the end of the month. It'll take time to sell it off unless I can find one buyer to take it as a job lot. That's unlikely but depending on what I do once those final orders are fulfilled, I might have a bit of time on my hands anyway.'

'Before you start work, you mean?'

'Yes. And this is just between us, Rach, as I haven't had a chance to mention that email to Adam, yet. It's not the solution I was hoping for, but one that could potentially take a lot of worry away.'

We stand and hug. It's full of regret for what might have been, and concern for what's to come.

'It's all such a waste… Ivy, isn't it?'

Now my eyes are filling with tears. 'I know, Rach. But I have a friend whose life fell apart through no fault of her own and now she's happy. Change isn't something to fear but to embrace, and for whatever reason I sincerely hope we're all going to get through this and come out the other side the happier for it.'

I can feel Rach's shoulders shaking as she starts laughing and I pull back. 'Ever the practical, but always the optimistic and I love that about you.'

'Do you? Or do you secretly wish I'd throw caution to the wind?'

Rach turns to straighten the cushions on the sofa, which were perfectly placed before she sat down. That's why she's good at icing cakes – because she's a perfectionist and has endless patience. When she turns back around, she's smiling.

'Ivy, wearing your business head you know what you're talking about and I trust your judgement implicitly. Thanks for reining me in a little but also for giving me some hope. I'll never have a boss like you ever again, my dear friend, and I know that, which is why I can't see myself working for anyone else.'

It's the end of an era but where will it lead us next?

By Friday morning the checklist of things to do is mostly ticked off. Storage facility rented; removers booked for Saturday the twenty-ninth – just over two weeks away – and cleaners booked to come in first thing on the following Monday morning, ready to hand back the keys later in the day.

Riverside Garden Centre is open seven days a week and Delia is happy for us to start moving in our stock on the Sunday. Having signed on the dotted line, it all seems painfully real now but Rach is like a totally different person. Everyone whose path she crosses gets a flyer stuffed in their hands, and she even asks if they're prepared to take a few to distribute to friends and family.

'Oh, Ivy, before I forget.' Rach stops me as I'm carrying a full tray and she's on her way back to the kitchen. 'I'm going to get some posters printed off as signage once we move to Riverside. Does our new venue have a name?'

I shake my head at her. 'Rach, it's one month. Is there any point in giving it a name?'

'There might be,' she replies, 'if we get enough customers for me to talk Delia into leasing it to me.'

She's full of optimism and it would be unfair of me to dampen her spirits. 'It's not like I have a business to sell on, Rach, so feel free to use *The Cake and Coffee Emporium* if you like, for some sort of continuity.'

She reaches out to squeeze my arm. 'Thank you, Ivy.'

'Rach, you'll need to draw up a business plan and there are things like insurance, and health and safety, to consider.'

'Don't worry, I'm enlisting the help of my whole family. My brother is an accountant and an adviser to business start-ups.'

Just because it won't work for me, Rach really wants to give it a shot. I draw her to one side. 'If you're really serious about this, then you need to talk to Delia to see what terms she could offer you.'

Her eyes light up. 'You don't mind if I get the ball rolling?'

'Of course not. I'm not giving you anything, Rach; I wish I were. Just don't jump into it without getting independent advice. Take a few days to think it through. Talk to your parents and your brother. As far as I'm aware, Delia hasn't had any further enquiries but I'm sure she'll tell you if there are any interested parties. You'll need to get a handle on what your overheads will be.'

'This means more than you could know, Ivy. It's my dream.'

It was mine once upon a time but now it's changed. After a long phone call with Cristabel Parker from Mawsley House on Tuesday evening, she invited me along for an interview early yesterday evening and she's made me a formal offer for the position of catering manager. I still haven't mentioned it to Adam yet. If I accept the job, I'll be taking on staff at the start of January ready for the launch sometime in February. Even if Rach isn't interested, maybe the other girls will be.

My dad once told me that a good plan involves a set of clear objectives and a little flexibility to cope with the unexpected. For some reason it has always stuck in my brain, but never has it been as relevant as it is right now.

I glance up at the clock. Another six and a half hours and I'll be in the car driving down to Cornwall. I didn't think it was a good idea at first, but now I can't wait to get away from here. I need to feel Adam's arms wrapped around me and then dive under the duvet with him. Sometimes the world feels like a hostile place and he's my comfort zone.

As I pull into the cobbled courtyard, it's enchanting. Lights from The Farmhouse, the adjacent rental cottage – Penti Growan – and Smithy's Cottage, which is attached to The Farmhouse Bakery, bathe the vast open space in a warm glow.

I park the car by the wall in front of the small barn and even before I turn off the engine, Adam comes hurrying over.

'At last. You said you were going to be another thirty minutes when you stopped for petrol,' he complains, as I slip out of the driver's seat. He pulls me in to him, planting his lips on mine and letting out a slight groaning sound. 'Oh, how I've missed you!'

I grin up at him. 'That's good to hear, although I'm sure you and Riley have had some fun.'

'Aren't you going to say how much you missed me?' He pulls a sad face, making me chuckle.

'Okay, maybe I did. It's been eerily quiet at home, that's for sure.'

Adam picks me up and twirls me around, almost losing his footing on the uneven cobbles. 'You're here now and we have the whole weekend. And I'll be able to drive you back early on Monday morning in your car, as I have an interview.' Adam can hardly contain his smile.

'Oh... that's brilliant news!'

'I'll head straight back here afterwards and Riley is going to pick me up from the train station. This is it, Ivy, the chance I've been waiting for to put my years of experience to good use. I've worked for enough foremen who were promoted before they were ready, to understand what it takes to lead a team.' He's buzzing. 'Let's grab your bags and get you inside. I'm cooking a romantic dinner for two and there's just time for you to take a quick shower and unwind a little before I dish up.'

This wasn't quite the reception I was expecting, but Adam needs to talk and I think I'll save my news until tomorrow.

'Should I pop in to say hi to Jess and Lola?' I query, as he escorts me over to Smithy's Cottage.

'No. I told them I was planning a quiet evening for two. They understand what a tough week you've had. And tomorrow morning I thought we'd take a walk along the cliff path before a late breakfast. After that, I'm prepared to share you, and tomorrow evening the four of us are going to The Trawlerman's Catch.'

'Really?'

'Yep. Riley's staying over, as Lola is having a sleepover with Daisy.' He raises his eyebrows, giving me a wicked grin, which makes me laugh.

'Aww… I'm glad they're managing to get a little alone time together and they want to spend some of it with us. How special is that? I'm guessing Cappy isn't around?'

'He's back in Gloucestershire getting his house ready to rent out and won't be returning until early next week. Riley and Jess are taking advantage of having The Farmhouse to themselves.'

As Adam swings open the door to the cottage and I walk into the hallway, I feel my worries begin to melt away. The smell of scented candles, mingled with the aroma of something delicious cooking in the oven, is comforting. It might not be our home, but it is for this weekend and I fully intend to enjoy every single moment of the time we have together. My best friend's farm has become a little sanctuary for us over the past year and a bit. Admittedly, usually we come prepared to roll up our sleeves and get stuck in but even that's been special. Tonight, however, I know that Jess will understand that Adam and I need a little time to get our heads around the next phase in our lives.

IVY
Renweneth Farm, Cornwall

5

Nothing Lifts the Spirits Like Reconnecting with Nature

'This is bliss, isn't it?' Adam and I wander hand in hand over the scrubby moorland, our eyes fixated on the dazzling blue sea in front of us.

'What's that programme you like watching... *Stunning Seaside Properties*, or something similar? Anyway, this is what dreams are made of, Ivy, isn't it?' Adam's voice is wistful. 'It's funny, because I'm here working and yet somehow it manages to feel like I'm on holiday. Out in the fresh air everything smells different and even when I can't catch a whiff of the sea carried on the breeze, I can actually smell the trees.'

I know exactly what he means.

'You're used to working in built-up areas and on large housing developments, Adam. How anything even remotely green manages to survive given the traffic congestion and the jungle of concrete, goodness knows.'

'Hmm... and yet there's lots of land everywhere. Instead, people are squashed into tiny spaces. It never made sense to me; still doesn't.'

I gave his hand a little squeeze. 'When Jess accepted Cappy's offer to take over the farm, I thought she was crazy leaving her family and friends behind to go it alone with Lola. That wasn't the case at all; it was a challenging opportunity and, yes, she was daunted by it at first, but it also gave her hope for a better future.

As it turns out, being crazy is hanging on to the past when it's obvious things aren't working out.'

As we reach the cliff path we stop to gaze out over the bay. Turning to our right, I catch a glimpse of Penvennan Cove. From here it's partly shrouded by a forest of trees that slopes gently down to the road leading to the beach. Only the far side of the wide expanse of sand and shingle is visible, where the cliff rises up again. Sitting atop the limestone promontory, Lanryon Church is an unmistakable landmark.

'That's where we're at, isn't it? Having to accept that change is unavoidable and hoping that whatever decisions we make are the right ones.'

I throw my arms around Adam's waist, burying my head against the thick fisherman's jumper we bought in Polreweek, the summer before last. It was our first visit to Renweneth Farm after Jess took over. Things were very different back then. Everything looked forlorn and a little neglected. Now she's giving it life as she continues to press forward.

'Yes, I suppose it is. How optimistic do you feel about this interview with Greystoke?' I pull away to gaze up into Adam's eyes and what I see is hope and enthusiasm.

'I've already had a video interview and it's mine if I want it, Ivy. It's a family-run company and they want me to meet the office staff. You know, shake hands, because everyone is a part of the team. It seems that walking out on that contract job because I wasn't prepared to cut corners swung it for me.'

'I'm so glad,' I reply, softly. 'Honesty should count for something, Adam. The fact that we'll be spending time apart isn't going to be easy, but I can see how happy you are.'

'I told you something would turn up. I won't know what sort of start date they're anticipating until we meet up on Monday, but I'll be fine to finish off the work here, with Riley. If I get a few days free after that, I'll be around to help with the move to the garden centre.'

He tugs on my hand and as we start walking again I draw in a deep breath, thinking it's time I mentioned my own news. Before I can begin, Adam turns to face me, a little frown furrowing his brow.

'I had a chat with the guy who does my accounts. He said the fact that I'm going from self-employed to employed with a higher income, could be a good thing in terms of getting a mortgage. The future is beginning to look an awful lot brighter than it was a week ago.'

As the seagulls flying overhead wheel, dip and dive, their raucous calls grate on my ears and it's a bit of a jolt to be brought back down to earth. My situation isn't settled and I don't know why I'm dragging my feet. Not wishing to dampen Adam's mood, I tell him about Rach and ask if he thinks it's wrong to encourage her.

'Don't forget that you're used to managing a bigger operation and having responsibility for staff. If Rach is starting small and her family are there to get hands-on and give her some serious financial support, she might be able to grow it into something worthwhile. It'll be a shame on one hand, as you'll miss working together.'

'I know. I want her to succeed, Adam, really I do. But bills need to be paid and it's all about being in a prime location. Even then, remember the early days after I first set up? Some days were so quiet, I could have curled up in the corner and cried. Mum and Dad were worried sick I'd end up losing everything. They warned me how hard it would be but, just like Rach, I was following my dream.' And what I learnt is that even when you're successful at what you do, you're only as strong as your weakest link. My landlord played me for a fool and shame on me for falling for it.

'It's time to focus on the future now, Ivy. If I'm going to be bringing in more money, then in the short-term it will take the pressure off you. We've talked about starting a family – I know that's not an option right now, but I don't want it to be something we keep putting off. Who knows what position we'll be in this time next year? Let's enjoy our walk and when we get back, I'll treat you to croissants for breakfast.'

'Treat me?'

'You can choose anything you want from The Farmhouse Bakery, including freshly ground coffee to go!'

It's hard to keep things back from Adam, but now my thoughts are in overdrive. Maybe he won't be thrown when I tell him about the job offer at Mawsley House. We're both so desperate to put down some real roots. It's a waiting game, though, because until you have a contract in your hand, nothing is guaranteed. I learnt that the hard way. It's constantly been two steps forward and one step back, but based on the law of averages alone that can't go on forever, can it?

'It's so good to have you guys here,' Jess says, raising her glass as we sit around a table at The Trawlerman's Catch. Spirits are high tonight after we all enjoyed a leisurely afternoon walking around Polreweek with Lola, before dropping her off at Daisy's house for the sleepover.

'I'm glad Adam talked me into popping down for a break. I only hesitated because I haven't been in the best of moods this past week and I didn't want to spoil anyone's weekend. But getting away was absolutely the right thing to do.'

We chink glasses and Jess gives me a reassuring look.

'You've supported me through my troubles, Ivy, and that's what friends are for. If you need any help with the move, I could always drive up to Stroud for a few days.'

Her offer is touching when she has so much to do here. 'Ah, that's sweet of you, Jess, but all the contents of the shop is going into storage for now. The garden centre has everything we need to fulfil the outstanding orders.'

Riley shakes his head, sadly. 'It's such a shame to have to shut down a successful business, Ivy. Will you look to start up the click-and-collect service again when you've found a new location?'

'I'm looking at other options right now.' All eyes are on me, but this wasn't exactly the way I wanted to break my news. 'It's likely that Rach will try to give it a go working from the garden centre.'

Jess looks stunned. 'You said it was a couple of miles down a narrow country lane – wasn't that why you decided not to consider it in the first place?'

'Yes, but she's going to talk to the owners this coming week about reopening the café, too. Rach's parents are backing her and her mum is going to be hands-on, so they'll be able to keep their overheads low to begin with.' I pull a face. 'In my opinion, it's still one heck of a risk and I've been totally honest with her about that. However, it's one Rach, and her family, are prepared to gamble on. As from the end of November I'll be walking away.'

Well, that killed the jolly mood. There's an immediate shift in the atmosphere and a lot of nervous eye contact going on around the table. I frown, wondering what's going on. Adam looks at Jess, as if prompting her, and she gives him an indignant look.

'Sorry, I didn't mean to blurt that out,' I apologise and Adam is the first to respond.

'Look, Ivy, I was speaking to Jess this week and—'

Riley immediately takes over the conversation. 'Adam has been worried about you, as has Jess. With the future of The Farmhouse Bakery still uncertain—'

I glance around, feeling slightly confused. 'I thought that was sorted, Jess? You said you were going to employ a couple of people and run it yourself.'

'Hmm…' Jess looks rather cagey. 'Servers I can find; bakers are few and far between, Ivy. Vyvyan has had some interest from a couple of people looking for a commercial let but the businesses aren't quite right for the farm. At the moment I've drawn a blank.'

Adam injects. 'What Jess means is that it's a potential opportunity, Ivy.'

'For what?' I ask, puzzled.

Did Adam get me down here this weekend for something other than a relaxing break?

Jess shifts uneasily in her seat, glaring at Adam, and he clears his throat before speaking. 'Look, Ivy...' He reaches out for my hand and he sounds emotional. 'It's not working for us back in Stroud and if you agree that I should take this job with Greystoke, then I'm going to be away most weeks Monday through to Friday evening.' He pauses for a moment and I can see this is coming from the heart. 'Jess and I have been talking; she's come up with an idea you might like to consider.'

I turn to look at my best friend in the whole wide world and wonder why on earth this is the first I'm hearing about it. 'Jess?'

My eyes wander over to Riley and I can see he's feeling distinctly uncomfortable.

'Ivy, you're like a sister to me,' she replies. 'You're a part of my family, as I am yours. You love coming to the farm. Is it that much of a stretch to imagine yourself living and working here?'

I close my eyes for a second and Adam's clasp on my hand grows tighter. I let out a disbelieving laugh. 'You can't be serious.'

Adam looks at me for a brief second before lowering his eyes. 'It's not a million miles away from Stroud, is it?'

I clear my throat uneasily. I thought my news might cheer him up but now I can see he might think differently. 'I've been offered a job as catering manager at Mawsley House Conference Centre near Stroud.'

Jess does a sharp intake of breath but recovers quickly. 'That's wonderful news, Ivy. And cause for a celebration!'

Adam's forehead is pinched. 'Why didn't you tell me?'

I do a half-turn, my eyes trying hard to gauge his gut reaction but he simply looks thrown. 'I wasn't sure what you would think. It's still sinking in and I haven't accepted it yet.'

Our food arrives and Riley, bless him – in between eating – ever so delicately changes the subject, to the relief of all of us.

'I'm trying to talk Jess into creating a water feature in the centre of the farmhouse courtyard. What do you guys think?'

Thankfully, Adam and Riley launch into a dialogue about how to pipe the water across to the cobbled area for the proposed new feature. I'm sitting here envisaging the expressions on our families' faces if we told them we were moving away. They'd think we'd lost our minds.

While we wait for dessert to be served, I slip out to the cloakroom. No wonder Adam was so gushy about how wonderful our walk along the cliff path was and how incredible it must be living by the sea. Yes, I do love those programmes where people up sticks and start over again, but not us. That was never the plan. If we're going to think about having a family, I'll need Mum's support more than ever. She's expecting to be as hands-on as she's been for Ursula, since the arrival of my niece, Tillie.

As I splash a little water on my face then mop it dry, a mix of emotions run through my head. Suddenly the door opens and Jess walks in.

'Ivy, please don't blame Adam. It was my fault. I was just throwing ideas out there and I'm sorry, because I should have spoken to you first.'

Now I feel bad that she feels it's necessary to apologise.

'It's a kind thought, Jess, and I am grateful but this is your dream. You walked away from some really bad memories and now you have a much better quality of life. Yes, you're working hard but you're happy and I'm thrilled for you, Lola and Riley. But for me and Adam, Stroud is home and always will be. We're simply navigating one of life's little hurdles and both feeling a little sorry for ourselves. Everything passes with time.'

'I know, Ivy. It's just that... Adam was so downhearted. Vyvyan isn't having much luck finding the right tenant and what do I know about running a shop? I wondered whether fate was giving me a nudge in your direction...' She tails off, awkwardly.

'Adam and I love spending time here – you know that. But this is like taking time out from our everyday lives and that's what makes it so special for us. I wouldn't want to lose that feeling.'

Jess leans in to give me a hug. 'Sorry. We were all having a good time and I found myself wishing you were a part of it, too.'

She doesn't get homesick for Gloucestershire. What Jess misses are the people she loves. That's the price you pay, though, because no dream is perfect. I'm prepared to sacrifice having my own business so that, fingers crossed, Tillie has a little cousin she can grow up with. Not someone she sees a couple of times a year.

'Come on, let's get back before they talk themselves into installing a huge fountain when all I want is a simple pebble pool with the sound of trickling water,' Jess groans.

I start laughing. 'Riley loves reclamation yards and I bet he already has something in mind. Seriously, Jess, you need to take control of this idea quickly.'

We've known each other for too long for me to be cross with her. Besides, Adam had a part to play in it too. I'm just surprised it's something he'd even consider doing. Then I realise Jess has been doing what a good friend does, letting the two of us offload to her. It was precisely what I needed, but when it comes to Adam, I'm shocked that he would even consider The Farmhouse Bakery as a suitable solution.

Neither of them have thought this through properly. Not only are they not standing back to see the bigger picture, they're ignoring the two biggest obstacles. The first is that Adam would miss having regular contact with his family equally as much as me. What he's forgotten, is that Jess had a valid reason for leaving Stroud. Old wounds cut deep and everywhere she turned there were reminders of her past. In contrast, the times she spent at the farm over the years reflected only good memories, so coming here was a way of freeing herself from the past.

The second thing they've overlooked is that I'm a confectioner and a café owner. The Farmhouse Bakery is simply an outlet for an established bread shop that also sells a few cakes. Is Adam expecting me to take a step back in my career so that we're not both under pressure? If that's the case, he needs to be upfront with me because I have no intention of going backwards.

Lying in bed in the dark next to Adam, I can feel the tension in him. He thinks he's upset me by confiding in Jess but who else was he going to open up to? And now I feel bad for not opening up to him about all of the things whirling around inside my head.

Do I continue to lie here quietly in case he wants to clear the air, or wait and see what happens in the morning? The night ended on a high note as it was fun, so I don't really want to spoil that. Instead, I roll into him, snuggling down beneath the covers ready to close my eyes.

'It seemed like a good idea at the time. Like me, Jess doesn't know how best to help. She just came up with an option I thought might turn out to be the perfect solution,' Adam confesses, shattering the silence.

As I ease myself up on one elbow to look at him, even in the shadows his expression is forlorn. 'Then why didn't she talk to me?'

'Ironically, the conversation that triggered it didn't start off being about you at all, Ivy. Jess was feeling a tad frustrated and muttered something about if only she could find someone like you. I picked up on it and one thing led to another.'

'Like me? The Farmhouse Bakery is doing well because it's being run by locals, people with years of experience making a wide range of specialist breads. You've been inside the shop and the cake section most certainly isn't the main focus. Locals and campers alike love fresh bread and it's what keeps them coming back. Even if I could deliver on Jess's expectations while turning it into a more profitable business to make it worth considering, you know how delicate my relationship is with Ursula, right now. I only get to see my niece when she's at Mum's and it would break my heart not to be able to watch Tillie as she grows up. I thought family was important to us both.'

'It is, Ivy,' he replies, tenderly. 'I just didn't engage my brain at a time when I was at a low ebb, wondering how we're going to get ourselves back on track. I didn't mean to put pressure on you, honestly I didn't. I just want you to be happy and you've been so stressed that I can't even imagine what's going on inside that head of yours.'

Now I'm feeling a tad guilty because Adam is right. There are things I should have talked through with him but my focus has been on getting through each day.

'Adam, the only reason I was considering the catering manager position is that I'd be hiring a team again. As it turns out, Rach wants to go it alone so she won't be interested. Grace is seriously thinking about working lunchtimes at the Heritage House Inn in Stroud as it's convenient. Lisa is applying for an admin job at her daughter's school, so the holidays won't be a problem. And Chris says that maybe it's time she retired.'

'It sounds like you're all heading off in different directions and that's often what change sparks. So now you can relax and think about what's best for us. I will admit that I was surprised you'd even consider it, but maybe it is the right way to go.'

I turn to face him, puzzled at this about turn in his thinking.

'There are some positives, Ivy,' he continues. 'No more financial pressures, a salary coming in each month and the perks that go with it.'

'Perks?'

'When we're ready to start a family you'd be able to take paid maternity leave. Ursula isn't hard-hearted enough not to come around if you got pregnant; not least because Tillie would have a cousin to grow up with. In a way, maybe life is doing us a favour. It's not always about bigger and better, sometimes the stress that comes with building a little empire isn't worth the price to be paid.'

Has Adam lost faith in me and my ability to follow my

dreams? My stomach begins to churn. 'It was a means to an end, Adam. A temporary step to make sure none of my team were out of a job until something more suitable comes along and I'd be off again.'

'Oh, I see.'

The silence between us is heavy and I can't bear it. 'I'm not looking for an easy option, just the right opportunity and until it comes along I'll take whatever I can get.'

Adam heaves himself up into a sitting position and one glance at his face and I can see he's panicking. 'In my defence, I thought Jess's offer was a chance for you to set up a new business next to the sort of cottage you've always dreamed about living in.'

I let out a sorrowful sigh. 'Oh, Adam. Smithy's Cottage is beautiful, but moving to Cornwall? You can't be serious. When we're ready to start a family, I'm going to need Mum close by more than ever because by then I'll have a new business. I want to be free to determine my working hours, babe, and get that perfect balance. But I also know that Ursula couldn't cope without Mum's help. If we are blessed with a baby, I want our parents to be a daily part of our child's life because I think that's a wonderful thing, don't you?'

Adam pulls me into him, wrapping an arm around me comfortingly. 'And I'll do whatever I can to help make that happen, Ivy. I've no doubt at all that within a couple of weeks I'll be in employment. I know it's not quite how we saw our future going, spending our working week apart, but at least we won't be constantly worrying about money.'

'I'm not disagreeing with you, but please stop trying to protect me when I'm perfectly capable of sorting out my own business affairs,' I state, firmly.

'I know but it's a good job I haven't crossed paths with your landlord, because I don't think I could have restrained myself if I had. He strung you along until the last minute with no thought for your situation whatsoever. I just don't want you looking back on the decisions you make now with regret.'

'Me neither and I'm determined not to make the same mistakes again. Life isn't fair, Adam. We've both learnt that lesson to our cost.'

'Which makes it even more important not to rush into anything. It's been an emotional roller coaster, honey, and it isn't over yet. Being apart has been agony because when we were able to talk I had so many questions that were left unanswered but I didn't have the heart to ask them.'

'So you talked to Jess and Riley instead, and thought you'd come up with a rescue plan,' I reply, edgily.

Adam frowns. 'I can see now why you might think that, Ivy. All I'm asking is that tomorrow you make time to have a quiet chat with Jess and let her down gently. The offer was a genuine one; the bakery has become a real problem for her at a time when she's under a lot of pressure. But if it's not right for you, that's fine by me.'

Now the guilt is really setting in. 'Okay, I owe Jess that. It's just that I wasn't expecting such an outpouring from you all and I felt... ambushed.'

'Ambushed? Oh, Ivy, it just came out all wrong – that's all – and then each of us seemed to make it a bit worse. No one is going to put pressure on you, but I'd hate for you to look back at some point in the future and think *if only*.' He gives me a gentle squeeze and I run my fingertips down his arm as his muscles tense. Adam is my rock in every way but this isn't a good idea.

'I don't want Jess to think I'm being ungrateful, Adam,' I reassure him. 'But most of all I was confused and a little taken aback, if I'm being honest. Knowing that the three of you had been hatching a plan without involving me, stings a little.'

Adam's face is mostly in shadow and I can't gauge his reaction until I hear a regretful sigh.

'I'm so, so sorry, Ivy. It's just that when I arrived here I had some sort of epiphany. The black cloud of doom and gloom that had been hovering over my head for the last couple of weeks disappeared and life suddenly felt simpler. I could imagine us living here, welcoming family, as Jess welcomes us. Being at the farm is like stepping off the treadmill for a while and all that was missing was you.' His tone is apologetic but there's a poignancy to his words that snatches my breath away for a moment.

What surprises me is that while Adam can be a bit of a dreamer at times, it's unusual for Jess to encourage it.

'Well, let's focus on having a wonderful weekend. Now, can we finally lie down and try to get some sleep?' I reply, determined to lighten the mood between us. 'You know I find it hard to drift off because it's so darned quiet here. It seems like everyone is tucked up in bed by ten o'clock.'

He scoots down the bed, half lifting me with him. 'It's called healthy living, Ivy. Early to bed, early to rise and all that. I... um... told Jess you'd be up for a walk before breakfast... just the two of you.'

'That's fine. I'd rather have the chat sooner, rather than later. There's no point getting her hopes up.'

Adam is already yawning as I snuggle up next to him. The silence around us makes me react to every tiny little sound until Adam begins gently snoring. Then, within seconds, my own eyelids start to droop. I imagine my hand in his as we walk along the beach, the breeze whipping my hair into a frenzy as he half turns to gaze at me as if he's the happiest man in the world. I can't remember the last time I saw that look on his face and I find myself swiping away a single teardrop as it rolls down my cheek. It's time to stop feeling sorry for myself and get my act together.

6

Getting Carried Away

'You and Riley are still very careful around Lola,' I reflect, as Jess and I meander our way across the scrubby moorland, ignoring the well-trodden route cutting across to the cliff path.

'Lola can see that our life here is happier with Riley in it; it's merely a case of her getting used to the fact that very soon our inner circle of two, will become three. That's a huge step, not least because it's beginning to sink in that Riley will go from being our friend, to her stepdad.'

I can understand them wanting to take it slowly. 'Oh, Jess. Moving into Renweneth Manor will change everything for you, Riley and Lola, won't it?'

She lets out a disparaging chuckle. 'Yes, but making it happen will come at a cost both financially and emotionally. Riley rescued a derelict shell and turned it into his home. Now he's going to be doing the same thing for us, but on a larger scale.'

'But it'll be hard for him to turn his back on the cottage.'

'Yes, it will. If Riley can negotiate having Ollie for weekend stays on a regular basis, that's when he'll tell Fiona about us. Hopefully, she'll be fine with it and Riley will then be able to bring Ollie to the farm to meet everyone. Lola can't wait. But equally as important is the fact that with Riley having his son here to stay, it will make the manor feel like *our* home.'

I give a little laugh. 'By then he'll know every single inch of it up close and personal!'

'He most certainly will. I sort of understand why Riley's reluctant to share our news with his ex. Look how unsettled I felt about Lola's first stay with Ben in Stroud. There was no way I was going to let her go if his girlfriend, Naomi, had insisted on staying under the same roof. Lola hadn't seen her dad in person for months and what they needed was some bonding time alone together to reconnect properly.'

'But Lola has accepted Naomi being in Ben's life now, so it's a fleeting thing,' I point out.

'Yes... but it might have been a very different story if we hadn't handled the situation in the way we did. Riley has only seen Ollie a couple of times in the four years they've lived apart. Admittedly, it wasn't his choice, but it's not about pointing a finger, it's about what's right for Ollie. And Riley needs to gain Fiona's trust at the same time as rekindling his relationship with his son.'

Jess turns to look at me and I can see a hint of unease in her eyes. She knows that encouraging Riley to reconnect with Fiona is the right thing to do given the situation, but that doesn't mean it's going to be easy on any of them.

'How old is he now?'

'He's eight.'

'Around Lola's age, then.'

'Yes.'

And then they'll get the happy-ever-after ending that they all deserve. Why does life always feel like a waiting game, though?

'Well, at least you have a plan and Fiona will no doubt come to appreciate what you guys are doing in order to make it work for everyone.'

Jess reaches out to grab a dry stalk of grass and I notice a red patch on the back of her hand.

'Is that a burn?'

'No, I brushed up against a pine branch when I was moving a planter and for some reason it always irritates my skin. It'll clear eventually – it just itches like mad.'

'Do you still have that aloe vera plant I gave you?' I check.

'Of course! It's on the windowsill in my en suite. Why?'

'Not all varieties are medicinal, but the one I bought you is. Just cut off one of the spiky leaves. It will weep, so put it on some paper towel while you trim off the narrow, serrated edges, then cut off a section, say two inches, and slice through the middle to expose the gel. Rub it over the back of your hand and let it dry. It acts like a moisturiser but it also cools the area, plus it has antibacterial and antiviral properties.'

She turns her head to give me a little smile. 'How come I'm the one who ended up on a farm and not you? You're much more into living off the land with all your organic ingredients and natural flavourings.'

Jess indicates to a huge, flat-topped rock and we make our way over to it.

'Hmm... and I was the one who simply wanted to settle down and have a family, wasn't I?' I muse.

'And I laughed at you, thinking you were mad not to grab life's opportunities to throw yourself into a career that could set you up for the future. Which was precisely what you ended up doing. We switched roles,' she replies and laughs, as we take a seat.

We're sheltered by a small outcrop of trees and it's nice not to be buffeted by what is a rather chilly breeze. I pull a scrunchie from my pocket and tie my hair back into a ponytail.

'Yeah, we did, but it wasn't exactly planned, was it, Jess?'

'No. Getting pregnant was not on my agenda at the time,' she concedes.

'And setting up on my own probably wasn't the best move for me, but I was driven to it. People have no idea what goes into the food they're buying. It's madness to take the natural goodness out of things only to replace it with man-made alternatives to get the same result. Natural is best and that's why I like to know where my ingredients come from, even if some of the suppliers can't afford to jump through the hoops to get certificated.'

'That's precisely why I thought this might work for you, Ivy. You're as passionate about your business as I am about mine. For me that's the key to making the farm a success. I only want people on board who care about whatever it is they produce.'

Jess has so much energy and enthusiasm that I can't blame Adam for getting drawn in. But it's as much about the setting as anything else and that's escapism, not reality.

'What exactly did you and Adam discuss?'

She has the grace to look a little awkward, suddenly staring down with great interest at her hiking boots.

'He was so conflicted when he first arrived here. Adam is torn between the chance to earn a good living and the thought of leaving you while he's working away. This job offer he's so excited about has put him on a guilt trip because he knows that it's going to be tough on you both. He understands what you're going through and doesn't like the idea of you spending so much time alone while you're um—'

'Not in a good place?'

Judging by the look on her face, maybe that's not quite the right choice of words. 'Unsettled. Adam is... he wants...' Jess is struggling and I know why.

'Adam feels it's his job to look after me and I feel it's my job to look after him.' Jess and I both start laughing. 'It's what makes us good together, Jess. He wants to build things and create that way. I want to...' I flounder, not sure how to describe what I want.

'Be honest, Ivy. Did the café turn out to be your dream come true?'

We look at each other intently.

'Yes and no. I loved that we built a good customer base: people who cared if the honey was organic and appreciated that we didn't use bleached flour. But...' I pause, trying to unravel my thoughts, which are like a tangle of knots. 'With rent, rates, staff costs, insurances, taxes and paying more for good quality produce, I felt like I was... I don't know... going against the flow. I could so easily have cut some of my overheads but as I deliberately chose not to do that, I paid the price. My landlord was only interested in making money and if I'd offered to up the rent considerably, maybe things would have ended differently.'

There. I've said it. It doesn't exactly make me sound like an astute businesswoman, but it's the truth.

'Oh, Ivy, don't you see what's happening?'

I look at her, quizzically. 'What do you mean?'

'One door shuts and another one opens. Jory and Alice are proving that the bakery can make a profit and a reasonably good one. It's an opportunity waiting to be snapped up and the rent will only be a fraction of what you pay now for a prime high street location in Stroud.'

'But that's only one consideration, Jess, and in fairness the income would be a lot less. My ultimate aim is to start again when I find the perfect location.'

'Adam is worried about you, Ivy.' Her voice softens. 'He's seen a change in you that scares him and he's hoping you'll take it a little easier in future.'

My darling husband isn't one for opening up about his feelings to other people but he's obviously even more comfortable talking to Jess than I thought.

'But… it's not a working bakery, Jess, it's a shop. They don't bake anything on site, they simply transport the bread and the cakes here from their premises in Polreweek.'

Jess is still fiddling with that long stalk of dried grass, batting it to and fro. 'You've been inside and seen the size of the kitchen. Riley can make whatever adjustments you want so it works for you. And, yes, it would answer a prayer for me, as I need the right person. Someone who understands the ethos behind creating a little community.'

'I understand where you're coming from, Jess, and it's a truly lovely thought, but I feel like I've had the stuffing knocked out of me and I just need time to get my head around my next steps. The truth is, Stroud will always be home to me.'

As we glance at each other I see a fleeting look of sadness pass over her face.

'You're family – you and Adam. I'll level with you, Ivy. The Farmhouse Bakery is at the heart of what I'm trying to achieve here and suddenly I'm back to square one. I know you'd make it work, but more than that you'd turn it into something very special indeed. All I'm asking is that you give it some thought.'

I was hoping to let her down gently, but I wasn't expecting a passionate plea for help. A lump rises up in my throat as I'm shocked to see that Jess is getting emotional.

'Oh, Jess!' I pause, struggling to find the right words. 'You were always the adventurous one whereas I—'

'It's a lot to ask – I know that – but what if you gave it a try? If it goes well and you end up seeing this as your home, somewhere to finally put down roots, I'm willing to rent you the shop and let you buy Smithy's Cottage.' As I go to speak, she puts up her hand. 'And before you tell me it's not doable because of your present situation, none of that matters to me, my friend. You can rent both until you're in a position to consider it as an option.'

'Oh, Jess... you really mean it, don't you?'

'I do. I was thinking we could look at creating a walled courtyard garden for the cottage so it's less like a rental property and more like a family home.'

I gaze at her amazed. 'How?'

'By moving the access to the retail outlets in the small barn. It doesn't have to be via the courtyard. Customers could enter from the pavement outside through the double gates that lead directly into the old forge.'

My head is spinning. 'And you've talked all this through with Adam?'

Jess looks at me guiltily. 'Sorry... we shared a bottle of wine one evening after Riley left. I was feeling down and it was just the two of us sitting at the kitchen table talking. Adam's a good listener. I told him that it means a lot to me that Renweneth Farm is a place that not just holidaymakers, but also friends and family gravitate towards. We're not a million miles away from Stroud and you two always look so at home when you're here.'

'But we're not locals, like Alice and Jory, Jess. You're running a business and while it's tempting to surround yourself with the people you love, I'm not the perfect fit for the bakery.'

She scoffs at me. 'Why not? With the campsite, the weekly markets, the small barn retail outlets... it's only going to get busier, Ivy. The Farmhouse Bakery is in the courtyard, facing The Farmhouse. I really don't want to turn it into a convenience store, but it could be so much more than just a bakery. The cobbled area could easily be turned into an outdoor café in summer, which is something the campers would love.'

'But to consider selling Smithy's Cottage to us Jess, that's terribly kind of you but don't you need it to give you a regular income?'

'Yes, but I also need more cash in the pot if Riley and I are going to make Renweneth Manor liveable again. You'll turn the bakery into something wonderful and to have you and Adam on our doorstep, imagine how amazing that would be. If you take that step and it doesn't work out for whatever the reason, there's one condition attached to the offer.'

I look at her, questioningly.

'You give me first option to buy it back from you at market value. That way you don't have to feel guilty if you want to move on and I won't end up with strangers living on my doorstep. I can reconsider the options going forward at that point. But, Ivy, I really think you'd thrive here alongside the other small businesses, each supporting each other.'

'In my dreams maybe,' I reply, sounding a tad wistful. 'I'm imagining my mum's face now... and my sister, well, if she can't visit me when we live close by, we'll lose all contact. Tillie is growing up fast and it's only because of Mum that I get to...' I grind to a halt, feeling that Jess isn't listening to me anyway.

As our eyes meet, she can see I'm simply being honest with her, but it's obvious she's gutted. I admire Jess because she's determined to turn every obstacle in life around but while I've learnt a lot from her, I've never been a risk-taker and that's what this would be. My pride has already been dented seeing my business reduced to nothing and, even though we're friends, I'd be putting myself under a different sort of pressure.

For a start, I don't know anyone when it comes to looking for staff. Back home, word of mouth alone was how I pulled my awesome team together. In a small community like this, if I took someone on and it didn't work out that could prove to be a bit of a nightmare. The last thing Jess needs is to bring in an outsider who unwittingly starts to make waves. What was Adam thinking?

IVY
Stroud, Gloucestershire

7

Good News and a Few Tears

After my chat with Jess on Sunday morning they could all see that I was overwhelmed, so no one mentioned another word about the bakery. And yesterday morning, when Adam drove us home in my car, we were both subdued. Understandably, he was a little anxious about his meeting with the owner and one of his sons, at Greystoke, but it wasn't just that. I kissed him goodbye feeling tearful as we pulled up outside the building company's offices, and Adam handed me the keys to the car. Wishing him good luck, I drove away realising that our old life was disintegrating before our eyes. Nothing would ever be quite the same again.

I spent the rest of the day working, while Jess's offer went around and around inside my brain like it was on a relentless ticker tape. I came to the conclusion that it would be sheer madness to even consider adding yet another drastic change into the mix. There's too much happening all at once and Tuesday at The Cake and Coffee Emporium the mood is decidedly sombre. Rach and I have been head down going through the motions while trying to maintain that welcoming atmosphere our customers naturally expect. It's gruelling. When the phone in my pocket starts to buzz, I ignore it until I'm done serving and then I head back to the counter.

A quick glance shows it's a text from Adam and as I open it my heart skips a beat.

Greystoke's just emailed me through a formal offer! Give me a quick call if you can?

Rach, who is buttering scones, looks up.

'Problems?'

'No, it's good news for a change. Do you mind if I head out back for a couple of minutes? Mum should be here any time now.'

'Go! I can manage.'

Up until now it's all felt rather surreal, but as I press the phone icon the reality of what's happening hits me in the gut.

'Ivy, I just had to hear your voice. It's happening, it's really happening!'

Adam is brimming over with excitement and it's wonderful to hear. 'I'm so proud of you, Adam. Why wouldn't they snap you up?'

'I didn't really believe it but now I've had the official email I'm in! The only thing is, my start date is Monday, thirty-first of October.' His tone evens out apologetically.

'It's fine,' I reply, brushing off his concerns. 'The removal men will have everything here at the café moved into the storage unit on the Sunday anyway. On Monday Rach and I will be setting up at the garden centre.'

'The good news is that first week I'll be office-based, shadowing my boss and doing a few trips out to a couple of their sites. I'll be home every night.'

He sounds awkward and I hasten to reassure him, as I don't want anything to take the edge off his elation. This is a big deal. 'Look, don't keep worrying about me. I'll be fine and we need to go out and celebrate your good news as soon as we're able. How are things at the farm?'

'Great. Riley and I finished the roof about mid-morning. Now we're getting stuck into insulating the walls ready to start plaster-boarding the area that's going to be used as a yoga studio, apparently. Jess is a dab hand at it and with the three of us it's flying up.'

It's a relief to hear that Jess is over her disappointment, as I'd hate for there to be a sense of unease between them while Adam's there.

'You'll get everything done in time before you leave them to it?'

'It'll be tight, I admit, but Riley is relieved that we'll have the worst of it out the way.'

I don't like to ask whether that means Adam won't make it back to Stroud for the weekend if they need to work through. There's an awkwardness between us still; a half-finished conversation Adam and I started on Sunday after my chat with Jess. He was visibly shaken when I said I felt a little angry, and undermined, by his lack of faith in my decision-making when I was supporting him in his endeavours.

'You'd best get back to work then.' I laugh, trying to sound jolly.

'Yep, better had. You and Rach are off to the garden centre this afternoon?'

'We are. Mum and Grace are covering for us and Lisa said they can give her a call if they get swamped, but we'll only be gone a couple of hours anyway.'

There's a pause and I hear Adam draw in a deep breath. He stops suddenly, as if he was about to say something but changes his mind at the last second. 'I'll give you a call tonight,' he replies. 'Take care. Love you, honey!'

I know you do, Adam. But that voice in my head remains unspoken. *We'll get through this, I promise.*

ADAM
Renweneth Farm, Cornwall

8

Accepting That Life Is a Rocky Road

When I called Ivy last night she could hardly string a few words together, saying she had a really bad headache. I didn't keep her talking for long and although she texted me first thing this morning, it was brief, saying she was better but had overslept. I've been on edge waiting to call her and couldn't hang on any longer.

When I walk back into the small barn, both Riley and Jess immediately look up.

'Ivy's fine,' I reassure them. 'She's feeling much better and looking forward to celebrating my new job.'

Jess retracts the blade on the knife she's using to cut a sheet of insulation and walks over to me. 'She didn't say anything else?'

'No. Just that she and Rach are off to the garden centre in a bit, as she ended up going home sick yesterday. They're hoping to talk the owner into letting Rach give it a go.'

'Ivy really is going to accept that job at Mawsley House?'

I look at Jess, shrugging my shoulders. 'I have no idea. After she tore into me about feeling undermined, I've backed right off ever since.'

Jess frowns. 'I think you're doing the right thing, Adam. Ivy has more than enough to deal with in the short term and doesn't need to add even more decisions into the mix. Now that your situation is sorted, it should help take off some of the urgency.

I'm really sorry I complicated things. I should have known better and I didn't mean to add to your worries.'

Riley, too, has now stopped work and comes to join us. 'Listen, guys. You both meant well, and Ivy knows that. I don't think any of us realised just how fragile she was feeling last weekend.'

Jess's expression is dour. 'It's my fault. I got excited about the thought of having the two of you here, to be a part of this.' She slaps her hand lightly against her forehead, holding it there as if *she* has a headache now.

'And I went overboard, which tipped her over the edge. Poor Ivy—' I admit, guiltily.

'What's up with Ivy?' a voice booms out from behind us. 'Goodness, you lot have been busy.'

We all turn around and Jess rushes over to throw her arms around her granddad.

'Cappy! At last – I thought you weren't coming.'

'What have I missed? Because you're all looking glum considering things are moving on in here,' he questions.

Jess releases him and Riley and I shake his hand.

'Come on up to the farmhouse and I'll tell you all about it,' Jess replies, sounding rather dejected. 'I think we could all do with a strong coffee.'

Both Riley and I nod our heads and then get back to work. When they're out of earshot he turns to look at me.

'Ivy won't even entertain the idea?'

'It seems not. I thought…' I stop mid-sentence. What did I think when she flung at me that she felt everyone was putting pressure on her? That wasn't the case, but in hindsight I can appreciate why she thought that. And Jess… well, Jess is enthusiastic about everything in life. To the Nth degree. 'I hoped that Ivy would see this as the perfect solution.'

Riley seems surprised. 'Perfect?'

'Look, you can't repeat this to anyone, especially Jess.' I give him a pointed look and get an instant "Of course" by way of response.

'We're all aware that it takes a lot of guts to set up your own business and there are no guarantees it will pay off. I simply thought that this was an easier option for Ivy.'

Riley lets out a rather caustic laugh. 'You can say that again… it doesn't pay to take anything for granted these days, especially when it comes to business.'

I nod my head in agreement. 'Ivy is a first-class baker and the end product really matters to her. Her motto is *you are what you eat* and in an industry that pushes sugar to the excess, she's about everything in moderation.'

'Even when it comes to cakes?'

'Everything she makes has only the best organic ingredients. No additives. No enhancers and the flavourings are natural, as nature intended. You won't see her plastering on the icing sugar or the butter cream.'

'Don't people expect a sugar rush, though?'

'You'd think so, but it's the reason why her shop is so successful. Treats without the guilt – or the regret – she often tells me. She makes what she calls *drizzles* and many customers aren't even aware they're eating healthily. If she'd been able to afford a bigger place to begin with, and had a better landlord, she'd be sitting pretty now.'

'I didn't realise. I'd simply assumed she was just a normal, run-of-the-mill baker.'

'No. Not Ivy. The problem is that she sees how Jess turns her dreams into reality but Ivy doesn't think she has the same level of resilience. She takes the knocks personally, as if it's a failure on her part. However, if she goes for that job as catering manager, I can see now that her dream will be over, even though I suggested it might not be a bad idea. I regret that, because I think she was fooling herself, knowing how tough it would be to set up somewhere new in the future.' Being able to share that with someone is like getting a load off my chest. I couldn't say that to Jess, because she's so close to Ivy. Riley, I know, won't breathe a word of this to anyone. He can see how hard it is for me to acknowledge what I'm saying.

'Mate, I'm sorry. No wonder you feel badly about what happened last weekend.'

'Ivy is trying to be as strong and determined as Jess, but inside she's starting to doubt herself. And that's not Ivy, but because she won't talk about it I don't know what to do.'

'Then do nothing.'

I look at him questioningly.

'It sounds crazy, wrong even. I know that and I only give advice if I think it might be useful.' He looks at me and I indicate for him to continue. 'Let me give you an example. I'm going through issues with my ex with regard to having at least some contact with my son – Ollie. I gave up my right to have any input into his life when Fiona threw me out. I messed up, big time, and I hold my hands up to that. I'm there if either of them needs me in a practical way but, as time is passing, Ollie wants to know more about his father. I never stopped caring about him, not for one moment, but he doesn't really know that. However, Fiona is in the driving seat, and I respect her wishes. If I don't, I'll lose him forever. What I'm trying to say is that sometimes it's not straightforward; you can't just cut to the chase.'

As his words sink in, I realise there's a lot more to Riley than I first thought. He wouldn't be in Jess's life if he wasn't fully committed because he realises Jess and Lola come as a package and the same is true for him and Ollie. I'm glad I opened up to him.

'You think doing nothing is the least damaging path to take? I can't afford to get this wrong.'

'Go home this weekend and be there for Ivy. If she wants to talk, simply listen and be supportive. Maybe all Ivy needs now is a little space and time to decide what she wants to do next. The decision is hers, mate; you know that.'

'It's just that here… well, it's all set up and she'd be free to do her thing. Whenever Ivy looks at Lola, I see the longing in her and, if we lived here, I genuinely think it wouldn't be long before

Ivy and I could have it all. A good life, a steady income and a place we'd be happy.'

Riley reaches out to put his hand on my shoulder. 'I'm miles away from my family and most of my lifelong friends have forgotten me, hidden away down here in Cornwall. I don't think that would be the case for you and Ivy, as it isn't the case for Jess and Lola. But Ivy must come to that conclusion herself, and if she doesn't, then you have to accept it, Adam.'

Cappy appears carrying two mugs. 'Here you go, lads. Jess said she'll be along shortly. She's just putting on a slow-cook casserole for this evening. Sorry to hear about all the upheaval, Adam, but congratulations on the new job!'

Gabe Newman is a grand old chap and his late wife, Maggie, left a huge hole in his life. So big that he couldn't stay at the farm and headed back to his family in Gloucestershire. Jess taking over was a huge deal for them all, but now she's got him back for the next six months as farm manager, while she and Riley press on with the next phase of the redevelopment.

'Thanks, Cappy. Is everything sorted back in Stroud?'

'A friend's nephew and his fiancée are renting the house, so it's in good hands. I put a few things in storage, but it was all new anyway. I didn't take anything much with me from the farmhouse, mainly personal belongings. Jess has recycled a few things but the rest of it is in one of the rooms in Renweneth Manor still, I believe. It's all dark wood, which I always hated but Jess likes to paint things and breathe new life into them.' He rolls his eyes.

Riley and I laugh, congenially. He's not fooling either of us. He'd have been disappointed if Jess had ditched the lot of it.

'Ivy's having a bad time of it, by all accounts? Landlord from hell, I gather.'

'Yeah, he's not the nicest of people, Cappy. She's been a good tenant. The property was in a prime spot, but she had problems with the basic facilities from day one.'

LINN B. HALTON

'Then Ivy's best off out of it,' he declares, firmly.

'I agree but it's a bitter blow, Cappy. Ivy wanted to really build her business and now it's back to square one.'

'Give her my love when you speak to her next, Adam, won't you? She's a lovely young woman and you're a lucky man, but then you know that. Right, my coffee's getting cold in the kitchen, so I'd best get back. Then I'll get settled into the farmhouse. It's good to be back, like coming home. See you later.'

I glance at Riley and his eyes widen. 'Like coming home?' he repeats, sounding delighted. 'Jess will be over the moon when I pass that on. But as for what we've been talking about, my lips are sealed. So, we won't be rearranging the layout, then? I really do need to know where the entrance is going to be.'

I grimace. 'I guess not. I simply want Ivy to be happy and if that means we stay close to family in Stroud, so be it.'

'It's a shame, Adam, but that's life. There's no point in changing the access to the barn from the street side if Smithy's Cottage is going to be a rental property. I guess Jess has some decisions to make about the future of the bakery. Personally, I think it's a mistake if she decides to employ people to run it. If they don't bake on site, then she still has the problem of finding a suitable supplier. If that's the case, then surely she's better off trying to get an established bakery to rent it as an outlet? I agree with her parents. They're really concerned that she's spreading herself a little thin with so many things to manage.'

'Maybe that's why she wants Cappy here permanently,' I point out.

'Hmm... but for now he'll only commit to six months.'

'That's a shame, because this place is full of memories for him. I understand it can't be easy but he seems delighted to be back.'

'What was Maggie like, Adam?' Riley asks. 'Everyone speaks of her so fondly. When I was working part-time for a building supplies company, I made a few deliveries here back in the day, but never had the chance to speak to her.'

I stop to consider how best to describe a tiny woman who was a literal force of nature. 'Maggie was the sort of woman who looked meek and mild but boy, did she have gumption, as Cappy always said. She was fearless. The sort of woman who would tell you straight that you're talking nonsense and if she did, you knew she was right.' I start laughing, remembering some of my more memorable conversations with her. Including the one where she told me that I should get a move on and propose to Ivy because the poor girl was getting tired of waiting.

'Hey, honey. How did it go this afternoon?' After my conversation with Riley, I've decided there was a lot of truth in what he said. Ivy is naturally feeling overwhelmed and all she needs is a little time and space to weigh up her options. When she's ready, I'll be there to support her no matter what she decides to do next; we're there for each other through the good times and the bad, which is all that matters.

'Delia was rather hesitant, and I could see that Rach was disappointed but it was time for her to step up and she did. Delia has agreed to let her rent the space on a rolling three-monthly basis. Rach was honest, saying that as long as she covered her overheads – which she'll keep to the minimum to begin with – that was fine. If the summer months see some return on her advertising, then it will allow her to get a van. The idea is that in the winter months the online click-and-collect hamper/takeout option will include a home-delivery service. Delia seemed impressed but she stressed that their focus is firmly on the wholesale side now. It sounds like they have no intention of doing any advertising other than in trade magazines.'

Even though that probably wasn't quite what Rach hoped to hear, Ivy doesn't sound concerned on her behalf. 'Do you think she'll make it work?'

'I don't know, Adam. But I was impressed with how she dealt with Delia and her first attempt at negotiating terms. Oh...

I have some other news! One of the estate agents rang and left a message. There's a shop on the other side of town that's been empty for a while because it has a serious rising damp problem. The owners are struggling to find a builder at the moment, so they can't estimate when exactly it will be ready. However... the agent has managed to get the owners to agree to letting me have a look around tomorrow morning.'

I don't say what instantly comes to mind, which is that's quite a job they're looking at. It'll involve knocking the affected areas back to bare brick, treating the problem and replastering. It might even mean digging out the floor and tanking it, if that's the root cause of the water ingress. 'It's not a quick job, Ivy.'

'Once the work has been done the rent is thirty per cent more than I'd ideally like to pay. However, it's a larger unit but as it's not on the main thoroughfare the price per square foot is lower. How that trade-off will affect the takings, I have no idea, but at least my regulars will be able to find us.'

It's time to ignore my reservations. 'In which case, it's well worth a look.'

'Cristabel from Mawsley House left me a voicemail earlier on to give her a call when I have a moment. I did say I wanted to take some time to consider her offer, so I won't get back to her until after the viewing. Poor Mum, her time isn't her own at the moment but she's excited at the prospect of a new premises.'

Suddenly there's a lift in Ivy's voice and an alarm bell goes off in my head. I thought she had already made her decision, so why is she getting her hopes up over what, at best, is a long shot? The last thing she needs now is another disappointment but it tells me one thing, that her dream is still alive, so I keep it upbeat. 'Knowing Sarah, she's in her element helping out at the café. There isn't anyone I know who does afternoon tea like your mother, Ivy – it's where your passion came from in the first place.' My reminder makes her laugh.

'And did you manage to calm down and get stuck in after you broke your exciting news to Jess and Riley?'

'I did. We all did, in fact, although Cappy's back and Jess disappeared for a while to help him settle into the guest room at The Farmhouse. Lola was so excited to see him when she arrived home. Misty had disappeared for a while and they both went searching for her. It was obvious she was hunting something and apparently the mice have set up a new home in one of the raised vegetable beds behind the manor. It all needs clearing out, but for now it's her new hunting ground.'

'Jess will be advertising Smithy's Cottage for rent then, if Cappy is still saying he's only back until the work on sorting the car park and facilities for the hay barn is completed.'

'I guess so. Apparently, the other cottage – Penti Growan – is booked solidly through until the end of March already.'

'Vyvyan will be happy about that. And it won't be long before she'll be advertising to fill the concessions in the small barn.'

'Riley told me that there's a waiting list of interested applicants so it shouldn't take much to get that sorted. We're just dry-lining the studio area on the mezzanine and it's quite an impressive space.' Suddenly, we're talking properly again and it's a huge relief.

'I'm sorry I've been so grumpy, Adam. I wasn't angry with you, but I was angry. Mainly with Mr Williams for not being upfront with me. I owe Jess an apology, too. Once I get tomorrow out the way I'll give her a call and have a heart-to-heart.'

'It would put her mind to rest, it really would. She meant well and I did, too. Whatever you decide to do, you know that I'm one hundred per cent behind you, Ivy, don't you?'

'If I didn't have you by my side, I don't know how I would have survived this last couple of weeks with my sanity intact, Adam. And the timing was awful, wasn't it, which just added to the pressure. At least you're settled and perhaps tomorrow I'll be in a similar position. I'll either have a job, or maybe a couple of months' wait until I get the keys for a new property. I didn't think I'd be hearing myself say that was even an option.'

'Hang in there, Ivy. There's always room in our lives for hope.' If the damp problem is easily fixable, even though the shop is tucked away, Ivy will come up with an idea to get the customers through the door and we'll all be supporting her.

IVY

Stroud, Gloucestershire

9

Not Quite the Answer I Was Expecting

Thursday kicks off with a big uptick in the general mood at the café when I quietly take Rach to one side and tell her about the potential new premises. We all know the old bicycle shop; it's been empty for a while and has changed hands several times. Not one of the owners so far has made a start on the work but, hopefully, this time around they'll get on with it.

Rach raises her hand, fingers crossed, as if this is the little miracle we feared was no more than an impossible dream. 'Oh, Ivy. If this works out we can all breathe a huge sigh of relief.'

'It's hard to believe that this was once a dingy kebab shop, so we know that anything is possible.'

In between serving, we natter away, but we're both clock-watching. About an hour later, Mum appears.

'Right, I can't keep the estate agent waiting,' I half-whisper to Rach. 'Wish me luck!'

She chews her lip anxiously, as Grace walks through from the back room to take over.

'Are you off somewhere nice?' she asks.

'Not really. I'm just in the mood for a bit of fresh air and a quick look around the shops,' I reply, breezily. Nothing would delight me more than to come back with some good news, but it pays to be cautious.

Mum is chatting to a customer but catches my eye and inclines her head in the direction of the clock on the wall. 'I'll see you after my break.' I yank off my apron and leave Grace and Rach to it.

Rach has so much potential. Before I took her on she was a waitress at a local restaurant but in her spare time, after putting her daughter to bed, she'd be in her kitchen whipping up novelty birthday cakes for family and friends. I think she could easily turn her hand to making wedding cakes but as long as she's baking, she's smiling.

'Um... right. The landlord did tell me that a company was due in to clear this out but obviously there's been a delay. Just mind where you step.'

It's dank, miserable and smelly. Mum and I exchange a worried glance.

'Is the floor safe?' I ask, hesitantly.

The estate agent glances around as if he isn't quite sure. 'As far as we've been told, it is. The damp problem is mainly at the back but you'll see it's also affected that far wall.'

When he says *affected* that's obviously estate agency speak for black mould.

'A builder was supposed to be starting in a week's time, but they pulled out due to staff shortages, apparently. The management company are hopeful of finding a replacement quite quickly to get this place back up to spec.'

I'm trying to ignore the obvious and in my mind's eye I think about where the tables would go and the best place for the counter. In its current position, on the left-hand side as you step through the door, it simply wouldn't work.

We traipse around rather gingerly, and I think even the burly estate agent is a little on edge hoping nothing furry suddenly runs out in front of us. The kitchen is a good size and there's a cloakroom with two toilets off a small corridor alongside it. Upstairs is a bathroom, two bedrooms and an office.

'It will all be redecorated once the damp problem has been sorted, naturally.'

'Is there any room for negotiation on the rental price?' If you don't ask, you don't get.

'You could give it a try, but they'll probably only consider dropping it after it's been on the market for a minimum of a few weeks once the work has been completed.'

It's not what I wanted to hear, or see, and my hopes are dashed. This could be ready to go in three months, but it could also drag on with no firm target date for occupation.

'Okay. Thank you so much for showing us around at such short notice.'

He gives me a knowing look. 'It's not quite the right location for you, is it, Mrs Taylor? I can't think of anything else likely to come up in the foreseeable future, but if I do get a lead, do you want me to keep in touch?'

'As you can appreciate, time is fast running out for me and if I don't find something very soon, I've got a tough decision to make.'

'That's a real shame. My wife works at the solicitors, Bradley's, just around the corner and twice a week she calls in. Carol? Short blonde hair.'

'Oh, yes! I didn't realise… strawberry twists and apricot tarts if my memory serves me right.'

'Yep. Our Tuesday and Thursday treat.'

As he sees us out and I step through the door, there's no doubt at all in my mind that this would be the wrong move. We all shake hands and as we walk away, Mum is very quiet indeed.

'What did you think?' I ask, wondering if I was expecting too much.

She laughs. 'It's hard to imagine it looking and smelling good, but this is a quiet backwater. You certainly couldn't put tables outside because of the vehicular access. Looking around it's a bit of an odd street, Ivy.'

Mum's right. A bookmakers' shop, a computer repair outlet, a place that sells plastic model kits, and a fabric store that looks like it's been here since the Eighties. Beneath the layers of peeling paint around the windows, the wood is probably rotten to the core.

'Do you think I'd be making a mistake if I take the job at Mawsley House Conference Centre?'

Mum stops in her tracks, a pained look on her face. 'Ivy, it's a job, a good one, but – oh, my love – honestly? It's not you. The thing is, are you ready to let go of your dream just to pay the bills? Only you can make that decision, but it will be a sad day given the success you made of what is quite a poky little shop.'

We both start laughing, as we link arms and increase the pace. 'It was never big enough for my lofty dreams, was it, Mum?'

'No, but you made a success of it and I'm proud of you. Life is going to be different for you once Adam's working away, and maybe taking on something bigger would put a little too much pressure on your shoulders.' I can sense her unease and it takes me by surprise. 'Ivy, whatever decision you come to, don't settle for something that will end up making you miserable. I'd hate that, my darling daughter. It would break my heart.'

Mine, too, but anything is better than nothing.

'Mum, what if an opportunity came up but it involved moving… some distance away. Should I consider it?'

We draw to a halt within sight of the café and she turns to look at me, her eyes scanning my face. 'Don't you even think about using your family as an excuse to hold you back, Ivy. You've a cousin in Wales and another living in Lincoln. Your aunt is always going between one and the other for her little jaunts away. All that matters is that you're happy. Is Adam aware of it?'

I nod my head. 'Yes, and he thinks it's a good idea.'

'But you don't?'

It's hard to explain how I'm feeling but I've always been

honest with Mum. 'This sounds silly, but I'm scared to even think through the implications.'

She narrows her eyes at me disapprovingly. 'Which tells me that you haven't totally rejected it, Ivy, but you're doubting yourself. Don't do that, my girl!' Her tone is emphatic. 'If it makes sound business sense, and both you and Adam are up for it, then it's something you should give some serious consideration to before you say yes to that job.'

Talk about back to the drawing board; Mum knows me better than I know myself. I was rather hoping she'd say I'm being too impatient; maybe if I wait a little the right property might come up so I can welcome my regular customers back. The problem with making life-changing decisions is that it's a total leap of faith. The other side of that coin is the fact that anything could go wrong. Now what do I do?

'Ivy, this is a surprise. Did you mean to dial Adam? He's been nervously checking his phone for the last hour, expecting a call from you.'

'No, Jess, I… I wanted to have a quick word with you first.'

'Oh, I hope nothing's wrong. Adam said you went to look at a new premises this morning and he's been on edge.' Her concern is touching.

'Everything's fine, but the shop isn't for me. That's why I'm calling. Before I talk to Adam, I just wanted to check whether your offer still stands?'

I wasn't expecting total silence before Jess stutters 'Oh, oh, um… yes, of course!'

'You paused for a brief moment there; it's not a problem if you've had a rethink.'

She starts laughing. 'Not at all! Can you hang on for a couple of minutes?'

'Yes. Why?'

'Something I've just remembered… I'll call you straight back.'

I should have asked Jess if she was free to talk first as I know how busy she is. I imagine her working off a ladder reaching out to fill in holes, or something equally crazy. When my phone kicks into life, I start laughing.

'What?' Jess demands.

'I forget that you're working on site. Sorry if it's not a good time to chat.'

'It's not that.' She lowers her voice, a little breathless, and I can tell she's walking. 'I had to run over to see Cappy. Riley and Adam are in the small barn and they're just about to start bricking up the entrance from the street. I asked him to stop them. He'll come up with a suitable excuse. Talk about timing!'

'You didn't mention me, did you?'

'No, of course not. I told Cappy I was having second thoughts and I'd explain later. So, come on, what's happening at your end?'

I let out a loud groan. 'Oh, Jess. Even Mum is worried about me accepting the job at Mawsley House.'

'Then come here, Ivy. Give it a go. Adam is already on board with the idea and yes, you'll miss everyone you leave behind, but we're not a million miles away. And one thing we have here is plenty of accommodation on the doorstep, with the campsite. Smithy's Cottage has a lovely guest bedroom; in fact, you could even turn the office above the bakery into accommodation.'

I blurt out a shocked exclamation. 'You've thought of everything!'

'I have, Ivy,' Jess admits, her voice sincere. 'I won't lie, you will miss people – I know because I do, even after all this time. But the quality of life here is very different and everyone is eager to come visit. When they do, they recharge their batteries and go home feeling happy.'

'Jess, be straight with me. I sort of thought you hoped that Cappy would move back to the farm on a permanent basis and you'd earmarked Smithy's Cottage for him.'

'That was the idea at first, but you try telling Cappy what

to do. He insists the guest room in The Farmhouse suits him perfectly. I think a part of that is because he can now spend time enjoying the memories he had there with Grandma, rather than focusing on his sense of loss. It's gone full circle and the more time he spends at The Farmhouse, the more at home he'll feel. He sees Smithy's Cottage as an income stream and if someone rents it out, he'll be happy.'

'Ah, now I understand.'

'Admittedly, the pressure is on to start work early in the New Year on renovating Renweneth Manor, as we're hoping to have phase one completed by August. If it all goes according to plan, Cappy will decide to sell his house in Stroud and move back permanently as Lola, Riley and I move into the manor. That's what I feel Grandma would have wanted.'

'Aww, Jess. But what about your parents? They like to keep an eye on Cappy.'

'Are you kidding? Mum is constantly fretting over him, precisely because she knows he isn't happy there. She just doesn't know what to do about it. My job is to entice him back here permanently when the time is right and make sure there's enough income coming in to keep Renweneth Farm going for years to come.'

Jess takes my breath away at times. How can I refuse my friend's generous offer? The truth is that I can't.

'Ivy? Are you still there?'

'I am. I guess the next phone call I make will be to Adam. Oh, Jess, are we really going to do this?' I draw in a deep breath, unable to believe what I'm about to set in motion.

'We are!' Jess states, firmly. 'And we'd better get a shift on, because Vyvyan is now looking to lease out the new stalls in the small barn. By mid-November, Renweneth Farm is going to be turned into a Christmas village and the bakery will be in the centre of it!'

Just listening to Jess makes my head spin. I mutter a silent prayer that I'm up to it, because her expectations will be high.

'A lot of friends and family will be descending upon Renweneth Farm this Christmas,' she continues, excitedly. 'Somehow or other, we'll fit them all in, I promise you, Ivy. Oh, it's going to be amazing. Make that call now, because I can't step out into the courtyard with a grin this big on my face without sending them all into a tizzy!'

Rach didn't take the news about the old bicycle shop well, yesterday. She was just as despondent as I felt.

'It obviously wasn't meant to be, Ivy. At least you left no stone unturned. Under normal circumstances you wouldn't even have considered it.'

'I shouldn't have said anything... I didn't mean to get your hopes up, Rach. Even Adam tried to bring me down to earth when I told him about what was wrong with the property.'

She'd shaken her head, sadly. 'It's hard to listen when what someone is trying to tell you isn't what you want to hear.'

'It's tough to accept that it's really over. So, for you, it's back to the former plan. Most of the flyers you brought in have now been handed out and hopefully some of our customers will find their way to the garden centre. Have you had any contact from Delia?'

'Yes, she's about to email me over some paperwork in the next day or so. My brother will go through it in detail and then explain it to me in layman's terms.'

We spent the rest of the afternoon bantering about the length of our respective to-do lists, as I wrap up things at the café and Rach ploughs forward with her own plans with renewed vigour. Mine weren't far off being complete, but Rach's list was growing and any spare moments we got she was picking my brains.

'You remind me of me, when I was first setting up this place.' I'd grinned at her. 'Buzzing with excitement on one hand, and nervous as heck on the other.'

'It's a little more than nerves,' she'd admitted.

The end of an era is a turning point you never forget and this was a particularly poignant one for us both.

'Did you get any sleep at all last night, Ivy?' Rach asks, as we get ready to open up this morning.

I guess that the dark bags beneath my eyes are a bit of a giveaway.

'Off and on. My head is fit to burst at the moment.'

'Have you made a decision about your future?'

I draw in a hesitant breath. 'I've been offered an opportunity that is a huge risk but Adam has convinced me it's worth a shot.'

Rach's ears perk up. 'That's not your style, Ivy. You always err to the cautious side and that's one of the things I respect about you, because you never wear those rose-coloured spectacles.'

'You're going to think I've lost my mind on this one,' I declare. 'Jess has offered me the chance to take over the bakery at Renweneth Farm.'

'You're moving to Cornwall?' Rach's expression is one of disbelief.

As I tell her about Jess's offer, her face brightens. 'Oh, Ivy! It sounds idyllic but I thought it was the place you and Adam go to relax and unwind. Not to live.'

'In my wildest dreams it's not something I ever saw us doing, Rach, believe me.' The reality of having made the decision is still sinking in this morning and my stomach begins to churn. 'I rejected it out of hand when the subject first came up because it's crazy, right? But Adam is convinced it's the right thing to do. My parents' reaction shocked me, too. It's true to say that we all shed a tear, but they said Cornwall is their favourite place to visit and they're excited for us.'

Rach frowns, giving it some thought. 'Well… we'll all miss you, Ivy, but I'm glad you didn't take the job at Mawsley House. It was kind of you to think of us all, but what worked here for our cosy little team wouldn't have worked in a corporate setting.

However, it's a brave choice and a real upheaval for you, given everything you still have to sort out at this end. Your head must be spinning. Adjusting to being apart from Adam, starting from scratch with a new business and settling into a new home. That's a tall order. Having Jess there is a big positive, though, and I hope it turns out to be as wonderful as it sounds.'

Without warning, Rach throws her arms around me and we hug, like sisters about to part.

When we step back it is a glassy-eyes moment. 'To be honest, I get times when I feel that none of this is real; but Jess will expect me to hit the ground running when I get there.'

'And you will,' she replies with a smile. 'That's one of your strengths; you'll soon pull together a plan of action.'

I purse my lips. 'Hmm… I fear it's not going to be quite as easy as it might appear. Finding the right staff when I don't know anyone, is going to be a challenge. And the customers are used to locally baked speciality breads, so I'll need to find the right supplier.'

Rach pulls a sad face. 'It's overload isn't it, everything coming all at once? I'm excited for you, though, Ivy. From what you've told me about the farm, it's an idyllic place to live and work. Maybe it is exactly what you need and at least you're going into what is in effect a brand-new building. No more dodgy wiring to worry about or faulty fire alarms.'

Rach can tell how anxious I'm feeling and she's trying to bolster my confidence but the weight of everything just seems to be pressing down on me.

'Oh, Ivy, you look completely drained. Sit yourself down,' Rach insists. 'I'm going to make us both a strong coffee. We can grab a quick twenty minutes and still be ready to open on time.'

As she beavers away behind the counter she's firing questions at me. 'Is the bakery available now?'

'No, the current people are due to move out at the end of the month. I'm going to call Jess at seven o'clock this evening to discuss a few details. On Saturday morning, Adam and I are heading down there and Jess is going to arrange for me to meet with the woman who is running it. I'm hoping to agree some sort of a handover arrangement.'

However, there's no way I can get everything set up so that The Farmhouse Bakery doesn't close its doors when Jory and Alice hand the keys back to Jess. I can't be in two places at once and I'm committed to being at the garden centre until the end of November, when Rach officially takes over. Neither Jess nor Adam seem to understand it isn't quite the easy option they think it is. But at the same time I'm beginning to feel excited about getting stuck into a new challenge.

IVY
Renweneth Farm, Cornwall

10

The Craziness Is About to Begin

Bright and early Saturday morning I walk into The Farmhouse Bakery hoping to be able to ink in some of the unknowns in what is now quite a detailed plan of action. To say that this meeting is important is an understatement.

Alice Rowse walks towards me, smiling, and her handshake is equally welcoming, which bodes well. We're not total strangers, as she and her husband were at the Renweneth Farm end-of-summer party. I stopped to have a brief chat with them, as you do when you're circulating.

'Ivy, it's lovely to see you. Come this way.' Alice turns to the woman serving, indicating that we're heading upstairs. There are three people waiting, but two of them are deep in conversation and not in the least concerned about queuing. It makes me grin to myself, as I'm used to office and shop workers who rush in for takeout and expect to rush straight back out.

I follow Alice up to the office and almost need to pinch myself at the thought that very soon I'll be the one running the bakery.

'Thank you for taking time out to chat, Alice. I so appreciate it.'

Ironically, it was a phone call from Rach the night before last that solved my biggest problem – that I can't be in two places at once. At the garden centre, Rach and the girls will be working for me until the end of November, after which any orders coming in will be Rach's responsibility. But that assumed I'd be there working alongside them. After talking to Grace and Lisa, who both agreed to do extra hours to cover if necessary, Rach insisted they could cope without me. She said it was the least she could do in return for what I'd done for her. The reality is that all I'm able to give her is an online business that has only been going a few months. Its value is negligible, because the bulk of the orders were as a direct result of the leaflets and window display advertising at the café. Maybe the garden centre café is waiting for Rach to slowly turn it into her dream business. I was just touched that the three of them stepped up to help me out in my time of need.

My meeting with Alice this morning is crucial because a smooth transition depends on several things slotting into place and that's why a lot depends on what she has to say.

'Anything at all Jory and I can do, Ivy, you only need ask. We feel awful walking away, as we love what Jess is doing here. It's about to take off in ways none of us really appreciated and Jess has the vision all right. A dear friend of ours, Anna, is going to take one of the units when they're ready. She runs her jewellery business from home and sells a bit online, but she's thrilled about being a part of this.'

'It's a great opportunity and that's so good to hear, Alice.'

'Jess said you run a successful café in the centre of Stroud and do all the baking on site. She mentioned that you also have a website and do online orders. It seems Jess has found just the right person to take over and Jory and I are thrilled about that.'

Even Jess doesn't understand this is going to be a totally fresh start. I'm not selling a business, as The Cake and Coffee Emporium won't exist after the end of the month. There is no goodwill to capitalise upon. I'd love to sit here and nod my head as if everything is going to be just fine but putting my pride to one side, I need Alice to understand I have a real dilemma.

'Sadly, it'll be a case of setting up a completely new website for The Farmhouse Bakery. My aim here is to use local suppliers, as I did in Stroud, and feature them. And, obviously, encompass everything that a trip to Renweneth Farm can offer.'

'Oh, I see. We assumed you were just expanding your business.'

'No, my landlord sold the premises and the café is shutting down the same day as I'm due to pick up the keys here. The earliest we could get a van for the move to Cornwall was Saturday the fifth of November. Even that's going to make it tight to organise the packing in time, as Adam is also starting a new job.'

Alice frowns. 'Oh, Ivy! We assumed we'd be handing the keys straight over to you. It's a real shame to close the doors for the sake of five days.' Clearly Alice, like me, thinks that's a bad idea.

'I've arranged for the steam ovens and kitchen equipment we're bringing with us to be installed on the Sunday. But as things stand, I don't have any other options.'

There's a tap on the door and the woman from downstairs carries in two cups of coffee. 'Sorry to disturb you but there was a lull and I thought you might appreciate this.'

'Wenna, this is Ivy who is taking over the bakery when we leave.'

We exchange smiles. 'Hi, Wenna, it's lovely to meet you and thanks so much for the coffee.'

'You're very welcome, Ivy.'

In the background there's a tinkling sound and Wenna's eyes light up. 'Another customer by the sound of it; I'll leave you ladies in peace.'

As the door shuts Alice looks directly at me. 'I meant it when I said Jory and I will do whatever we can to help, Ivy. We were really excited to be a part of this community and Jess was very understanding when our situation changed overnight.'

Here goes. If you don't ask, you don't get. 'I appreciate you'll have a lot going on back at your own shop in Polreweek, given that you're expanding the business, but I wondered if you'd consider continuing to supply the bakery with bread going forward? My parents have offered to come down and do whatever they can that first week and at least that would ensure the customers have some continuity. The new patisserie side will be up and working a week later.'

Alice wrinkles her brow and it's all I can do not to cross my fingers as I wait for her response.

'It'll be all go back in Polreweek for us, coping with building works and baking, but I know that Jory will make it work.' She looks pleased and the relief is immense. 'And Wenna lives in one of those cottages just off the lane down by the crossroad. I'm sure she'd be very happy to continue on here to provide cover, but she will need some help.'

'That would be amazing, Alice, it really would.'

Alice is helping Jess out, I get that, but she's also doing something wonderful for me and it's a lifeline.

'You're a baker who specialises in confectionary, I hear?'

'Yes. I only bake bread very occasionally at home and one of my main concerns was disappointing your customers.'

Alice's cheeks begin to colour up. 'Ah, that's kind of you to say that, Ivy. We are doing good business here, it's true, and we've been pleasantly surprised at how many regulars we have already.'

'In all honesty, Alice, I don't think I'd be doing anyone any favours by turning the bakery into a simple cake shop and café.'

I stop to drink my coffee and Alice's eyes sweep over my face. 'And Jory and I will still feel like we're a little part of it here.'

My heart leaps in my chest. 'Alice, you have no idea how happy that makes me!' I admit, with deepest sincerity.

'If small businesses like us support each other, then we'll all have a bright future. Let's head down and have a word with Wenna, shall we? We took her on for the trial here and have offered her a job in Polreweek. To be honest, if you wanted to keep her, I think she'd jump at the chance to stay as the bakery is almost on her doorstep.'

Finally, there's a light at the end of the tunnel... It's just a tiny glow but it's my job to ramp it up. I can do this; I know I can!

There hasn't been much to smile about these last few weeks but this afternoon everything is different. Laughing and joking while we watch Riley and Jess walking hand in hand together in front of us, the old Adam is back.

'No pressure, guys,' Jess calls out, 'but Vyvyan rang me this morning to say all of the stalls are now taken in the small barn.'

'Now that calls for a celebration!' Riley instantly responds.

'And it means we need to come up with a name.'

Adam's quick off the mark. 'I think that's best done over a pint, don't you agree, Riley?'

'I do. Let's head down to Penvennan Cove. Have you ever been to The Lark and Lantern, Adam?'

'No.'

'It's going to be your new local so it's about time we checked it out. It's about a thirty-minute trek from here or a ten-minute drive,' Riley confirms. 'How did your chat with Alice go this morning, Ivy?'

'Great,' I reply, glancing at Jess, who immediately turns to look at me with interest. 'I'll tell you about it when we get to the pub.'

We banter as we walk, and I reflect on the fact that when Jess was married we never did things together as a foursome. Ben only joined in if we were going somewhere – the cinema, or bowling. Long walks and chilling out together was never his thing.

Me, I just love being out in the fresh air. When the weather's good in Stroud, once the lunchtime rush is over, I often wander out to sit on a low stone wall to munch on a sandwich. The birds are never far away and gravitate towards me knowing I won't ignore them. Gazing out over the town as it slopes down towards the precinct, in the background the green hills create a wonderful backdrop. It's often described as 'the Covent Garden of the Cotswolds' and it's where I was born and brought up. And now, here I am, walking a cliff path and trying to get my head around the fact that in a couple of weeks' time this will be home for me and Adam.

'I can't believe the progress you guys have made this week, especially considering Adam deserted you to sneak off to his job interview on Monday,' I acknowledge.

We're sitting in the conservatory at The Lark and Lantern. The bar is packed and it's a little quieter in here as we wait for our food.

Riley is quick to respond. 'We don't hang around.'

'You can't when the boss is working alongside you,' Adam jests.

'Jess has given me a firm deadline by which to get the job finished,' Riley remarks, 'so Adam and I worked four very long days, didn't we, buddy?'

Adam's used to that, and he simply shrugs it off. 'You won't hear a moan from me when I'm working inside in the dry. It won't be long before I'm back on the building sites again with my boots constantly caked in mud.'

I know he's joking but it's a reality check all the same. I notice that Jess is rather fidgety, and Adam gives me a pointed stare to broach the subject in the fore of everyone's thoughts.

'The removal van is booked for Saturday the fifth of November. With clearing out the café and organising things at the garden centre, that gives me four days to pack up our personal things at the house ready for the move.' Adam gives me a bit of a guilty look, but it will be his first week on the job and there's no way he can ask for time off. 'I've already paid the rent to the garden centre through until the end of November and fingers crossed the profit will cover all of my costs, including payroll. After that, Rach and her mum will be on their own.'

Jess looks relieved. 'At least you'll be walking away giving them a fighting chance of building something, Ivy. How long do you think it will be before the bakery here will reopen?'

'It won't shut. Wenna has agreed to stay on, but I need to find someone to work alongside her for that first week.'

Adam reaches out to place his hand on mine. 'I knew you had some good news when your frown turned into a smile earlier on.'

'Even better,' I continue. 'Alice and Jory will continue to supply the bread so that'll keep the locals and the campers happy, Jess.'

She beams at me. 'Now that's what I call a seamless transition. I think a toast is called for.' They all turn to glance at me.

'Oh, right... here's to new beginnings. Exciting new beginnings.'

We chink glasses as two waitresses descend on us, carrying loaded trays.

'Three catch-of-the-day specials and who's for the Treeve Perran Farm sirloin steak?'

Adam puts up his hand and as the plate is lowered in front of him, I grin to myself.

Judging by the look of approval on his face, he could easily get used to this.

About an hour after we arrive back at Smithy's Cottage, I get an unexpected text from Jess.

If you hear the screech of car tyres in the courtyard in the next five minutes, Riley and I are off to spend the night at his cottage. 🔑🚗 Cappy is going to take Lola to see a film and then they're stopping off to get fish and chips on the way home. I'll be back after breakfast tomorrow. Have a lovely evening! 😊

I'm beaming as I type my reply.

Have fun... I know you will. Enjoy every single second!

IVY
Stroud, Gloucestershire

11

I'm Back on My Feet

'I'm glad the weekend went so well down at the farm, Ivy. Dad and I were a little anxious until you rang. How's Adam doing?' Mum asks, as she watches me brushing fruit purée onto the top of a tray of freshly baked vanilla cupcakes.

'He's like his old self again. Nothing keeps him down for long and he's really looking forward to starting his new job.'

A customer calls out and I look up, stopping to wave as she takes a seat. It's the estate agent's wife, Carol. Grace engages her in conversation as she wipes down the table and then takes her order.

Mum glances around. 'It's unusual for Rach not to be here on a Monday.'

'She asked if she could take the day off to get a few things sorted. It's all beginning to feel very real for both of us. Grace kindly offered to cover.'

'You seem brighter today, Ivy.'

'After making the decision I was reeling for a bit, Mum. There's a lot to organise still, but I feel more in control now.'

'What's happening about the house?'

Grace hurries over, grabbing a tray and pressing a button on the coffee machine before leaning into me conspiratorially. 'You know that shop you looked at, Ivy?'

Mum and I turn to look at her, all ears. 'The old bicycle shop?'

'That's the one. Well, Carol just mentioned that there's a

serious structural problem and they'll be shoring it up ahead of the work starting. Good job you didn't go for it. Sounds like it could take a while to sort that out.'

'There you go,' Mum jumps in. 'You could have wasted a lot of time and effort if you'd pinned your hopes on that place and you'd be back to square one just like that.' Mum snaps her fingers and Grace nods her head in agreement.

I think about the charming bakery down at the farm and, as Adam pointed out, Smithy's Cottage is my idea of a dream home. It's just that little voice of self-doubt that sometimes makes itself heard. Jess is a dynamic force, whereas I'm more the slow-and-steady type. Staying in Stroud, my main worry would have centred around covering the overheads; down at Renweneth Farm my chief concern is meeting my best friend's expectations. So, I guess I'd better start brainstorming now. A little tingle of excitement begins to work its way down my spine and my face lights up.

Mum grins at me. 'At last!' she declares, sounding happy. 'I haven't seen you with a look like that on your face for quite a while and it's good to see it. I'll tell your dad there's no need to worry; our girl is back on form and that's all that matters to us, Ivy.'

12

Saying Goodbye Is Never Easy

It's Monday the 31st of October and what was once a thriving and vibrant café is now a bare shell of a building. With the removal lorry on its way to the storage facility, this is it. Rach looks at me and we both turn to glance around.

'Well, even sad and empty it still looks a darn sight better than the day we moved in,' she declares. 'Do you remember how much grease we scraped off the tiles in the kitchen?'

I laugh, trying hard not to grimace at the memory of it. 'Everything was sticky, wasn't it?'

'It didn't take us long to get it looking good,' she reflects. 'It's wrong, Ivy, what's happened.' Her tone instantly changes. 'Mr Williams was a nightmare landlord from day one. He was happy to take your money but never happy to deliver on his promises, was he?'

It's always easy to be wise in hindsight and, looking back, I ignored the warning signs every step of the way.

'Some lessons have to be learnt the hard way, Rach. If something is cheap, then there's usually a catch. The truth is this place was all I could afford at the time. I saw what I wanted to see... the place we turned it into. We worked our socks off, didn't we?'

'It was *the* place to come for cake and coffee. How many businesses close and their customers bring them good luck cards to wish them well in their next endeavour?'

'I know; it was touching, Rach.'

She stares at me, pointedly. 'You didn't let our customers down, Mr Williams did. He should have had the decency to level with you about what his intentions were. I can't understand why you aren't angry.'

I sigh, dejectedly. 'What's the point, Rach? I launched the business on a shoestring budget and I was lucky to find this place. The lesson it taught me was that growing a business is one thing, but there are other factors that you ignore, or take for granted, at your peril.'

We both go quiet.

'With Jess, though, you know exactly where you stand,' she points out.

'Yes, but there are other pressures. The community know Jess and her family; they don't know me and Adam. Every decision in life comes with a different set of risks. And, of course, I'm going to miss everyone. I feel like I'm leaving a part of me behind. My heart belongs in Stroud, even though Cornwall is the place I love to go to unwind. I just hope that it turns out to be the right decision all round.'

Rach pulls a sad face. 'Has Ursula been in touch?'

'No. I was hoping that when Mum told her I was moving to Cornwall she'd pick up the phone and give me a call. Admittedly, our last conversation didn't end well, but how could I stand by and see her pandering to Nate when he was constantly going off and doing his own thing? He's a husband and a dad, and he needs to remember that.'

Now I sound angry. That's because people mean more to me than anything else. A relationship is a two-way thing and if his heart isn't in it, he should be honest with Ursula.

'At some point she's going to tire of listening to his excuses and empty promises. All you can do is be there for her when that day comes,' Rach replies, sadly.

'I know. Oh... before we lock the door for the last time there's one thing we must do... Where did I leave my bag?'

I look around and then realise I left it in the kitchen and I hurry off to retrieve it.

When I return Rach is gazing out the window. It looks bare now the decals have all been taken down. It was emblazoned with a huge picnic hamper advertising the online service on one side and the café's logo on the other.

I carefully lift out a tea towel and unwrap two champagne flutes before handing them to her. Grabbing the bottle I loosen the cork and it shoots into the air, making us both squeal as a fountain of bubbles spray down on us.

'Oops… guess I should have carried it a bit more gingerly.' I grin at her as I half-fill the glasses. 'I think we should each propose a toast.'

Rach chews her lip, frowning. 'You go first.'

Ooh, this is harder than I thought and I take a moment to still the disparate thoughts whirling around inside my head. 'It's been quite a journey. All those days when the fire alarm kept going off, driving us and our customers mad, but we also had a lot of fun and laughs along the way.'

Rach lets out a gentle sigh.

'I read an article once about how to succeed in life,' I continue. 'The person said that to understand your past, you should look to your future. It didn't seem to make any sense at all to me at the time but, for some reason, it's suddenly popped into my head now.' I know I'm rambling but it's a light-bulb moment. 'We turned a greasy old kebab shop into a little haven of a cake and coffee shop with a difference. What we baked here could have graced the shelves of any little French *pâtisserie*, but with a healthy twist. I'm gutted that we're parting ways and having to start afresh, Rach, but the fact we did it once proves we can do it again. So here's to a successful future for us both, because we're used to rolling up our sleeves and making things happen.'

We're both glassy-eyed as we chink glasses and take a moment to compose ourselves.

Then Rach clears her throat. 'Oh, Ivy... ever the positive one and that's what I admire most about you. You've taught me so much, and I don't mean just about baking. You had a dream, but you're not a hopeless dreamer – you're too practical for that. It's why problems don't faze you; you simply focus on finding a solution. Working alongside you has given me the courage to strike out on my own, mindful of the risks, but with the help of my family we're determined to make it work. Thank you, Ivy, for everything you've done for me, past and present. Now the future is down to me.'

That final toast is a poignant one as we stand for a couple of minutes, looking out at the shoppers as they pass by for the last time.

'Onwards and upwards,' I say, with great positivity, as we empty our glasses and I pack them away. 'I'm only a phone call away, Rach, if you need a listening ear. And I'm hoping you and the family will come to visit us in Cornwall when you get a chance to have a break.'

She starts laughing, her eyes twinkling. 'Now that's an offer I don't intend to refuse!'

NOVEMBER

NOVEMBER

IVY
Renweneth Farm, Cornwall

13

Goodbye Stroud, Hello Cornwall

It's Saturday the fifth of November and with four burly men hanging around in the courtyard drinking coffee and talking about football, Jess and I are anxiously clock-watching. We didn't get here until gone one o'clock, but it only took an hour for Riley, Adam, and the driver and his mate, to carry our boxes into the cottage. Although we've served notice on the house, Adam will be living there for the next month at least, so it's mostly personal stuff and smaller items. Sod's law is that having completed his office-based first week, his time will be split between two sites north of Gloucestershire.

Finally, Jess clears her throat and gives me the nod. The bakery shuts at three o'clock and I walk over to the door, reaching out to turn the handle and feeling somewhat ceremonious. Technically, I became the official tenant a week ago but hearing the tinkling sound of the bell as I hold the door open for the last customer of the day to exit, I feel a tad emotional.

'Welcome home,' Wenna calls out, as she rushes around the counter to greet me with a hug. 'I can't even begin to imagine how you're feelin', Ivy.' She laughs. 'Nervous and excited in equal measure, I expect!'

She pulls back, grabbing a bunch of keys from the pocket of her apron and holding them out to me. 'It's all yours. I've wiped everything down. Erica couldn't make it this morning as Daisy has tonsillitis, so Jess stepped in for the morning rush.

There's not much left, just a few rolls and I've bagged them up for you.'

I'm lost for words. Jess kept that very quiet. I'd assumed she was in and out the bakery keeping an eye, not dipping in to serve customers.

'Wenna, I can't thank you enough, really I can't.'

Her cheeks begin to colour up. 'It was my pleasure, Ivy, and I'm lookin' forward to workin' for you. Thank you for the flowers – it was so thoughtful and rather touchin', actually.'

I give a little smile. 'I couldn't be here to welcome you on your first day under new management, but I guess so far it's been pretty much like just another week at the bakery.'

'A busy one,' she declares. 'Erica was here from nine each day until we closed at three. Jess kindly did the school runs with Lola and Daisy. Anyway, those guys look like they want to get back on the road before the storm hits. Everyone's gutted about having to cancel the big firework display tonight but let's hope we get away with as little damage as possible.'

'Fingers crossed it runs out of steam before it gets here. We will have some sort of relaunch party once I have the confectionary side up and running, don't you worry. Did my delivery arrive safely?'

'Yes. Riley assembled the rackin' in the kitchen as you instructed and Erica and I loaded up the shelves. We marked it up in sections, so there's one for sacks of flour, dried fruits et cetera. The organic honey and maple syrup we stored in one of the wall cabinets.'

'Perfect!' I do love it when a plan comes together.

The tinkle of the bell makes me turn around to see Adam standing there looking bashful. 'No pressure but...'

'It's all yours.'

They crowd in as Wenna grabs her coat. 'See you on Monday bright and early, Ivy. Have a great weekend all and let's hope the storm passes quickly!'

I give her a fleeting smile as Adam takes the removal guys

upstairs. Suddenly, Riley looms up in front of me. 'Do you have a copy of that plan you drew up for the kitchen? Adam thought it was in the car, but I've just checked, and it isn't there.'

It's hard not to roll my eyes but then it's been a chaotic day. Slipping off my backpack, I pull out a clipboard and pass it over. 'Tell him not to lose this as they're my originals.'

Riley gives a cheeky laugh. 'Maybe I'll keep hold of it and give it back to you once the kit is in place.'

Suddenly I'm standing here all alone, as it begins to sink in. We're here. This really is it and there is no turning back. A nervous shiver runs down my spine and I shake it off, determinedly.

Jess seems to have disappeared and I go in search of her. Upstairs, the guys are in the kitchen and Adam has a tape measure in his hand, checking one of the measurements. I saunter into the other room to see Jess standing there, staring out the window, which looks out over the main road.

'That was quite an emotional moment for me,' I admit. When Jess turns to face me, she has tears in her eyes. 'Oh, please don't start me off!'

I stand next to her as we both draw in a deep breath. 'This means so much to me, Ivy. Our friendship got me through some really bad times in the past. Ben leaving me and then losing Grandma… coming here, wondering whether taking Lola away from her family and friends was the right decision to make. You were my tower of strength. And now you and Adam are going to be a part of this. From the bottom of my heart, I really do hope that Renweneth Farm soon begins to feel like home to you both.'

We link arms and I give her a comforting squeeze.

'I still can't quite believe it if I'm being honest. But it is exciting, and I can't wait for the electrician to arrive tomorrow. Riley is a star finding someone to work on a Sunday, isn't he?'

Jess chuckles. 'He is, Ivy. You know, it means a lot to him – and me – the way you and Adam accepted him into our little circle.'

'He makes you and Lola happy, Jess. That's all that counts.'

'Ivy, where are you? We have a problem,' Adam calls out. 'One of the freezers is too tall as the ceiling slopes away in the corner.'

I burst out laughing. 'Two builders scratching their heads and they're asking me to come up with a solution?'

Jess grins back at me. 'Come on, the layout just needs a bit of rejigging, that's all. Let's go sort them out.'

It's our first night in Smithy's Cottage and although we're both exhausted, neither Adam nor I can sleep. Admittedly, a lot of that is down to the frightening sound of the wind as it gusts overhead. Thankfully, we seem to have caught the tail end of it and there haven't been any loud crashes yet. But lying here in the dark, a single exceptional gust could change the situation in an instant.

'Hey, relax.' Adam draws me against him, tightening his clasp on me. 'Cappy, Keith and Len spent most of the afternoon strapping things down and they know what they're doing. There'll be some debris from the trees but that'll be about it.'

'I know and I appreciate how lucky we are as it could have been much worse. Some poor souls somewhere will, no doubt, be mopping up and trying to make things good as we speak.'

'Yep. It doesn't bear thinking about, does it? And all those expensive fireworks Jess bought and the advertising Vyvyan did for the bonfire party. It would have been a nice little earner and a great community get-together,' Adam whispers, sleepily. 'It's such a pity. What a memorable party it would have been to look back on, like we'd arrived in style.' He begins to laugh softly, making the bed shake.

'They won't go to waste; she told me she'll use them for the festive celebrations they're planning for Father Christmas's visit to the farm on the twenty-third of December.'

'In that case, I can't wait. I want to make sure he has our new address.'

I give a little giggle. We're safe and warm, and that's all that matters. Most of the boxes Adam and I brought with us have now been unpacked, although the bakery still has a stack to go through but they're mainly kitchen utensils and small equipment.

When I roll over to face him, he shifts his position. 'What are we going to do about the furniture at the house – you know, when you move out?'

In the twilight I feel the movement as he shrugs his shoulders. 'I don't know. I haven't had time to think that far ahead.'

'Jess said that if we want to put our own furniture in here, then she'll get everything packed up and stored in Renweneth Manor. Nothing will be wasted and a couple of items in here are family heirlooms. Things that remind her of her grandma.'

'I guess there's your answer, then.'

'The thing is...' I pause, not quite sure how Adam will take this. 'Is there anything at the old house that would look right in here?'

Adam reaches out to touch my cheek, running his thumb gently down to my chin. 'A forever home means everything should be perfect, honey.'

'It's not just an excuse for me to go shopping, Adam, really it isn't.'

'I know.' His tone is one of acceptance and I truly believe that he agrees with me. 'We've fallen on our feet here, Ivy. You're earning from day one and yes, you have your work cut out for you turning the bakery into your vision for the future, but money isn't quite the issue it was for us. Now I wonder why we couldn't see everything was stacked against us. We were working simply to keep afloat.'

It's a sobering thought that in the space of just a few weeks we've gone from fearing our nest egg would be all we had to keep us going, to both having a reliable income again.

'The bakery is making a reasonable profit as it stands but that will grow now that we'll be making our own cakes and pastries on site. The only problem I have is that I need to employ someone part-time to help with the baking. Wenna is brilliant at serving and, being local, a lot of the customers already know her. But I need someone I can train up to work alongside me, not least to cover if I'm sick, or take a day off.'

'Is that why you approached Erica to give Wenna a hand last week?'

'Yes. I know she runs her own little business from home, but Jess said that she's either rushed off her feet or twiddling her thumbs. She also has a stall at the Tuesday market Jess runs, although she bowed out this week as she was behind the counter at the bakery. I really owe her in a way that money alone can't repay.'

'It's crazy on market day,' Adam warns me. 'Seriously, Ivy, you'll need two people serving. I've seen the queues for myself. Jess is talking about holding two market days in the run-up to Christmas. Cappy and Vyvyan have been busy organising that between the two of them.'

'The parking issue is a real thing, then?'

'It certainly is and if it weren't, Cappy would see through it. Jess is really motoring now she has Riley on board, but she's often being pulled in too many directions at once.'

'Jess is still banking on convincing him to stay permanently as her general manager and, in truth, he's the sort of man who needs something to keep him occupied.'

Adam lets out a subdued 'hmm'. In the interim silence it's obvious the wind has dropped, which is a relief. 'I wouldn't take it as a given, Ivy. He feels a bit awkward about the situation between Jess and Riley.'

'Why? It's obvious he approves of their relationship.'

'It's nothing to do with that, Ivy. From what I've seen, Cappy is very happy to get involved when Jess needs him but, longer term, I think he sees it as a role Riley should take on. And if he doesn't feel there's a point to him being here, he'd be like a fish out of water. Pun intended.'

I start to chuckle. 'Aww... Cappy is such a lovely man and

both Jess and Lola love having him here. Riley, too. Why can't he see that? It's obvious he isn't happy back in Gloucestershire.'

'But he feels that having handed over the project to Jess, it's not fair of him to interfere now Riley is in the picture. Although, we were talking about boats the other day, as you do when you're looking out at the ocean, and I think it's still his dream to own one.'

'He mentioned to me once that he used to go fishing with Erica's husband, Charlie. Maybe they'll pick that back up?'

'Maybe.' He starts laughing to himself.

'What?'

'Jess is Jess. Can you see her giving up easily? He belongs here and we all know it, except for Cappy. Jess will think of something.'

'Like she did with us?' My voice is questioning because I'm serious.

'Is it wrong to propose something that turns out to be so right, Ivy? I don't mean to sound selfish here, but when I'm away working, I know you're safe.'

I give a little snort. 'Oh, and I wasn't *safe* living a mile or two from my family in the heart of the sleepy Cotswolds?'

He utters a little groan. 'You know what I mean. I'm not trying to undermine you, Ivy, please don't think that. It was the former bicycle shop or working at Mawsley House. Sorry, but the first one is a disaster and now you know that for a fact. It's going to take them months to rebuild the entire rear wall of the building. The second option would have had you tearing your hair out. Having to cut corners in order to stay within a budget set by someone above you who only cared about the profit margin would have gone against the grain.'

My man knows me so well.

'At least I listened.' It's an admission driven by guilt for dismissing Jess's offer at the very start.

'Ivy, don't ever change, will you? One of us needs to be the cautious one and that job falls to you. I'm happy-go-lucky, except when everything goes wrong at once and then I have no idea what I'm doing. All I can say is that coming here and working alongside Riley and Jess, Renweneth Farm felt like a haven to me. That's what I wanted for you, a place where you can grow your business and don't feel as if you're on your own even when I'm not here to support you.'

I lay my head against Adam's chest, listening to the sound of his heart beating fiercely as he tries to reassure me.

'I appreciate that and, believe me, Adam, what you're sacrificing to make our future secure. Not just in terms of taking on more responsibility, but in accepting that to realise our dream it means spending time apart.'

'Anything for you, Ivy. So, you'll talk to Jess and when you have time we'll turn this into the home we've always dreamt of having?'

'Yes!'

'I guess I'll be selling off the old furniture, then. It'll give me something to do to fill those long evenings while we're apart.'

It's a sobering thought. But no matter where we were based, accepting time apart from each other was inevitable. Absence makes the heart grow fonder, as my mum says, and my job is to ensure that when Adam is here, we can make the most of our precious time together. There's more to life than just work and in a setting like this everything we need to relax and enjoy ourselves is literally on our doorstep.

'Mornin' all, something smells good,' Cappy says, as he steps into the kitchen at The Farmhouse.

'Ah, there's a catch, Cappy,' Riley replies, pulling a long face. 'There's no such thing as a free meal around here, Jess wants to thrash out the plans to get us all in full-on Christmas mode.'

Lola is sitting on the floor, playing with Misty and she immediately joins in. 'Are we trimming up the courtyard, Mum?'

'That's a part of the plan, Lola, but there's a lot to do.' Jess sounds like she means business.

Adam and Riley are busy frying bacon and sausages. I'm buttering the rolls Wenna bagged up yesterday, having reheated them for a couple of minutes. The kitchen smells both savoury and yeasty, no doubt making everyone's mouths water.

Jess is busy laying the table and indicates for Cappy to take a seat. 'You're in charge of the decorations. Do you want to fill us in?'

Cappy starts laughing. 'It's Sunday morning, these two have only just arrived,' he points out, looking at me and then at Adam, 'and you're cracking the whip!'

Lola jumps up to join Cappy at the kitchen table. 'I'm with Mum. We need to trim up. The Farmhouse Bakery, too, Ivy.'

'I know. It's on my list!' I smile, wondering how on earth I'm going to find time to fit it all in.

'We need cans of spray snow,' Lola enthuses.

Jess points in Lola's direction. 'That's my girl! I'm thinking I should earmark next Sunday to put the festive decorations up. We'll need to get as many hands on board as we can. Cappy, can you see if you can find us some additional help? I know it's going to be a crazy weekend, as we're kicking off the first Saturday market and officially opening the Courtyard Hub. There's so much happening this week, though, that I can't see what other chance we'll get.'

Cappy gives Jess a wink. 'I'm on it. You decided on the name at last. It has a good ring to it. How's that final list of jobs coming along, Riley? The clock is ticking and if you need someone to pick up the slack, you only have to say.'

Riley turns, holding a spatula up in the air. 'Jess has given me to the end of Wednesday. The leaseholders will have access on Thursday and Friday to move in. I might be glad of a bit of help getting the last two countertops in place.'

Adam turns to look at Riley. 'Anything I can do before I head back later today?'

Riley chuckles. 'Thanks, mate, appreciated, but I've got to make them yet.'

'And the bays are all taken?' I ask.

'Vyvyan had a waiting list before the work even started,' Jess confirms. It was just a case of getting the contracts signed.

My eyes stray over to Adam, who is standing next to Riley in front of the range, but he doesn't turn around. Is it my turn to speak up? I wonder.

Clearing my throat, I launch in. 'I was thinking of running a couple of festive-themed workshops at the bakery. Making and decorating Christmas biscuits... that sort of thing.'

Lola sticks up her hand, as if she's at school. 'Can you do one on a non-school day, please Ivy, then I can help. It sounds like fun and I bet lots of kids in my class would love to come along.'

Jess stops what she's doing. 'What a brilliant idea. Maybe we could tie it in with one of the market days?'

'Hmm, that sounds good to me,' I reply, feeling encouraged. 'And I'll be expanding the menu to include a healthy version of hot chocolate.'

Adam immediately turns his head to look at me. 'There's a healthy option?'

'There is. It's the one I make for you at home,' I laugh.

'Oh, well, I can vouch for the fact that it's great, as I didn't notice any difference.'

Cappy raises his eyebrows at me questioningly.

'Raw cacao powder, almond milk, a little vanilla from a pod, dark organic maple syrup and a pinch of sea salt,' I inform him.

'Never heard of salt in hot chocolate before, but I'm willing to give it a go!'

'The eggs are ready so grab your seats and we'll serve you at the table, won't we, Adam?' Riley gives him a nudge.

'Sure will. I hope you all like your bacon American style.'

'That'll be super crispy then.' Jess giggles.

Thankfully, the sausages look fine, so all is not lost.

As we take our seats there's a buzz of excitement in the air and we're all feeling it. The only dampener is the thought of saying goodbye to Adam when he sets off for Stroud late afternoon. He's got an early start tomorrow and the site he'll be working at is a forty-five-minute drive away. For both of us it will be day one of our new routine and partings are a part of that. It was different waving him off from Stroud when he was giving Riley a hand, because I had a familiar routine and lots of people to call on if I needed help or some company. It's a case of taking it one day at a time for now and hope that I can cope with whatever comes my way. The last thing I want is to go bothering Jess.

14

Team Spirit

Monday morning dawns and the grey clouds come rolling in. It's five-thirty and I've been awake for a good hour, lying here thinking. In my head I'm checking off the list of things to do in case there's anything we missed over the weekend.

I can't help thinking about Rach and how she's feeling this morning. As they work through the online orders, the newly named Olive Tree Café will also be open for business. I'm glad she's moving forward with determination, but without any advertising other than the flyers we distributed to our customers at The Cake and Coffee Emporium, it's a case of hoping for the best.

Adam and I have agreed we'll catch up each evening as we both need to focus on what we're doing, so I text him a simple *Good morning, love you! x* and jump out of bed. I'm impatient to step across the threshold of The Farmhouse Bakery and switch on those ovens.

'My, what a lush smell! That cake display looks amazin'. You must have been up with the lark,' Wenna exclaims, as she steps inside. 'The bread van has just arrived, so I'll leave the door ajar.'

It's eight-thirty on the dot and we have thirty minutes to fill the display cabinets and shelves behind the counter.

'Mornin', ladies.' A burly guy backs through the door, a large covered crate in his hands.

'Fred, this is Ivy, the new owner.'

'Hey, Ivy. How're you doin'?'

'Great thank you, Fred. Do you want a hand?'

'I'm fine, thanks. I know you'll be eager to get this lot unpacked.'

I follow Wenna through to the back room to hang up her coat. It's little more than a lobby really, as the shop takes up almost the entire floor space from front to back.

'Fred usually hangs around to take the empty crates with him. It saves us storin' them here.'

'Oh, right. We'd best get moving then.'

It doesn't take long, and I follow Wenna's lead. We line the wicker baskets on the shelves with fresh sheets of greaseproof paper. 'We'll need to order some more of these,' Wenna points out. 'We're okay for greaseproof bags but as they come from the same company that might be somethin' you want to order sooner rather than later.'

The yeasty smell makes my stomach rumble but there's still a lot to do.

'What are your plans for the tastin' room?' She tilts her head in the direction of the opening that leads into what Jess told me was originally a small greengrocer's shop.

'I guess for now we continue doing what Alice did.'

'The customers do like being able to wander in and try a few of the products but it's a wasted space, isn't it? I can't fathom why they didn't have the whole wall taken down in the first place.'

'It was like that to start with because it was originally two separate cottages. I'm not sure it's even possible to take out a supporting wall that's almost three foot thick, hence the door-sized openings down here and upstairs.'

'It's a pity my great-granddad isn't still with us. He was the blacksmith here back in the day. He'd have known these cottages inside and out. My dad was delighted when I told him about the renovation work and he loved the thought of Smithy's Cottage as a name.'

How lovely to hear that Wenna's family have a connection to the farm going way back.

'It's good to see the buildings being brought to life again, isn't it? Now all I have to do is make sure the bakery becomes the heart of the courtyard. That will mean setting up a self-service-style café once the patisserie side is running smoothly. The tasting room, as it is now, is perfect for me to encourage customers to wander in and try some new and exciting combinations of flavours. Market testing is crucial at this stage, as there is only me until I find an assistant baker and establishing what will sell well is key. I'm still reaching out to find local, organic suppliers but it all takes time.'

Wenna's face breaks out into a smile. 'That sounds excitin', Ivy. Jess mentioned somethin' about utilisin' some of the cobbled area too, in the summer.'

'Yes, it'll be an extension of the café. The bakery just isn't big enough to provide a waitress service,' I concede. 'But before long, people will be able to take their trays through into next door or sit outside on benches when the weather is behaving itself.'

'You've certainly got your work cut out for you!'

As we pick a few things to carry through to the tasting table, we chatter away.

'I would like to consider running a couple of workshops – icing cakes and making biscuits, that sort of thing. We could trial a few sessions between now and Christmas. The other thing I'll need to sort out quickly is the staffing situation. For now, I'll get the ovens going early and you can call me down if you need help but it's not ideal. At the very least, on market days we're going to need two people behind the counter.'

'Have a word with Erica. She couldn't do full-time, obviously, but between you and me, she's always glad to earn a little bit extra.'

'I did wonder, as she was keen to come to my rescue last week. Isn't the takeaway meal service keeping her busy?'

Wenna pulls a face as she slices up a round cob loaf into small pieces and I turn a layered strawberry-infused sponge square into bite-sized cubes.

'It's been hit and miss but it's the delivery side that's the problem. She's focusin' now on the market stall she has here every Tuesday. Have a chat with her – Jess can vouch for the fact she knows how to bake an excellent cake.'

I smile to myself. 'I've tried them, too. Thanks for the heads-up, Wenna.'

'Anythin' I can do, just say, Ivy. Workin' here is perfect for me. My husband, Gryff, works from home and uh... well, I like to be close by.'

It's not my business to pry, so I carry on slicing and dicing.

'He suffers from epilepsy, you see,' she continues. 'It's under control but just occasionally somethin' will trigger an attack. Gryff gets a warnin' sign ahead of it; his sense of smell changes and he knows what's comin'.'

'If you ever get a call, Wenna, just drop everything and go.' I can't even imagine what it must be like not knowing if, or when, something like that will happen.

'Thanks, Ivy. He'll only call me if his mother isn't around. She lives a mile further along the lane. She knows how to handle it. Gryff hates being fussed over, but for me, just knowin' that I'm so close is a comfort.'

The tinkle of a bell, as the bakery door opens behind us, heralds our first customer. Let the day begin!

We bustle out ready to roll up our sleeves and find three people waiting.

'Good morning,' I launch in, 'what can I get you?'

'Well, I only came in for our usual loaf,' the gentleman says, scratching his head as he stares at the confectionary display. 'No doubt the wife will give me a tellin'-off if I don't take back a couple of cakes. Jess has been spreadin' the word saying it was all changin'.'

'And I told you that you were in for a treat, Albert!' Jess joins in, as she steps through the door.

'The bread still comes from Rowse's Bakery in Polreweek,' I reassure him with a welcoming smile.

'That's good then and we'll try two of those fancy cakes, I think.'

Wenna is busy bagging up some rolls as her customer, too, browses our display. Behind them, Jess is standing there looking rather smug.

When it's her turn to step forward I pick up the tongs. 'I'm not here to buy.'

'It's on the house.' I chuckle.

'I don't want to make a dent in that perfect display. I've only popped in to say there's a team meeting this evening at The Farmhouse at seven, if you're free. If you've run out of steam by then, I'll bring you up to date with what's said tomorrow. I did notice that you started very early this morning and no one's expecting you to contribute yet.'

Another customer enters and I walk around the counter. 'Jess, come and try a sample.'

As soon as we're out of earshot she leans into me. 'How did you sleep?'

'Like a log but I woke up early. I was just anxious to make sure everything went smoothly. Ovens can be temperamental, but all the kit survived the move.'

'Well, it all looks wonderful, Ivy.'

'It's a limited range to begin with, as I'll be guided by what sells well and trial something new every day. Let's hope I got the volume right, I'd hate to run out. Alice gave me a detailed breakdown of what bread products she sold each day over the eight-week trial and I ordered from her based on the overall average daily sales.'

Jess reaches out, placing her hand on my arm. 'Just relax, Ivy. Take a deep breath because everything is going to be just fine. You're taking it up a notch and customers are going to love that. It's more up-market and that's just the sort of experience the holidaymakers are going to appreciate, too.'

I pick up one of the small plates and Jess takes a cube of sponge cake. Seconds later she takes another. 'Seriously, Ivy, having temptation on my doorstep might be a huge mistake. I'd forgotten how moreish your cakes are. Riley is going to be in his element, but I'll let him discover that for himself.' She laughs. 'Right, I'm off to show two of the new leaseholders around and you just might get a little influx of customers popping in once the tour is done.' She gives me a knowing wink as she turns on her heels and hurries off to start her working day.

As Jess exits, two more customers enter and my worries begin to melt away. Wenna is bantering with them both, so they're obviously locals. I'm so lucky she wanted to stay on as at least there's some continuity. People trust people they know, and I can't wait to become another familiar face and a part of the community. The only problem is I have no idea how long it takes to become accepted in a small village setting like this.

'Hey, honey, how did it go today?' Adam sounds upbeat, which is a good sign.

'Better than I'd hoped. Wenna knows everyone and when I say that, I mean it. Her great-granddad was the old smithy here at the farm.'

'Really? I don't think Jess is aware of that. You sound happy.'

'I am. We sold out of virtually everything, but that was more down to the information Alice gave me when it came to ordering a delivery from Rowse's Bakery. I underestimated when it came to the cakes; I don't even have enough left to take to this evening's team meeting.'

'Ah, you're officially on the committee now!'

'I guess I am. How was your day?'

Adam gives a little laugh. 'It's a good team of guys but it's a steep learning curve. They all know what they're doing, so I'm just shadowing the foreman, learning how to troubleshoot the problems and when to report back up the line. A couple of the guys live close by, so we're meeting up in Stroud for a pint later this evening.'

A wave of relief washes over me. It was either going to be his thing, or a huge mistake and that would have been a nightmare. We're both committed now and there's no turning back.

'I missed you last night,' I admit and then instantly regret voicing my thoughts out loud.

'Me, too, Ivy. But I'm in my element, I really am. My job has potential to take me much further once I've proven myself. It's like I've suddenly found my niche. Some of the guys have always worked for someone; I've experienced both sides. When you work for yourself, you solve your own problems and that gives me an edge. All I need to familiarise myself with are the protocols and the contacts I'll need on speed dial. They won't sacrifice quality for cost when it comes to manpower, or materials, but obviously the skill is in knowing where to draw the line and let management make the judgement call.'

He sounds confident, and in his stride but, oh, how I wish he were here next to me right now because I really need a hug. I glance at my watch and it's time for me to head across the courtyard.

'You sound happy and that eases my mind. Right, I'd better get myself over to The Farmhouse.'

'I love you, honey.'

A sharp stabbing pain hits me square in the chest, as his words echo around me. 'Love you too, babe.'

'Hey, I was thinking... dangerous, I know,' he jokes. 'How about at the weekend we head into Polreweek and see if we can begin the hunt to furnish Smithy's Cottage?'

My stomach dips. This weekend is going to be hectic, both days by the sound of it. 'Um... I haven't had time to find someone to come in and help Wenna on Saturday, yet. I need to talk to Erica first. It's top of my list for tomorrow, I promise.'

'Oh, right. Well, our shopping expedition can wait until you're more settled. I don't suppose you've had a chance to talk to Jess about it, anyway, what with all that baking.' I can imagine him sitting there grinning to himself.

'No. Not yet.'

'You do need to find a baker, Ivy,' he stresses. 'It's too much for one person.'

I know he's right. 'I'm working on it. There's a lot going on here at the farm this weekend though, as we're getting ready for Christmas.'

He mutters a little sigh. 'It's still early days and whatever you need me to do, I'll be there for you until everything is up and running properly. I know the pressure you're putting yourself under, Ivy, but please don't overdo it. I might not bake, but I can serve.'

'And also hang decorations? Because I have boxes and boxes of them on the way.'

Adam gives a tut. 'Are we going to be working *all* weekend?'

I bite my tongue, tempted to blurt out that you can't have your cake and eat it, but sarcasm, as they say, is the lowest form of wit. Even so, it hasn't sunk in that I've gone from a team of five, including my Saturday lady, to just two for now.

'It's going to be full-on but the evenings and nights will be yours,' I promise in my best sultry tone.

'All right. But will you do me a favour?' Adam asks, in serious mode.

'You know I will.'

'When you jump into bed tonight, whatever time, give me a call? I won't answer, but just leave a voicemail saying goodnight.'

Aww… my heart squishes up inside my chest. 'You know me, I never say one word if I can say twenty.'

'I'm banking on it, Ivy. Love you more than you can know and thanks.'

'For what?'

'For having faith in me that this job was the right way to go and being brave enough to face the move to Cornwall. I know you're playing catch-up, but it won't always be this crazy.'

'No, Adam, it won't – I promise you that. Enjoy your outing to the pub with some of the guys and we'll speak tomorrow night. Love ya, babe.'

'Love you, too, Ivy. Always and forever.'

As I lie back on the sofa, my heart is aching. It's going to feel like forever until Friday is here and I can feel Adam's arms around me once more. Adam was right, Smithy's Cottage is perfect for us and so is the bakery, but before I can think about making the cottage ours I have a massive to-do list to work through.

With Cappy, Riley, Jess, Vyvyan, Keith, and myself, sitting around the kitchen table in The Farmhouse, it feels more like a group of friends getting together than a meeting.

'Right,' Cappy interrupts the general chatter to gain our attention. 'Unless we want to be here all night, we'd best make a start. Maybe our marketing manager would like to kick us off.'

'Thanks, Cappy. And welcome to your first meeting, Ivy.' Vyvyan gives me a beaming smile and there's a little chorus of "hear, hear". 'Wearing my marketing manager's hat, this coming weekend is going to be a big one for Renweneth Farm. Before I go through my update, what's the latest on the new interim parking arrangements?'

Cappy jumps straight in. 'We'll be testing it out at tomorrow's market.'

'Any little hitches can be ironed out ready for Saturday,' Jess adds. 'Can you just do a run-through of the changes for tomorrow so everyone is aware?'

'Keith's been hard at work and I think we've come up with a temporary solution that will avoid cars queuing in the road.' Cappy turns to look at Keith, who opens the notebook in front of him.

Popping down with Adam for the occasional weekend to lend a hand, I never really appreciated what was involved in keeping Renweneth Farm running. Everyone around this table has a real part to play and from now on that includes me. However, it seems I have some catching up to do... and quickly, to get up to speed!

'We informed the owners of the camper vans and caravans in the over-winter storage area of the move. All but two of them gave us permission to go ahead. The other owners wanted to choose their new pitches and they called in to move their vehicles themselves. We then cordoned off the big area to the right-hand side of the entrance to the campsite for overspill parkin'. I've two signs to put up first thing in the mornin' to finish it off.'

'And are you happy with the temporary arrangement, Keith?' Jess checks.

'We don't have a choice, Jess. A cordon means campers have to stop their vehicles on the way in and out to reach field two. But until Cappy has that meetin' with the plannin' office and the highways guy about a second point of entry off the main road, it's the best we can do.'

'We've also erected some fencing around the toilet and shower block adjacent to the hay barn, Jess,' Cappy says, taking over. 'The cordon makes it clear that anything beyond that is restricted to campers only.'

Jess nods her head. 'Do you have a date yet for the meeting, Cappy?'

'I had an email this morning. It's being held on site this coming Thursday. Do you want me to give you a shout?' Cappy checks.

'I'll probably be tied up, I'm afraid,' Jess replies. 'The small bar... sorry, the Courtyard Hub leaseholders will be moving in ready for the grand opening on Saturday.'

'We were oversubscribed in the end, Jess, so we have a waiting list if anyone drops out. A couple of our former market stallholders are leasing space in the hub but I managed to sign up a few new people to replace them, so we're at maximum occupancy across the board.' Gosh, Vyvyan is certainly on the ball. But then I already knew that. She took time out to advise me on my lease negotiations and I feel bad now, not just because the landlord was wasting everyone's time but realising just how busy she is here at the farm.

'What was the outcome when you canvassed opinion about the last seasonal Saturday market before Christmas, Vyvyan?' Jess enquires.

'The majority voted to hold it on the Friday of that week, instead. I hope that's okay with you, Jess. You've been so busy we haven't had time to sit down and go through it together. I took the liberty of amending the date in the advertising that's been going out. With Christmas Eve falling on a Saturday, it was cutting it too fine for many of the stallholders. Not just collecting the meat and veg orders, but also the craft stalls taking bespoke orders right up until the week before Christmas.'

Riley gingerly sticks a finger in the air. 'Um... I'm just checking, but has anyone thought about the signage to direct our new customers for the hub to the right entrance?'

Jess raises an eyebrow, giving a little laugh. 'As if I'd forget something like that! I've ordered two smart new signs and they'll be here on Wednesday morning. One to go next to the entrance to the courtyard and one for the pavement next to the wrought-iron gates the other side of the row of cottages.'

'Ah.' Riley nods his head. 'Perfect. I'm guessing that'll be my first job when they arrive, then. For some reason it's not on my list of jobs to do.' He gives Jess a mischievous smile.

'Sorry, Mr Fix-It, slapped wrist for me! Before long, even the private access door you created from the courtyard into the hub will need bricking up. I'm hoping that *is* on your list, Riley?' Jess beams at him.

'It is. And that's my next task once I've finished in the hub.'

'Is this to do with the changes at the bakery?' Vyvyan enquires, glancing first at Jess, then at me.

Jess shakes her head. 'Not directly, we're creating a walled garden for Smithy's Cottage. It will make it more private.'

Vyvyan seems surprised. It looks like the offer Jess made Adam and me isn't general knowledge.

'The amount of foot traffic going past the front of it into the hub would have been a problem,' Jess continues. 'There's a perfectly good alternative entrance and it seemed like the sensible thing to do. Obviously, Ivy is still finding her feet at the bakery so it's a case of watch this space. Unless you have anything you'd like to add, Ivy?'

I clear my throat nervously, as all eyes are suddenly on me. Being a part of something bigger is a role that's completely new to me and although I'm a little nervous to be in the spotlight for the first time, I don't feel out of place.

'Thanks, Jess. I just wanted to say that there will be some changes in the coming weeks starting with the patisserie section. The tasting room will also be turned into a self-service seating area so people can stop for a coffee and a cake. Jess mentioned the possibility of putting some additional tables in the courtyard during the summer months, too.' Heads are nodding. 'I'm looking to take on two people willing to work flexibly if you could spread the word. One additional server and a baker.'

I pause to look at Jess, before I launch into the next bit. She seems happy enough. 'My intention is to run a couple of workshops in December icing Christmas cookies and cupcakes. And, ready for Saturday, I'm kicking off the festive vibe with a big display of Christmas cakes that will be up for pre-order via the bakery, and the website once it's live.' I make a mental note to dig out the number of the developer who helped me troubleshoot a few online problems I had in the past. It's a job he can take off my hands and it'll be well worth the cost.

Vyvyan's eyes light up. 'Ooh, the workshops will definitely go down well as it's something a little different.'

Jess nods her head in agreement. 'It's all about getting the right balance of products and crafts, as we have a limited amount of stalls. Vyvyan does a good job of ensuring we don't double up on anything.'

'Is it okay to have someone walk around the market stalls

on Saturday, then, with a sample tray to launch my Christmas range? It won't upset anyone?'

Vyvyan gives me an encouraging smile. 'I'd say that would go down very well indeed. I can't wait to sample some of the cakes I've been hearing about myself, Ivy.'

'If you need another pair of hands, I'm sure Lola would be only too glad to help out,' Jess adds.

Riley gives me an apologetic grin. 'I'd offer to do it, but I'd probably scoff more than I'd hand out.'

So, Riley will be here, even though he doesn't officially work Saturdays and obviously Lola will be helping out, too. It's lovely to see everyone pulling together but one thing really stands out: Jess requires a team around her because it's a lot to handle. And that means everyone rolling up their sleeves. I'm glad I forewarned Adam, but now I'm beginning to panic a little as there's a lot to do in just a few days.

15

It's Time to Roll Up My Sleeves!

It's my first experience of market day at Renweneth Farm and I was hoping to grab five minutes to wander around the stalls, but Wenna and I haven't stopped. By late morning I'm flagging; having turned on the ovens at six this morning, I've been on my feet for five hours straight.

'This is crazy, Ivy.' Wenna looks indignant. 'You need a break. I'm goin' to make a phone call. My neighbour, Kate, doesn't work on Tuesdays and she might be free to pop in for a few hours. At this rate you might need to get bakin' again a bit later. What do you think?'

My feet do feel like lead and my back is aching. 'Oh, Wenna, that would be amazing, thank you!'

It's wonderful to see people flooding through the door, but the tasting plates are all empty and when Wenna disappears to make the call I try to step up the pace. My cheeks are aching with all the smiling I'm doing because I'm so grateful for every single customer who sets foot across the threshold. But, oh my, I need to sort out some permanent help ASAP because market days are certainly lively. No wonder Alice and Jory were torn at having to walk away from Renweneth Farm because there's a lot of potential here.

However, Alice and Wenna managed just fine because all they had to do was serve, but now that the word is going around that the bakery sells *posh cakes*, everyone is eager to sample them. And when they do, they head straight back to the queue to make a purchase. The problem is that I can't serve and bake at the same time! Although at this rate, I'm going to run out of some of the basic ingredients if I don't get another order in pretty quickly.

'Erica, it's Ivy from the bakery.'

'Oh, Ivy, hi!'

'Is it convenient to talk… you're not cooking?' I know exactly what it's like when someone calls while I'm in the middle of something and a quick chat turns into twenty minutes of juggling things to make sure nothing burns.

'It's fine. I'm clearing up after having loaded three slow cookers with beef stew. How are things at the farm? I had to cry off from taking a stall today to get ready for Saturday.'

'Of course, Saturday is going to be a big day.'

'I hope so, as I need to sell as much as I can. Is it busy today?'

'Yes,' I reply, realising I sound a little stressed. 'We're rushed off our feet, and Wenna called in a friend. I was up early baking and am only just able to put my feet up for half an hour.'

'It's gathering speed, then?'

'I just can't bake the cakes fast enough. I wondered if you knew of anyone with some time on their hands who knows how to follow a recipe to the letter.'

There's a brief pause. 'What sort of hours are you offering?'

Is she asking for a friend, or for herself? I wonder. It's worth a shot. 'In the short-term, the priority is getting someone in two evenings this week. I have a lot of fruit cakes maturing that need icing ready to set up my Christmas window display ready for the weekend. I'll be taking pre-orders and need to get as far ahead as I can,' I explain. 'Longer term, I'm looking for someone to work four mornings a week, from six until about eleven, and every Saturday.'

'Let me make a call. There's someone I know who might be

interested in a permanent position. Aside from that, if you're desperate I could rejig my schedule and make myself free tomorrow and Thursday from mid-afternoon, if that's any help?'

I scrunch up my eyes, as it's precisely the answer I hoped to get. 'Oh, Erica – you're a total star!'

'It's no problem and the extra cash will come in handy. My other half, Charlie, is home both days. Jess is tied up this week getting everything ready, so he's offered to take both Daisy and Lola to school. I can start as early as you like. Do I need to bring anything with me?'

I breathe a sigh of relief. 'No, just yourself, Erica. Honestly, you have no idea how happy that makes me. Shall we say three o'clock tomorrow?'

'Perfect. Looking forward to it!'

As the line disconnects, I glance down at my sock-covered toes, giving them a little wriggle. Putting my legs up on the desk as I sip my coffee immediately eases that tension in my back. Wenna is right; I do need to take regular breaks and sorting out my staffing issue is a top priority.

Sitting here relaxing, I keep thinking about Rach and how she's doing at the garden centre but, like me, she'll be up to her eyes in it. Building a new team isn't easy and in some respects we're both going through the same thing. Her mum has never worked in catering before, albeit that she taught Rach a lot of what she knew.

Fingers crossed, people wandering around looking at the plants will smell the coffee and head straight for the café. I do hope that some of our old customers pop in to try it out, too. But oh, how I miss our banter as we worked side by side and welcoming a constant stream of familiar faces.

An elderly gentleman with a walking stick came in this morning and Wenna made a beeline for him. They exchanged a few words in Cornish and it made me smile. As he was leaving, the person in front of him was about to close the door and he called out *'Ullon yaw! Leave it abroad.'*

I looked at Wenna blankly and then watched as the young woman smiled, stood to one side, and let him pass. He gave her a grateful wink. Apparently, it means *wait a minute, don't shut the door*. The thing I've noticed in the short time that I've been here is a real sense of loyalty and kinship between people, regardless of whether there's any blood ties. People look out for each other and even Erica's husband doing the school runs on his days off to help not only his wife, but Jess, too is typical. One for all and all for one. I simply love it!

Now it's time to get back to work and get to know Wenna's neighbour, Kate, a little better. Judging from the laughter filtering up the stairs, there's a lot of merriment at the bakery today. Goodness knows what Saturday is going to be like.

'Wenna's just locked up and here are the keys, Ivy. Where do we start?' Erica looks like she means business as she stares at the pile of boxes on the stainless-steel countertop.

'This little lot need icing and decorating.'

Her jaw slackens. 'That's a lot of cakes, Ivy.'

'I know it's a tall order and we need to work quickly, as on Saturday I also want to showcase as many of my patisserie range as possible. Fortunately, I have two full days in the kitchen as Wenna's friend, Kate, is going to cover for me.'

'That wouldn't be Kate Enys, would it?' Erica queries.

'Oh.' I laugh. 'I don't know her surname. She popped in to help out for two hours at the drop of a hat, which impressed me.'

'She's the person I was thinking of when you rang me yesterday. Kate started up a business from home making novelty biscuits a while back but ended up having to take a part-time job to keep afloat. Now she's just got the part-time job but at least it's better than nothing.'

I feel bad now, as I didn't really get much time to talk to Kate, but I will.

As Erica and I start to unpack the boxes, she turns to grin at me. 'You certainly know how to store a rich fruit cake, Ivy.'

'I've had enough practice over the years. I made these six weeks ago. The Cake and Coffee Emporium was infamous for its display of Christmas cakes,' I say with some pride. 'They've been skewered and brushed several times, with a dark sherry. I covered them in marzipan the day before we made the big move.'

In tandem we unwrap the foil outer layers, then slip off the string around the middle to tease open the greaseproof paper and suddenly the kitchen is filled with a whole array of nostalgic smells.

'Oh,' Erica groans, 'I haven't used sherry for years. It reminds me of my gran and the cakes she used to make. I'm getting orange peel, cherries, raisins…'

'They don't call it *rich* for nothing.' I smile. 'Instead of refined sugar, I use an organic honey mixed with a little freshly squeezed orange juice to sweeten it.'

The cake Erica has unwrapped is an eight-inch square. 'Is this homemade marzipan?'

'Yes. You'll notice it's applied thinly. We'll do the same with the traditional fondant when we cover them. The final decorations are non-edible but fun and are reusable as decorations.'

'What a clever idea!'

'The problem I have is that traditional cakes are still extremely popular, but I also offer a healthy options range, which are tray cakes with naturally sourced toppings. They're delicious but don't keep for weeks like an old-fashioned fruit cake.'

I go in search of the box of decorations to show Erica and when I begin laying them out, I can see she's impressed.

'Oh, Ivy. You put so much thought into what you produce. These could be plucked off the cake and hung on the Christmas tree.'

'That's the idea. I can't bear the thought of making fondant snowmen and filling a child's stomach with even more sugar. Kids love some of the new flavours for the frostings I've developed over time, as long as no one mentions the word *healthy*,' I declare with a smirk.

Erica laughs. 'I bet a lot of adults have the same reaction. Anyway, let's make a start. How many cakes do you have in total for the window display?'

'Fifteen, although they range in size from six inches to fourteen inches.'

'We'd best make a start then. Gosh, it really does smell like Christmas in here already,' she remarks, wistfully.

It's just after eight o'clock when Erica and I look at each other and give a weary sigh. 'I've had enough – I don't know about you,' I admit.

'Same again tomorrow? I can get here at noon if you like. Is Adam driving down tomorrow night after work?'

'Yes, and I can't wait. Waving him off last Sunday seems like a distant memory already,' I laugh.

We pop the finished cakes into airtight containers, and I load the dishwasher while Erica wipes down the countertops.

'Come on,' she hastens me, 'you look like you're done in.'

'Hmm. I started at six this morning. It's a good job I've got stamina.'

She chuckles at me as I switch off the kitchen light and we make our way downstairs. I glance around, noting that everything is pristine, ready for the morning. Wenna and Kate did well.

'Right, it's time to go. Goodnight, Erica, and thank you so much for coming to my rescue. You have no idea how much I appreciate your help because I couldn't do this all on my own. Noon tomorrow it is, then.' I lean in to give her a grateful hug.

'Aww… you're going to do wonders here, Ivy. Sleep well; I know I will!'

With the door ajar, I watch Erica walk over to her car and give her a wave as she drives off. In the gloom I hear a voice calling out. 'Ivy!'

The front door to The Farmhouse is open and, in the doorway, the shape of Jess is illuminated. I lock the door to the bakery and hurry over.

'My goodness, you look exhausted,' she blurts out. 'Have you eaten?'

'Not since... I don't know,' I groan, easing my shoulders back and tilting my head from side to side to relax my upper torso.

'Come on, I'm just about to grab something. Lola's in bed; she had dinner with Daisy and Charlie earlier on. Was that Erica you were waving off?'

I step inside, slipping off my coat and hanging it on one of the hooks.

'Yes,' I reply, keeping my voice down.

'Oh, Lola's not asleep, she's reading. Her door is shut, and I'll pop up later as often she falls asleep before switching off the light. Cappy is at the pub with Riley, Keith and Len. Take a seat.'

I love The Farmhouse kitchen. It's everything you would expect, from the flagstone floors to the huge range cooker. The hand-painted units look homely and who doesn't love a large, scrubbed pine table?

'I bet you haven't stopped either,' I remark.

Jess turns to look at me. 'It's been crazy and tomorrow is going to be just as bad. Riley and I have been hanging shelves, assembling displays, and generally helping our newcomers get ready to move into the hub. It's starting to come together but we have stacks of recycling that Riley will have to deal with tomorrow. One of the leaseholder's vans broke down on the way here, so one of the bays is still bare. She's bringing racks with her, too, for displaying handmade cards. Here you go. I made two large lasagnes as Riley will probably stay over tomorrow night. It's going to be an early start on Saturday.' She beams at me.

'How do you manage now Cappy's living here?'

'Oh, Riley uses the pull-out sofa in the sitting room. It's

annoying...' she rolls her eyes '...but it's nice having him here under the same roof.'

'Oh... of course. I don't suppose you get any time together on your own anymore, even if Lola has a sleepover with Daisy.' That thought hadn't occurred to me.

'It's awkward, that's for sure. I'm sleeping in what was Cappy and Grandma's bedroom and while Granddad's back... well, it wouldn't feel right somehow.'

'What impresses me the most about Riley,' I admit, 'isn't just that he's so respectful to Cappy, but he always has your back. He loves the farm just as much as you do, Jess.'

'That's how I know he's the one, Ivy.' She joins me at the table, and we immediately tuck in.

'This is really kind of you and just what I need. I've got to watch the time as I said I'd call Adam around nine.'

'Cappy suggested that Riley and I try to grab more nights together at his cottage. It was lovely to have some quality time, not just because it's frustrating not having any privacy, but to talk about our plans for the future.' Jess looks at me from under her eyelashes and I burst out laughing.

'Is that *all* you talked about?'

'Maybe not. At some point I want a ring on my finger.' She raises her eyebrows and now we're both laughing like fools.

'Oh, Jess. Still, with Cappy here at least you have a live-in childminder.'

'Yes, but she'll probably talk him into letting her stay up late, so we've decided it has to be at the weekend. We're both so tired these days it'll probably be more about falling asleep in each other's arms, than it will be rolling around under the sheets. Anyway, what's going on at the bakery?'

Jess passes me a basket of bread and it makes me smile. A few hours ago this Cornish cob loaf was sitting on the shelf in the bakery.

'Thanks. Oh... so much that my head is reeling. I want to capitalise on Saturday's big opening of the hub and another bumper market day. Adam warned me Tuesdays are crazy but is it always like that?'

Jess nods her head, putting her hand up to her mouth as she swallows. 'Yep, pretty much. Word is really getting around. Thankfully, Cappy, Keith and Len have the parking under control for the time being, but Saturday is likely to be even busier. We've arranged with Pengali Farm to use one of the fields opposite as an overspill car park, if needed.'

I stifle a yawn between mouthfuls of food. 'Do you know Kate Enys? She's a friend of Wenna's. She's covering for me while I'm prepping for Saturday.'

'I did see her in the courtyard; I just didn't realise she was helping you out. I don't really know her, only in passing,' Jess remarks.

'She kindly offered to work three days as a favour. I'm badly in need of a second server, but Kate already has a part-time job. I'm not sure if it will fit in with her existing commitments.'

My plate is empty, and I sit back feeling pleasantly full. 'That hit the spot, thank you. So, aside from being busy everything is ticking over all right?' I check.

'Vyvyan said there's a bit of a problem. Someone who didn't get a space in the hub isn't happy and she wants to talk to me about it. It's all go right now, so I had to put her off until Monday. We were due for our regular meeting where she brings me up to date with bookings on the campsite and the cottage. However, I'm running behind on processing paperwork, which means I've paid out money that isn't on the spreadsheet yet and that makes me feel uncomfortable.'

'I don't know how you manage it all, Jess. And yet you're still smiling.'

'It's all doable if I keep on top of it; the problems occur when I don't. Once this weekend is over things will calm down a lot.'

I nod my head in agreement. 'That's the point I'm at right now. I could do with two of me, but I'll have an additional pair of hands here tomorrow night; I just haven't told him how late we'll be working.'

We exchange knowing glances.

'Poor Adam, I hope he isn't expecting a restful weekend. How's his new job going?'

'He's enjoying it and doing a bit of socialising with his new colleagues.' I try my best to stifle yet another yawn, but Jess gives me a pointed look.

'Go on, get yourself back to Smithy's Cottage before you fall asleep at the table. I don't think you're going to be able to stay awake long enough to call Adam,' she warns.

'Hmm... I might text him because I think you're right. I just want to sink into bed.'

As she sees me out, Jess watches as I pull on my coat.

'Ivy, you've no regrets... have you?'

'Oh, Jess – not at all. It's my first week and judging by the reaction we got today, my problem is going to be keeping up with demand,' I reply, firmly.

'Good. That's all I wanted to hear.' She wraps her arm around my shoulders and gives me a squeeze. 'It's so good to have you here, Ivy. It won't always be this chaotic. Well... I hope not. Sleep well.'

'You, too, Jess. And thanks... for everything.'

ADAM

Renweneth Farm, Cornwall

16

Signs of the Changes to Come

'Hi, Mum. How are you and Dad?'

Mum gives a nervous little laugh. 'It's all good here, my son. Are you on your way to the farm?'

'Yes, it's not far now. Sorry I didn't have time to pop in to see you this week, but I've spent a bit of time socialising with some of the guys. It looks like a couple of them are earmarked to work on my first project.'

'Do you know where it's going to be?'

'No. There are two possibilities, one is in Wiltshire and the other in Devon, a place called Parklands. The decision on which one will be down to timing, although I've just learnt that there might be a bit of a planning hitch with Parklands, I'm afraid.'

'We'll keep our fingers crossed for you. How was Ivy's first week?'

'Crazily busy, by the sound of it.'

'Busy is good, but I do hope the two of you get some time to simply rest and relax.'

'Ivy has already warned me that this weekend is going to be intense. They're gearing up for the festive season now and, as it's the first Christmas for the bakery, Ivy's putting a lot of pressure on herself to get it right.'

'Ah!' she sighs. 'It's all change, isn't it? We'll all be establishing a new tradition this year.'

Inwardly I groan. Every Christmas since we got engaged, Ivy

and I take it in turns to visit one set of parents one day and the other set the following day. This year Jess had invited us down to the farm, so Mum was prepared for that. The plan was that by the following year we'd have a place of our own in Stroud and just the two of us would spend Christmas Day together at home. On Boxing Day we'd invite both families round, creating a new tradition. However, a permanent move is another thing entirely and, suddenly, it's the things we took for granted that mean much more than we'd realised.

'We'll sort something out – you know it. My company shut down for two weeks and I'll be pressing Ivy to make sure she has enough cover to take some time off.'

'It doesn't matter when we celebrate Christmas, goodness knows we don't have enough room to get everyone together these days, anyway. Your dad was talking about organising a big meet-up between Christmas and New Year.'

'What, everyone?'

'Why not? Now that would be a real party and we could do it once a year.'

I give a little laugh. 'Seriously, Mum, can you imagine organising that?' There are a lot of us.

'I can and I will. All that matters to your dad and me is that you don't lose touch with the wider family. And, when you're settled, we'll pop down for the day and take you and Ivy out to lunch. Talking about food, why don't you pop in one evening next week for dinner?'

They're used to me calling in at odd times over the weekend, especially Saturday afternoons when Ivy was at work. I feel guilty that in future I'll be heading home to Cornwall. 'Great. You tell me which evening works for you and I'll be there.'

'I'll find out if your dad has any evening meetings planned and text you. There's some controversy about a new roundabout the council are proposing, and he's joined this action group to fight it.'

Dad is a bit of a campaigner when it comes to avoiding public money being wasted. He's not one to go off about something unless there's a reason but he says if people don't stand up and speak their piece there's no point complaining after the fact. And he's right.

'And, Adam, tell Ivy we miss her, won't you?'

Oh, how I do, too but I'm on the last leg of my journey. 'Of course. Speak soon, Mum – love ya!'

As we disconnect there's a bleep on the dashboard and Riley's voice fills the car.

'Hey, mate. I got away a bit early. Another hour and I'll be pulling into the courtyard. I thought I'd surprise Ivy.'

'Well, just to make you aware that the lights are on in the bakery, so chances are she'll still be working when you get here. She's had a lot of extremely long days, so Jess says she'll be tired.'

'Thanks for the heads-up. I'll tread carefully.' I half expect him to say he'll see me in a bit and ring off, but he doesn't.

'How's the new job going?'

'Smoothly, I'm glad to say. It's like the good old days.'

'Ha!' Riley gives a belly laugh. 'That makes you sound ancient, Adam.'

'Well, I've been in the building game since I was sixteen, when I started my apprenticeship. Back then you were taught the trade the right way. Nowadays, seriously, some of the guys I've worked alongside are cowboys. Whether that's due to poor training, or laziness, I don't know.'

He gives a throaty laugh. 'Some of these big companies have a lot to answer for, don't they? I've experienced that for myself. It was why I ended up teaming up with an old friend to start a business. Nothing's guaranteed, though, is it?'

He's in a reflective mood this evening, which is rather puzzling. 'No, it's not. How are things with you... in general?'

'Heh! Heh! It's that obvious something's up, is it?'

Oh, please don't say you're having problems with Jess. 'It is a bit.'

'Fiona has been in touch to say that Ollie is ready to spend some one-to-one time with me here, in Cornwall.'

Hmm... I thought that was what Riley wanted. 'That's good news, isn't it?' I venture.

'Yep, but I need some advice as, naturally, Fiona started asking questions about where I was working and what I did in my spare time. She was fishing, checking whether anyone else lives at the cottage. I answered truthfully that I was employed doing building work at a local farm and that he could come any weekend because I have no commitments.'

'Fiona doesn't know about Jess?' I reply, trying not to sound shocked.

'No, of course not. We rarely speak. This is a big deal and my chance to re-establish a bond with Ollie again. But what if something slips out and I inadvertently mention Jess's name. I'm not good at keeping secrets and if he says something to his mother it's going to look bad, isn't it?'

'What does Jess think?'

'I talked her into agreeing that we wouldn't tell Fiona yet, but what if I put my foot in it?'

'Mate, that's not an easy situation to find yourself in but I'd say stick to the plan and relax, just watch what you say.'

'There's so much riding on this, Riley, it brings me out in a cold sweat.'

'You're not scared of Fiona, are you?'

There's a slight pause. 'No, but I know how her mind works. She hasn't forgiven me for messing up her life and now she's finally giving me a chance to get to know my son again, I don't want to mess that up too.'

'It's not as if Ollie and Jess are going to cross paths, is it? But at some point, there'll be no avoiding the conversation. Where are you? It sounds like you're walking around.'

'I'm staying over at The Farmhouse tonight as we have an early start tomorrow. I'm outside in the courtyard. Drive safely and no doubt we'll catch up in the morning.'

'I think Ivy has a list of things she wants me to do,' I warn him.

'Hmm... I know the feeling, Adam. And thanks for the advice!'

When I pull into the courtyard the lights from the bakery shine out across the cobbles and they glisten after a recent shower of rain. I lock the car and hurry over, peering in through the main bakery door to see Ivy moving a stepladder around. I give a gentle tap. She looks up and immediately breaks out into a beaming smile.

I'm glad to see it's locked as she's clearly on her own. When she welcomes me inside, I throw my arms around her and begin to gently walk her backwards, nudging the door shut with my elbow.

'You're early!' she exclaims. Then my lips are on hers and words aren't necessary. As usual, one kiss is never enough, and I'm loath to let her go.

'You smell delicious. Sort of like peaches and cream,' I banter.

'It's probably a splash of liqueur from some of the cakes I've been making ready for tomorrow. How was the journey?'

'Good. I got caught in the early rush hour on the outskirts of Stroud but it wasn't quite as bad as I was expecting. The boss said he's okay with me leaving a bit earlier on a Friday. I don't always clock off on time and he says it's give and take. Anyway, wow – this is all looking lovely.'

She does look tired, but I can tell she's buzzing as she points out the changes. The coffee station has been moved to the left-hand side of the counter, so the staff have more room to move around.

Her cheeks are rosy, and her face is a little shiny. Most of her hair is tucked up into her signature houndstooth baker's beanie cap, but a few strands have escaped, and she looks so cute.

'I love the new T-shirt. I hope you have one for me.' It's white, long-sleeved and with *The Farmhouse Bakery* embroidered in a hand-written font. Together with black trousers, she looks every inch like the professional baker she is.

'I do,' she replies, 'all my staff have been kitted out. Well, you, me and Wenna for now but I'm working on it.'

'I'm staff now, am I?' I query, frowning.

'Tomorrow you will be if we get swamped.'

But it's the window display that she's really excited about. 'Do you think it's too much?'

'You've done all this by yourself in the last few hours?'

'Erica offered to stay but she's worked tirelessly today again with only two thirty-minute, breaks. I sent her home an hour before we closed with my grateful thanks. Come and look at the Christmas cakes. You'll need to step outside while I uncover the displays.'

At least the fine drizzle has stopped, and I stand back patiently awaiting the reveal. Either side of the main door into the bakery, the glass panes have been lightly sprayed with snow at the very top and in a wavy line along the bottom. As Ivy carefully slips off the large white cotton cloth in the first window, individual domed glass cake stands are supported on white pillars at varying heights. The array of Christmas cakes is a visual feast. The window on the other side of the door is a mirror image, although all the cakes are different shapes and sizes. She hurries out to join me.

'It's a work of art, Ivy. In fact, all of the cakes are a work of art.' Covered in plain white icing, each one is topped with a unique Christmas decoration. There's a cluster of small golden baubles, a series of wooden hearts sporting tiny red bows, a duo of golden bells and even a ruby red sleigh filled with tiny little presents.

'It's going to take me another couple of hours to do the other two windows, I'm afraid but I'm thrilled with how it looks, babe.'

I place my arm around her waist, pulling her closer as my eyes scan along the entire rank of cottages. The second two windows are in total darkness, as the lights in what Ivy calls the tasting room are switched off.

'Once you arrange for the tables and chairs to be delivered, will you make use of the second door?'

'It'll make sense, as we often have a little queue wrapping around inside the shop. It means we'll have a way in and a separate way out.'

'I think you've outdone yourself with these two windows displays, Ivy. I really do.'

As I encourage her back inside, Ivy's eyes are gleaming. Only the tiny dark smudges beneath them tell me we need to get a move on.

'What can I do to help?'

She gazes around at the part-opened boxes littering the main part of the floor. 'Let's carry these through into the cake-tasting room. I ordered some rather wonderful white metal trees. If you can clean the inside of the windows, wipe down the sills and give them a quick spray of snow so that all four of them look the same, I'll start unpacking the trees. But first, I'll grab us some coffees and a little snack. Erica very kindly brought me in one of her slow-cook casseroles, all ready to go. It'll be ready about nine o'clock.'

I glance at my watch. 'Hmm… we've got an hour then. I'd best get busy.' As she turns to walk back into the main part of the shop I call out, 'I love you, Ivy Taylor. You made me a proud man indeed the day we tied the knot.'

She turns to gaze back at me. 'Aww, babe! Love you, too… maybe even three. Might even make it a five if you agree to carry around some trays of samples at the market tomorrow.'

I groan. 'Ah, I knew you had something in mind. I didn't think you'd really allow me behind the counter. Even dressed up to look the business.'

'Oh, you'll look the business all right. And who wouldn't want to clamour around a good-looking man offering freebies? You're a part of my marketing strategy.'

She starts giggling to herself as I grab a cloth to get cleaning.

'I nearly forgot,' she says, excitedly. 'Renweneth Farm Bakery has a website. It's a bit basic at the moment, but people can go online to order their Christmas cakes. Over the coming weeks I'll be adding more photos of the bakery and all sorts of local information about the farm and the area in general.'

'How did you manage that on top of everything else?'

She looks at me and winks. 'It's not what you know, but who. Remember Sean Hannity from IT Solutions and Web Design?'

'The guy who fancies you and bailed you out when the old website went down?'

'Don't be so ridiculous.' She rolls her eyes at me. 'One five-minute call, an hour pulling together the basic information and taking photos to email to him, and he set it up within three days slotting it in around a big job he's doing.'

'Hmm,' I muse, raising an eyebrow. 'I bet he doesn't do that for everyone wanting something done quickly.'

With that she walks off chuckling to herself. And he does fancy her.

IVY

Renweneth Farm, Cornwall

17

It's Time to Turn Up the Heat

Nothing beats waking up in the morning lying next to the man you love and watching him as he lies on his back snoring. I smile to myself. Adam is my idea of the perfect man. He makes me feel safe; well, with muscles like that anyone meaning trouble will stop and think twice. But he's the only man I've ever met who made me feel… special. He worries about me, like I worry about him. And in a world where everyone is trying to prove themselves, we're old-school. Everything we do is for *us*, as a couple. I don't want a string of bakeries and Adam simply wants a job that utilises his skills, where he can earn what he's worth. Together we're building the future we want, not striving to conquer the world.

Suddenly one eye opens, and he peers up at me. 'Was I snoring again?'

'Only a little.'

'What time is it?'

'Just after five. Go back to sleep.'

He groans softly as he rolls onto his side. 'I didn't get to the gym once this week and boy am I feeling it. I've got a couple kinks in my upper back that the shoulder press would soon straighten out.'

'There's bound to be one around here. Why not check with Riley?'

'I thought you had my weekend all planned out for me,' he teases, as I nestle into him.

'You could escape for a couple of hours. A lady named Kate is helping Wenna and me behind the counter today. If I'm not needed, I'll be upstairs baking.'

Adam grimaces.

'I know,' I reply, sadly. 'But if the window displays inspire customers to place their orders, fruit cakes need time to mature. Unfortunately, I still don't have a baker to help me.'

'Ah. All that spiking and drizzling of brandy, or whatever you do.'

'Sherry, actually. No one likes dry cake, do they? And it takes time, unless my customers want a crumbly cake that doesn't slice well. I am sorry, Adam, but I will make it up to you, I promise. As soon as I have someone on board who can fill in for me, I intend to take every Saturday off.'

'I'm jolly glad to hear it.'

He eases himself up, plumping the pillows before getting comfortable again. As he reaches out for me in the gloom, I snuggle closer, laying my head on his chest.

'My mum's a bit down about Christmas,' he admits. 'She's talking about arranging a big family get-together, between Christmas and New Year. I just thought I'd warn you and they both send their love.'

'Oh, this was always going to be a different Christmas, wasn't it, but now I feel really bad.'

'Me, too. And once I move out of the old house it's going to really sink in that Cornwall is our home now. They're talking about coming down for a visit once we're settled. But Smithy's Cottage doesn't feel like ours yet and your focus is understandably on the bakery.'

Adam doesn't just witter on. If he mentions something, then I need to tune in and read between the lines.

'My mum is stressing a little, too, although she's making a concerted effort to stay upbeat. We speak every day and I can't lie and say it isn't full-on here, but that's to be expected. Leave it with me. As soon as I get a chance, I'll work something out, Adam. Maybe we can get our parents here together one Sunday and I'll make lunch for us all.'

He lays his head against mine. 'Thanks, Ivy. They're bound to worry and want to see exactly what we've got ourselves into. Once they have, I'm sure they'll agree this wasn't a whim, or even a risky move. Maybe we should have a family open day and invite the lot of them,' he starts laughing and the bed shakes.

'That's not a bad idea.' I sigh. 'The only problem is having time to arrange it. As soon as I resolve my staffing problem, I'll be on it. And if all these Christmas cakes that I'm baking don't sell,' I jest, 'I know what I'll be wrapping up with a red bow and giving everyone this year. Right, I hate to say this, but I need to shower and get to work. If you're going to be handing out free samples, I've got to bake them first.'

By the time Wenna taps on the door, all the ovens have been on for nearly three hours.

'Ivy, the windows look amazin'! And what's that gorgeous smell?' She's wearing her new uniform quite proudly, I see.

'Fruit cakes, carrot cake with orange cashew frosting, cupcakes with mango lemon frosting… you name it, we have it!'

As she goes to shut the door Kate arrives, looking a little flustered. 'Sorry, I was worried I'd be late. Is it all right if I go use the cloakroom to change? And wow – Christmas is coming. It all looks so festive in here.'

'Yes, feel free and thanks. Adam and I ended up working very late last night to get it finished off.'

'Seriously, Ivy, this is really something. Jess is going to be overwhelmed. It's not just a bread shop that sells cakes, it's like gazing into one of the windows in a posh French *pâtisserie*.'

'Exactly the look I was aiming for!' I exclaim. 'When we open the café, I want our customers to feel they're coming here for a real treat. Something a little different. We'll focus on the various flavour combinations rather than labelling everything healthy and organic, which puts some people off. A lot of people have allergies these days, so if anyone asks about specific ingredients, I have a leaflet you can give them. It lists everything in each product we offer.'

Kate is back and she saunters up to us. 'And the bonus is that you can charge a premium because you get what you pay for. It's all good for business. That's where I went wrong,' she says, sounding a little jaded. 'I didn't charge enough.'

I don't quite know what to say and even Wenna casts me an awkward glance.

'Ah, one of the timers is bleeping, so something's ready to come out the oven. If anyone wants to order a Christmas cake, try to get them to do it online. I've printed off a pile of small handouts with the name of the website on it. For those who are old-school, there's a price sheet and an order book next to the point-of-sale. Just take a name, address, a telephone number, and a collection date. I must dash, but I'll explain about the healthy alternatives later.'

I rush upstairs, taking them two at a time and as I pull out a large tray of blueberry cinnamon chia bake, my stomach rumbles. As I'm about to slip it into one of the cooling racks, there's a tap on the door. I look over to see Jess's smiling face.

'Hey, you! Adam's doing a great job with those lights outside and the windows look lovely, Ivy. You must be delighted.'

She looks pleased but I realise I might have made a bit of a mistake. 'I meant to check with you first before putting up the lights, Jess, but with everything going on it slipped my mind. You didn't have a master plan… did you?'

She raises her eyebrows at me. 'I wish I did. We've a ton of decorations but no plan. Sadly, it was so far down my urgent to-do list this week that I'm berating myself for not giving the job of organising it to someone else. You've saved the day, Ivy, as the bakery is like a Christmas cave. Riley is on car-parking duty with Cappy and Len today, so nothing will be put up until tomorrow, I'm afraid. However...' she gives me one of her happy smiles '...the hub looks incredible. Do you have a moment to pop in and check it out before we open up?'

There's a ping as another timer goes off.

'Let me pull these out and I have twenty minutes until the next timer goes off.'

Two minutes later we're on our way, dodging Fred as he carries in the first crate of bread. 'Wenna, the cakes are in the first of the two cooler racks. I won't be long.'

'Thanks, Ivy.'

As Jess and I make our way across the courtyard into the side entrance to the hub, she gives me a quick glance. 'Are you going to take Kate on permanently?'

'Today's her last day but I did express an interest. She said she'd think about it and get back to me. Why?'

Jess gives me an uneasy look. 'I don't like talking behind someone's back, but I've come to learn that Kate can be a little temperamental at times.'

I nod my head. 'Thanks, I'll take that on board.'

As Jess swings open the solid single door, which replaced the original wooden sliding one, she grins at me. 'This is going sometime next week, now that everyone has moved in. Riley is going to start work on your walled garden too.'

My face lights up at that thought, although with so much on my plate, turning the cottage into our home seems like a far-off dream.

As we stroll around The Courtyard Hub, I can't believe the transformation. It's warm and inviting, nothing at all like the draughty, workshop-style barn it was, except for the ceiling height. One half of it is still open right up to the wooden rafters; the other half now has a half-glazed walled mezzanine. Overhead there are several skylights that flood the entire place with daylight. Riley has put up lots of strands of twinkling lights and what was a compacted dirt floor now has a rustic feel with reclaimed wooden boards.

'What's going on upstairs?' I ask, pointing.

Jess leans in, lowering her voice. 'It's going to be a yoga studio but there's a bit of a dispute. I'll tell you all about it when we have a quiet moment.'

Dividing panels split the main area into individual bays. There's a bookshop, a stationery and card bay, a health food concession with an array of nuts, dried fruits and grains, a large corner section with a display of bespoke shabby-chic repurposed furniture. There's even a pottery section with a working potter's wheel, where customers can watch the pieces on display being made. The final one is a jewellery stand. A young woman sits sideways on to us at a bench behind the sales counter, creating a new piece as we watch.

'Jess, this is amazing,' I half-whisper, not wanting to be a distraction as we turn towards the exit. 'What a vision you had.'

'No, it was Grandma's vision, Ivy. I just hope I've done it justice. It's Vyvyan who ensures we have as wide a variety as possible to interest our visitors.'

As much as I'd love to browse, I need to get back and Jess appreciates that as she ushers me out the side door. 'Your garden is going to be very private, Ivy,' she says, adamantly.

'Oh, how I'd love to stay and chat, but I can't afford to burn any cakes today. The more free samples we give out, the better. And it's almost nine, so you'll be opening the gates to the hub.'

'Lola's excited about helping Adam.'

'And he's delighted to have a sidekick.'

'You know, Ivy, Grandma would be so happy to know you're a part of this. Alice and Jory have good hearts, but you're going to turn the bakery into something really special and when Adam's here, Riley has a mate to chat to.' She holds up the keys in her hand and they give a little jangling sound. 'Right, it's not quite like cutting a ribbon but they'll all be waiting for me to do the honours. See you later.'

I close the door behind me, and Adam reappears. He's standing there, arms crossed, looking up at his handiwork with an expression of satisfaction on his face.

'You finished in the nick of time,' I remark. There's already a queue forming outside the bakery and people are peering in at the window displays. Seconds later, the door swings open and Kate ushers the customers inside. 'The lights were expensive, but well worth the cost. Thanks for sacrificing your lie-in, babe. What would I do without you?'

I give him a quick kiss on the cheek.

'I'm just about to go inside and change ready for my next task.' He grins at me. 'It sounds like the market is already in full swing.'

'Yes, and I should be in the kitchen getting those trays ready for you. Oh.' I turn, hearing my name being called. 'Lola! Have you come to help Adam?'

'Mum said I had to report at nine o'clock sharp,' she informs me, that sweet little face of hers sporting a serious look for a second before she's distracted. 'Ooh, I love the lights, Ivy!'

'Come on, let's head into the bakery and you can give me a hand while Adam changes his clothes. And I have a rather nice-looking baker's hat for you, too, Lola.'

Her eyes gleam. 'Can I taste the cakes first, Ivy? Just in case people ask what they're like.'

Lola links arms with me. I give Adam a wink as we turn and the two of us head for the bakery. 'Of course you can. It's a vital part of the job!'

My aim each day is to have all the ovens turned off, and the kitchen sparkling clean, by eleven o'clock. I go straight downstairs to relieve Wenna so she can have a coffee break and, when she returns, Kate decides to head out to stretch her legs and take a look around the hub.

'Has it been like this all morning?' I lean in to Wenna as she appears next to me. I wrap a rosemary and sea salt loaf, placing it in one of the paper carriers and grab the tongs to put half a dozen rolls into a bag.

'Yes. It's a pity we can't fit more than two people behind the counter, but we'd only get in each other's way,' she replies before turning her head.

Her customer points to the shelf. 'Can I have one of those, too, please? The long one.'

I glance at Wenna, frowning. 'I hope we don't run out of bread. You've set aside the usual orders, haven't you?'

'Yep. Did that first thing. I'd say we've already had at least a third more customers in so far compared to this time last Saturday.'

'Really?' I thought it would be a bit busier and I upped the order a little, but at this rate the shelves behind the counter will be bare several hours before we close. That's not going to impress our customers.

'It might be worth givin' Alice a ring and see how they're fixed. You never know, they might be willin' to do a second delivery if they have anythin' spare.'

'Kate seems a little subdued; is everything all right?'

Wenna glances at me. 'I don't know. She seemed a bit put out sayin' she hadn't seen spaces advertised in the hub – that's why she's gone to check it out. Vyvyan has tried to spread the word as far as she can.'

When Kate reappears to take over she's frowning. 'The hub has a nice vibe going on. I'd have loved to have been a part of that if I'd known. I guess it's all about who you know.'

I don't think either Wenna or I quite know what to say.

'Ivy,' Wenna jumps in, 'I expect Adam and Lola's trays will need toppin' up.'

'I'll get straight onto that, Wenna. I'd like to have a little wander around the market anyway, to see how it's going. I'll see you in a bit, ladies.'

★

'Just in time!' Adam and Lola both come hurrying over as soon as they spot me.

'I didn't want to venture into the crowd in case I dropped one of the trays,' I admit.

Lola takes Adam's empty tray off him, placing her own on top, holding it out to him. He scoffs the last three fingers of cake in quick succession, and they hardly touch the sides.

'Oh, yum… this is downright cruel, Ivy. I'm starving.'

I shake my head at him. We're both aware he had a hearty breakfast, as he cooked it and builders-sized bacon sandwiches aren't exactly a snack.

'Here you go.' He places the empty trays underneath my arm as I hand them both a replenished one. 'You're allowed to pinch a few as you've done such a brilliant job. It's certainly making people head into the bakery. I've just had to top up the display before I could come across.'

'That's what we wanted to hear, wasn't it, Lola?'

She grins, ear to ear. Jess walks past and stops when she sees us. 'I'm just going back to The Farmhouse to grab a quick cup of coffee. The queue at the bakery is too long to get takeout,' she bemoans. 'Lola could probably do with a break, so give me five minutes and I'll go and make you both a drink. Hot chocolate, Lola?'

She nods her head enthusiastically. 'Ooh, yes please, Mum. This is great fun, isn't it, Adam?'

Adam doesn't look quite so enthralled and Jess gives me a bit of a smirk. 'I'm sure Cappy, Vyvyan, Keith, and Len will be glad of a hot drink, too. I'm on it, guys.'

I wish them luck and take a couple of minutes to stroll around the stalls. Everyone seems to have a list in their hands and I haven't even begun to think of Christmas shopping.

Erica waves and I give her a thumbs up as she's serving a customer and has two people waiting. When I start making my way back to the bakery, I pull the phone from my pocket and call Alice.

'Ivy, how's it going? I've been thinking of you. It's a big day at the farm for you all.'

'Bigger than I imagined it would be, Alice. It looks like I underestimated my order. I don't suppose there's any chance you could spare anything. It doesn't matter what it is but as the market doesn't shut until four, I don't want bare shelves for the last couple of hours.'

'Oh, I didn't know you'd extended the opening hours.'

'Yes, we close at five now.'

'Leave it with me. I'll have a word with Jory and he'll sort something out. Fred's here at the moment, so I'll give him the heads-up to be on standby. It'll probably be about an hour and a half. Is that all right?'

'Wonderful thanks, Alice. You truly are a lifesaver.' A bakery with no bread would be a major embarrassment for me today of all days.

'Hey, it's a partnership we're proud of, Ivy. Everyone in Polreweek is talking about Renweneth Farm today.'

'I was going to ask if you'd be happy for me to include your logo, as well as the Renweneth Farm one, on the printed bags and greaseproof wraps? I'm also going to ask Jess if I can design a bespoke one for The Farmhouse Bakery. I just thought it would be rather nice as it would link us all together.'

'I love that idea. Text me your email address and I'll get that sent over to you.'

'Perfect! And I won't make the same mistake next Saturday, Alice, I promise you!'

18

Be Careful What You Wish For

It's time to go home and I thank Wenna and Kate for what has been a hectic day behind the counter. Seconds later I'm unlocking the door to Smithy's Cottage.

'Only me, Adam,' I call out.

'I've been counting down the minutes,' he replies. 'I'm in the sitting room and I'm too lazy to move. My face muscles are aching, having spent so many hours smiling at people. It's more exhausting than laying bricks.'

I slip off my jacket and join him, sinking down onto the sofa and groaning as I lie almost prostrate.

'It's my legs and my back that are complaining,' I moan.

'Mine, too. I do a lot of walking, but I guess I end up sitting down a bit more than I realised.'

'Did you manage to grab something to eat?' I check.

'Jess heated up some of her homemade pasties and brought them out to us shortly after Erica picked up Lola. She's having a sleepover with Daisy. We're invited to dinner at The Farmhouse for seven this evening.'

'Ah, that's so thoughtful. Honestly, I don't know where Jess gets her energy from. There's no stopping her. I just want to crawl into bed.'

Adam's eyes widen. 'Now that sounds like a good idea to me.'

'To sleep,' I reply, emphatically.

'Let's just sit here and catch our breath for a bit, shall we?'

I snuggle up, nestling my head against him. Adam goes quiet and I listen to the regular rhythm of his heart beating in his chest. Is one beating heart just like another, or do we each have a unique rhythm? I find myself wondering.

'Riley is going to make a start this week on bricking up that side door to the hub and turning the space into a courtyard garden for us.'

Adam gives a warm 'Hmm' of approval. 'Jess will do anything she can to keep you here, Ivy.'

'You mean to keep *us* here, Adam. I think Riley will be around a lot more at weekends in future. Jess said he values and appreciates your friendship, and that makes her very happy.'

'Riley knows a lot of people around here – he should do as he's done jobs for a lot of them,' he points out.

'Knowing people is one thing, forming a bond with someone you feel comfortable sharing your innermost thoughts with is another thing entirely.'

'You know, Ivy, the hardest thing about upping sticks and moving away is putting distance between yourself and the people you've always had around you, isn't it?'

'Yes, babe, it is. But when Riley came to Cornwall it was slightly different for him; none of his family, except his brother, kept in touch. As for his friends, they soon drifted away. He lost everything and it's only now he's piecing together a new life. So, if you want to slope off with him for a pint at any time, just do it. He'll drop everything if I ask for help and that's the very least we can do, to repay his kindness.'

I smile to myself. I've discovered this week that it's not just the cakes that entice Riley through the door to the bakery, but he's popped in a couple of times just to check that everything is fine. He even insisted on putting up a few shelves for me, when he saw the stack of cake tins I had piled up in boxes with nowhere to put them.

'I'll remember that. Riley's a sound chap, someone you can rely on. Changing the subject... do you know what's up with

Cappy? He's been walking around in a bit of a mood, which isn't his style. It might have been purely coincidental, but I didn't see Jess and Cappy standing around chatting once today.'

I give a shrug, too comfortable to move my head and look at him. 'Things were certainly running smoothly from what I could see. Everyone seemed happy and the turnout was incredible. Alice had to bail me out with a second delivery of bread.'

'Oh, that's good news. Anyway, this new courtyard garden… I'm quite excited about it. I know for a fact there's soil under the cobbles if you want a couple of flower beds once the wall is up.'

I shift, uneasily. 'Adam, as exciting as it is, what if we can't pull it off? You know, getting a mortgage.'

Adam tilts his head to one side, trying to catch my eye. 'That's a ridiculous thing to say, Ivy. Unless you don't think the bakery will make a profit and we'll need to subsidise it.'

'Moving-in costs aside, so far the daily takings have exceeded my projections, which were based on Alice's weekly sales figures for the last month and a cautious estimate for the new patisserie range. Of course, it could be a bit of a novelty factor, as the locals are all coming in to check me out.' I laugh.

'Have you burnt through the money you set aside to expand the old café?'

'No, I still have a couple of thousand left. I'm keeping that to one side, as I know Jess would love an outdoor seating area once I have time to turn the tasting room into a café.'

He gives a low, rumbling laugh. 'Then our nest egg is still intact. In three months' time my probation will be over and my accountant says I can probably get a mortgage based solely on my salary. We're in a great position, Ivy, so what's worrying you?'

I pause, trying to pinpoint the problem. 'It all seems too good to be true, Adam.'

'Ivy!' Adam admonishes me, as he reaches out for my hand. 'You, of all people, know better than to think negatively. Yes, it's going to be hard work to begin with, being apart and getting things set up here. But think about where we were just a few weeks ago. Yes, you've swapped one lot of worry for another, but stressing over empty shelves means the business is doing well. And all the hard work you put in this week made Jess determined to get the courtyard in full-on festive mode tomorrow.'

'You think so?'

'I know, for sure. Even Riley said tomorrow morning we hit the ground running. Don't underestimate the impact you've already made, or what you've achieved in a short space of time, Ivy. Now, why don't we go upstairs and lie on the bed for an hour, or two? I want to be refreshed so I can enjoy Jess's generous offer. The last couple of months we've ended up just the two of us on a Saturday night sitting in front of the TV. Yes, we're both tired, but we're not stressed, not like we have been. And tonight we'll be among friends who appreciate what we're doing. Not just for us, but for something much, much bigger. I'm looking forward to it.'

Suddenly, I find myself looking at this past week in an entirely different way. This was the right decision to make, and Adam needs me to acknowledge that. Even if my income doesn't count for mortgage purposes as the business is so new, that doesn't mean we don't have an additional income stream. I've spent so long worrying about money, the future and how we're going to cope, that I've forgotten how to simply *be*. To enjoy each day as it comes. Maybe this is payback time for all the hard work we've put in, in the past. It's time to stop worrying and do what comes naturally and that's to follow my passion.

'Oh, Adam,' I sigh, happily. 'You're right. I want our garden to be filled with pots but I also want some climbers creeping up over the walls. Roses – naturally – honeysuckle, clematis, hydrangea… ooh, and jasmine!'

'That's my girl. We work to live, but we don't live to work, Ivy. That's not what we want out of life. I don't need a huge house, but what I want is a home; a place where we can escape from the world when we lock our door. I know you'll still be renting the bakery for a while to come, but maybe not forever.'

That thought blows my mind. Adam and I are an integral part of Renweneth Farm now. Somehow, I need to find a way of getting our families together so they, too, feel a part of our life here. I don't want them to feel abandoned, or distant. I want them to come and visit, spend quality time with us. I don't intend on working long days forever, but I do need to find the right people to help me. And maybe think about turning the office above the bakery into a guest room as Jess suggested.

'Come on,' I say, easing myself into a standing position and offering to pull Adam to his feet. 'Let's grab a couple of hours' sleep. Then, we can take a leisurely stroll along the coastal path before we head over to The Farmhouse for a wonderful evening with friends. I think we deserve it.'

Adam and I walk hand in hand across the courtyard, each of us carrying a bottle of wine. As we pass Penti Growan Cottage, adjacent to The Farmhouse, the door opens and the couple staying there step out.

'Evening!' the guy calls over to us.

'Oh, hi,' I call back.

'The bakery looks lovely all lit up,' his partner says, joining in.

'Thank you. It was quite a day. We're off to The Farmhouse to celebrate,' I hold up the wine bottle in my hand.

Adam steers us in their direction.

'We're off to The Lark and Lantern at Penvennan Cove. We've heard they do excellent pub grub there.'

'We've only eaten there once but we really enjoyed it. Another place you might like to try is The Trawlerman's Catch – it's on the way to Polreweek,' Adam suggests.

'Thanks for the tip. Enjoy your celebration.' They both smile as we begin walking again.

When we hear their car pulling out of the courtyard I turn to Adam. 'They think we're locals,' I muse.

'Well, Ivy, we are.'

It seems we're a little late as when Cappy throws open the door to The Farmhouse, there's a buzz of chatter coming from the kitchen.

'I was half-tempted to come looking for the pair of you,' he states as we hold our bottles out to him. 'You didn't have to do that, but thanks. Come on in, there are glasses on the side and a couple of bottles of wine to choose from. I'll add these to the stash.'

'Adam, Ivy... at last!' Riley welcomes us and he looks so at home standing at the range stirring something and wearing a navy-blue apron. 'I've been cooking for hours.' He swipes the back of his hand across his forehead and Jess bursts out laughing.

'Ignore him. Help yourself to a drink and grab a seat.'

Adam indicates with his hand for me to sit down, then he walks over to join Cappy.

'It's lovely to get together,' I remark, giving Vyvyan and Keith a warm smile and pulling out a chair. 'What a successful day it's been. How was the parking, Keith?'

'Pretty smooth, although it was manic late mornin'. We had a couple of new arrivals at the campsite and one of them was towin' a brand-new Compass Camino caravan. It was a real beauty, but he was a bit of a nervous driver.'

Cappy looks across at us. 'Nervous? He had a good two-foot clearance either side of him, but he insisted we got a few of the parked cars to move. I've never seen anyone make such a hash of a manoeuvre before as he turned into the gate.'

Oh, Cappy's fired up tonight and Jess changes the subject.

'Everything was fine in the end. Anyway, tonight we have one of Erica's posh fish stews with garlic and saffron. And crusty bread from The Farmhouse Bakery. I managed to grab the last two cob loaves on the shelf.'

'You were lucky,' I inform her. 'I ended up going home with a couple of bread rolls. Adam wasn't too impressed, were you, babe?'

'You can't get much in a roll, Ivy,' Adam points out. 'Hard work is it, Riley, stirring that pot?'

They grin at each other. 'I'm not allowed to let it stick. It's hot work.'

A little *miaow* announces the arrival of Misty. She's such a gorgeous cat and a typical grey and white short-haired breed with luminous, citrine-coloured eyes.

'She's looking for Lola,' Riley remarks. 'She'll wander around for a bit and then head into the sitting room to gaze out the window. You miss Lola, don't you, Misty?'

'Hey, girl.' I lower my hand, and she wanders over to sniff it. But it's fleeting and she heads straight past to her food bowl.

'I think you can start dishing up now, Riley. I'll slice up the bread. That stew smells delicious.' Jess grins at him.

Keith asks Adam how the new job is going and I'm content to sit back and take it all in. This time last week Adam and I were enjoying the first evening together in our new home; now we're celebrating what has been a hectic, but unbelievable first week.

'Any news from Rach?' Jess asks.

I shake my head. 'No. Not yet. I thought I'd wait until she rings me.'

'Oh, Ivy.' Vyvyan catches my eye. 'I saw you had Kate serving today but as you asked, I've got a couple of names and numbers I've written down for you. One of them is a lady looking for a few hours' work a week serving and can be flexible, but she doesn't bake. The other one, Chelle, isn't a trained baker as such but she does make novelty birthday cakes in her spare time. Remind me to grab that piece of paper from my bag before I go.'

'Thanks, Vyvyan. We had orders for fourteen Christmas cakes today. I couldn't believe it.'

'Make that fifteen.' Vyvyan raises an eyebrow at me as I start laughing.

'Sixteen,' Jess joins in. 'Actually, I'll probably need two given how many mouths we'll have to feed this Christmas.'

'After dinner let's have a wander over to look at the window display and we can pick out our cakes,' Vyvyan adds.

'Give Ivy a rest, ladies,' Cappy interrupts the banter. 'Although, I did get a taste of that, what was it? Like a finger of cake with mango and lemon frosting. It was very moreish.'

'Ah, there was hardly anything left, which is why I didn't bring anything with me. I'll save you a couple of slices on Monday, Cappy. Promise!'

'Don't feel too sorry for him, Ivy,' Adam interrupts as he passes me a bowl of steaming fish stew, making my stomach rumble. 'If he had one sample, he had at least half a dozen from me. Don't know how many from Lola, though.'

Whatever was troubling Cappy, his mood has improved and there's a lot of laughter and banter as we sit together, eating. It's good to be among friends we regard as family, and now we're getting to know Vyvyan and Keith, too.

At one point I glance over at Riley while Jess is talking and he's staring at her, hanging on every word. You can't fake the look of love and he's got it. At least tonight he's staying at The Farmhouse again, ready for the big trimming up tomorrow.

Adam touches my elbow with his hand. 'You're deep in thought.' His voice is low as our eyes meet.

Oblivious to the chatter going on around us, I gaze at him adoringly. 'I was just thinking about how lucky we are to have each other.'

'I think I'm the lucky one, Ivy. We're here because of you.'

It's almost ten o'clock by the time the table is cleared, and the conversation starts to wind down.

'Anyone fancy a nightcap?' Cappy asks.

I'm sure he means a small tot of rum, or brandy, but I have another idea.

'If anyone fancies a cup of hot chocolate, we could walk over to the bakery. It doesn't take long to fire up the machine.'

Glancing around the table, my suggestion seems to have gone down well, as heads nod.

'If we all wrap up,' Jess suggests, 'we could have a wander around the courtyard and think about where we're going to start tomorrow. There's a tree being delivered first thing in the morning.'

'And wait until you see the boxes and boxes of garlands, lights and trimmings Jess has ordered,' Riley says, shaking his head as he looks at her. 'I don't know where we're going to put them all.'

Jess batts her eyelashes at him. 'We're not talking about trimming up a house, Riley. This calls for large, statement decorations. Go big, or go home, is my motto.'

As we filter through the hallway to grab our coats and then out into the courtyard, Jess points towards the bakery.

'Ivy has the right idea. She's kept it simple and with the colourful string of lights running the whole length of the roof above the row of cottages, it looks really pretty.'

It's the first time I've had a chance to stand back and gaze at the bakery from this angle. In the darkness, the lights were worth every penny.

'You put a lot of thought into those window displays, Ivy,' Vyvyan adds. 'The cake displays are gorgeous, but I also love the other two windows with the forest of white trees. Are they wooden?'

I pull the keys from my pocket, as we approach the door. 'No, they're metal. What I loved about them is the differing sizes.'

Adam hurries over to turn on the lights and then fires up the coffee machine.

'Oh, before I forget...' Vyvyan reaches into her shoulder bag and pulls out a piece of paper. 'Here are those names and telephone numbers.'

'Perfect, thanks so much.'

Jess, Cappy and Keith have all wandered into the tasting room and Vyvyan joins them. Adam and I slip off our coats and get busy.

'Anyone prefer coffee to hot chocolate?' I call out.

'Coffee for me, please,' Cappy replies. 'A cappuccino would go down well, thanks, Ivy.'

Adam grins at me. 'Who would have thought we'd be here, doing this?'

A little buzz courses through me as I realise how different the bakery looks already, compared to the day when I took possession. When I opened The Cake and Coffee Emporium it was the result of almost a year's hard work, pulling together my business plan to convince the bank to give me a loan, finding premises and getting everything set up. The irony is that if it weren't for that experience there is no way I could have taken on this challenge.

Adam disappears with the tray while I clear up. When I step through the opening to join them all, they're standing looking out over the courtyard.

'We're talking about where best to put the tree, Ivy.' Jess turns to look at me. 'So far, it's a tie, so yours is the deciding vote. I will admit that I had my heart set on having it in the centre of the courtyard.'

'What are the options?' I ask.

'In front of the return wall opposite Penti Growan Cottage. That means you'll get the best view of it from this room, which is a shame.'

'Play fair, Jess. Stop trying to sway Ivy's decision,' Cappy states quite firmly.

She's right in what she says. If it were in the middle of the courtyard, we'd be looking out onto it from the bakery side.

'Imagine when there's a storm at sea and the winds come rolling in,' Riley points out. 'It'll be safer protected by the stone wall around Renweneth Manor's garden. Once it's in situ, we don't want it toppling over every time it blows a gale.'

Now I feel awkward.

'Come on,' Cappy says, genially. 'You and Adam grab your coats and we'll wander back outside.'

'I do love the idea of it being a centrepiece,' I remark. I gingerly turn in a circle, careful not to spill the cup of hot chocolate clasped in my hands.

'If it helps,' Riley interrupts, 'the stone wall I'm building this week to make a garden for Smithy's Cottage will end about...' he strides over to the narrow end wall of what is now The Courtyard Hub '...about here.'

I glance at Adam, excitedly. 'I was expecting a small walled garden, not a mini courtyard all of its own,' I exclaim.

'The idea is to keep it the same height as the other walls. I was going to make the entrance an archway, to mirror the one into Renweneth Manor. You can have either a fancy metal gate, or a wooden one. The choice is yours, guys.' He turns to look at me, then Adam.

'Well, I'm about to arrange for a removal van to collect the tables and chairs I have in storage. It won't be long before the tasting room is turned into a café and I'm not sure I like the idea of my customers getting a peek inside the garden. What do you think, Adam?'

'I'm easy, but metal would be more in keeping.'

'Then I'll have a scout around. I'll find something that will give you privacy, but has a bit of character, which I can refurbish. So, back to the tree. What are we doing with it?'

'I agree with Jess, but I also think Riley has a point. In a storm the wind sweeps across the courtyard. That makes it four-three...' I pause. 'But doesn't Lola get a vote?'

Cappy gives a belly laugh. 'Of course she does! We'll see what she has to say tomorrow morning. Right, that hit the spot, thanks Ivy, but I'm ready for a small nip of something a bit stronger before I turn in for the night.'

I collect the disposable cups and Jess walks over to saunter back to the bakery with me. 'You're definitely going for the café, then?'

'It's the best use for the size of the space, Jess. I only have indoor furniture though and I know you were hoping for some outside seating.'

She looks around to check no one is within earshot. 'I'm sure Lola will vote for putting the tree by the wall, so I have something else in mind that might do the trick.'

I give a little chuckle. 'Does it involve more work for Riley?'

She raises her eyebrows. 'It does, I'm afraid, but I think you'll love it.'

'Even more than the garden?'

'I told you, Ivy. I want this to be your home for as long as you're happy here. Now let's get shot of these cups and turn in for the night. Tomorrow is going to be another busy day!'

19

Surprise!

I knew it was going to be all hands on deck, as Cappy referred to it, but it seems that he's pulled people in from all over. The courtyard is buzzing and there are even more willing helpers beavering away over at the hay barn.

Lola and Jess have two volunteers to decorate the tree, which sits neatly tucked back against the beautiful stone wall surrounding Renweneth Manor. Jess has sent Riley and Adam in search of some old benches she thinks were stored up in the attic of the old house. I'm not quite sure what she's planning, but she seems pleased with herself.

I'm helping Keith and Vyvyan assemble some rather unusual metal snowballs. They're three foot in diameter and sit on resin plinths. The metalwork consists of fretwork panels as intricate as lace and, sprayed white, they look stunning. They come in sections, with fiddly little nuts and washers and there are six of them in total. The first one took the three of us about forty-five minutes to work out but we're getting a bit quicker with each one.

'Ivy!'

When I hear my voice being called and I look up, my jaw drops. 'Mum, Dad!'

'Surprise!'

'Sorry, guys – I wasn't expecting this,' I apologise.

Vyvyan shoos me away with her hand. 'Go. We can manage. Look at your mum's face – she's so happy to see you!'

I hurry over for a group hug. 'It's good to see our girl smiling,' Dad says. Mum's speechless.

When I step back, she looks teary-eyed. She holds up a finger to her lips while she takes a couple of deep breaths. My lower lip begins to wobble.

'Now before you take us to task for just turning up out of the blue,' she blurts out, 'I needed to see how you were doing. Your dad said I should have warned you but... well, I had to see for myself how you were settling in.'

'When you told us it was crazily busy, we weren't expecting this!' Dad scratches his head. 'Look at that tree, Sarah. It's a beauty.'

I wave out to Jess and both she and Lola come hurrying over. 'Oh, my goodness,' she declares. 'Paul and Sarah – how lovely to see you both!'

Dad looks at Lola and does a double take. 'My, you've grown. Jess, your little girl isn't so little anymore.'

I realise it's probably eighteen months at least since my parents last saw them.

'We're not here to stop you. We just wanted to say hello and see if there was anything we could do to help.' Mum looks a little embarrassed but Jess waves that off with her hand.

'Oh, visitors are always welcome, Sarah. Lola, why don't you show Ivy's mum and dad around while we go and make everyone a hot drink?'

Mum's eyes light up. 'Oh, that would be lovely. We've seen some photos, but they really don't do it justice, Jess. Where's Adam?'

'He's with Riley, fetching something,' I reply.

Mum turns on her heels, trying to take it all in. 'Oh, look at the bakery, Paul!'

In the last photo I sent them, the windows weren't decorated, and the lights weren't up.

Lola takes charge. 'We'll start with the most important thing on the farm. My treehouse.'

Jess and I start laughing as she leads them away.

'Come on, let's head to The Farmhouse and make a brew.' Jess says, as we watch the three of them walk away from us. 'It's obvious you weren't expecting this little visit but I'm glad they came. Your parents need to see that you're happy, Ivy. I'm just relieved that they're both still speaking to me.'

'As if they wouldn't. If you take the orders for hot drinks, I have a perfectly good machine doing nothing in the bakery and I'm sure I can find something suitable to slice up to go with it. I'll get things started.'

'From the way Riley rolled his eyes when he and Adam headed off to Renweneth Manor, he knew it wasn't going to be a simple case of carrying a few things across. Even so, they're taking their time.' Jess pulls a long face.

'They're two strapping guys and between them I'm sure they'll figure it out.'

To someone like Jess anything is possible if you just put your mind to it, but patience isn't her strong point. Sometimes in business it's a balancing act and it's possible to push forward too quickly. You have to fully evaluate the pros and the cons, or risk living to regret a decision.

From a practical point of view, I knew I was pushing my luck not shutting the bakery down until I had everything, including the staff, all set up and ready to go. Without Alice and Jory's cooperation, Wenna agreeing to stay, and Erica and Jess filling the breach, it wouldn't have been an option anyway. That first meeting with Alice was the deciding factor.

I wasn't simply trying to impress Jess, though; it was a business decision. Any break in continuity when the bakery had only been open a couple of months, and was already being taken over by new management, would have sent out the wrong signals. Not just for the shop, but for Renweneth Farm.

Vyvyan and Jess end up circulating with the trays of hot drinks and fingers of rich fruit cake. When, eventually, I manage to get back outside I'm surprised to see Riley, Adam, Mum, Dad, Lola and Cappy sitting on two benches in the middle of the courtyard.

'What's this? Sitting down on the job already?' I call out as I walk across to join them.

Adam grimaces. 'You obviously have no appreciation of how hard it is to manoeuvre these things around very tight turns in two narrow stairwells. And there are another five of them to dig out. Seriously, the attic rooms are stuffed full of old furniture. I mean, it's a bonus, but it took some doing getting these out.'

Riley looks directly at me. 'What do you think, Ivy?'

Jess appears at my side, offering the tray of cake around to some appreciative 'oohs' and 'ahs'.

'I think my customers will be delighted to be able to sit and enjoy a coffee out here when the weather's fine. What's the plan, Riley?'

He turns to face Jess. 'Care to enlighten us?'

The intimate look they exchange makes my heart squish up.

'I'm imagining all seven in a circle with enough of a gap between each one for people to walk through, rather than climb over them. In the middle…' She pauses, and Riley sits upright. 'In the middle, I think the boys would look perfect.'

Now we're all puzzled. 'The boys?' Cappy asks.

'My two metal stags. I mean… what's more Christmassy than that? Oh, and they'll need something behind them but I'm sure Riley will find the right thing. Not the giant snowballs; that would be too fussy. Something simple and white to make a nice contrast.'

We all start chuckling as Riley raises his eyebrows to the heavens. 'Do you see what I have to put up with? Can you be just a tiny bit more specific, Jess?'

Mum and Dad seem amused but then it's the first time they've met Riley and I'm not even sure they know he's the main man in Jess's life now.

'Tall, white, chunky,' she replies, before picking up a piece of fruit cake and popping it into her mouth. 'Mmm… Ivy, this cake is gorgeous.'

Once our break is over, Mum and Dad offer to join in rather than heading into the cottage for a look around.

'We can do that in a bit, Ivy,' Dad states, emphatically. 'I'm going to give Cappy a hand over at the hay barn.'

'And I'm going to help Lola put up some bunting in *the hub*, wherever that is,' Mum retorts with a laugh.

It's so good to have them here and seeing them having fun joining in. Maybe one day soon Mum will talk Ursula and Tillie into coming down with them for the day for a visit. Well, that's the dream and if it means apologising to my sister for speaking my mind, I'll do anything to make it happen.

'I could have made lunch for us all, Mum,' I point out.

We're sitting in the conservatory at The Lark and Lantern, waiting for our food to arrive.

'Nonsense! The pair of you have had a hard week and you've been on the go all weekend. The whole point of popping in to see you was to take you out for a leisurely, if rather late, lunch.'

It's half past two but Renweneth Farm is now a Christmas oasis, and we can all, finally, relax.

'Cheers, Adam and Ivy!' Dad raises his half-pint glass. 'If we hadn't seen it with our own eyes, we wouldn't have believed it. All credit to Jess, she knows what she's doing, and Cappy seemed very content. It's just a shame that Maggie isn't here to see it.'

I let out a gentle sigh. 'I know. She left a big hole in his life but I'm glad Jess has managed to lure him back.'

'Is it for good?' Dad asks.

I shake my head. 'No. Six months. After that, who knows what will happen.'

'I can't see him walking away, Ivy,' Mum replies. 'Renweneth Farm isn't exactly a little set-up, is it? What I hadn't appreciated was how important the bakery was. It's the heart of the courtyard, isn't it? No wonder you've been working flat out, but you must be happy with what you've achieved, Ivy.'

'I am, Mum. I couldn't have done it without Adam's help though.' I turn to gaze at him adoringly. 'What he needed this weekend was a rest; what he got was two days of non-stop work.'

Adam laughs it off. 'Handing out cake samples isn't exactly work and, let's be honest, I usually spend a couple of very intense hours at the gym. I don't need to do that here. There's always something to give me a workout.'

'Those benches are solid, aren't they?' Dad comments.

'They sure are and beautifully weathered. A bit of a sanding and a coat of varnish, they'll go on for years to come. Knowing Ivy, she'll want to expand it a little in the summer but Jess was right, it's a real focal point for the courtyard now, as is the tree.'

I'm already ahead of him. We'll need some trash cans and a couple of those tall bar tables with umbrellas, where people can stand around chatting while they enjoy their cake and coffee.

'Smithy's Cottage looks beautiful from here, Ivy,' Mum adds.

'I know. It's my dream, isn't it? I just imagined it being in the Cotswolds.'

Mum looks directly at me, narrowing her eyes. 'I think you're better off here, Ivy. With Adam away, I'm sure it's a comfort that you have a group of people on your doorstep if something goes wrong. Riley is a very personable man; a great builder, too, from what Cappy was telling us, isn't that right, Dad?'

My father nods in agreement. 'I might be wrong, I have been before, but I'd say Jess and Riley are pretty close.'

Adam gives me a nervous glance.

'You could say that.' I turn to grin at Adam. 'I'm sorry it's been a rather chaotic few hours but thank you for rolling up your sleeves and joining in. That's what it's all about here and it means a lot. Your next visit will be more relaxed. It's a shame to visit Renweneth Farm and not make time to wander over the moor or take the cliff path down to Penvennan Cove.'

Dad's expression is very matter-of-fact. 'You two are living the dream. We miss you both, but you'll make a good life for yourselves here. It isn't right to work as hard as the pair of you do, not to get your just rewards. It's a weird world we live in, that's for sure. We're proud of you both and now, having seen the farm for ourselves, our minds are at rest.'

I realise that we need to get Adam's parents here as soon as possible, because no matter what he tells them, our life here is a big unknown to them too.

Waving goodbye to my parents was a tad emotional, but by the time Adam's bag was packed it was a real struggle to keep my voice steady and a smile on my face. The weekend has been a whirlwind of activity, but it was also full of laughter, camaraderie, a sense of achievement and, most of all, it reminded me of why I love Adam. He was as torn up about leaving me as I was to let him go, but he stayed strong and all I remember, as I wearily climb the stairs to bed, is his beaming smile. 'I'm counting down to Friday night, honey. The clock is already ticking.'

'Not fast enough for me, Adam,' I half-whispered in the gloom. 'Not fast enough for me. Travel safely, my love.'

Even though I'm tired, I know I won't fall asleep until he texts to say he's back in Stroud. Will it get easier? I wonder. Or will our partings always feel like my heart is being torn apart? But he's right, the clock is ticking and if I achieve my goal, it won't be long before things are running smoothly at the bakery and our weekends will be all about enjoying our new lifestyle by the sea.

After such a frenetic Saturday, Monday at the bakery seems almost sedate by comparison, even though there's a steady stream of customers. It's nice not having the pressure of a queue and after the early rush, Wenna simply calls me down from the kitchen if she needs my help.

Kate was going to think about whether she could fit in doing a few hours each week at the bakery and let me know first thing, but by lunchtime she still hasn't been in touch. I give her a ring as I really do need to get something sorted quickly.

'Hi, Kate, it's Ivy.'

'Oh, Ivy. I said I'd phone you.'

Hmm, I might have caught her at a bad time, as she doesn't sound very happy. 'Sorry, I don't mean to bother you but uh… well, tomorrow is market day again and—'

'Look, I'm not sure whether I want to take on anything else right now.'

Goodness, this isn't quite the way I was expecting the conversation to go as she seemed pretty keen when I first mentioned it. 'Oh, I see. The thing is, Kate, I need to employ a part-time server quickly and if you're not able to commit long-term I understand. Either way, I'm very grateful for what you did last week.'

'I can't do anything this week anyway, Ivy. Maybe this isn't going to work out.' And with that she cuts me off.

I wander down to see Wenna, making myself a coffee while she's serving a customer and then offering to make her one.

'I just talked to Kate; she seems to have gone cold on the idea of working here. She was rather short with me and I wondered if I've done anything to upset her?'

Wenna goes very quiet. I can tell by her expression that something is up.

'What did I do?' I ask, feeling mortified.

'Nothing, Ivy. You didn't do anything wrong; it's just that I saw Kate yesterday and she was saying how she wished she hadn't given up on her business. I think you just inspired her to have another go but she's rather missed the boat here.'

'Oh, right. I see. Well, she should have just said that; there's no need to feel awkward about it. I just wanted to know if she was interested, as Vyvyan gave me the numbers of two people. One of them makes novelty birthday cakes, so it sounds promising.'

I pass Wenna her coffee, and she looks disappointed. 'Sorry, I didn't mean to get your hopes up. I thought Kate was over it and was enjoying having a regular income. Maybe she's decided to go full-time, who knows? Oh well, I'm glad you've got a couple of options.'

And just as we're about to sip our drinks, three people come in at once. When the last woman steps forward Wenna turns to me.

'Ivy, have you met Rose Tregory?'

I offer my hand and we shake but I can't say I recognise the face.

'I'm Len's wife,' the woman informs me. 'He covers for Keith and does a few extra hours here and there. I've heard a lot about you, Ivy. How're you settling in?'

'Oh, of course – Len! It's nice to meet you, Rose. It's still early days and there's a lot to do but it's coming together nicely.'

'Your window displays are gorgeous, and doesn't the farm look amazing? I will admit that I haven't bought a single thing for Christmas yet but seeing all this is putting me in a very festive mood. I only popped in for some bread and a couple of cakes, but I might as well order a Christmas cake while I'm here.'

'We love taking orders, don't we Ivy?' Wenna laughs, reaching for the new laptop and whisking Rose over to select the one she wants as I head back upstairs.

I'm three steps up when the bell on the door tinkles and I turn to go back down. It's Jess and she hurries over to me looking a tad flustered.

'Are you okay?'

She does that thing with her eyes that indicates something has gone wrong. 'Go on up to the office. I'll make you a quick coffee and I'll be straight up.'

It takes me a couple of minutes as Rose and Wenna pull me into their conversation, but when I walk through the door Jess is slumped in the chair.

'Oh dear. What's up?'

She shakes her head, wearily. 'I told Vyvyan to let the mezzanine studio in the hub to a lovely lady named Flo. She knocked on my door one day and over a cup of tea poured her heart out. Flo is very passionate about what she does. She'll be running yoga and well-being classes, as well as individual sessions, both during the day and a few evenings. I've given her free rein, so she'll have her own key to the gates. From my point of view, it was the perfect solution.'

'And great for the other retailers in the hub I should imagine, as attendees will be walking past the bays to get to the mezzanine. Let me know when I can sign up for a class, as that's exactly what I need to relax me.' I laugh, but Jess doesn't join in. 'Oh… she hasn't pulled out, has she?'

'Vyvyan already had someone who was interested in renting the space but the woman never responded when she emailed her to say the space was available. So, in good faith, I told Flo she could have it. But Flo was never on the list of interested parties. As far as I'm concerned, it's a done deal and I gave her my word.'

'It's your property, Jess; you can choose whoever you want.'

She sips her coffee, looking downcast. 'The thing is, the other person is an old friend of Cappy's and my grandma's. Flo hasn't signed the lease yet and he knows it; she's meeting with Vyvyan tomorrow to get the paperwork tied up. Since the day I took over Cappy has never interfered with any of my decisions. However, he approached me the other day and asked if I could do him a favour and *sort something out* to accommodate Prudie Carne. What, exactly, he didn't say and now I'm facing a real dilemma.'

I give her a sympathetic look. 'Awkward.'

She gives a little groan. 'That's putting it mildly. It's an impossible situation to find myself in. What would you do?'

Jess has always been there to offer me advice when I've had problems, so I can't leave her hanging. 'Why don't you give Flo a ring and explain what's happened. Perhaps she'd appreciate sharing the space and reducing her own overheads. It's quite a big studio, after all.'

Jess frowns, her mind ticking over. 'Prudie is a painter and well known around here. She wanted to turn the space into an art gallery and also hold weekly art classes there. This Prudie has a cheek because she was the one who didn't get back to Vyvyan and yet she's been challenging her because she knows she was first on the list. Now she's escalated it by getting Cappy involved.'

'Visitors won't be able to wander around the gallery if there's a yoga class in full swing. Besides, it's a little late to kick up a fuss, isn't it?'

'She told Vyvyan she's been away and returned to a backlog of emails, apparently. That's hardly Vyvyan's fault and I don't know what Cappy is expecting. There just isn't anywhere to put her.'

An idea pops into my head. 'If Flo has a set weekly programme, presumably it wouldn't be the end of the world to accommodate a couple of slots for Prudie's classes?'

'Flo's a nice lady and if it were as simple as that, she'd probably be prepared to work something out. She's drawing up a new timetable of classes for the hub as we speak, so it might not be too late. But even so, there isn't a blank wall large enough on the ground floor to house an exhibition and that's the problem.'

My brain is chuntering away. 'But there are two good-size walls in what will soon become the bakery's café.'

Jess does a double take. 'Are you serious, Ivy?'

'Why not? Extra traffic through the door would be good for business. Why don't you float the idea and see how it's received?'

Jess is beginning to perk up. 'Oh, Ivy, you're a lifesaver. Seriously, Cappy has been a bit moody for a while, and I think it's because he felt embarrassed to go back to Prudie empty-handed. They go way back, but she moved away to work at a prestigious art centre in Clifton, Bristol. She wasn't here when he lost Grandma, but he bumped into her when she had an on-site meeting with Vyvyan.'

'I noticed her stall at the market on Saturday. I'm fine with it, Jess. To be honest, as long as she's willing to leave cards we can hand out to anyone who expresses an interest, I wouldn't be looking to levy a charge. After all, it's local artists and that's good for the community.'

Jess gives me a beaming smile before draining her coffee and jumping to her feet. I walk around the desk, and we hug each other. 'Going back with anything at all takes the pressure off and I'll have a word with Flo next. I'm fine if she wants to come to a private arrangement with Prudie. Some of the artists might even be interested in signing up for Flo's classes. You never know.'

'Before you rush off... although the office is great, I don't really use it. My laptop is always alongside me in the kitchen when I'm working. If my memory serves me right, you did sort of mention the possibility of me using this as a guest bedroom.'

Jess chuckles. 'I told you, Ivy, use the space however it works best for you. And talk to Riley about installing a shower in the biggest of the two cloakrooms.'

'I did wonder why one was double the size of the other. With the disabled toilet downstairs, it didn't really make any sense.'

'Ah, that was Riley's idea,' she remarks, as I follow her out onto the landing. 'He's all about flexibility. If the shop idea hadn't worked, this could easily have been turned into a three-bedroom cottage with a full bathroom.'

Thank goodness, for me, that wasn't the first option Jess went with. Having a guest bedroom in Smithy's Cottage, and with a relatively simple fix here to gain another generously sized spare room, Adam is going to be over the moon.

'I hate adding to Riley's workload, Jess.'

'It's not a problem, in fact...' She lowers her voice, as the sound of laughter filters up the stairs. 'I'm looking for smaller jobs to keep Riley busy through until Christmas. We need him to help on market days and I don't want to make a start on Renweneth Manor just yet. Come the New Year, I'll know exactly what funds I have to kick-start the final project.'

I draw in a breath, feeling excited for her. 'I bet you can't wait.'

She nods her head, enthusiastically. 'When he first looked at the plans, Riley told me whatever ultimate budget I have in mind, to double it.'

'Oh, Jess... I know you're sinking every penny you have into it, but the farm is thriving, and you'll get there. Now go and sort out your little problem with Flo, then give Prudie my number. We don't want a grumpy Cappy walking around with a long face, do we?'

Jess lets out a sigh. 'The thing is, Cappy never asks for anything, Ivy, and I felt really bad about it. But I put Vyvyan on the spot, too, and I have apologised to her. It was an impulsive decision on my part when she's the marketing manager and I should have told Flo to talk to her directly. Right, let's go mend fences... not literally, I hasten to add. That would be all I needed.'

ADAM

Stroud, Gloucestershire

20

Blowing the Monday Night Blues Away

When Mum texted at lunchtime to say Dad was home this evening, I didn't like to refuse the offer of joining them for dinner. Mondays are hard for me. I usually keep myself busy in the evenings listing items of furniture to sell online. Bit by bit, the old life Ivy and I had for the best part of two years is being dismantled. But Mum wanted to hear all about the farm and how Ivy's doing. I knew she had a whole string of questions to ask me and I don't want my parents to feel left out.

Two hours later, I'm back at the house and eager to call Ivy.

'Hi, honey, how was your day?'

What comes back at me is one word. 'Amazing!' I can tell by how bubbly she sounds that it's been a good one.

'Tell me all about it.'

'Hmm… tell me about your day first,' she replies, playfully. Is she hesitant in case I don't feel quite so jolly tonight?

'I had dinner with my parents and, to be honest, I'm feeling like a bad son. So much is happening and I realise that I'm not keeping them in the loop. They were bowled over with the photos I showed them and I could see them visibly relax. I've literally just arrived back.' It's funny but I never refer to this house as *home* now because it isn't. 'Anyway, the boss called me into the office as I was just about to leave work. The Wiltshire project is being delayed but the one based in Devon is ready to break ground next week and it's mine!'

She gasps. 'Oh, babe… does that mean—'

'It means I'll be home every single night. It's just over thirty miles away from Renweneth Farm. A place called Parklands and it's no more than an hour's drive.' I can't stop grinning to myself, imagining the look on her face.

There's a loud 'Whoop, whoop!' and I yank the phone away from my ear until she's finished.

'I thought that might go down well.' I chuckle.

'Oh, Adam… you have no idea how hard it was to let you go yesterday. But I too, have some good news.'

'I thought you might. You sound upbeat.'

'If I wasn't before, I am now.' She giggles. 'No more waving you off late Sunday afternoon and lying in bed waiting for you to text that you've arrived back safely. Anyway, you'll love this. Jess is happy for us to convert the office in the back room above the bakery into a bedroom. And… wait for it… you know that second cloakroom on the landing is like walking into a large closet? Well, that's because Riley made it big enough to turn it into a shower room. There's plumbing in the walls ready and waiting.'

'So, both sets of parents could visit us at the same time and stay over? That's a bit of a relief, to be honest. I've been stressing over how we're going to make it work but this makes it a lot easier.'

'I knew you'd be delighted. And… drumroll…'Ivy keeps me in suspense for a couple more seconds. 'I have a baker and a server to help Wenna.'

'Erica and Kate came up trumps?'

'Sadly, that's not how it worked out. Erica's hopeful that doing two market days through until Christmas will give her business the boost it needs. As for Kate… she was supposed to give me a call and when she didn't, I chased her. She was a bit *off* with me and made it clear that she's not available. Fortunately, Len's wife – Rose – is thrilled to be joining the team. I'm going to give one of Vyvyan's contacts, a lady named Chelle, a trial as my baking assistant. She makes novelty birthday cakes in her spare time and sent me some photos of her work. I think she's exactly the sort of person I'm looking for.'

'Great. How did Len's wife get into the picture?'

'She popped into the shop this morning and I met her for the first time. Later in the day, when I told Wenna the good news about Chelle, she was thrilled but disappointed to hear about Kate. Then she suggested I give Rose a call. I did wonder whether it was a bit of a cheek, but Rose was over the moon about it. Both her and Len are retired and he's usually here a couple of days a week anyway, either covering for Keith, or helping whenever there's a two-man job at the campsite. I think Rose is going to love working here, if for no other reason than she'll enjoy the company. I'll work Monday to Friday and we'll sort out a rota with a rolling day off for Wenna, Rose and Chelle.'

I've never seen Ivy looking as tired as she did when I arrived last Friday, so this is brilliant news. The dark smudges under her eyes told me that she'd been overdoing it. Jess has always been an inspiration to Ivy, but in some ways they're two very different people. It reminds me a little of the story about the hare and the tortoise. Except that there's no real sense of competition or mockery between them; their temperaments are just different.

Jess is like a whirlwind to be around, and she has a dogged determination. Ivy puts her heart and soul into everything she does, but usually she prefers to go at a more measured pace. I didn't say anything as I know Ivy just wanted to prove herself, but she's been pushing herself too hard for my liking.

'Ivy... don't take this the wrong way, but I don't want you turning into Jess mark two; and I mean that in the most caring way possible. Jess is amazing, and I'm one of her biggest fans but you're different.'

'I just didn't want to let her down, Adam. There's too much at stake for us all.' Ivy's voice dips.

'You won't, Ivy. I seriously doubt anyone else could have hit the ground running like you have. And we'll repay Jess for the wonderful opportunity she's given us. For now we're just renting the bakery and the cottage but being appointed to a project means I'm off probation ahead of time. HR are drawing up my permanent contract this week.'

'Oh.' Clearly, Ivy wasn't expecting that.

'My accountant says we might pay a bit above the going rate, but he thinks he can sort out a mortgage based on my income alone.'

'Adam! I can't believe it... and Jess so badly needs an injection of cash. Please don't repeat this, but she's scratching around to find jobs to keep Riley occupied while she considers how to finance the first phase.'

That gives me cause to pause for thought. 'Are you saying Jess is strapped for money? I mean... her overheads are increasing, but I thought with all the new income streams—'

'No, that's not what I'm saying, Adam. But Renweneth Manor is huge and Riley has warned her it's going to be a money pit. She's putting everything on the line to kick it off in the New Year.'

Even I swallow hard at that one. 'Including the lump sum she got when she and Ben sold their house?'

'I hope not. She's been watching every penny and setting as much aside as she can to boost the fund. But if we were able to buy the cottage... oh, Adam, this could change everything for all of us.'

'Don't say anything just yet. No doubt it'll take a few months to get a mortgage offer tied up, but it's certainly looking good, Ivy.'

'It really is within reaching distance, isn't it?'

'It is, Ivy. But I don't want you working so hard you get sick, do you understand? As long as you're making a profit, that's all we need. I'd rather have some time with you, than more money in the bank.' There, I've said it.

She clears her throat, nervously. 'Understood. And I want our weekends to be relaxing, Adam. Fingers crossed, I might have found the perfect team. The courtyard doesn't just need a bakery, it deserves a fully-fledged café and now I can make that happen.'

'But it doesn't have to happen overnight, Ivy. Why not delay it until after Christmas when things will be a little quieter.'

'And lose the impetus generated by the additional market days between now and December?' she replies. 'What's good for the farm is good for us, babe. It'll keep the visitors coming back at a time when the campsite is quieter. Together with the hub, the farm is now a little community of its own and I need to capitalise on that.'

'Okay, point taken and I'm sorry, Ivy.'

'For what?'

'I thought coming here was a no-brainer option and I was surprised by your initial reaction. Seeing the work you've had to put in, I can now understand your reservations.'

'It wasn't a working bakery, Adam. It was a sales outlet for Alice and Jory's shop. Thankfully it still is in a way and that custom will continue, but that alone wouldn't have made it a viable business for anyone else to take on. It's the profit from the patisserie and the café that will turn it into a little goldmine.'

Ivy is the sort of person who just gets on with it and sometimes I think she doesn't fill me in with the detail because she knows it'll go over my head. 'Just don't go exhausting yourself, honey. I thought coming here it would be less pressure for you but that was me being clueless and naïve. I'm proud of what you've achieved and whatever you need from me when I'm here, you got it.'

On our wedding day we vowed to support each other's dreams as we build a life together and that's exactly what we're doing.

'Adam, I'm in a real quandary and I don't know where to turn. I instantly thought of you, mate.' Riley does sound troubled.

'What is it?'

He lets out a deep sigh. 'I'm having Ollie this weekend. As you know, it's the first time and I told Jess I won't be around, so she's on board with it.'

'So… what's the problem?'

'Fiona rang just now to firm up the details. She's insisting on driving Ollie down after school on Friday. I didn't really have a choice in the matter…' He tails off for a moment. 'Fiona sort of invited herself to stay overnight. I jumped straight in and said I'll drive him back on Sunday afternoon but how will that look to Jess?'

'Mate, just tell Jess the truth, that you didn't offer to put Fiona up. She'll understand. Hopefully, next time you have Ollie to stay for the weekend it will just be the two of you.'

He gives a disparaging laugh and I can tell he's not convinced it's going to be as easy at that.

'Fiona is a bit unpredictable and she calls the shots when it comes to Ollie. What makes it even worse is that Lola keeps asking me when I'm going to bring him to visit and I keep saying soon.'

From the little I know about his situation I understand that Fiona has sole custody of their son, but I remember Jess mentioning that it was Ollie who asked to reconnect with his dad. Surely his ex won't stand in their way?

'Anyway,' he continues, 'I won't be broaching the subject with Jess this evening, that's for sure. Cappy's a bit upset about something and Jess is trying to sort it out. Rumours are flying apparently about some sort of misunderstanding over rental space at the hub. It's unusual for Cappy to get involved, but I've been trying to keep out of it. I figured if they need my help, they'll ask for it. How are things with you?'

'I've not long got off the phone with Ivy. It sounds like she's staffing up and the other good news is that I'll be working at a place called Parklands, near Plymouth, from next week.'

'Thank goodness for that. Does it mess things up as you're in the process of emptying out the house in Stroud, aren't you?'

'Yes, it does rather, but my parents have offered to step in and take over. I'll have a car full of personal stuff when I arrive on Friday night, but the rest has to be sold off, or taken to the local charity shop.'

'It's the end of an era but I know you'll both be relieved.'

'Too right. Thankfully, it's a good-size project, so I'll be there for at least nine months by the sound of it.'

'I bet Ivy's face was a picture when you told her. So much has happened in such a short space of time and it will be nice to establish a routine.'

'You can say that again, mate!'

What I didn't have the heart to mention to Ivy is that my mum and her next-door neighbour visited the garden centre to buy some plants and stopped for a coffee. She said it was almost lunchtime and there was only one other person in there, and it looked like he was one of the gardeners.

When I think about all the hard work Ivy has had to put into taking over an existing business, albeit it a young one, I realise how astute she is. She warned Rach that, in her opinion, a café in the garden centre wasn't a viable option as it was too far from the main road. Sadly, hard work alone doesn't always guarantee success; it's about spotting the right opportunity. I guess that comes with experience.

IVY
Renweneth Farm, Cornwall

21

The Past, the Present and the Future

Tuesday is crazily busy; even with Wenna and Rose behind the counter I'm constantly up and down the stairs to lend a hand. With Renweneth Farm all decked out there's a real festive buzz to market day and it feels more like a Saturday.

Just as I'm locking up, Jess appears at the door looking decidedly jaded.

'You look like you're in need of a coffee!' I exclaim.

'Oh, am I… What a day it's been and not in a good way. I didn't mean to stop you, though, as I know you've been on your feet all day.'

I roll my eyes. 'I'm used to it.' I laugh. 'The good news is that Rose joined us today and, thanks to Vyvyan, I think I might have found my assistant baker.'

'Oh, thank goodness!'

'Her name is Chelle. She's a bit nervous as she's never worked in a commercial bakery before, so I suggested a trial run. I really didn't want anything to put her off as she's a really chirpy person and will fit in well. We're going to have three intense baking days together.'

Jess follows me over to the coffee machine and then we make our way into the tasting room. 'Sorry about the stools. The table and chairs are arriving on Friday.'

Jess's face brightens. 'Oh, you do move fast.'

'It won't be a full waitress service. People will be able to queue up to buy a cake and a coffee, and then come in here to sit and enjoy it. I want to have the team working together smoothly before I'm pulled away to set up the café properly. I've pencilled in Tuesday, the sixth of December as the official launch date. What do you think?'

'That sounds good to me! I was surprised how many people took advantage of the benches in the courtyard, today. Even though it's chilly, it was good to see them chatting while enjoying their hot drinks and pastries. The café is going to be a great addition, Ivy.'

'I think so, too, Jess.'

'That's partly why I popped across to see you. I've spoken to Flo and Prudie but have decided that Vyvyan should take over the negotiations from here.'

'Is Cappy giving you a tough time?'

Jess nods her head, miserably. 'Flo is prepared to be amenable, but Prudie isn't easy to deal with and I'm fed up going back and forth between the two of them. I just wanted to check you haven't had a rethink about renting wall space for the artwork if Vyvyan can tie something up for the workshops in the studio.'

'It's not a problem at all, Jess. And, honestly, as long as we don't have to get involved, I'm happy to let Prudie display the paintings for free. Do ask her to call in so we can have a chat.'

'Thanks. There's um... been a bit of backlash and it would really help to get Prudie sorted out sooner, rather than later.'

'There has? About what, exactly?'

'Out of the blue, Kate approached Vyvyan for a stall. We didn't have a space so she put her on a waiting list. However, the very same day rumours started getting back to Vyvyan that we're being selective about who we offer space to. She's calling it discrimination.'

'In what way?'

'It's true that we have a quota of food versus crafts and what we term general items as we want customers to see a wide range of products. Even so, Vyvyan simply told her the truth: that we didn't have an available space.'

'That's ridiculous, Jess.' I laugh dismissively, but she's deadly serious.

'I know, it's ludicrous but she began mumbling about it to anyone prepared to listen, saying we wouldn't allow her a pitch because we don't want competition for the bakery.'

'Wenna mentioned something about Kate wanting to restart her business. I wonder if that's why she was off with me when I rang her? It's weird, as she'd given me the impression that she was seriously considering joining us at the bakery permanently.'

Jess frowns. 'I don't really know Kate but I've heard a few rumblings about her, which is unusual. I don't pay any attention to gossip, but the gist of it was that she has a bit of a chip on her shoulder. It seems that might have had some truth to it.'

'Even though we already have one handmade biscuit stall and two other takeaway food stalls, unfortunately, Kate's grumbles reached Prudie's ears and she mentioned it to Cappy. Now he's wondering what's going on.'

'Surely he can see how silly this is? Prudie had no claim over the studio; she didn't respond to Vyvyan and missed the boat. As for Kate, why should she jump the queue?'

'To my surprise, he's expressed his concern about it. When I took over, I promised him that I'd make this a community that helped to promote local businesses.'

'And you are! Oh… is this about me taking over the bakery because I'm not from here?'

'That seems to be the way she's spinning it.' Jess sighs.

'Honestly, if some people don't get everything handed to them on a plate, they play the victim card. I just didn't think Kate was like that.'

'When Cappy was telling me what he'd heard – via Prudie – I laughed. But he was serious and said that if we want the community to support us, we must support the community. I thought that was precisely what we were doing here and, I'll be honest, I was a little offended. I pointed out to Cappy that I'm an outsider too and so is he! Flo isn't Cornish, but she's lived here most of her life. Kate's husband was born here, but obviously she wasn't. At that point he sauntered off, looking a tad sorry he'd raised the subject in the first place. He just hadn't thought it through but I can see why he tackled me.'

This is unsettling for us all.

'Tell Prudie that she can call in any time at all to check out the space and I'll make her so welcome she won't be able to refuse the offer. I think it'll be wonderful for the customers too. And Prudie would be an unreasonable woman indeed, if she isn't prepared to compromise on the timing and days of her classes with Flo.'

'I agree and thanks, Ivy. It means a lot as I hate being out of kilter with Cappy. I know Prudie is disappointed, but it was down to her. Cappy got involved as a kindness, in case there was anything we could do but now it's all become very messy indeed. Anyway, Vyvyan has squeezed Kate in and I hope that's the end of it.'

We lapse into silence as we sip our drinks. It's such a waste of time and energy sorting out little disputes like this and I know Jess has a lot more important things to worry about.

'Is everything else okay with you?' I check.

'Yes. Riley won't be around this weekend, so Len is going to work on Saturday. It's Ollie's first sleepover at the cottage. Riley is excited, but understandably nervous.'

'Oh, that's wonderful, Jess. Hopefully, it's the first of many more to come.'

'Ironically, Saturday evening I was going to stay at Riley's cottage again.' She looks wistful. 'However, Fiona rang him and brought the visit forward a week. I'm thrilled for him, though, as he's waited a long time for this.'

'Fingers crossed it goes well for him.'

'I'm sure it will be fine; he's wonderful with Lola. Anyway, I'd best get back as I'm going to put in a casserole. Do you want to eat with us this evening?'

'Thanks for the offer, but I've a mass of paperwork to get through and a stack of recipes to photocopy for Chelle, ready for tomorrow. I'm going to encapsulate them and pop them into a ring binder. I'll be marking it top secret, of course!' I laugh and Jess's face breaks out into a warm smile.

'And how's Adam doing this week?'

'Good. From next Monday he'll be working less than an hour's drive away so he'll be home every single night.'

Her smile grows exponentially. 'Oh, Ivy, that's the best news ever. Onwards and upwards, it's bound to get easier with every passing day, isn't it?'

As I lock the front door and turn to walk towards Smithy's Cottage, I stop in my tracks. I knew Riley was making a start on the walled garden in front of the cottage but didn't realise he'd been working on it today. There are three courses of freshly mortared stone butting up to the end wall of The Courtyard Hub. Several rows of cobbles have already been taken out. He's even pegged out where the gate will be and the return wall that will join onto the cottage itself.

I stop to gaze around, taking in the Christmas tree, the giant metal snowballs and the strings of lights around the courtyard. This does feel like home, and while I might be an outsider, in my heart I know this is where I'm supposed to be. I'm not going to let anyone make me feel guilty about it. I'm passionate about the cakes I make and proving that they don't have to be loaded with refined sugar to make them taste good. I'm a woman on a mission because you are what you eat. I've lost count of the number of conversations we have where customers are curious about the ingredients and the flavours; I see that as a positive thing that I'm bringing to Renweneth Farm.

As I let myself into the cottage, I make a mental note to ask Vyvyan when Flo's classes are due to commence. I fully intend to sign up for one of her evening candlelit yoga sessions. Maybe

I'll be able to talk Adam into joining me… With that I burst out laughing. He's always going to be more of a gym man, and I have no doubt he'll be looking into that next week.

By nine o'clock I'm in bed, albeit with piles of invoices and to-do lists spread out around me. When my phone kicks into life I think maybe Adam forgot to tell me something, but I'm surprised to see that it's Rach.

'Hi, lovely, how are you doing?' I ask.

'Bearing up. How's it going there?'

Oh dear, that's not what I was hoping to hear. 'Truthfully, it's been exhausting.'

'I know that feeling. I'm calling to pick your brains, Ivy. You were right about the café. Luckily the hampers are doing well but we've lost a few orders because people aren't prepared to pick them up. Dad has decided to take early retirement and he's going to spend some of the lump sum he'll get from his company pension on buying a delivery van.'

My heart almost stops for a moment. 'That's a big step to take, Rach.'

'I know, but you don't know until you try and my brother has overhauled the website to include a whole range of Christmas hampers which has seen a huge jump in orders.'

'Well, that's a good omen and I'll be keeping my fingers crossed for you.'

'I just wondered whether you had any other ideas to boost our income that would justify running a vehicle once the Christmas rush is over.'

'Ooh… let's brainstorm!' I reply, enthusiastically. It's just like the old days when Rach and I would regularly update our menus to keep our customers coming back time and time again. 'How about… hmm… catering for children's birthday parties? Maybe offering themed ones?'

'Now there's a thought. That could be a nice little earner and very doable once we have the van. Mum suggested a wedding breakfast but honestly, Ivy, I think that would be a stretch too far. Most will want both hot and cold, and while the kitchen here is big enough to cope with it, I'm not sure I am. Sandwiches, cakes and little savouries is where I draw the line.'

I continue to cast around for ideas. 'How about phoning around some of the conference centres, to offer executive buffets?'

'For workshops and corporate training events, you mean. Hmm, that might work. We could also do a leaflet drop to some of the larger offices and business premises within a reasonable radius.'

'You might get a better result from that rather than placing ads in the local papers and magazines. It's labour intensive but the personal touch may well be worth the effort.'

A positive-sounding 'Hmm...' echoes down the line. 'If I drew up a list, once Dad's on board he could probably fit that in around his deliveries.'

'I'm glad you're being realistic, Rach, about what you branch off into. Just from a manpower point of view, if it all ties in nicely, you can take on extra staff as you need them. If you provide a full-blown menu, it would be a steep learning curve. I'm not trying to put you off, but even I'd blanch at that.'

'Thanks, Ivy. Mum was getting excited about it and I felt awful rejecting her idea but you've given me some great options to think about. Sandwiches, gourmet savoury nibbles and cakes we can cope with but delivering hot food for a sit-down meal is another thing entirely.'

'Precisely. Have you been into Stroud recently?'

'Yes. The old shop has been gutted. The latest news on the street is that there are going to be two concessions in there. The guy who bought the building will be running his own shoe repairers and key-cutting section and he's subletting to a luggage and handbag outlet.'

'Clever idea. If you don't need the space, why not utilise it to the fullest? I've offered to let a local artist use some of the wall space in what will be the new café here. She also represents a whole group of avid painters so if she goes ahead, it'll hopefully add a bit of colour to the place.'

'Artwork?' Rach sounds surprised. 'It sounds like you're really settling in well, Ivy. How's Adam?'

We end up chatting for about half an hour, and she brings me up to date with both Grace and Lisa's news. It's strange knowing that nothing there will ever be the same again. For several years the four of us worked side by side most days, but life moves on.

'Thanks for calling, Rach. To tell you the truth, you have been on my mind. The early days are usually frustrating, with constant setbacks, but eventually the hard work will begin to pay off.'

'Hopefully, before we run out of money,' she jokes, but she doesn't sound too disheartened.

'And remember what I said, if you ever get a chance at the weekend to take a trip down to deepest Cornwall, you'd be very welcome to stay overnight.'

'Thanks, Ivy. I'll keep that in mind.'

There's a tinge of sadness as we disconnect. It's hard when someone who has been a big part of your life is no longer around. We had some good times, a lot of laughter and days when everything seemed to conspire against us. Burning cakes, the burglar alarm going off two, three, even four times a day and battling with a landlord who never returned calls. But I also remember our lovely regulars, people we'd often stop and chat with. I'm sure it won't be too long before it's like that here. I stifle a yawn. This little lot isn't going to get sorted out tonight and it's time to pack it all away. Tomorrow is another day.

22

Rumours and Speculation

On Friday morning I awaken to the sound of howling wind and when I open the curtains it's blowing a gale. I'm eager to get to work as it's a big day for me.

By ten o'clock, everything in the bakery is in full swing when I get a text to say the removal van will be here shortly. It's the first time since I took over that we've used the front door to the second half of the bakery and I insert the key in the lock, swinging it open. When I look out, Riley is inspecting his handiwork on the new wall.

'Morning!' I call out. 'I'm just checking the lock works. Will the removal men be in your way if they bring the furniture in through this door?'

He saunters over to talk to me as the wind seems to whip the words out of his mouth and disperse them on the air. 'No, it's fine. I'm not sure whether I should find something else to do this morning but as long as it doesn't rain, if I can get at least a couple of rows of stonework done I can always cover it up with polythene if it starts raining.'

'Exciting!'

'Thanks, it's a labour of love – stonework – but I want it to end up looking like it's been there forever.'

'Jess told me this side of the bakery was once a greengrocer's. I bet that was popular in the day.'

'Yes. From all accounts it was the definitive farm shop, selling what they produced here off the land. Originally, Renweneth Farm owned a lot of the fields on the other side of the road. Over time, much of the land was sold off to pay taxes and keep them afloat.'

In the midst of our discussion, Vyvyan arrives with a guest in tow. I recognise her from last Saturday, when I had a wander around the market stalls. Give Prudie her due, she's open to any opportunity that comes up and even a stall isn't beneath her. She was only selling prints and cards that day and had a helper, but she had several ring binders open on the table with photos of some really fine paintings.

'Ivy, this is Prudie Carne,' Vyvyan says, introducing her warmly.

'It's lovely to meet you, Prudie.' I give her a welcoming smile. At a guess I'd say that she's in her early seventies; even from the way she's dressed, you can tell she has an artistic flair. There's a wonderful touch of flamboyance to her outfit: wearing a silk scarf with ducks on it draped around the shoulders of her heavy, navy-blue woollen coat.

'Same 'ere, Ivy,' she replies, as her eyes dart around the room.

'It'll take a couple of weeks to get the café up and running, but I'm working towards a launch date of Tuesday the sixth of December.'

'We're all looking forward to seeing it open, Ivy,' Vyvyan enthuses. 'It's a great addition to the courtyard.'

'Thank you, Vyvyan. Please feel free to wander around, Prudie. I should imagine ambience is everything when it comes to displaying artwork.'

She gives me a pointed look. 'Most people don't appreciate that, Ivy. It's a lovely buildin' all right and the natural stone walls work well. It's also much bigger than I expected. Rentin' two walls could suit my purposes.'

'Oh, um... as long as you can leave a pile of cards for customers to pick up if they want more information, I'm more than happy to let you display here for free. I think my customers will be delighted to have something interesting to gaze at while they sit and enjoy their coffee and cake.'

'That's very generous of you,' she replies, peering at me.

'I know that Jess is keen to showcase as many local talents and artisan skills as possible. The next step up from a cottage industry isn't always easily affordable and we're all here to support each other. That's what attracted me to Renweneth Farm in the first place.'

Her eyes scan my face intently. 'I was told that you and Jess go back a long way.'

Vyvyan eyes me suspiciously; this is beginning to feel like an interview.

'Yes, Prudie, we're childhood friends and both passionate about making a difference in our own ways.'

Prudie walks over to the corner and turns to gaze back across at the opening through into the bakery. 'Your cakes are a little different I gather, but I see from the bread on display that you've managed to maintain a relationship with Alice and Jory Rowse, despite their quick exit.'

'Yes. Alice was extremely helpful in making the handover a seamless transition.'

'That was good of her, under the circumstances.' Prudie raises an eyebrow, as if she's doubting me.

I glance at Vyvyan, not wishing to say anything out of order, and she immediately comes to my rescue. 'The timing wasn't quite right for the Rowses, Prudie.'

Prudie turns around, suddenly taking a much more detailed interest in the room.

As I trail around behind her, I can't help wondering what exactly Kate has been saying. Prudie isn't the sort of woman to spread gossip, so clearly when – as Jess said – she pulled Cappy into it, no doubt Prudie did it in good faith. However, I can understand why Jess is upset because what business is it of anyone's why the Rowses left?

'I think I can make this work, Ivy. Probably better than the studio which, on reflection, is a little out of the way, being two flights up.'

Am I supposed to be grateful? It feels like Prudie is doing me a favour, not the other way around. A quick glance at Vyvyan's face and I notice that her lips are pressed tightly together; I'm not the only one feeling Prudie has a bit of a cheek.

'Most artists struggle throughout their entire careers,' she continues. 'Few have the luxury of makin' it their day job. I think this will do us nicely.'

That's a relief; I don't know what Jess would do if Prudie had rejected it out of hand.

A man walks through the door. 'All right, missus? Is it okay to unload the furniture?'

'Yes. Please do. Just stack it all on that side of the room for now, thank you.' I turn back to Prudie and Vyvyan. 'Come and let me show you around the bakery and then we can have cake and coffee in my office upstairs. The ingredients are all organic and I only use natural sweeteners. There are no chemicals, additives, or manufactured flavourings.'

Vyvyan gives me a look of sheer relief as we head off. If Kate thinks Jess ousted the Rowses to hand the bakery over to her best friend, I can sort of understand why she was paranoid when Vyvyan turned her down for a stall.

When someone jumps to a conclusion without knowing the facts, not only do they make themselves look silly, but careless words can cause damage. Kate obviously doesn't know Jess at all, as that's not the way she operates, and neither does Prudie. If it concerns her, I'm sure she'll ask her own questions as, clearly, Prudie's not the sort of woman to hold back.

When I wave off the removal guys, it takes just over an hour to get the remainder of the tables and chairs into some semblance of order, but instead of a hollow-sounding room, it already looks the business. It's actually going to cost me very little to get it all set up properly but I have more pressing priorities right now.

Eventually, I make my way upstairs to see how Chelle is doing. 'Sorry about that. It took a bit longer than I'd anticipated. Any problems?'

I glance around at the cooling racks, and it all seems fine to me.

'I'm having problems with this vegan frosting,' she admits, staring down into the bowl in front of her. 'It's very lumpy.'

Oh, that doesn't look right. 'Did you melt the coconut oil first?'

Chelle looks at me and then checks the recipe. 'Oh… right. My eyes skipped over that bit. I'm so sorry, Ivy. This isn't going to be usable now.'

'Hey, it's not a problem. Just start over again and I'm sure it'll be fine.'

'It's very different to what I'm used to, Ivy. I mean whipping avocados, maple syrup and cacao powder together with coconut oil is a first for me.'

'You'll get used to it. And let the oil cool a little once you've melted it, not so much that it starts turning solid again, just enough to bring it to room temperature. The good thing about this healthy frosting is that, if it's kept refrigerated, it keeps for five days. It's one of my favourite recipes.'

Chelle gives me an artful grin. 'Never in my wildest dreams would I have considered using avocados in a mixture to ice a cake. But I'm learning,' she says, emphatically.

'Does that mean you'll be coming back next week?'

I await her answer with bated breath.

'I'm learning something new every single day, Ivy, and that's quite something. If you think I have what it takes, then I'd love to accept your offer.'

Yes! I stop short of punching the air, but this is such a relief. If I'm ill, there would be no cakes. And if I'm going to keep my promise to Adam, I'll need someone here every Saturday morning to top up whatever we're running low on. You can't have a bakery running out of cakes, can you?

It's been a satisfying day in many ways, although I realised this afternoon that there's still a lot to do. With new Christmas orders coming in daily, baking must take priority. Just extending the opening hours to five o'clock has had an impact on takings and makes it a long day for me. That's fine Monday to Friday, but I'll need weekends to recharge my batteries. I'm hoping Wenna and Rose will be able to cope with the vast majority of the serving, and with Chelle beavering away in the kitchen, they'll be able to call on me if they get swamped, and on their respective days off.

I'm beginning to run out of steam, so I put down my notepad and pick up the phone.

'Hi, Mum, how are things with you and Dad?'

'It's all fine here, Ivy. I bet you're clock-watching until Adam arrives.'

I laugh, indulgently. 'It's agony. Every time I glance up it's like time is slowing when I want it to speed up.'

'Aww... not long now. Have you, um, spoken to your sister recently?'

My heart sinks in my chest. 'It's her turn to call me and she's not been in touch. Is Ursula still talking about getting back with Nate?'

Mum pauses, thrown by my response. 'Oh, I didn't realise... He moved back in a week ago.'

'Really? Hasn't she been through enough?'

Mum clears her throat, nervously. 'I know what you're thinking but little Tillie is thrilled to have her dad home again and it's different this time around, Ivy.'

'Hmm... this is what, the third time she's given him another chance?' I remark, sounding decidedly jaded. My sister is four years younger than me. When she found out she was pregnant, it was at the time Adam and I were planning our lavish wedding.

Ursula and Nate simply walked in one day flashing their wedding rings after a quick trip to the registry office with only their best friends as witnesses. We were all in shock and hurt to have been excluded because if we'd known, we'd all have pulled together to help them. They hadn't known each other for that long and none of us were really surprised when it all began to fall apart.

'Whatever we think, Ivy, it would be wrong of us not to give Ursula our support. This time she's laying down some rules. No more raucous nights out with the guys for Nate. It's time he started acting like a married man and taking responsibility for his actions.'

'He's giving up his snooker club and no more following his favourite football team around the country?'

'Apparently, that's what he's agreed to.'

'Yes, well… seeing is believing. I'll reserve judgement until he's proven he won't slip back into his old ways.'

Nate's a nice guy when he's not being selfish. His problem is that he gets talked into things far too easily and most of his friends are single. At twenty-four, he's the only one with a child.

'That's probably why she won't call you, Ivy, and that's a real shame. There are going to be things she won't discuss with me, or your dad, so if she does get in touch please, please don't upset her. Just listen and bite your tongue. It'll either work this time around, or it's over for good.'

They never had a clean break from each other anyway, and I chided Ursula for agreeing to go on date nights with him. How can you get over someone if they're constantly in and out of your life, especially when they don't give you what you need – like a sense of security and stability. It's madness.

'All right. I hear what you're saying. You can tell her I won't rant if she needs to talk. But it's hard to see her struggling and what sort of example is it for little Tillie, when one moment her dad is there and the next he's gone for several months at a time?'

'I know. But she's made it clear this is his last chance, Ivy. Anyway, did the furniture arrive safely?'

'It did and now I'm on countdown to launch day. My new baker, Chelle, has officially joined us and will be working four mornings a week and covering for me on Saturdays.'

'Oh, Ivy, what a relief that must be for you!'

'It is, Mum. It's important that Adam and I grab as much quality time as we can together at weekends,' I confess. 'Ever since we got married it's all been about working hard and saving money. Hopefully, very soon I'll be in a position to be less hands-on in terms of the daily running of the bakery. Instead, I'll be creating new recipes which I find energising and it puts me in my happy zone. As Adam says, "a happy wife means a happy life", and that's the aim.'

'That's so good to hear. The pair of you have had a trying time of it lately and you should both take advantage of those marvellous sea views and the wonderful cliff walks.' There's a lift in her voice that tells me she's smiling to herself.

'The other news is that two of the walls in the café are going to be turned into an art gallery. A local lady, who's quite well known in the art world herself, is promoting a group of Cornish artists. She came to look around this morning and we're getting together on Monday to decide how best to showcase the paintings. I might need to get Riley involved.'

'How wonderful for your customers.'

'Yes, I thought so, too. And I want to give back to the community, even though it's only some free wall space.'

'It's the thought that counts, Ivy. Just don't put too much pressure on yourself. It's still early days.'

'Don't worry, Adam and I won't always be rushed off our feet, Mum. We'll all have some wonderful times together here at the farm, I promise you. With a spare room at Smithy's Cottage and turning the office above the bakery into a guest room, we're reserving them for parents, so maybe you guys might consider coming here for Christmas. I could get something sorted close by for Ursula, Tillie and Nate, if he's still in the picture.'

Mum sucks in a deep breath. 'Oh, Ivy!'

'If anyone else wanted to come down, Jess said we could possibly look into renting some of the caravans that are stored on the campsite over winter. Honestly, Mum, some of them are luxurious. It would certainly make our first Christmas here a memorable celebration.'

'Well, Ivy, that sounds like a truly wonderful idea.'

'I'm thinking of suggesting to Jess that her guests and friends join us at the café on Christmas Day. We might as well go big.'

'Let's be optimistic and say that Nate, Ursula and Tillie will want to be there, too. I'll have a chat with her and no doubt she'll ring you to talk about it.'

Oh, Mum, you hate it when your daughters aren't talking to each other. Hopefully, this will get us back on track.

'I'm home,' Adam calls out as he swings open the front door. 'I see that Riley's been hard at it.'

I rush down the stairs, straight into his arms.

'I know... Riley reckons unless he's rained off, he'll have it finished by the end of next week.'

'And then we'll have our own private garden.'

Adam stoops to kiss me and suddenly none of the worries whirling around inside my head are important. My man is here and everything in my little world is just fine.

'Come on, I'll give you a hand emptying the car. Did you manage to fit everything in?'

'Everything I need. Mum and Dad are going to do a few runs to the charity shop and there are a couple of things they'll advertise for sale online. You wouldn't recognise the old place now; it's a shell.'

I grin at him in the twilight as we walk over to the car.

'We made some good memories there, but I'd rather be here. This feels like home, Adam; it really does.'

'It's funny you should say that, as the moment I got in the car a feeling of contentment washed over me; this is our new life. Up to now, I've had one foot still anchored in the past and, at weekends, one stepping into our future. Suddenly, it's all beginning to feel very real.'

As we stop for Adam to get his car keys out of his pocket, I glance at him anxiously.

'You don't have any regrets… do you?'

'No,' he answers without even pausing for thought. 'None at all.'

'Good, then it's time to invite our families here for Christmas. I want it to be a special one. We can turn the café into a winter wonderland and I reckon we can seat forty people easily, maybe fifty. It would be a nice way to repay Jess and her family by including them on Christmas Day. For once she could take a back seat and simply enjoy herself. What do you think?'

'I think you're amazing, Ivy. You haven't stopped since you got here and I know how tired I am, so you must be feeling the same. But, well… our first Christmas at Renweneth Farm, we want it to be a memorable one. I'll talk to my parents and you have a word with Jess.'

'I'm beginning to get that tingly, festive feel. Imagine how excited everyone is going to be experiencing Christmas in Cornwall!'

Waking up naturally on a Saturday morning, with absolutely no need to rush out of bed, feels decadent. Normally, the first thing on my mind is to get those ovens turned on to bring them up to temperature in the bakery, but I know that Chelle will manage perfectly well without me.

'Are you pretending to be asleep?' I whisper and Adam opens one eye for a brief moment.

'No. Just resting while I can.'

'I was wondering if you were up for a little shopping trip in Polreweek this morning.'

His eyes spring open.

'For the cottage?' he checks.

'No. Now that all your clothes are here, we're going to need a bit of a sort-out before I can turn my attention to that. I meant for our guest room in the bakery.' I laugh.

'Hey, I did get rid of some stuff while I was packing, you know.'

I roll over onto my side, leaning on my elbow to glance down at him.

'Hmm... I could tell. But first things first. The desk is now in pieces stacked up in the rear corridor in the bakery. It's not really in the way but it will need moving at some point. In the meantime, it won't take long to turn it from an office into a bedroom. A couple of items of furniture, some bedding and a blind. I also have enough left in my budget to cover the cost of the fixtures and fittings for the shower room. I don't think it's right Jess foots the bill for that.'

Adam gives me a sleepy grin. 'That's fair enough.'

'She suggested you have a word with Riley to make the arrangements and if we want to store anything temporarily in Renweneth Manor he'll lend a hand. He's not around this weekend, though.'

Adam yawns and stretches his arms out in front of him, flexing his muscles. 'He did mention it.'

'He did?'

'Oh... I mean—'

'You've been talking to him?'

Adam gives me a guilty look. 'He rang me for a chat... just guy stuff, no big deal.'

'Oh, I see.'

Why is Adam being cagey?

'Is it anything to worry about?'

'No, of course not! Riley is stressing over Ollie's visit and it helps to talk.'

'Okay, I trust your judgement and I like Riley; he's a good man but he messed his life up once. It would be awful if his ex-partner suddenly changes her mind about the visit.'

'It'll all work out, I'm sure.'

I guess it's a good sign if Riley is reaching out to someone and I can understand him being nervous. He dotes on Jess and Lola, and it's hard to imagine Renweneth Farm without him here. However, to make the dream complete I'm sure being able to bring his son here for regular visits is a big part of it for him. Let's hope the weekend goes smoothly.

ADAM
Renweneth Farm, Cornwall

23

Suddenly Everything is Falling into Place

'Before we head off to Polreweek, can I ask your advice about something?' Ivy gives me one of her beguiling smiles.

'You know I'm all yours whenever you need me, honey.'

'Then step this way,' she says.

I close the front door behind us and then follow her.

'Morning,' Ivy calls out as we walk into the bakery.

Both Wenna and the other lady, whose name has slipped my mind, give a cheery "Morning" back. I raise my hand to acknowledge them, feeling a bit awkward. It doesn't help that there's at least half a dozen people waiting to be served and they instantly stop chatting to look at us with interest.

However, it's good to see the tasting room is no more and the tables and chairs pretty much fill three-quarters of the space. In fact, it could accommodate another three or four tables, if necessary.

'You must be pleased, Ivy. What else is there left to do in here?'

She looks at me as if she's going through a mental to-do list. 'There are a couple of paint touch-ups around the doorframe where the delivery guys knocked the woodwork. It wasn't their fault – the wind kept catching the tables. And I have one of those trolleys on order for our customers to stack their trays in when they leave, plus a couple of recycling bins. I've decided I'll be splitting my time between the kitchen and the counter when needed. It's hard to know how busy we're going to be but for now I think we have enough staff to manage.'

'It's hard to predict what sort of difference it's going to make, isn't it?'

'I'll probably look for one more person if I can find someone who is able to step in when needed for a couple of hours here and there. Especially during the summer. I'll put the word out and see if I get any interest.'

I sidle up close to her, lowering my voice. 'Who's the other lady behind the counter again?'

'That's Rose, Len's wife.'

'Ah, and she's here permanently now; see, I do listen.'

'I know it's confusing, but hopefully there won't be any further changes. Anyway, Prudie — the artist lady – wants to meet with me on Monday to finalise our arrangement. Which roughly translated means she's coming to tell me what prep work she wants doing ahead of the paintings being hung. My thoughts were that the two white walls would be best, but I could tell she had her eyes on the large stone wall opposite the opening. I draw the line at having holes drilled in it.'

I stand back to look around and I can see why, from a sales point of view.

'If she uses the white wall on the left-hand side it's almost as big and will be easy to get fixings,' I comment. 'With the natural stone wall, it will probably be better to either have display stands in front of it, or maybe see if Riley could make up some sturdy, narrow timber frames. Three or four should do it. If he anchored each one to the ceiling and the floor and painted the wood in a colour to match the stonework, it would look like the paintings are floating on the wall. I think that would do the trick. I'll give him a call to forewarn him.'

Ivy links arms with me, snuggling up close. 'I knew you'd come up with something. I'm not in favour of stands, as they'll restrict the floor space. Thanks, babe. Prudie is the sort of woman who doesn't mess around and I didn't want to be caught off guard and allow myself to be talked into something I'm not happy with.'

'I'll be talking to him about the shower room anyway, so I'll mention the frames in here at the same time. I guess if you go with that, you'll want it done ASAP?'

'Naturally!'

'This woman... Prudie, sounds a bit demanding considering she's getting the space for free.'

'It's a goodwill gesture and trust me, it's the right thing to do. It'll take a bit of pressure off Jess. In fairness, Prudie's more discerning than demanding, but I want to remain firmly in control of the situation.'

She tugs on my hand, eager to start our day.

'It was just a flying visit Wenna, Rose,' I remark, as we pass the counter. 'Have a great day, ladies.'

'You, too!' they both call out, as we leave them to it. I still feel like a bit of a stranger around here but that's all about to change.

Ivy chatters away excitedly, giving me the latest news about her sister, as I ease the car out onto the road. There's a significant queue waiting to drive into the main car park and it's good to see it so busy. Ivy and I both wave to Cappy, as he puts up his thumb to indicate that it's clear for us to turn left. The car park is obviously full and he's now directing them to the overflow field opposite the farm.

'Gosh, Ivy, the café could turn out to be a little goldmine. Even if it's only exceptionally busy on market days in the winter, imagine what it'll be like during the holiday season.'

'I'm thinking the same thing but the busier we get, the more flexibility it will give me to take on extra help.'

It's good to hear her sounding so positive and upbeat.

'Anyway,' she continues, 'as you saw for yourself, people seem to enjoy standing around chatting while they wait and no one seems to mind. Let's hope it was just chatter, though, and not gossip.'

'It's probably a bit of both,' I laugh. 'Riley's list of jobs just keeps growing and now we're adding to them.'

'Oh, I don't think Jess has anything major planned for him now until work begins on Renweneth Manor.'

LINN B. HALTON

'Maybe not, but when it does it'll be a major headache for him. He's going to need a lot of help from a whole variety of different trades and the place will need gutting first. I was thinking of offering to take a week off work in the spring to lend a hand. What do you think? Just to pay them back for everything they've done for us.'

Ivy reaches out to place her hand on my leg and it's comforting to feel her touch. Even being in the car together these days is a treat.

'It's very thoughtful and I'm sure both he and Jess would appreciate it.'

'I want to be a part of it and I do miss getting my hands dirty at work. Well, maybe not when it's pouring down with rain, or when it comes to levelling concrete.' I laugh to myself.

'But you are happy?'

Out of the corner of my eye I can see Ivy nervously waiting for my response.

'I love the new job. I've had many a foreman over me who wasn't an all-rounder, so I know how to keep the guys happy. If you treat them fairly, they treat you fairly in return.'

We lapse into silence. It's a nice little run into Polreweek but we're heading for an industrial estate on the outskirts of the town. I get to a point where I ask Ivy to put the postcode into the sat nav as The Design Cave isn't quite as easy to find as I'd hoped.

'It's much bigger than I thought it would be,' Ivy's eyes light up as we eventually pull into the car park. 'I'm rather excited.'

'You, excited about shopping? You're the least shopaholic woman I've ever met.'

'This is different, Adam. This is our forever home and I'm nesting.'

I glance at her, pulling a face. I have no idea what that means but it sounds expensive.

When we step through the sliding glass doors, I let out a low groan as Ivy mutters, 'Ooh, this is my idea of heaven! Adam, look at that sofa. Now that's country style with a touch of elegance. Oh my!'

Sofas?

She's off and I increase my stride to catch up with her, realising that this is going to take a while.

'Do you like it?' she asks, running her hand over the brushed fabric. 'It looks like silver, and it has a classic look.'

'I thought we were here to buy a bed and a few bits and pieces. Are you going to fall in love with everything you see?'

She stands back, gazing around. 'Pretty much. Come on, over there the stands are full room-size displays. Oh… look at that beautiful bed; I think the white chalk-paint finish would be perfect for our guest room!'

It's wonderful to see her looking so happy. And even though it's not really my thing to get excited about furniture, bedding, and curtains, it's giving me a bit of a buzz too.

'This is going to cost a lot of money,' I moan, 'isn't it?'

'Sadly, I think you're right, Adam, but it's going to be worth every penny. Pinch me please, because I think I'm dreaming – everything I could ever want under one roof!'

'I think I'd better go and get a trolley while madam begins shopping.' I'm not even sure Ivy is aware I'm talking, as she's already hurrying away from me.

What a day. Lying here in bed staring up at the ceiling in Smithy's Cottage, it really does feel that our life is finally falling into place. We'd been doing all the right things; working hard at our jobs and saving every penny rather than spending it, but it felt at times that we weren't getting anywhere. It's funny but looking back on our old lives now it was very much like being on a treadmill. While it's running it's tricky to step off, so you keep on going. If you keep pressing forward, the belief is that at some point you'll reach your goal. Except we never did.

I had doubts about coming here, sure I did. It was a major

decision to make and the fact that I had to talk Ivy into it didn't sit well with me. What if I let her down again and the job wasn't what I thought it would be? Plus, there are always sacrifices to be made and yes, it's not been easy at times but here we are. Making our way to the till today with two shopping trolleys filled to the brim, and an order for a list of furniture, put the biggest smile on Ivy's face. Almost as big as the one she was wearing the day she walked down the aisle towards me.

'Are you still awake?' Ivy whispers in the darkness.

'I haven't been able to nod off yet.'

She yawns, rolling over to face me. 'Too much going on inside that head of yours?'

I lean in to kiss her cheek and pull her closer. 'This is what it's going to be like now, at least for the biggest part of the next twelve months. No more wishing you goodnight over the phone. What do you have planned for us for tomorrow?'

Ivy places her head on my chest. 'Jess has invited us to Sunday lunch. Cappy is cooking. You don't mind, do you?'

'No, of course not.'

'If it isn't raining tomorrow, we could take a walk down to Penvennan Cove and stroll along the beach; you know, blow those cobwebs away. After lunch, how about we draw up a plan for the garden? Now we can see the footprint we have to play with, we can get designing. I don't want all the cobbles taken up.'

'That's still a fair bit of work, you know, Ivy.'

'Yes, I do appreciate that, but fortunately I just happen to be married to a builder.' She starts laughing.

'You know, Ivy, you're the best thing that ever happened to me and I have no idea what I've done to deserve you. I guess I've a couple of tons of cobbles to shift, then. Riley said if we wanted to take them up, I can barrow them around to the rear of Renweneth Manor. Have you ever been inside the manor?'

'No. Jess talks about it a lot, naturally, but if she's not working or looking after Lola, she's entertaining. She never takes a day off.'

'Now who does that remind me of?' I declare.

'All I can say is lucky you!' Ivy giggles. 'Now stop talking. I'm tired and you're keeping me awake.'

This time her yawn sets me off and it isn't long before my eyes begin to close, as I listen to her breathing growing deeper and deeper. This is what it's all about; being together in a place we know is where – for whatever reason – we were destined to be.

When I open my eyes, I can hear noises coming from the kitchen down below and while I wait for Ivy to appear with coffee, I pick up my phone only to discover it's dead. When I search around for the lead and plug it in, within seconds there's a ping and then another, in quick succession.

I hope you're having a better Saturday night than I am. Fiona is now insisting on staying tonight as well. She said it would save me the drive tomorrow. There wasn't anything I could do about it. Now Ollie's gone to bed and she's being nice to me. I think I might be in trouble.

The next text was nearly two hours later, just before midnight.

I've never faked a migraine in my life but it was the only thing I could think of. I'm either naïve, or a sucker. Goodness knows what Jess will think. One night was unavoidable given the circumstances but two nights is going to look suspicious. Give me a call when you can.

I groan out loud. Riley, how could you have not seen that coming? I quickly text him back to let him know my phone was dead and as things might be a bit fraught at his end, I'll call him a bit later.

'Who's that you're texting at this time on a Sunday morning? Most people have a lie-in, you know. Well, those who don't have kids. I suspect my sister has been up with Tillie since five o'clock.'

'Oh, just a text I missed last night as my phone was out of charge. Are you worried about Ursula?'

I fold back the duvet cover as Ivy puts a tray on the bedside table, handing me a mug before she settles herself down.

'I just don't want to see her hurt again.'

'She's only avoiding you because she knew what your reaction would be.'

Ivy turns to give me one of her stares. 'Are you saying I'm not sympathetic?'

Now this is where I struggle. It's a touchy subject because Ivy's sister doesn't deserve the way Nate's messed her around. A man gets to a point in his life where he can't put his mates before his partner. At his age I didn't have a regular girlfriend in tow, but I like to think that if I'd got a girl pregnant, I'd have stepped up and left my laddish ways behind me.

'You know that's not what I meant but he's not a bad guy, Ivy. He just needs to grow up a bit. Ursula loves him and if she wants to give him yet another chance, as tough as it is to stand back and watch, it's her decision.'

Ivy doesn't sulk; her silence simply means she's thinking it over and I sit here hugging my mug.

'Mum said more or less the same thing. Honestly, Nate's a fool. He has a darling little daughter and a wife who thinks the world of him. I'm sure he adores them but he's such a... flake.'

'I agree.'

'Sorry, let's start again. Good morning, babe, how did you sleep?'

'Like a log.' I grin at her. 'And so did you, as at one point I woke up and you were snoring.'

'That's very ungentlemanly of you to point that out.' She beams at me. 'Especially as I brought you coffee in bed.'

'I agree.'

'Can I have a potted olive tree for the garden?'

'Where did that come from?'

'I thought if you're just going to say *I agree* I'd reel off a list of things and see what I could get away with.'

'Yes, to the olive tree.'

'Does your coffee taste all right?'

'It's fine. Why?'

'Hmm... it tastes a bit funny to me. I'll pop down and make myself a cup of tea instead.'

'That's probably because you don't usually snore and you did most of the night.'

'Oh, not the mouth wide-open thing!'

I give a little chuckle. 'You were just totally exhausted but don't worry, you still managed to look cute. Stay there, I'll make it for you.'

'Can you grab my notebook and pen from the coffee table? We can start planning the garden when you get back.'

It's not quite the start to our Sunday that I had in mind, but I'm sure at some point before Ivy's ready to leap out of bed, I'll think of something to entice her to stay a while longer. It's time to turn on the charm and I know she won't be able to resist.

'Riley, are you free to talk?'

'Oh, I'll need to grab a notebook to take down some details. Can I call you back in a couple of minutes?'

'Sure,' I reply, trying not to laugh. Notebook? Details? I'm guessing Fiona is glued to his side.

I'm in the former office at the bakery double-checking we can fit in a king-size bed, a wardrobe and two bedside tables. It's a while until my phone kicks into life.

'What took you so long?' I demand.

'Don't ask... This weekend has turned out to be a complete and utter nightmare,' Riley groans. 'Thankfully, Ollie's having a great time. He likes exploring and the garden backs onto moorland, so for him it's a real adventure.'

'And Fiona?'

His sense of exasperation is troubling to hear. 'Mate, I'm out of my depth. I thought it was over between us and now I'm not so sure that's how Fiona sees it. I don't know how I'm going to wangle my way out of this one. She's already talking about another visit and I don't think she means just Ollie.'

IVY
Renweneth Farm, Cornwall

24

The First Day of Our New Routine

Yesterday was blissfully relaxing. Aside from indulging ourselves designing the little courtyard garden of our dreams, it was wonderful not counting down the hours until Adam packed up the car and drove off.

A wet and windy Monday morning isn't exactly the best start for Adam's first day on his new job at Parklands and I can tell he's a little anxious by how quiet he is. The site doesn't open until eight o'clock as it's in an established residential area, so when I leave at six to start my working day, he still has an hour to kill. Just knowing that he'll be home at the end of the day it's a different sort of goodbye. I give him a big hug, a lingering kiss on the mouth and wish him the best of luck.

It's too windy for an umbrella and I fasten the toggle on my hood as I scramble to unlock the door to the bakery in the dark. Once the lights are on it's comforting and Chelle appears a few minutes later. Tapping on the door, she peers through the glass and that round, rosy grin of hers is a real tonic.

'Morning, Ivy.'

'Not the nicest of them, Chelle.'

'No, it's not.'

'The coffee machine is on. I'll head up to the kitchen and start warming the ovens.'

Even before I reach the top of the stairs my phone starts

pinging, once, twice and then three times in quick succession. When Chelle walks in I'm chuckling to myself.

'Adam just sent me through pictures of three different shower cubicles. I only left the house ten minutes ago and Riley's already been in touch to say he'll be installing it today. I guess it's too bad to work outside.'

'Ooh, he'll be in your good books, then. Here you go.' She places the steaming mug down next to me.

'Thanks, Chelle.'

I quickly text Adam back having selected the second option. He instantly replies.

Riley will pick it up on his way in and he'll be there about nine. Best not mention how the weekend went. It wasn't a disaster, just stressful.

Oh dear. Drive safely and I'll see you later! x

'I guess we're going to be in for a bit of noise today.'

'Yes, but it'll be nice to get the place as you want it, Ivy.'

Chelle starts carrying across some bags of flour as I assemble the first mixer, then she heads over to the fridge to get a tray of eggs and some butter.

'This is our forever home now and it's good to finally be putting down roots.'

'It can't be easy, though, being parted from family and friends,' she acknowledges.

'No. It isn't. But I intend to make the time we have together when they visit us a more meaningful experience. Popping in to see both sets of parents for the odd hour here and there after work, it was just to catch up. On Christmas and Boxing Day we alternated between them but this year I want to get everyone together, here at the farm.'

'My word, now that sounds like an ambitious plan!'

'Ever since I started up my first business, I've worked six

days a week. Adam worked Saturday mornings six until noon virtually from the day we started saving up to get married.'

'That was in Stroud, was it?'

I think back, nostalgically. 'A few miles away, actually. We were married in a little parish church and the reception was held in a charmingly rustic barn on the outskirts of a sleepy little town in the Cotswolds.'

Chelle smiles across at me. 'Ah, I bet it was lovely.'

'It was, but not quite as perfect was coming back from honeymoon to a rented house I never really felt at home in. That spoilt it for me. That's why the bakery and Smithy's Cottage means so much to us both.'

'Take it from me, you've fitted in from day one and I'm glad to be on the team. Right, what's on the list today?'

'Well.' I grin. 'You'll be pleased to see it's a fair bit shorter than Saturday's.'

'Ah, we'll be able to make a few more Christmas cakes, then.'

'Yes, the orders are mounting up. I'm not complaining, but we do need to get ahead. I can't abide a crumbling fruit cake. It should slice perfectly and it only does that if it's given time.'

'I know, tell me about it. Don't you just hate the supermarket ones that look the business but fail to deliver?'

'That's why discerning people come to bespoke little bakeries like this one,' I laugh. 'And we'll show them how it's done.'

Just after ten o'clock Wenna appears in the doorway.

'Ivy, you know Flo – the lady who's doing the yoga classes in the hub? She's got a pile of leaflets and was wondering if you'd be happy to take a few for the counter.'

'Oh, of course! Tell her I'll just wash my hands and I'll be straight down.'

I've been hoping to bump into her; the couple of times I've popped along to the hub she's not been around.

'Hi, Flo, I'm Ivy.' I hold out my hand and we shake.

'It's lovely to meet you, Ivy. There's no pressure, but I wondered if any of your customers might be interested in yoga classes at the hub.'

I grin at her. 'You can sign me up and I'll put a pile of leaflets on the counter.'

'I don't have a lot of free slots if you were thinking of one of the evening sessions, as most of my regulars from the church hall are following me here.'

I glance down the list of classes. 'A Wednesday or a Thursday works for me,' I confirm. 'I know Jess was thinking of signing up too. Step into the corridor and I'll just give her a call.'

'Oh, that's very kind of you.'

I click on Jess's icon and it rings for a little longer than usual. 'Hi, Ivy.'

'Sorry, bad timing?'

'No, ugh… just not the best start to the day. How can I help?'

'Flo's here in the bakery and I'm signing up for the Wednesday evening yoga class. Do you want me to add your name, too?'

'Oh, please. My back is in so many knots, anything I can do to relax my muscles will be a welcome relief. Sorry I can't stop to talk but we'll catch up later, and give my best to Flo, tell her she's a star.'

I frown to myself. 'Jess says to sign her up and that you're a star.'

Flo looks around rather nervously. 'I'm late getting these leaflets out because it's the second lot I've had to get printed. Prudie Carne isn't an easy woman to deal with. I know she does a lot of good for the local artists, well Cornish artists in general, and she's well known, but my can she be stubborn. Someone's been spreading rumours that it wasn't first come first served. They're wrong. I took the space because it was free at the time and yet Prudie thinks something underhand is going on. I don't want to upset Jess or Cappy – their hearts are in the right place – but wasting fifty pounds on a box of leaflets that ended up in the bin because the slots I offered Prudie for her painting sessions didn't suit her is out of order.'

I grimace. 'Jess would be horrified if she knew that, Flo.'

'Sorry, I didn't mean to offload and I really don't want to make a fuss as the studio is perfect for me. I just hate being at odds with anyone, Ivy. It goes against the grain with me. Still, it takes all sorts. At least we came to an amicable agreement in the end but, for whatever reason, Prudie feels she's been snubbed and it still rankles that she can't use the space as her gallery.'

I shake my head, sadly. 'Between you and me, she's going to use two of the walls in the new café area. Not only will it brighten the space up, but she'll get a lot more footfall through that room than she would upstairs at the hub.'

Flo smiles at me, knowingly. 'Some folk are never happy, however much you bend over backwards for them, but she should count herself lucky. Anyway, thanks for taking the leaflets and for being a team player. It means a lot to me.'

'You're very welcome. And I'm really looking forward to Wednesday's class.'

'Great, come ready to relax and stretch your way through an hour's gentle workout. Now I'm going to join that queue, as healthy and delicious is right up my street. I'm on my way to my sister's house for coffee and she'll be delighted if I take her in a little treat. Enjoy your day!'

By noon on the dot the kitchen is sparkling clean and Chelle is glad to get away from the sound of drilling and hammering. What will be the new shower room is just the other side of a plasterboard wall that abuts our stockroom and on one occasion we both look over, half-expecting Riley's drill to come through the wall.

Jess texts and asks when I'm breaking off for lunch and when I tell her I'm free, she says the cheese and tomato toasties are in the pan. I tell Wenna I'll be back to relieve her at one o'clock and make my way across the courtyard.

How is it even possible to wear a waterproof coat and find the wet still seeping in? I muse. It's like the wind has one task and that's to make me feel damp and miserable.

When Jess answers the door, initially she looks a little distant.

'Are you all right?'

'Just confused and—' She lets out a shriek as Misty appears out of nowhere almost causing her to fall over.

I stoop to pick the cat up. 'Hey, what's the hurry?' I ask, giving her a stroke.

'She hates the rain and keeps going to the cat flap thinking it'll stop, but it's in for the day by the look of it. So she's having these bursts of manically running around like her tail is on fire and keeps getting under my feet.'

Gosh, it's not like Jess to be short-tempered, but her nerves seem frayed.

'Come on, let's get you some chicken treats, Misty, as I need you to calm down.'

Miaoooooow, Misty wails, clearly not at all happy.

The smell of the melting cheese makes my mouth begin to water, as Jess indicates for me to take a seat. Flipping over the sandwiches, she then sorts some treats and silence reigns.

'Tea, coffee, wine?'

'Wine? You really have had a trying morning, haven't you? I've just had a coffee but I'd love a glass of water. Is there anything I can do?'

'No, it's almost ready.'

'Where's Cappy?'

Jess turns to look at me over her shoulder. 'He seems to have a lot of lunch meetings lately. He never used to be that sociable. Maybe Saturday nights but not on a Monday. Sometimes I think he goes off with his paperwork to find a quiet table in the pub as there are fewer distractions.'

'As long as he's happy. What's happening with you?'

'If I'd known what Riley was battling with at the weekend, I'd have been on edge the entire time, which is exactly why he didn't come clean with me.'

'Ollie's first visit, you mean?'

'Yes. That's why he was a little late arriving over at yours. He called in to have a chat as soon as Cappy went off to do the school run with Lola and Daisy. Honestly!' She pulls the frying pan off the heat and leans against the edge of the counter. 'The one thing I thought I'd made crystal clear to Riley is that we don't hold anything back from each other. I couldn't believe it when he said it wasn't just Ollie who stayed for the whole weekend, but Fiona, too! What was he thinking?'

Her eyes are flashing as she wields a knife to cut the hot toasties in two, before carrying the plates over to the table.

'Here, grab a napkin. Help yourself to salad.'

It's not just our lunch that is steaming; Jess is really angry and I can totally understand why.

'Everything Riley does revolves around you, Lola and the farm, Jess. You have nothing to worry about.'

She looks away, rather guiltily. 'Look, I'm not an unreasonable woman and when he explained I did calm down, but it was a shock. I've been stewing over it for the last couple of hours and I guess I succeeded in winding myself up.'

'You're the love of his life – that's obvious. And you can't surely be questioning his commitment given everything he's done here at the farm.'

She sits back in her chair staring ahead of her, unable to take a bite.

'No and I understand that when Fiona changed the arrangements at the last minute Riley didn't really have a choice in the matter. She wanted to drive Ollie down to Cornwall and I get that. It's the first time he's stayed with his dad.'

At least she's putting herself in Fiona's shoes.

'It's a long drive, so obviously when she asked if she could stay overnight, it would have been unreasonable of him to refuse. After all, it's a three-bedroom cottage but...' She pauses, ominously. 'When it was obvious on Saturday morning that Fiona was including herself in the plans they were discussing over breakfast, he should have said something. He told me Ollie was very relaxed and looking forward to going to the beach and skimming stones. In this weather – that's kids for you.' She gives a little laugh. 'What concerned me was the fact that it didn't sound like Riley made any attempt to put her off. At all.'

We're both toying with our food and I reach out for the salad tongs.

'He simply wanted the weekend to go well so that next time Fiona won't have any reason to refuse a stay. By then, hopefully, he'll feel comfortable telling her about you and Lola.' However, her expression tells me she isn't totally convinced of that.

'Riley gave Fiona everything she asked for when they divorced because he says the break-up was his fault entirely. He put work before his family and lived to regret it big time. When Fiona did allow Riley to visit, or call, he didn't know how to keep four-year-old Ollie occupied. She wouldn't let Riley take him off to the park, or the cinema, so what did she expect? Unless that was the whole point.'

I gasp. 'You think she did it purposely because she was punishing Riley?'

Jess shrugs her shoulders. 'I don't know, but when she eventually made it clear to him that his visits unsettled Ollie, he had no choice but to back off. Now Ollie is older, he's obviously curious about Riley's life but it seems Fiona is, too.'

Jess is obviously feeling anxious about the whole thing but I guess, given the situation, that's only natural. 'Surely, the fact that you, too, have a child might make the situation a little easier for the future?'

She leans forward, scarily attacking her sandwich with a knife and fork, her brow wrinkled. 'Oh, Ivy... when it comes to Fiona it seems Riley is incapable of saying "no". Riley needs to be straight with her now, as he has to decide what he intends to do with the cottage once he moves to the farm.'

'And he doesn't want to?' I push the food in front of me around the plate, feeling sad about the tricky situation they find themselves in.

'He's scared of her reaction. Riley has a small team of men ready to start on Renweneth Manor on the ninth of January to gut the place, top to bottom. Given the way Fiona invited herself to stay, either he needs to stand up to her, or see a solicitor about formalising some sort of access to his son. What's the point in starting the renovation work if we have this huge question mark hanging over us? It could take months and months to get it sorted. And what do I do, move in with Lola because Fiona is still messing Riley about?'

Suddenly I'm chewing my lip rather anxiously.

'Tell him exactly how you feel, Jess. Riley will understand and he'll do something about it.'

She sighs. 'I know. It was just upsetting to think of them spending the weekend together. And here I am, scrabbling around to get the funds sorted to turn a wreck into our dream home. It makes me feel a bit silly, actually.'

I pause for a moment, wondering if this is the right time, or not to raise the subject. Then I decide it might lift her spirits. 'If it helps, Adam's sought financial advice and we may be able to apply for a mortgage a bit earlier than we first thought. We'd need a firm purchase price for Smithy's Cottage to get a mortgage in principle before we could proceed.'

Her eyes widen. 'Oh, Ivy, that's wonderful news. Not just for you, but it would really help ease the pressure for me, too. However…' she reaches out to touch my arm and give it a squeeze '…don't feel any sort of obligation. If it ends up being too much of a stretch for you guys right now, that's not a problem.'

'We're not going anywhere, Jess, and the place feels so right for us. I can't wait to get the courtyard garden sorted once the wall's finished. Adam is already backtracking and saying I might have to be patient. He says landscaping in winter when the ground is frozen is a task too far.'

We both laugh.

'Men, eh? All it needs is a couple of pickaxes.'

I know we're being silly but somehow, we've both managed to lift our spirits. Anything is possible, right?

'I'll ask Vyvyan to book a valuation and she'll be in touch as they'll need to gain access to the inside. I'll give you a copy of the report once it's back. At least you'll have a figure. But come April I'm hoping there will be more in the pot than I anticipated, as I always err on the cautious side when doing my income and expenditure forecasts.'

As we finish our lunch, I don't like to raise Fiona's name again, as Jess seems to have pushed that to one side for now. Even though it's obvious she's a little concerned to find out the three of them spent the entire weekend together. But an estranged dad will do anything to reconnect with a son he loves and, in her heart, Jess understands that.

25

And Just Like That the Grey Clouds Begin to Roll Away

I say goodbye to Jess and step out into the courtyard. The rain has stopped and the sky is slowly starting to clear. Just to see a swathe of blue far on the horizon is a joy and I might be feeling a tad over-optimistic, but the sun itself might even put in an appearance before the day is done.

'Right, Wenna, it's your turn. Go and grab some lunch with Gryff.' It's nice that he works from home, and they can grab a quiet hour together. It's not quite the same eating alone.

'It's been steady this mornin' and we've had another three orders for Christmas cakes. Is everythin' good with Jess?'

'Yes. She's fine, just busy. I really don't know how she manages to keep track of everything.'

'She'll turn her hand to anythin', will Jess. I've a lot of admiration for her.' Wenna pulls on her coat as I stand behind the cake display.

'And what does madam fancy for dessert today?' I enquire, with mock seriousness.

'You spoil us, you know. What haven't we tried yet?' Wenna muses, working her way from the top to the bottom.

'How about a raspberry bomb? It's the first time Chelle has made them, and I think I'm going to try one, too.'

I lift one off the platter onto a small plate. As I cut it into four bite-size pieces, the all-natural, luscious raspberry filling oozes out. It's easier to eat with a fork, as the outer coating of sponge is drizzled very lightly over the top with a thickened organic honey infused with bay leaves. As we each pick up a piece, there's a wonderful, gooey stickiness that makes us instinctively lick our fingers afterwards.

'Oh, my goodness, Ivy. That is delicious.'

'Have another piece. Chelle really has this recipe nailed. It's one of my favourites and I think the new baking-paper cupcake cases look really smart. I must take a box over to Jess at the end of the day. What do you think of the new logo?'

'Country charmin',' Wenna states, gobbling down her second piece and rolling her eyes as she reaches for a napkin. 'Gryff is goin' to love this one!'

As I pop two into one of our smart new greaseproof bags, I can't help sighing with a real level of satisfaction. The Renweneth Farm logo is an artist's impression of Renweneth Manor in its heyday and now, next to it, is a similar one of the bakery. The wrap for the various breads only has Rowse's logo, but I think it adds that authentic artisan touch. I'm proud to sell their bread as it's such a high-quality product. If it's worth making well, it's worth the extra little touches that tell the customer what they're getting was made with love.

'Thanks, Ivy.' I hand Wenna a bag with two raspberry bombs. 'Before I head off, Riley might be glad of a coffee. I was just about to make him one, when you came in. See you at two!'

I'm just about to call out to Riley to come and take a coffee break, when the doorbell tinkles and in steps Prudie. Two paces behind her is Cappy. Maybe it wasn't a working lunch for him down at the local pub, after all, and my heart sinks in my chest.

'Ivy,' Cappy bellows. 'My, it smells so good in here.'

'Can I get you a hot drink and a cake on the house?' I offer.

'No. We're fine, aren't we, Prudie?'

We? Why is he answering for her?

'I wanted to get Cappy's opinion about the best place to hang the paintings, Ivy. A second pair of eyes is always useful.'

Prudie does have a bit of a warm, soft Cornish lilt when she's not being sharp, and it helps to make her a little less scary, if I'm being honest.

'No, of course not. I'm keen to get the work done as quickly as possible so that it's simply a case of hanging the paintings when you're ready, Prudie.'

A customer steps through the door, so I have no choice other than to leave them to wander, which is precisely what I didn't want to do. It would have been helpful to have heard what they're saying.

'Good afternoon, what can I get you?'

It's impossible to make pleasant conversation with a customer and try to strain your ears at the same time. The only thing I catch is, 'Oh, Cappy, I don't think so!'

Then I hear the sound of Cappy chuckling. 'You know best, Prudie – you've been doing this a long time.'

Just as my customer leaves with one of the smart new carrier bags swinging from his hand, he holds the door open and two women step inside.

'Ooh, look at that for a display, Margaret,' one says to the other.

'Feel free to browse, ladies, I won't be a moment.'

I race up the stairs and into the new shower room, almost making Riley jump out of his skin.

'Ivy. What's wrong?'

'Prudie Carne is here with Cappy and I'm serving as Wenna's at lunch. Could you come to my rescue?'

He straightens, pushing a pencil behind his ear. 'I'm on it!'

'She can display her paintings on the two plaster-boarded walls, but no stands anywhere, as that will restrict the floor space. And I don't want the natural stone walls drilled. If that's the way she wants to go, it's a problem. Adam sugg—'

He puts up his hand to stop me. 'We spoke about that this morning. I'll sort her out, don't you worry. You get back to the shop.'

Mondays are quiet but, like Wenna said, it seems to be a steady stream and, frustratingly, I miss the entire conversation. Prudie and Cappy hurry off with little more than a wave and a fleeting "thank you".

Riley loiters and when we're finally alone, he looks at me and bursts out laughing. 'They weren't being rude,' he hastens to explain. 'I said that you'd put me in charge of doing the necessary work.'

Well, that's something. I felt like I was the hired help as they breezed out of my shop.

'Prudie wanted the impossible but she's not getting it. However, we did come up with a compromise she quite liked.'

'Maybe I should charge her,' I grumble, begrudgingly. 'I'm doing the woman a favour.'

'Don't worry, it's going to look fine. I'll talk you through it.'

'Let me just make us both a coffee first.' I hand him a set of tongs and a plate. 'Help yourself... you can't overload with sugar, not in here.' I laugh.

'That's why Adam doesn't have a spare ounce of fat on him.'

'Ooh, I'm so glad you mentioned that.' Riley looks at me quizzically. 'Now that he's here permanently we're going to need to set him up with a gym membership. Where do you go?'

'It's about a fifteen-minute drive – halfway between here and my cottage. It was a farm but they turned all the buildings into holiday lets and the gym is a part of the complex. It's reasonably priced and they've got some good equipment. If you like, I'll suggest to Adam I take him there as my guest one evening.'

'Ah, Riley, that's really kind of you. Right, here you go.'

He's just stuffed half a banana and rum raisin slice in his mouth and is carefully carrying the other half on his plate, so I grab both mugs while he follows me into the café.

Wiping his mouth on a napkin, he tilts his head in the direction of the stone wall facing us. 'You were right, she has a bit of a thing about stands but I told her straight it's a safety issue as a child could potentially pull it over.'

'You did? Brave man.'

'I might look a pushover, but I'm not.' He grins at me, popping the other half of the slice in his mouth in one go.

He points, silently, at the wall to our left and I wait while he finishes chewing. 'That hit the spot. Hmm. Anyway, um... oh, yes, I told her that anyone looking in through the window would instantly see the art, so she agreed that will be her main feature wall. And she couldn't argue that white is definitely the best background colour.'

It sounds like Riley wasn't having any nonsense.

'However,' he continues, 'just because Cappy was looking a little like he wished he hadn't come, I decided to keep the peace. Prudie was beginning to look like she needed a win as she's in love with the stone wall. After all, what does a general builder like me know about art?' He grins at me. 'I'm going to fix two bespoke runners at floor and ceiling level. It's based on Adam's idea of a minimal framework. She can slide them along to suit the size of the paintings and can hang maybe a dozen large ones, more if they're smaller. When people step through into the café they'll be met with a wonderful contrast against the beautiful old stone.'

'And she was happy with that?'

'Cappy was very impressed, but I got the feeling Prudie felt she was settling.'

'Settling? Poor Flo wasted fifty pounds on printed flyers, only to bin them because Prudie wouldn't agree to the time slots for her art classes. Flo has been running her business for years and now some of her clients have had to change slots because of one woman! It's insane.'

'Prudie does have a lot of standing in the community, Ivy, and it pays to be on her good side. Trust me. Jess will thank you for this. Prudie's family have always lived here but she's travelled far and wide, retiring twice no less and coming back here not that long ago, after a long spell away. But she's spent her entire life extolling her love and support for Cornish artists and her homeland. She can be a bit testy at times but if you stand firm, you'll earn her respect.'

'Well, thank you for keeping her happy. I didn't mean to create a lot of extra work for you, Riley.'

'Oh, this is as much about healing a bit of a sore point between Jess and Cappy, as it is pandering to Prudie. You have no idea how grateful Jess is to you for accommodating her.'

'I just want to do my bit, Riley. And… um… how are things with you?'

Just as he opens his mouth to speak, the bell on the shop door tinkles and our coffee break is over. I shrug my shoulders at him, gather up the mugs and the plate, and scurry away apologetically.

'Your man is home,' Adam calls up the stairs and I rush down into his arms.

'I must be dreaming because it's only Monday!' I tease him.

He lifts me off my feet as I plant a kiss firmly on his lips and walks me very gently backwards into the kitchen/diner.

'How was your first day?' I can tell it went well because his eyes are shining.

'It was great. I have a good crew and a few familiar faces. Now it's time to prove I can do the business. I was thinking that it might be a nice gesture if, on Friday evening, I offer to take them all up to the pub for a quick half after work. What do you think? It might be a nice way to end our first week.'

'A bit of male bonding is always good.'

'Whatever you've got in the oven, Ivy, smells really good. I'm starving.'

'A rib-sticking beef casserole that's been slow-cooking for the last six hours. Do you want to shower first?'

'To be honest, I'm not really that messy. The only mud is on my boots.'

He grins back at me as he takes a seat at the table.

I stop short. 'Oh, darn it! There's something I forgot to do. Can you give me five minutes?'

'What is it?'

'I put a box of cakes together for Jess and I left them on the counter. I want to pop them across. Everything is now sporting the new logo and she'll love it.'

He puts his hand up as he gets to his feet. 'Pass me the keys and I'll pop them over to her while you dish up.'

'Ah, thanks, babe.'

The minutes tick by and by the time he finally returns I'm poised with a ladle in my hand.

'What took you so long? Here you go. Help yourself to Rowse's sea salt and rosemary bread – and I did a few roast potatoes, but you can serve yourself.'

'It's not a meal if there isn't a potato on the plate,' he retorts, giving a little laugh. 'Lola came running up behind Jess and when she saw the box her eyes lit up. Jess said "thanks" and the new logo got a big thumbs-up.'

He begins eating as I continue to serve myself. 'I'm so glad you've had a good day, because I've got something I need to mention.'

Adam leans back in his seat, a dunked piece of crusty bread oozing the rich beef gravy dripping back into the bowl in front of him. 'Uh-oh.'

'Now don't panic but...' Maybe this is something I should raise after dinner but I'm too excited. 'Jess is going to get a market valuation on Smithy's Cottage.'

His entire face lights up. 'Really? What sparked this?'

I tell him that I had lunch with Jess, but don't elaborate. Adam attacks his food with relish. When he's hungry, he prefers to just eat but he's more than happy to listen to me. I ask him how much he thinks it'll cost to renovate the manor and he appears to be giving it some thought but really he's just hungry as he wolfs his food down.

Eventually he sits back in his chair. 'In all honesty, Ivy, I reckon Jess is looking at two hundred and fifty thousand minimum to renovate the entire place. And that's not going overboard with the finishes. Labour costs are going to be high.'

'She's hoping Riley will have enough rooms done for them to vacate The Farmhouse in August at the latest.'

As we sit facing each other across the dining table, he scratches his head. 'The trouble is that it's a lot of unglamorous, boring things that drain the budget. Gutting the place and putting in the basics will gobble up at least half of that, maybe more if it needs a new septic tank. That alone could be an additional thirty grand in one go.'

'But Riley knows that, right?'

'Sure, he does. Just between us, though, Jess doesn't always listen. It's obvious they need to be out of The Farmhouse and living the dream, but until the place is stripped out, who knows what problems they'll find? I'm assuming it's all solid, because the walls are pretty thick but none of these old buildings have foundations.'

Adam scoops back his mop of curly blond hair, suddenly looking weary, and I can see that he's concerned for them.

'When you're emotionally invested in a place it's easy to hear what you want to hear and let the rest go over your head. Even if they don't discover anything untoward, and don't lose their heads when it comes to the finishes, it's going to be a stretch.'

He's almost done eating but my appetite seems to have disappeared.

'That wasn't all Jess wanted to talk about. Fiona stayed at the cottage with Ollie the whole weekend. She was understandably shocked when he told her yesterday morning. Riley was a bit late arriving, but I wasn't aware of the reason why.'

'Yeah, well, I did warn him.'

That brings me up with a jolt. 'You knew?'

'Only that his ex, Fiona, had insisted on staying the first night. He didn't have a choice when it came to the second night, apparently, but believe me when I say he wasn't at all happy about it.' It's not like Adam to clam up but he immediately changes the subject. 'Anyway, I'll dig out that card for the mortgage consultant.'

'It would be nice if we could get something sorted, Adam. Jess is going to need every penny she can get. She helped to make our dream come true and I'd love to do the same for her. Imagine what a difference an injection of cash would make.'

'I'll give the guy a call and see what he says. When will Jess be able to give us a figure?'

'She said she'd ask Vyvyan to arrange for the valuation to be carried out as soon as possible.'

'This could be the turning point for us, Ivy. You always said you wanted a cottage; I just didn't think it was going to be possible. This is what you want, isn't it?'

Adam reaches across the table to clasp my hand in his. 'Yes. And I have some photos to show you of our new shower room next door. Let's clear this lot away first and then snuggle up on the sofa. I'll catch you up with what turned out to be quite a day. Riley came to my rescue by having a standoff with Prudie and Cappy.'

'He did? Well, I can't wait to hear all about that!'

DECEMBER

IVY
Renweneth Farm, Cornwall

26

Building Bridges

In one way, I can't believe that it's the fifth of December already. Sadly, in another way, I can as the last two weeks have been a real trial on a daily basis. Riley expected it to take a day, maybe two, for him to make the framing for Prudie's display on the largest of the stone walls. He said that putting up the fixings on the adjacent white wall, which is plasterboard, would be a doddle and she'd have plenty of time to unpack her paintings.

However, life has an annoying habit of teaching us that it's naïve not to expect the unexpected and when he hit a water pipe, I heard the cussing from behind the bakery counter and rushed in to help.

Now, here I am, nervously waiting for Prudie to arrive and she has just one day to turn two blank walls into an art gallery. I can't blame her for feeling put out, but it was a simple mistake, an accident. Riley couldn't find his pipe detector that day and after wasting half an hour he gave up the search. He was confident he knew exactly where the pipes were behind the plasterboard anyway, as he was the one who installed them. Except that he'd forgotten about the pipe that branches off to feed the radiator in the downstairs cloakroom.

Jess pops in and when she sees that the café is no longer sealed off, she immediately breaks out into a smile and gives me a thumbs up. There are two customers waiting but Wenna sends me off to join Jess the other side of the counter.

'It's a relief to see it opened up again,' Jess admits, keeping her voice low as we walk through the opening. 'No smell of damp, either. What a result.'

'A little water goes a long way,' I groan. 'Even though we managed to stop any ingress into the bakery, it's taken forever to dry the floor out in here, even with those industrial dehumidifiers going day and night. My biggest fear was the damp seeping into the bakery. Soggy cakes and bread would have been an even greater disaster. Bless Riley, his reaction was instant in sealing the opening so tightly, nothing got through.'

'Sorry that Riley and I weren't around yesterday to help you, Adam, and Cappy to get the furniture back in situ. We needed to get away and talk frankly, just to clear the air between us.'

She looks more relaxed, which is a good sign. 'And did you?'

'Yes and it was well overdue.'

'I hope you did more than just talk.' I grin at her.

'It was like our early days together.' She smiles, a hint of pink colouring her cheeks. 'Riley and I would be alone here at weekends if Lola had a sleepover with Daisy. We were working flat out on the bakery and Smithy's Cottage back then. It just—' She closes her eyes for the briefest of moments. 'It reassured me we're still on track.'

I give her a comforting smile. 'I've told you many times, you have nothing at all to worry about with Riley, Jess. He's a good man.'

'My heart tells me that. I just worry that Fiona still has a hold over him, which she does, obviously, because she controls all access to Ollie. Anyway, I challenged his reason for not telling her.'

I look at Jess, a little surprised at the uneven tone in her voice. 'You did?'

'I ended up getting upset and it just came flooding out. I asked if he was having second thoughts.'

'And?'

'He admitted that Fiona might be, but he said there is no going back for him. Living a lie wouldn't be in Ollie's best interests.'

'It sounds to me as if she didn't really think Riley had got his life together but anyone who knows him can see he's a worker. He's not the sort to sit idly by and wallow.'

'Maybe her stay made her stop and think that making a life in Cornwall is quite an attractive option. Who knows what her motivation is, but at least now she's aware of the situation.'

'But it's a setback, obviously. I can tell from your face.'

'Yes. I didn't hear the call but he was shaken when he returned to the room. Riley had his hopes set on having Ollie here at some point over the festive period. Maybe for a couple of days after Boxing Day. We were hoping that would make Ollie feel a part of our celebrations. We were planning to do an intimate rerun of Christmas Day just for him.'

'You thought Fiona would let Riley bring Ollie to the farm?'

'I couldn't see why not but given her reaction who knows what's going to happen next. If Fiona comes to her senses, Lola and I could go and stay at Riley's Cottage. She's with her father for the New Year, so it would make our last few days together rather special.'

There's a sound behind us and we both turn around. It's hard not to let my shoulders sag. 'Ivy, Jess... sorry to interrupt when you're deep in conversation.'

Aren't words and expressions supposed to match? I almost feel as if Prudie thinks standing around talking is a sin.

'I 'ope you don't mind me team bringin' everythin' through? Unless you 'aven't finished, of course.' At least Prudie sounds a little apologetic.

'No, please feel free,' I reply.

'I only popped in to check everything was ready,' Jess explains, and I give her a pointed stare. She doesn't have to placate Prudie.

'Well, I can tell from here it's all perfectly fine. It just took a lot longer than we'd 'oped.'

I'm not prepared to let Prudie get away with that, so even though I probably sound on the defensive, I can't stop myself from replying.

'Riley wanted to make sure everything was completely dry, Prudie. We had industrial heaters in here running on low all day Saturday, just to make doubly sure.'

The truth is, she should be grateful we've been so cautious. The last thing we wanted was for her to hang the art and find too much moisture in the air was affecting the frames, or worse, the canvases. Riley and I even went online to establish safe humidity levels, which he checked with his meter – that's how paranoid we've been.

'In 'ere, guys. Please stack those boxes very carefully indeed.'

Jess disappears without as much as a goodbye and I can tell there's no love lost between the two women. But I'm stuck here and it's going to be a long day.

'Can I give you a hand with anything, Prudie?' I offer, out of politeness.

'Goodness, no. Unpackin' and hangin' delicate pieces is for experienced hands only.' She doesn't even turn to look at me, her eyes firmly on the precious cargo being carried through. Suddenly, a professional-looking young man in a dark blue suit appears in the doorway.

'Oh, I wasn't expecting this, Prudie! What a wonderful venue.' His enthusiasm instantly lifts the temperature of the room a good couple of degrees.

I watch, entranced as he looks around, taking it all in.

'The light is perfect and…' He fumbles in his pocket, retrieving his phone. 'Ah, south is that way,' he informs us. 'Excellent. There won't be any problems with sun exposure in here during the height of summer. And the stone walls will also keep it at a nice ambient temperature.'

I'm sorry… are we displaying the *Mona Lisa*? I need to make a quick exit before I start laughing.

'Can I offer either of you a tea or coffee before you begin?'

'Earl Grey for me,' Prudie replies.

'I'm a cappuccino man. Two shots and heavy on the chocolate sprinkles, thank you. Are you *the* Ivy?'

He walks towards me, offering his hand, and we shake.

'No, just Ivy,' I say with a laugh, and he starts chuckling.

'Don't worry, given the little miracle you've managed to pull off, we'll have everything sorted before you close,' he assures me. 'It's going to add a real charm to this delightful little bakery. It's a dream location for us, really.'

Prudie simply scowls at him. 'We should make a start, Karl.'

And that was clearly my cue to exit.

When there's a lull in serving, I pull on my jacket and bobble hat to take Riley out a mug of coffee and a cake in a bag.

'Oh, the gate is up!' I exclaim, as I walk towards him.

'You have no idea how welcome a sight you are. Prudie Carne has been giving me the evil eye out the window. I know it was a rookie mistake, I didn't engage my brain before I started drilling, but she's never going to forgive me.'

'Please, Riley, don't feel guilty. That lovely young man, Karl, thought you'd pulled off a minor miracle. If there's any moisture left in the air, it's from the drinks I've just taken in to them.'

I hand him his mid-morning snack.

'Ah, thanks, Ivy, I could do with that. You and Jess really know how to look after a builder.' He gives me a wink.

'Well, you've created a garden for me, so you more than deserve a little looking after. Can I open the gate and see it from the other side?'

Even from this angle it gives the courtyard a completely different look. Smithy's Cottage is now private. When I walk through and close the gate behind me, as I peer through the small panel of fretwork metal at the top, I see Riley put up his thumb and smile to myself.

I didn't want a totally open gate as people would have been able to see through into the garden, so Riley had a special one fabricated. It's about eight foot high, the top two feet made up of a wonderful panel of intertwining ivy leaves with just enough tantalising little gaps to allow me to stand on tiptoe to look out, unseen.

The main part of the gate is made up of slim, four-inch panels with less than a half-inch gap between each. I can't resist and I walk over to the furthest corner to look back. Instead of a large expanse of cobbles bounded by the front of the cottage and natural stone walls, I imagine how it's going to look when it's landscaped. There will be some cobbles, but also flower beds, a bench and some pots. I could stand here dreaming all day, but it's time to get back to work.

As I walk past Riley, I stop to give him a quick kiss on the cheek. 'It's amazing, Riley. Thank you from the bottom of my heart!'

'I'm so glad this was the right thing for you and Adam, Ivy. Jess instinctively knew that she had to find the right person for the bakery and given what's been happening with the little upset and rumours, she was right. That's why she told me it's important that I keep you happy. It's nice to know I've succeeded.' He gives me an abashed grin. 'And I don't know if I've actually said it, but you make the most amazing cakes.'

Prudie and Karl disappear shortly before noon, so engrossed in their conversation that they don't acknowledge anyone as they leave the bakery. Is it a sign of trust, I wonder, that she's content to leave me to stand guard, or is it now a part of my job? I smile to myself. I don't know what it is about her that rubs me up the wrong way. I get the feeling that Jess has a pretty similar gut reaction, although the fact that Prudie runs to Cappy, rather than going directly to Jess, is out of order.

'Wenna.' I nod my head in the direction of the clock on the wall.

'Oh, it's later than I thought. Thanks for the prompt, Ivy.' She walks off to grab her coat and comes to stand next to me.

'You, um, mentioned once that Gryff paints. Does he have anything to do with Prudie?'

'Not really, although he's enrolled for one of her new classes at the hub. He finds paintin' relaxin', and I think he's pretty good, but I'm no art critic. He's a graphic designer by trade but at least if he has a brush in his hand he's not on his PC. She's mentored a lot of Cornish artists who have made a bit of a name for themselves over the years. And her work is wonderful. But the thing about Prudie is that she's good at takin' people who don't have much confidence in their abilities and makin' them believe in themselves.'

'Really?' Now there's a surprise.

'When I was a teenager, my mother once took me to an exhibition of Prudie's down in Truro and the one thing I remember was her sayin' that *beauty* is in the eye of the beholder. As long as somethin' is beautiful to just one person, the artist has done their job.'

I rather assumed Prudie was a bit of an art snob. 'That's good to know. I don't think she likes me.'

Wenna laughs as she opens the door for a customer. 'You just haven't caught her on one of her goods days. See you in an hour!'

For the next thirty-five minutes it's a steady stream of customers but a few are quite chatty, and I always enjoy that. Gradually I'm getting to know a little more about our regulars and, of course, everyone asks how the preparation is going for tomorrow's launch. The new *art gallery* seems to be on the tip of everyone's tongue at the moment.

When I finally get a breather, I make myself a coffee and saunter over to see what progress has been made for myself. What I see makes me catch my breath.

The large expanse of white wall to my left is now shimmering with a wonderful swathe of pastel colours. Starting with an explosion of green, the muted colours seem to ripple across the wall and, about halfway, almost seamlessly change into a mirage of blues. I'm intrigued and take a closer look.

All the paintings vary in size and shape; but the entire wall is like a series of snapshots while going walkabout in Cornwall.

From the gorse-covered moorland to wonderful vistas of the sea, and tiny fishing villages with colourful boats moored up along the quays, it's amazing. Different styles, but the colours of Cornwall are strikingly similar throughout.

Behind me the tinkle of the bakery doorbell pulls me away and as I turn on my heels, to my dismay, Prudie walks towards me. She's unaccompanied.

'Oh, sorry,' I immediately start apologising as if she caught me red-handed. 'I couldn't resist taking a peek. I assumed you'd both gone to lunch.'

'No. I dropped Karl 'ome to collect his car. He's gone to pick up some things from the printers for me.'

The eye contact between us is a little strained.

'Um... can I get you a cup of tea, Prudie, or will you be breaking off for lunch?'

'Tea would be nice, thank you, Ivy. There's no time to delay, so we're both workin' through.'

'This is amazing, Prudie. How many different artists will you be featuring in total?'

She pauses. 'Twenty-four, if my memory serves me correctly.'

None of them are priced yet, so all of these could be well outside of my budget, but I hope not. There's one in particular that my eyes keep straying back to. It's the view as you hit the beach at Penvennan Cove after negotiating the steep walk down through the trees. It looks out across the bay as far as the headland on the other side.

Prudie clears her throat, prompting me to make a move. 'Right, I'll get that tea for you.'

Three customers follow in quick succession, so it takes a little longer than I'd hoped, but as I'm finally getting around to it she appears at the counter, purse in hand.

'Oh,' I mumble, 'there's no need to pay. Wenna is due back shortly and I'll put together a little platter for you and Karl. It's nothing to make up a few rolls and a selection of cakes.'

'It's obvious you've run a caterin' business before, but it was in Stroud, wasn't it?'

I put her tea and a small jug of milk on a tray and place it on the countertop.

'Yes. My landlord suddenly decided to sell the property just before I was due to renew the lease.'

Her eyes widen a little. 'Ah, I see. It can't have been an easy decision for you and your partner, even if it was rather convenient.'

I look at her and it's clear she still has some sort of axe to grind.

'Adam is my husband, actually. I think you should know that it was Alice and Jory's decision not to take up a lease because they're expanding their operation in Polreweek. The decision to pull out was a reluctant one, but it was entirely their choice and, yes, it did leave Jess in a bit of a vulnerable position.'

Her eyes wander around the shelves and the displays as if she's taking an inventory. 'It's a pity that fact isn't widely known, Ivy. I've heard a few whispers goin' round, although I've come to learn that you have to take everythin' you hear with a pinch of salt. People do like to have somethin' to make a fuss about. It's good to hear that Rowse's bakery is goin' from strength to strength and a feather in your cap that they're willin' to be a supplier for you. That's gone down well with the locals.'

Is that some sort of back-handed compliment? 'Well, opening on market day should hopefully get a good stream of customers in to check out the gallery. I'm also offering twenty-five per cent off a cake and a hot drink, as a little enticement to get as many people through the door as possible.'

Her face brightens.

'We'll have a good supply of cards, and the phone number goes straight through to Karl at his gallery in Polreweek. He'll arrange collection with the customer. When he makes a sale, one or other of us will pop in to take the paintin' down and replace it with another. Any problems, Ivy, here are my contact details.'

She slips a business card out of her wallet and I take it, placing it firmly in my pocket. 'Perfect. I think the arrangement will work very well and I'm sure my customers will be just as delighted as I was when I walked into the room and saw the display.'

The door swings open and Wenna hurries inside.

'Ooh, that's a chilly wind out there,' she remarks, as Prudie walks off carrying her tray.

Wenna slips off her coat and on the way through does a little detour. 'You two looked comfortable nattering away when I walked in,' she whispers.

'It's not as strained as it was. Karl will be back soon, so I'm going to make them up a few rolls for lunch. Could you put together a little taster plate of cakes? I'm not sure what they'll like, so pick a few and cut them up as if they're samples.'

She grins at me. 'Will do. I'm glad she's lightened up a bit. The look she gives is usually worse than her bite. Well, mostly.'

27

The Café Is Open for Business

Iinvited Prudie and Karl to join us at noon to formally toast the opening of the café and the gallery. It has created quite a stir and the girls and I have taken it in turns to walk around with cake samples advertising today's special offer and handing out leaflets from a massive box Prudie had a courier deliver for nine this morning.

When they arrive the café is full to capacity and people are milling around. Prudie seems oblivious to the fact that Wenna, Rose, Chelle and I are all looking a bit hot and bothered. I lead them through to a small table set up in the far corner with an ice bucket on it and four champagne flutes. As if on cue, Jess rushes through the door. She looks like she hasn't stopped all morning and, as she's the one making the toast, I've been anxiously awaiting her arrival as I'm not one for making speeches.

Karl very kindly uncorks the champagne, which Jess told me was extremely expensive, but as I don't like the stuff it could be straight off the supermarket shelf for all I'd care. But Karl and I make a bit of a show as I hold the glasses and he expertly fills them. He's such a charming young man and very personable.

Jess, Prudie, Karl and I stand with glasses in hand and Jess starts speaking. A hush gradually works its way around the building and people in the bakery begin to gather in the doorway.

'Thank you everyone for coming to support this new venture today,' Jess begins, glancing around and smiling at everyone.

'I'm sure by now many of you will recognise Ivy Taylor, the new owner of the bakery. Ivy and her husband, Adam, are now an integral part of Renweneth Farm and I'd like to congratulate Ivy on the opening of the café.'

She pauses and there's a little round of applause. I can feel my cheeks begin to flame.

'It's a café with a difference and we're all delighted to welcome Prudie Carne, one of Cornwall's most revered, watercolour artists. But Prudie has also devoted her life to nurturing new talent and, in doing so, has spread the word about everything Cornwall has to offer. So it's with great pleasure and pride, that we welcome Prudie to Renweneth Farm and as you can see when you scan around, Cornwall is full of talented artists. I hope everyone enjoys the display. Please do share the news far and wide, because who wouldn't want to have a little piece of Cornwall on their wall to gaze at?'

I notice Cappy has joined us and he kicks off the applause with gusto. We all join in enthusiastically and Prudie smiles regally, nodding her head as her eyes connect with various people in the audience.

I'm just relieved it's such a good turnout and after a couple of minutes of standing around with silly grins on our faces, Jess and I make a beeline for the bakery. We've done our bit and people are standing in small groups chatting. Besides, it's hot and stuffy and my legs are beginning to feel a little wobbly.

Jess and I walk out to the back corridor to cool down.

'Are you okay?' she asks.

'Yes. It's just been crazy. Thanks for that wonderful speech. Oh, by the way, Vyvyan texted to say the valuer is due here at twelve-thirty, so I'll be heading off shortly to let him in. How are things with you?'

'Cappy helped me write the speech,' she admits. 'And the valuer won't say anything, they usually just walk around with a clipboard looking official. As for me, Riley has had a few nasty texts from Fiona. He's really upset and won't even talk about it.

The chance of us having Ollie here at any point over the festive holidays is looking slim. If you see him, don't mention it unless he raises the subject. Can you warn Adam, too?'

'I will. Oh, Jess, I think it was always going to be difficult. Why Fiona should care, I don't know because they've lived apart for so long they've had very little interaction.'

'I know. If she really loves Ollie, she'll come around because, like any mother, she'll want what's best for her child.'

'You have the T-shirt on that one, Jess.'

'Yes and I do sympathise with her. She'll obviously want to come to the farm to see it for herself and meet me and Lola. I want it to work for everyone and show her that we're going to make Ollie feel very welcome. But, best laid plans and all that.'

It's time to change the subject.

'While I think of it. Christmas Day we've invited both sets of parents and my sister and her family to come and stay. I'll need to sort some accommodation for Ursula if you know of any caravans that are free, but how about you all come to the café and we have one big Christmas dinner together?'

Jess's eyes widen. 'Really?'

'It makes sense. We'll make it extra festive and there will be plenty of hands to help peel veg and stir saucepans.'

'Oh, Ivy, that's an awesome idea. We'll get our heads together to make up the guest list so we know how many we're shopping for. I'll cook the turkeys in the range if you like. Anyway, you'd best get off!'

I glance at the clock and reach out to grab my coat. 'Where does time go?' I groan as we both hurry out the door, waving to Wenna, Rose and Chelle on the way out.

Jess is right and the guy says very little but as he's leaving a delivery driver walks up to the door. 'Smithy's Cottage? I have a delivery of furniture for you.'

I look at him blankly. 'You do?'

'The name on the delivery sheet is Mr Taylor. We did send him an automated text message and an approximate arrival time this morning.'

I have no idea where my phone is and Adam has probably been trying to get hold of me.

'It's not a problem. If you don't mind bringing everything in here. It's going to be a bit tight but I'll get it all moved later.'

'It's a king-size bed, two side tables, a wardrobe and two sofas, is that right?'

I hold my hand to my forehead as I nod my head. Why today of all days. I can't even get excited about it as tonight I'm going to be way too tired to unpack anything.

'As I said, put it wherever you can.'

I head through to the kitchen to grab a glass of cold water. It feels as if the world is spinning and it's time I took the weight off my feet for five minutes.

'Ivy,' I tell myself firmly. 'Stop stressing – it all went off well. Your job is done.' And just like that, I lower my breathing and feel an immediate improvement. I should do this more often.

Wednesday the twenty-first of December dawns and Adam is off work now and doesn't go back until the third of January. On the other hand, the bakery doesn't shut for another two days and will reopen the day after Boxing Day, so it's just another workday for me.

'Here's your to-do list, babe. It's mainly a supermarket run for soft drinks and wine, but it'll be a carload. Don't forget I'm at yoga tonight with Jess. Did you arrange anything with Riley?'

'Hmm, he's taking me for a free session at the gym he uses. I'm looking forward to it.'

Adam's phone buzzes and he starts frowning as he reads. 'It's from Cappy. Darn it... we're due for some snow this evening, Ivy. They're forecasting at least eight inches overnight but are saying the temperatures should climb tomorrow and there'll be a big thaw. I guess we're all going to be shovelling and gritting in the morning just in case. Cappy's got a hotline to the highways team and they've assured him they'll keep the road open for our bumper Christmas market on Friday no matter what.'

'The thought of snow is nice,' I muse, rather fleetingly. 'But any more than a couple of inches is a bit of a daunting prospect.'

'It'll be fine,' he reassures me. 'There are enough of us to keep the farm clear and they often get it wrong. It might not be quite as bad as they're predicting. So we're both out tonight, then.'

'I can't wait; my back has been killing me and I need to work out some kinks. It's nice for Jess and me to do something fun together, too. Anyway, I must go. Those cakes don't bake themselves.'

28

It's About to Get Hot in the Kitchen

The morning of Friday the twenty-third of December, the final market day of the year, finally dawns. We had another couple of inches of snow late yesterday evening before the temperatures plummeted and now everything is rock hard and glistening in the wintry darkness.

Even so, there's a tantalising air of excitement among everyone here at Renweneth Farm this morning, despite the extremely early start. I heard the gritter lorries drive past several times during the night, so if there is any further snowfall today, hopefully, they'll still be able to keep the road open. I don't know what we're going to do if our bread delivery doesn't turn up but then that would also mean our customers couldn't get through and that doesn't bear thinking about.

It's a little after five and I give Adam a parting kiss on the cheek. With his beanie hat pulled down over his ears, his thick padded jacket and a scarf wound around his neck to keep out the chill, he makes his way over to start scraping the windscreen of the car. Sometimes they do get the weather forecast right, although I think we seem to be one of the areas that suffers the heaviest of snowfall because we're exposed.

Wenna kindly offered to come in early today to lend me and Chelle a hand in the kitchen. She only lives a stone's throw away, but Adam said that as he was going to be up early anyway, he'd pick her up. Fortunately, Chelle's husband is able to drop her off on his way to work in his trusty old 4x4.

The irony is, that what was going to be a day of fake snowball fights has turned into a bit of a winter nightmare. Taking a moment to gaze out across the courtyard at The Farmhouse, I'm not surprised that all the lights are on. It does all look so pretty, though; it's just a little inconvenient today of all days.

I turn on the ovens and start carrying ingredients over to the stainless-steel bench when my phone pings, and it's Jess.

All good over there?

Yep! I think you lot were up about the same time as us. Adam's just gone to collect Wenna and then he'll be straight over. The road is clear. I heard the gritter lorries go past a couple of times during the night.

Thank goodness for that. Fingers crossed we pull this off today. We can't afford to fail! 😊 ❄️

I know... imagine being snowed in with enough bread, cakes, Christmas savouries and turkeys to feed an army. Cornish people are made of strong stuff. A couple of feet of snow isn't going to deter them.

Lol!

Hot savouries will be available on the house for helpers from seven o'clock onwards. Pass the word.

Thanks, Ivy. You're amazing!

Adam and I probably had less than four hours' sleep last night. We were both so fidgety that we kept waking each other up, so I guess it's no wonder I feel a little jaded this morning.

There's a tap on the door and I hurry down to let Chelle in.

'Morning, Ivy. Brr… it's freezing out there.'

'I'm just relieved to see you. Adam's gone to collect Wenna.'

She's already pulling off her bobble hat and slipping out of her coat as we walk.

'Right, I'll hang this up and we'll make a start. What's the plan? Are we sorting breakfast for everyone first?'

'They will need feeding but I doubt we'll see anyone until gone seven, as they'll be making sure pathways are clear of snow and salted, and the outdoor heaters and braziers are in place. I thought maybe I'd start baking while you focus on our Christmas savoury snacks.'

'Sounds good to me.'

When we walk into the kitchen and Chelle looks at the lists pinned on the noticeboard, she grimaces.

'It's not quite as bad as it looks,' I hurry to reassure her. 'The three lists on the right are for pre-ordered Christmas cakes that are boxed up ready for collection. Wenna's first task this morning is to mark all the traditional cakes as sold out on the website. We only have a small stack of boxes left in the stockroom. If we put them on the counter they'll go quickly.'

But Chelle's eyes are focused on the other list. The healthy alternative festive range, that our customers will be collecting tomorrow.

'We certainly have our work cut out, Ivy, to get this lot baked, decorated and in the fridge by the end of the day. First things first, though. How many savoury trays do you want me to make up ready to put in the oven?'

'As many as you can fit in the chiller cabinet to start with as we'll probably get through at least three when Jess's team come in to warm up.'

We don our baking caps and aprons and get to work. Another hour and a half, and Rose will be here for an early start, too.

Fingers crossed, Fred won't be far behind with the first of two bread deliveries due today.

'Oh, I nearly forgot!' Chelle disappears, clattering down the stairs and returning a couple of minutes later breathing heavily. 'I have a little something for everyone to mark the bakery's first Christmas.'

In her hand she has a paper bag and she opens it, pulling out a small box and handing it to me.

'It's to put on our caps.' She smiles.

I instantly recognise the logo of the jewellery concession in the hub and when I open it, inside is a beautiful little enamelled brooch. It's a little cluster of green holly leaves with three red berries. 'Ah, Chelle, that's beautiful. What a lovely thought. Thank you so much.'

'I think it will make the girls smile when they get here. Is it a bit early to pop in a Christmas CD?'

As I pin the badge to my hat, I give her an encouraging smile. 'Go for it. I'm starting with a tray of cinnamon buns, so another half an hour and it's going to smell festive in here. Let's get in the zone.' I smile to myself.

Moments later there's a sharp rap on the door announcing Wenna's arrival and Chelle's face breaks out into a broad smile. 'Ah, another pair of hands! Give me two minutes and I'll join you!'

As she clatters down the stairs, I know it's ridiculously early, but there's nowhere else I'd rather be and nothing else I'd rather be doing.

Wenna appears in the doorway, her cheeks flushed.

'Sorry, ladies, but we need another tray of sausage swirls as soon as you can.'

Chelle instantly looks up. 'There's three minutes left on the timer and they'll be with you.'

'Perfect! Adam is giving Fred a hand bringing in the delivery.

He said the journey was slippery in places but he didn't encounter any hold-ups.'

'That's reassuring. Have they both grabbed something hot to eat?' I check.

'Not yet. As soon as they're done, I'll make them both a drink and you might want to pop down to the café to say hello.'

I hear the sound of Cappy's hearty laughter filtering upstairs and I press on quickly, eager to get these cupcakes in before I take a break.

'Thanks, Wenna. I'll be down shortly.' She hesitates for a second and then I notice that she has a printout in her hand.

'There was a bit of an uptick in orders again yesterday afternoon.'

I can tell by the look on her face there's a problem and I stop what I'm doing to take the piece of paper from her. 'Have you had time to check the stockroom yet?' Numbers-wise, fingers crossed we might have enough traditional cakes as there were about a dozen at least in there yesterday morning when I had a quick look. However, I have no idea if they sold any of them yesterday.

'No, but as soon as there's a lull downstairs it's my next job.'

As she disappears out the door, I turn to face Chelle. 'There's another eight orders for the alternative festive range.' Her jaw drops. 'I know... I'll have a quick check that we have enough ingredients and then I'll jump online and mark them all as sold out. I guess we can say it's been a success but our day just got longer.'

'Thank goodness Christmas comes but once a year,' she jokes and I start laughing. 'I think I'd better get this batch of biscuits in and then get back onto the savouries, Ivy. Some of the stallholders will no doubt be needing something hot and we're down to the last three trays already. After that I'll start tackling that list.'

She glances at me for confirmation. 'How would I have managed if I hadn't found you? Look at us. We're a production line.' I giggle.

Chelle shakes her head at me, laughing. 'As long as we have customers, we'll keep feeding them. My challenge is to keep up with you. All those recipes are in your head but I still have to check every time.'

'A lot of trial and error went into honing each recipe to get the flavours right. You have no idea how many mistakes I made, Chelle, and how many batches ended up in the bin. That's the only reason why they're imprinted inside here,' I say, tapping the side of my head and then pulling off my plastic gloves. 'I think you're doing amazingly well. You want it to be right and I can't ask any more than that. OK, I'll pop this tray in, put the timer on and show my face. How do I look?'

'Hot.' She bursts out laughing. 'You know what I mean. Go, mingle, get a drink and take the weight off your feet. Oh, that tray needs to come out.' Chelle hurries over to the oven just as the timer goes off.

'I'll grab some gloves and take it down with me. When I get back you can go for your break.'

As I reach the turn in the stairs, Rose stands back to let me pass. 'Morning, Ivy. Ooh, good timing. We have people waiting for those. Are any of the trays of cakes ready to put out yet?'

'Yes, one entire rack ready to go in the stockroom. How was your journey in?'

'It was icy in places but Len's a cautious driver. I'm so happy to be a part of it, Ivy. He loves working at the farm and now I can see why. It's going to be an exciting day for us all.'

'Fingers crossed we don't get any more snow and I'm sure it'll be fine,' I reply, glibly. If my hands weren't full though, I'd have my fingers firmly crossed.

As I negotiate the remainder of the steps and make my way into the bakery, suddenly I begin to feel emotional at what I see.

When I glance at the clock, it's not eight yet and we're not due to open until nine, but Wenna is busy serving some of the stallholders. They all look very happy to be in the warm and I'm met with an array of smiling faces and several greetings. I stop at the end of the counter to let Wenna grab some of the savouries to refill the hot cabinet and she beams at me.

I mouth a silent *thank you* before turning and heading into the café. Adam immediately spots me and jumps up off his chair to hurry over.

'It's hot,' I warn him.

He gingerly backs away as I lay it down on top of the empty tray in situ. 'Help yourselves!'

Cappy and Len come straight over.

'Best not say that too loud,' Cappy chortles, 'or you'll have everyone crowding in.'

'All the traders have arrived?' I check. Some of them travel quite a distance and set off ridiculously early.

'Yes. It's a full house. Jess is beaming from ear to ear, and everyone is eager to go. Cars are already filtering in, so you'd best get ready for the onslaught.'

I turn to look out the window and even though it's still murky, the twinkly lights on the Christmas tree and around the courtyard contrast with what are now little hills of snow. The benches have been cleared and in the middle a brazier glows with red embers. In front of the bakery are two patio heaters and a couple of people are happily standing there chatting, hot drinks in their hands.

The sound of laughter makes me turn around to see Lola and Daisy come barrelling through from the bakery.

'Ivy!' they both call out in tandem.

Their eyes are shining, the tips of their noses red despite how bundled up they are.

Lola begins unwinding what must be one of the longest hand-knitted scarves I've ever seen.

'Hot chocolate, girls?'

'Yes, please,' they say in unison. 'Come and grab something to eat. There are sausage swirls, warm cinnamon buns, cheese twists and baked egg slices with ham.'

They go straight for the buns, and I smile to myself, as these are my healthy version and I doubt they'll even be able to taste the difference.

'I'll make the hot chocolate,' Adam offers. 'You take a seat, Ivy. I'll make you one, too.'

As I sink down onto a chair he stares down at me and I can see from the way his eyes smile how happy he is; today he really does feel a part of the wider team. Tomorrow our families arrive, and we'll be on countdown to our first celebration at the farm. I'm really hoping that Adam will love his present this year. They do say it's the thought that counts but this one was a no-brainer.

'Thanks, babe. I have ten minutes tops.'

He grins at me. 'Yes, ma'am.'

I walk over to sit with Cappy and Len, the girls choosing to stand looking out of the window as they gobble up their buns.

'The gallery works in here,' Len says, approvingly.

'It does. I hope people do take the time to browse. I already have a favourite,' I muse. 'That was hard work out there this morning, guys.'

Len gives me a wink. 'But what guy isn't keen to shovel snow? It takes us back to our childhood, Ivy, and brings out the kid in us.'

'You certainly don't feel the cold when you're doing it,' Cappy says and laughs.

'The big snowball fight will be for real when Father Christmas arrives,' I point out, warily.

'Hmm... that's something we weren't expecting,' Cappy replies, raising his eyebrows. 'Jess has already pointed out that what was supposed to be a fun thing, could turn into a bit of a health and safety issue if I'm not quick enough to duck and dive.'

Len and I exchange a harrowing glance as Adam appears, handing me a mug while balancing a tray on his other hand like a real pro. 'Here you go Jess, I'll be back in a second.'

He carries it over to the girls who are now sitting at the table closest to the window, chattering away as if they haven't seen each other for ages, rather than only yesterday.

'Why the frowns?' Adam asks, as he eases himself into the seat next to me.

'Instead of a fun bombardment of soft, fluffy fake snowballs to rain down on Father Christmas as he arrives, we're now faced with the cold, hard variety.'

'Oh… you're going to have to wear a safety helmet under your red hat, Cappy.'

'I was thinking the same thing, Adam.'

'How about a snowball game instead with a hard target? Then the adults can join in, too,' I suggest, thinking aloud.

Cappy stares at me. 'Like what exactly?'

'I don't know… maybe…' I stop to sip my hot chocolate, conscious that the seconds are ticking by and I'm needed upstairs.

Len's face brightens. 'How about setting up some targets and if they hit them, they get to ring a bell? You can't get more of a festive sound than that.'

'That's a good idea,' Cappy injects. 'It's easy enough to make up a couple of fixed wooden targets with a piece that pivots when it's hit, but where on earth would we get a bell at such short notice?' He scratches his head.

'There's one in the hedge in the second field,' Len replies.

'There is?' Cappy's eyes widen and we all look at Len, askance.

'I assumed everyone had spotted it. Something like that doesn't rot but if there's no use for it, it's not in the way either. It's been here as long as I have,' he chuckles.

There's nothing men like more than a challenge and I sit here grinning to myself.

'Sorry, guys, as lovely as this is I really must get back to baking.'

Cappy stands. 'And we've got a bit of unexpected work to do. If it saves me ducking and diving real snowballs, it'll keep Jess happy.'

Rose appears with a spray bottle and cloth in her hands to wipe down the tables. When we all stand up, she rushes over.

'Oh, I'm not shooing you out,' she apologises.

Len smiles at his wife. 'It's fine, m'dear. We're done and we need to get back to work. That hit the spot, Ivy, and you're all doing a grand job here. The bakery is a real credit to the farm.'

'Thanks, Len. That means a lot. I know I'm an outsider, but Renweneth Farm already feels like home for me and Adam.'

Len gives me a quirky smile.

'My father was Cornish born and bred, Ivy, but my mother's family were from Ireland. I was named after my great-great-grandfather on her side, he was called Leonhard, which is apparently the Germanic form of the name. I think we choose to settle where we feel a true connection with the people around us. The pair of you fit right in just fine.'

It's shortly after ten when Adam suddenly bursts into the kitchen.

'Have you heard what's happened?'

Chelle and I are singing along to 'Frosty the Snowman' and we immediately stop to stare at him blankly.

'No, what?'

'The oak tree with the big split in it up by the crossroads has come down. It's blocking both lanes and no one can get in, or out.'

I gasp and Chelle's hand goes up to her mouth as she exhales sharply. She turns to look at me and my stomach turns over.

'Has anyone been hurt?' I blurt out.

'We don't know. Someone who came to the farm to collect their Christmas order from the Treeve Perran Farm van was driving up to the tree at the precise moment it started to topple. Instinctively, he put the car into reverse and they were lucky, but it only missed them by inches. He said there were no other vehicles close that he could see but impossible to know what was going on the other side. The guy and his wife are in shock, but he managed to drive straight back to the farm. They're downstairs now having a coffee while Cappy reports it. Jess is on the phone to Pengali Farm as it's on their property. He's offering to organise a work party to assist the services to clear the debris when they get here.'

'What makes a tree like that keel over? It's probably well over a hundred years old.' Like me, Chelle is finding this hard to take in.

'And some. Cappy says a tree can rot from the inside out where there's significant damage. It was probably hit by lightning in the past. Eventually the rot weakens the roots. He's seen trees cut down where the inside has turned to something as fine as you'd see on a compost heap. Literally. With only a solid outer ring to hold it up, the weight of the snow on the good branches would probably have been enough to bring it down.'

It's a miracle no one was hurt. But what about all those customers making their way to the farm, who are relying on the bakery, the stallholders at the market, and the hub, to fulfil their Christmas orders?

'Is there anything at all we can do to help?'

'The people who are here can't get out, so they'll no doubt be glad to come inside to get warm and wait it out. Sorry, Ivy. I know how hard you've all been working. I'm going to jump in Cappy's 4x4 and head up to check it out, then report back.'

It takes me a few moments to gather my wits about me and then I hurry downstairs.

'Wenna, what time was Fred due with our second delivery?'

She excuses herself from her customer and comes closer, lowering her voice. 'Noon, so he'll still be on his rounds. It's awful, isn't it? I really do hope that no one has been injured.'

Breathing a sigh of relief, I take a second to compose myself. 'Adam's going to take a closer look. We need to squeeze in as many people as possible, as they can't stand around in the cold. Reduce the price of hot drinks and snacks by twenty per cent and we'll just keep going. Let's hope it gets sorted quickly.'

ADAM
Renweneth Farm, Cornwall

29

It's Time to Count Our Blessings

There's a small queue of cars ahead of me, all sitting with their engines turned off. In front of them, a vehicle has tried to do a U-turn, but it's now slewed across the road. *It's a tree. You saw it coming, man. Why drive up so close on a narrow part of the road with snow drifts either side and end up perilously close to a ditch?* I ask myself. The emergency services are going to have their work cut out as it is, without rescuing cars from ditches.

I gingerly pull into a snow-covered gravel entrance to one of the fields owned by Pengali Farm. This calls for a clear head and straight thinking, not idiots putting themselves, and other people, in danger.

As I press the key fob to lock the vehicle, a man walks briskly towards me. The snow crunches noisily beneath his boots.

'Quite a shock, isn't it? I don't suppose you live locally and know the quickest alternative route? According to the sat nav there's a couple of tracks a few miles back but I don't want to risk getting stuck with the kids in the car.'

'I'm from Renweneth Farm. The services have been called but it's going to take a while to get the road clear. About nine miles back there's a turning marked Holly Lane but I doubt the gritter lorries can get up there. It's potluck whether you'd make it through to the lower road without getting stuck. What's it like the other side of the tree?'

He grimaces. 'There are about a dozen vehicles in the same quandary but from what I can tell no one's hurt. There's some sort of market on apparently and they've decided to sit and wait. Quite a few cars have driven up and turned around but it's a risk as the sides of the road are so slippery. I've been tempted to follow one to see if I can get out but decided it's not worth the risk. Do you think it'll take long to clear?'

'An hour or two, once the emergency services get here, I would think. We're organising a work party of locals to lend a hand once they get started. There's a café at the farm if you need to use any of the facilities. It shouldn't be long before the work is under way.'

'Thanks.' He gives me an affirming nod and I let myself through the gate, closing it firmly behind me. It's a shock to see a tree upended, the substantial base with a gnarly clump of roots savagely ripped from the soil. I expected it to be much bigger, but then it obviously wasn't a healthy tree. It's still sad to see. I skirt around it, scrambling up a three-foot-high bank to where the fallen bough has ripped out a section of hedge. There's a hole and I try to peer through.

'Can anyone hear me? Is everyone okay that side?' I call out.

'Yes. The fire brigade is on the way, apparently.'

'We're arranging a work party of local people to lend a hand. There are facilities at Renweneth Farm if anyone needs them, or to warm up.'

'If we squeeze through the hedge, is it far on foot?'

'Ten minutes tops. There's a gate the other side of the tree. Someone will come and cut this back so you can get through safely. It won't be long.'

'Thanks, mate.'

I make my way back to the car, taking a moment to survey the scene. There's a long narrow lane leading up to two detached cottages; one is where Wenna and her husband live. Further on it widens out and there's a small village with a parish church. Looking at the angle the fallen tree is lying, it's hard to tell whether it's blocking the entire lane, or not, but I decide to check it out.

The ground is harder going this side as the heap of snow is at least three foot high and there's no gate. I end up clambering over the tree, dodging the splintered wood at a place where it's literally flattened the hedging. Even taking the greatest care, I end up ripping the back of my jacket when it gets snagged. The crown of the tree has totally blocked the track and, to my horror, there's a car with the tip of a branch smashed across the bonnet, all but severing it in two. The driver's door is open, and the airbags are deployed. The rear door is also open, and a man is sitting sideways on the seat with his feet on the ground, looking dazed.

'Are you all right?' I call out, as I hurry over to him.

'Just a bit shaken. The impact of the air bag knocked the livin' breath out of me. I've called the police.'

'I think it's best we get you checked out by a paramedic.'

Before he can object, I slip the phone out of my pocket and walk around to the other side of the car, pretending to check out the damage. I explain to the operator that the guy is having difficulty catching his breath, and he looks grey. When I return to the car, it's obvious he's still struggling and the cold doesn't help.

'How're you doing?'

'Sorry. Suddenly I'm feeling proper weird, light-headed like.'

'There's an ambulance on the way. I'm Adam Taylor, I recently moved into one of the cottages at Renweneth Farm.'

'I'm Jack Enys. I'm grateful you came along, Adam.'

'Don't worry. I'll get someone down from the farm to start clearing some of these branches so they can get to you.' I can hear a siren approaching in the distance, but I think it's a police car. At least some help is on the way. I run through a few basic questions and checks from my first aid course. His speech isn't slurred and when I touch his hands and his feet, he says he can feel them. 'Just slide your feet inside and lie back. Try to regulate your breathing, okay?'

I walk a few paces away from the car, while keeping watch on him and call the farm.

'Cappy, can you and Riley get down here quickly with a couple of chainsaws? I've just called an ambulance. There's a guy here whose car was hit and his breathing's not too good. They won't be able to get to him until some of the side branches are cleared. It's the lane on the left, leading up to the cottages. Can you bring some blankets with you, too? I think he's going into shock.'

'We're on our way, Adam. Just keep him talking.'

'How are you doing?' I open the rear door and lean in to place two blankets over Jack.

'Just c-c-cold, I can't stop my t-t-teeth from chattering.'

'Don't worry, it's just the shock. We'll soon warm you up a little.'

'I'd love a hot cup of tea. I live in the first cottage up the lane. My wife isn't home, but my next-door neighbour's husband, Gryff, is in.'

Cappy and Riley have already fired up the chainsaws and out on the road even more rescue vehicles are arriving. The sound of activity is reassuring.

'No problem. Would you like me to give your wife a call on the way to let her know what's happening?'

'I'd rather not worry her. I'm already feeling more clear-headed, just cold.'

'I'll be back shortly.'

Why didn't I think to ask Cappy to bring a hot drink with him, I berate myself and stride off purposefully. As I approach the two detached cottages, I get one of those déjà vu moments transporting me back to this morning. In daylight it's a nice little hamlet but in the dark and with only the headlights of the car to illuminate the lane, it didn't seem quite as far along. I knock quite hard on the door. When it opens, the man looks at me in surprise.

'Yes?'

As soon as I explain who I am and why I'm here, he doesn't hesitate and insists that I don't wait. I tell him it's a bit tricky underfoot, but he waves me off saying he'll be down directly. I hurry back to the car.

'Hey, Jack. I'm back. That tea is on the way. Gryff was very obliging.' I slip into the rear seat next to him.

Even inside the vehicle, my breath turns into a white, cloudy vapour.

'We've known each other since school,' he replies. I notice that Jack doesn't turn his head. His eyes are closed. 'Didn't think we'd ever end up livin' next door to each other.'

His teeth are no longer chattering but he sounds drained.

'Have you lived there long?'

'Four years. Moved here from the other side of Polreweek when... I... got... married.' He lapses into silence.

Instead of encouraging him to talk, I give him a running commentary on what's happening around us. I can see a blue flashing light as Riley makes cut after cut and Cappy and another man work side by side to throw the logs into a heap beside the lane.

'The paramedics are here!' I declare with some relief. 'You're going to be just fine, Jack. And Gryff's here, too with a flask. We'll let them check you over first and if they say it's okay, the hot tea will revive you I'm sure.'

'Thanks, Adam. Can you take my phone? If they cart me off somewhere, my wife – Kate – is on my contacts list. Can you let her know where they're taking me?' He slowly pulls it from his pocket and slides it across the seat, still sitting in a rigid position.

Jack hasn't turned his head at all since I lifted his legs into the vehicle and now I'm worried that his condition is beginning to deteriorate. 'No problem, mate.'

I swing open the door and one of the two paramedics immediately starts asking me questions, while the other one introduces himself to Jack. I mention the fact that Jack appears to have a problem with his neck and tell him about the difficulty he had breathing when I first found him. Afterwards, I walk over to Gryff, and he gives me a look of concern.

'You look like you could do with a cup of this yourself. Here.' He pulls one of the metal caps off the top of the flask and fills it to the brim.

'Jack is gonna be all right, isn't he?'

I take the cup from him, gratefully, and notice as I slip off a glove that my hands are trembling.

'I hope so, Gryff. At least he's lucid and didn't lose consciousness.'

'I'll hang around for a while, Adam. They might let him have a sip of this in a bit. It's mighty cold today. I bet they're in a panic up at the farm; it's a big day for them. Was it you who picked Wenna up, this morning?'

'Ironically, yes. I didn't think I'd be back this quickly, though.'

'How're they coping?'

'They haven't stopped since first thing but I'm sure they're keeping everyone going.'

He smiles at me. 'My wife is the sort of woman who likes to make herself useful and she was delighted when Ivy kept her on. After all, it's on our doorstep and everyone is talking about the new café. And with Prudie Carne telling everyone what a wonderful job your wife is doing, word will spread like wildfire.'

'That's good to hear, Gryff.'

'Yes. But then, Renweneth Farm is actively seeking to breathe life back into this area. It's tough for Cappy without his lovely Maggie by his side, but Wenna tells me that little Lola is the apple of his eye.'

There's movement around the car and one of the two paramedics walks over to us.

'We're going to manoeuvre Jack onto a spinal board and get him checked out at Polreweek hospital. He asked if you could let his wife know?'

'Of course. Tell him not to worry, I'll drive her there myself as soon as the road is clear.'

I thrust out my hand in gratitude and he shakes it.

'Thanks. I panicked a bit when Jack couldn't move his neck. I didn't know whether lifting his legs to get him into the back of the car and stop him freezing was the wrong thing to do.' A cold chill runs down my spine.

'You did just fine. You kept him awake and warm. It's probably just whiplash, but even that is painful, and recovery can take a long time. He hasn't lost any feeling in his legs, or hands, so it looks promising. I'll leave you to it then. We'll get the fire brigade to give us a hand getting him into the ambulance.'

Gryff unscrews the lid off the thermos flask and tops up my cup, then pours himself one.

'It's times like this I always think about what my gran always said in freak situations: *there, but for the grace of God, go I*. My granddad was a fisherman, and a lot of lives were lost at sea; he instilled in me the idea that it helps to have a bit of faith. I have my own personal beliefs, so I don't follow a set religion as such. But we don't know how lucky we are until we see some other poor soul suffering, do we? It's a sharp reminder not to take our blessings for granted.'

I finish the tea and hand the cup back, gratefully. 'Thank you, Gryff. I needed that. Jack left his phone with me to call his wife, so that's my next task. He said she's not at home, though.'

'No, Kate's at the farm. She's got a stall there today.'

'Maybe it's better that I go and find her then, rather than breaking the news over the phone. Thanks for the tea and the company.'

'My pleasure, Adam. Thanks for making sure Wenna got to work safely this morning; it was good of you.'

As I set off back up to the farm, they're already carving swathes into the tree. The sound of massive chainsaws going fills the air, but it's the human chain of people helping to clear the debris out of the road that is really heartening. People who were sat in their cars, locals and professionals, all working side by side in concert. The man directing the operations has his eyes and ears everywhere, and his calm but forceful guidance keeps everyone focused.

When I walk into the bakery there are people everywhere. Inside and out. The atmosphere is congenial, and Jess is keeping the kids occupied out in the courtyard by organising some fun games. As I make my way rather wearily up the stairs, it all seems a little surreal.

Ivy is buttering bread and Chelle is slicing a large ham; they both look up.

'You look drained, Adam.' Ivy hurries over to give me a hug. 'I've been worried sick. You've been gone for such a long time.'

'There's nothing to worry about. The road will soon be clear. Kate, who gave you a hand here, was her surname Enys, by any chance?'

'Yes, why?'

'It's her husband they've just taken off to hospital to get checked over. I promised him that I'd find her and drive her there.'

Ivy puts her hand up to her mouth. 'Oh no…'

'I don't think it's serious, but I need to get her there as soon as possible. You never know for sure with these things. She has a stall at the market today, I gather?'

'Just drop everything, Ivy,' Chelle says, firmly. 'I'll make up these sandwiches. You go off with Adam to break the news to Kate.'

I didn't mean to panic them, but I can't waste time. 'Thanks, Chelle.'

Ivy pulls off her hat and her apron and I follow her downstairs, lingering while she goes to grab her coat and a bobble hat. She waits until we're outside before she grabs my hand and squeezes it.

'Oh, Adam. Is he in a bad way?'

'Any sudden impact causes trauma to the body. Like any good first-aider, I checked all the basics. I think he's in shock but might have some sort of neck injury.'

We walk quickly and Ivy waves out to Erica and Daisy as we pass their stall. On the far side, squeezed into a corner, I recognise the woman standing behind a table laid out with homemade cakes and biscuits.

She glances at Ivy nervously and then at me. 'Kate, there's been an accident. I don't want to panic you, but Jack was in his car when the tree fell. He's alert and talking, the car was quite badly damaged and—'

She rushes around to look at me, her eyes full of fear. 'He's trapped in the car?'

'No. The paramedics have taken him to hospital to get him checked out. He didn't lose consciousness while I was with him, which is a good sign.'

She turns around to look at Ivy, her expression one of complete and utter distress.

'Just go, Kate. Adam will drive you. I'll get someone to look after your stall.'

I give Ivy a grateful look and with that we rush off, Kate wringing her hands, and I don't think that's down to the chill in the air.

IVY
Renweneth Farm, Cornwall

30

Ding Dong Goes the Bell and All Is Well

It took just over an hour to clear the main road past Renweneth Farm but there's still no news from Adam. He did send a text to say they were at the hospital and that he was going to hang around until Kate's Mum arrived. In the meantime, Cappy and Riley made their way back and took a well-earned break before getting into costume.

As I glance out the window, it looks like Keith and Len have everything set up ready for Father Christmas's arrival in fifteen minutes' time.

'Oh, Chelle, come and take a look!' I point across to the courtyard and she hurries over to join me. 'Jess, Lola and Daisy are all dressed up as elves. They have a little extra padding though.' I begin laughing.

'Oh, that's clever. Elf ski suits, what a fabulous idea and so apt, given the weather. My goodness, that's quite a crowd gathering. I think we're more or less done up here. What do you think? The noise level drifting up from downstairs has certainly dropped considerably so I'm guessing they're all beginning to filter outside.'

I turn around, smiling. 'And we should, too.'

'The kitchen is gleaming and even if we do run out before the end of the day, given what we've had to cater for, I think we've done an amazing job, Ivy.'

'High five, girl – we got through it!'

Our hands collide mid-air and then we both head into the stockroom. Four boxes of small bags containing half a dozen, bite-sized Christmas biscuits and a large gingerbread star have been lovingly wrapped ready for Father Christmas to hand out.

'Are we all set?'

'We are. Let's go join in the fun.'

As we head downstairs my pocket begins to buzz and I up the pace, eager to set my boxes down on the counter. It's Adam.

I'm on my way home. Jack is going to be all right. They're keeping him in overnight purely for observation. See you soon. Love and miss you!

'Why don't the three of you put on your coats and mingle with the crowd? Adam's on his way back and it's good news. I'll hang around to serve anyone who comes in, but there are only a handful of people in the café and everyone will be outside watching the festivities for at least the next hour.'

'If you're sure, Ivy, that would be great. Come on Rose,' Wenna calls over her shoulder, 'let's get togged up.'

'Shall I let Jess know the gift bags for the children are ready when they need them?' Chelle asks, joining me to look out, as she pulls on her coat.

'Please. I think they're doing the games first but she and the girls can pop in whenever they're ready.'

'Look at that bell, what a beauty!' Wenna remarks. 'The kids are going to love ringing it.'

'It's been exhausting but what a lovely day,' Rose sighs, contentedly. 'So many happy, smiling faces. And all the locals turning out to help clear the road so the festivities could continue. Renweneth Farm really has become the hub for our growing community in more ways than one.'

'Yes,' I reflect, wondering how on earth we've managed, but we did. 'Now, go and soak up the ambience.'

Rose opens the door and the little bell tinkles, followed by the strains of a beautiful choral rendition of 'The Holly and the Ivy'. I stand for a minute or two with the door ajar, breathing in the chilly air, to listen. It smells of snow and that slightly acrid assault on the nostrils of wood burning in the big brazier in the centre of the courtyard. The rumble of general chatter, laughter and screeches from the children playing chase sends a little tingle of joy running through me.

It takes me back to my earliest memory of heavy snowfall, but as I was probably... I don't know five, maybe six, it might only have been a few inches. At the time it felt like several feet. But I had this little padded all-in-one suit in cherry red with matching mittens. Dad and I went outside to build a snowman and I cried my eyes out a few days later when I woke up to find his head had fallen off as he started to melt away.

'Hey, you!' Adam looms up in front of me. 'You look sad.'

'I was remembering an old friend, one who melted away as soon as the sun appeared.' I laugh as I step back to let him inside.

'Argh.' He lets out a tired groan as he rolls his shoulders back before unzipping his coat. 'I'm glad to be home and you're all alone. Come here!'

I reach up to yank off his beanie hat and ruffle his hair as he throws his arms around my waist. 'That's better and I see you ripped your coat. It's been quite a stressful few hours for you, hasn't it? How's Kate doing?'

'Her parents turned up just after the doctor came out to let her know Jack's going to be all right. Unfortunately, he has whiplash, which is why he can't turn his head properly but they're only keeping him in overnight because of the impact with the airbag. His breathing has regulated, and she visibly sagged with relief.'

He grins at me before planting his lips on mine. When he pulls away, he just stares at me, smiling.

'Any chance of a coffee? I need to pop into the cottage for a quick shower and change of clothes before I do anything else. I won't be long, I promise.'

While I'm at the machine the doorbell tinkles and I turn around to see Jess sporting a wide smile.

'There's nothing you can say that I haven't heard a thousand times already,' she warns me. 'I know I look ridiculous, like you could bounce me off a wall, but you wait until you see Len.'

'Why? What's he wearing?'

'He's got one of these suits but he's a Christmas pudding. It's hilarious and worth every penny. I just popped in to say the games are about to start and ooh…' She walks over to the counter. 'Don't these Christmas bags look wonderful? You can count on me being a return customer next year.' She chuckles.

'Do you have time for a quick coffee? Or one to go?'

'A cappuccino to go would be great, thank you. Any news about Kate's husband?'

'Yes, he has whiplash but they think he'll be home tomorrow. You've literally just missed Adam; he's gone to take a shower. Here you go.'

'Thanks, oh… a chocolate holly leaf, very festive. Why don't you put a closed sign on the door and come out with Adam to have a wander, soak up the ambience? They'll all probably come flooding in for hot drinks after the games are over and Father Christmas has handed out the gifts. Cappy looks so realistic in his get-up. It's the blue eyes that do it and his sparkle.'

She's happy and so she should be. It took a lot of organising to make today happen and I'm thrilled it's been a success.

'Were there any problems with customers not getting through and giving up?' I ask, tentatively.

'I did a quick ask-around and most of the stallholders who had advance orders confirmed their customers turned up. Even the Treeve Perran Farm van are down to the last two but there's another hour to go yet. No one wants a surplus of turkeys left over the day before Christmas Eve, do they? But I said I'd take them off their hands if that's the case. I've space in the freezer.'

'I think it's little short of a miracle how well it's turned out, all things considered.'

'And silly me spent all that money on two fake snow machines. Look at it out there. Anyway, see you in a bit, Ivy!'

The kids are in their element. Turning the advertised snowball fight into a snowball game turns out to be great fun and everyone wants to have a go. There are three targets and if you manage to make the top tilt you get to ring the bell. And what a bell it is. In the end they hung it from a metal pole, suspended between two hefty chunks of a tree trunk. No prize for guessing where they got those from but it would have taken a dump truck to get them here so kudos to Cappy.

'Another hit!' Father Christmas bellows at the top of his lungs. 'Ring that bell!'

Everyone joins in chanting and a boy of about nine steps forward giving it his best.

'Dongggg!' The sound reverberates around the courtyard with a satisfying ring. It's such a silly thing and yet they're queuing up. The snowballs are going everywhere, of course, and a few are catching people, but it's enough to keep everyone entertained.

Adam squeezes my gloved hand and I turn to smile at him. We wander over to The Farmhouse where there's a *build a snowman* competition in progress. An area has been cleared and the snow left in distinct piles. There are four teams of two and Len is counting down the time.

They have ten minutes and it's down to the last three. One of the heads suddenly starts moving and as it rolls onto the floor there's a lot of screeching as a little girl runs after it. Members of another team are scrambling around for a nose, and someone tosses them a bottle top. Aww, one of the littlest contestants has just taken off his scarf to wrap around the snowman's neck.

'Ten, nine…' Len does the final countdown. 'Two… one and stop!'

I lean into Adam, gazing at the uneven line-up and smiling. 'They're all winners. And if we don't have another snowy

Christmas for a while, this is something that'll stick in their memories for a long time.' They all get a prize as it's not about winners and losers, it's about taking part.

We continue our journey around the courtyard. People are standing in groups chatting, one eye watching some of the fun and games. Adam and I wave to a few familiar faces from the market and when I spot Erica, she beckons us over.

'Ivy, Adam... I don't think you've met my husband, Charlie, have you?'

Adam sticks out his hand. 'We've a lot to thank your wife for, Charlie. She got Ivy out of a hole that first week helping to keep the bakery running. Merry Christmas!'

'Thanks, Adam, same to you and Ivy.'

I step forward. 'It's nice to finally put a face to a name, Charlie,' I say as he shakes my hand. 'I've heard a lot about you of course.'

'All good I hope.' He smiles back at me. 'Well, you've already made a bit of a name for yourself, Ivy. And the bakery lights up the whole courtyard. Adam, do you fish?'

He shakes his head. 'Never tried, Charlie.'

Jess suddenly appears at my side, her face radiant. 'Careful what you say, Adam, or the next calm day you'll find yourself on a boat.'

'Actually, I'd like to give it a go.'

'Cappy and I are determined to get out there again next year and we'll invite you along on our first trip. It's a bit of fun, even though we do get a tad competitive at times. We've had some wonderful catches and lots of occasions when we've come back with nowt.'

We all start laughing.

Jess touches my arm. 'I've come to steal the two of you away. As our newest residents we think you should both throw a few snowballs and get to ring the bell. Apparently, it's good luck but who knew?'

We excuse ourselves and follow her over to the targets. I slip off my gloves and pop them in my pocket. I haven't made a snowball for years but I don't rush the job. From distant memories of the boys pelting us girls in the playground at school, it has to be well compacted and firm.

My aim is atrocious and the first one misses the mark by a mile and there's a sharp "Oh" as I miss. I repeat the process and this time I zone out as I lean back and my eyes don't move from the target. It hits it square on and a little cheer goes up.

'Ring that bell!' The chanting begins and seconds later I'm surprised how satisfying it is as I grab the rope and yank it, the sound of metal on metal delighting the crowd.

Naturally, Adam scores on his first attempt and his ring has a lot more force behind it. He grins at me as he strides forward, planting a kiss firmly on my lips. 'Now that's a memory for all time, isn't it?' he whispers, a little breathless when he pulls away.

Riley and Jess walk over to join us and we have a group hug. 'It's quite a landmark day all round, guys.' As we pull apart he turns to Adam. 'Any chance you could give me a hand lighting the fireworks? They're all ready and waiting in the garden of Renweneth Manor. Father Christmas is just about to hand out the gifts and then the show will begin.'

'I'd love to. See you in a bit, honey.' Adam gives me a fleeting kiss on the cheek and he and Riley quickly disappear from sight.

Jess heads off to find her elves to assist Father Christmas and when I turn, suddenly Prudie is there at my side.

'It's quite a spectacle, isn't it, Ivy? Jess and the team have done us all proud.'

Goodness, she didn't say *Cappy* and the team and now she's a part of *us*? Well, I guess that technically she is, now I come to think of it.

'Karl's been back and forth quite frequently. I didn't know whether he's rotating the paintings or because of sales.'

'Oh, they're sellin' and better than we'd 'oped. We encourage our artists to be realistic with the prices they set. An unsold canvas just sits there, a sold one graces someone's wall and becomes a talkin' point. It's somethin' they appreciate every time they walk past it and that gives an artist a reason to continue.'

'I'm really glad it's working out. The feedback I'm getting has been very positive and people do linger to peruse the walls. It's funny, because you're right, it sparks a lot of conversation and memories, too. I've noticed that Cappy often wanders in there to sit quietly with a coffee, just gazing around.'

Her expression softens and at first I think that it's due to the delighted look on the children's faces as they each receive their present. But as I follow her gaze, she's staring at Father Christmas himself. Cappy's face beneath the fake whiskers is a joy to behold. He's having fun and it shows.

'When a man has the sea in his heart, Ivy, he longs to return to it. For Cappy some of those scenes will remind him of lost friends. But also of the good times he spent at sea, a lifetime of memories that swell his heart.'

I don't like to walk away from her, as I sense that she's feeling a little nostalgic for some reason. Maybe thinking of her late husband, although I have no idea if they had any connection to the farm in the past.

When the fireworks begin, the snow around us is forgotten and all eyes are turned to the heavens. Huge umbrellas of light burst open, the colours and explosions making us all gasp as they come and come again. It's the perfect end to what has been a truly memorable day in more ways than any of us could have expected. But it's also the start of a new tradition here at the farm and the bakery really was at the centre of it.

31

The Best Is Yet to Come!

Christmas morning is usually all about getting ready to jump in the car and go to exchange presents with family. This year our routine has been turned upside down in a good way.

With Adam's parents settled in the guest room at the bakery, my parents staying in Smithy's Cottage and Nate, Ursula and Tillie snug in one of the luxury caravans across the way, we come together at the bakery for breakfast.

There will be a total of twenty-eight of us in here this afternoon. When we extended an invite to Wenna, Gryff, Rose, Len, Chelle and her husband, Dan, Erica, Charlie and Daisy, as a thank you, we were delighted when they all accepted the offer. It just means that everyone who has been a part of the process so far will be there. Except Prudie, who regretfully declined as she's spending Christmas Day with her family at her daughter's house.

Jess texts to let me know that she started cooking the turkeys at three this morning and the first one is almost ready. Two more to go and she says The Farmhouse kitchen smells divine. She's organising her guests and they'll be leaving shortly.

'Right, everyone, are we ready to walk breakfast off?'

Many hands make light work and less than ten minutes later we gather in the courtyard, everyone keen to get a glimpse of the sea on this gloriously sunny, if frosty, Christmas morning.

*

Adam walks up behind me, throwing his arms around my waist as I tilt my head to look up at him. 'Now that's why we came to Cornwall,' I declare, passionately.

As the land falls away in front of us, all we can see from here to the horizon is a shimmery, silver-blue sea. It's like a vast piece of silk laid out, rippling as the soft breeze whispers over it. The fact that the temperature of it is freezing is neither here nor there. It's nature at her best.

I gaze along the path and see Cappy standing there next to Riley and Charlie, transfixed. The shrieks in the background come from Daisy and Lola who are jumping into little drifts of snow, although there's not much here at the edge of the cliff. It's something to do with the salt spray in the air, I've been told.

The seagulls are wheeling around above us, their constant, high-pitched calls ear-piercing. Even with the general laughter and chatter going on around us, it's still tranquil and relaxing. As long as you're wrapped up warmly winter is a joy and I could stand here all day just appreciating the scenery.

Ursula and Nate join us, Tillie sitting proudly on her father's shoulders. She's not a wee tot anymore, she'll turn two in April. Tillie has two favourite words, *no* and *Panda* – her cherished soft toy. Ironically, it's the one I gave her when she was born.

'Words can't describe this, can they?' Nate remarks, as he takes in the view. 'Thanks for inviting us, guys. I know we've been distant but we're back on course, aren't we, Ursula?'

She turns to grin at him. 'We are.'

Tillie is holding out her hands to the sky and then I realise she's pointing to the birds overhead.

'Noisy, aren't they, Tillie?' I say, copying her and she giggles.

'Birdies,' she calls out, patting her gloved hands together.

'I don't think you'd want to catch one of those,' I tell her, giving a little laugh.

We move on to join up with some of the others and I make a beeline for Mum, linking arms to stroll along with her.

'I received a Christmas card from Rach with a lovely letter

inside. She says they're giving up on the café idea but will continue to rent the kitchen facilities. They're focusing on expanding the business in other ways and she sounded hopeful.'

Mum turns to glance at me. 'I had heard on the grapevine but I'm glad she got in touch with you. Are you at peace now, Ivy… with everything?'

It's hard when something happens to you that is outside of your control but the ripples from it affect other people's lives almost as much as it does your own. It's easy to let guilt swallow you up and it did for a while.

'I think I'm finally there, Mum. Letting go isn't easy but yes, there's no point dwelling on the past, is there?'

She gives me a warm smile. 'Not when you have such a wonderful future ahead of you, Ivy. We all fear the unknown but it's seldom as bad as we imagine it to be. Everyone gathering together yesterday to trim up the café with fresh ivy, mistletoe, and bunches of spruce and eucalyptus was such fun. Normally, some of us are chained to the cooker on Christmas Eve.' She rolls her eyes, but they're sparkling with amusement. 'Others are left to lounge in front of TV. Here there's a real party atmosphere and last night my voice was a little hoarse from all the chatting and laughing I've done.'

'That touches my heart, Mum, because this is exactly what I hoped for. Jess always saw the farm as a place for friends and family to gather, not just customers. It seems that network grows by the day. Thank you for giving me the courage to take the risk.'

'Oh, my darling girl, your dad and I only ever want what's best for you.'

This Christmas is a little more magical than even my parents are expecting but that's something for a bit later.

Adam and I grab our coats to get a little fresh air. People are still content to linger around the dinner table, most too full to move yet but I need to walk it off.

'That was an amazing meal, Ivy.'

'It wasn't down to me, Adam. There were a dozen cooks in the kitchen and Jess certainly knows how to cook a turkey, or three,' I jest, but she does.

Standing here in the middle of the courtyard and gazing back at the bakery, I see that the lights are glowing both inside and out. It really is everything I hoped it would be and more, and this is a truly defining moment.

'I know it's been hard work and I appreciate just how much you've sacrificed to allow me to put my stamp on the bakery.'

Adam takes my hand in his, giving me one of his cute little smiles. 'Life happens *for* us, Ivy, not *to* us. Whether we choose to pick up the precious opportunities it presents us with is a conscious decision only we can make.'

'We certainly did that all right, although I had my doubts at the time. Luckily, it turned out just fine.'

'No, you simply weighed everything up, Ivy, before making a bold decision. You know me, I don't believe in luck, never have done. We make our own luck by being honest with ourselves and having the courage to believe we will succeed. Then it's time to get on with it without expecting everything to fall into our laps.'

Adam is right: hard work pays off but sometimes it takes a while to prove that.

'To some people, like Kate, that's how they perceive what happened to us, that we were lucky,' I reply, sadly. 'They don't know what we've been through and yet they're quick to judge.'

'That's the way people are when they're not happy, honey. In some twisted way it helps if they believe that other people have it easy and they simply don't get the breaks.'

It's troubling, as everyone deserves a chance but if they give up too easily, I can see how they can fall prey to that mindset.

'At least Kate had the good grace to apologise to me when she came to thank you for looking after Jack. It can't have been easy for her but given the trouble she caused I would have thought less of her if she hadn't.'

'Oh, that reminds me.' Adam's eyes light up. 'Earlier that day I was talking to Gryff and he said something I think you'll be delighted to hear. Apparently, Prudie has been going around telling everyone what a wonderful job you're doing.'

Now that does make me smile. 'Don't you just love it when people know they're in the wrong and then make an effort to put it right?'

Adam bursts out laughing. 'I seriously doubt that's how Prudie sees it, but I was impressed. I like to think that in the end, people judge us by what we do. We've prepared to be there for anyone if they need help. It's who we are and it doesn't matter whether it's a loved one, or a stranger.'

We lapse into silence as he places his arm around me. The happy noises emanating from the café filter out like a wave as we watch the merriment from a distance.

I draw in a deep breath and it's chilly on my teeth. 'The best thing about life are the little surprises that happen along the way,' I reflect.

'Some aren't so little Ivy,' Adam points out, 'but what a result.'

'I'm not talking about Cornwall, Adam. I have one more present for you.'

'Ivy, I thought we were doing token gifts only this year?'

'Adam, you know how I can't stomach coffee first thing in the morning? Well, I took a pregnancy test and it was positive.'

His jaw drops. 'We're having a baby?'

'Actually, I took three tests as I couldn't quite believe it and they were all positive. I don't think we should tell anyone yet as I'm probably only six or seven weeks, but I'll book a doctor's appointment after Christmas.' I grin at him. 'That was the last thing you were expecting, wasn't it? The timing is a bit unfortunate.'

Adam half-turns to stare into my eyes. 'No, it's the best gift you could ever give me, Ivy.' His voice is emotional and he throws his arms around me, hugging so tightly he takes my breath away for a moment.

'Six months ago, having a baby seemed like a distant dream that was fading fast. And now here we are… the seemingly impossible has happened. And, yes, it's a little scary going into the unknown but I wouldn't change a single thing, Ivy. Roll on the New Year because life is about to get a whole lot more exciting!'

'Today has been a reminder that, no matter what, when we all get together each time it's going to be a huge celebration. Everyday life goes on hold, and each moment is one to savour and enjoy in a very special way. It'll be like that when the baby comes.'

'Our life is never going to be boring, is it?' Adam pulls me into him, placing his lips on mine and a sense of peace and happiness washes over me. 'But now that I'm going to be a dad it changes everything. I guess it's time to set the wheels in motion now we have a valuation on Smithy's Cottage.'

His eyes are shining with happiness and my heart feels full.

'When my granddad was alive,' he continues, 'he said that *tomorrow* is the only thing a parent is supposed to live for. He was talking about the future generations of our family. Suddenly, it's not just about us, it's about the new life you'll be bringing into the world next summer. I'm a lucky man, Ivy. I know I say it all the time, but that's because it's true.'

And I'm a lucky woman. 'I love you, babe. No matter what problems life presents us with, together we'll find a way through it and out the other side. Each little hurdle makes us stronger and each success is a new high to spur us on. Always and forever, Adam.'

About the Author

LINN B. HALTON is a #1 bestselling author of contemporary romantic fiction. In 2013 she won the UK Festival of Romance: Innovation in Romantic Fiction Award.

For Linn, life is all about family, friends, and writing. She is a self-confessed hopeless romantic and an eternal optimist. When Linn is not writing, she spends time in the garden weeding or practising Tai Chi. And she is often found with a paintbrush in her hand indulging her passion for upcycling furniture.

Her novels have been translated into Italian, Czech and Croatian. She also writes as Lucy Coleman.

Acknowledgements

Writing the second book in this series of three involved several research trips back to Cornwall again, so a huge thanks to my Cornish friends who welcome me back for short breaks to reconnect and soak up the ambience.

Cornwall has always been an enchanting destination for me and whenever I visit, I return home feeling renewed and uplifted. The coastline is enchanting, but the landscape too, holds a powerful draw for me. And how I wish Renweneth Farm really existed, because it's a place I'd love to call home. One day, perhaps my husband and I will find our own perfect Cornish retreat...

I'd like to give a virtual hug to my inspirational commissioning editor, Martina Arzu – it's a sheer delight working with you! And to everyone involved in the process. From the creation of the stunning covers for this series, to the diligent eyes of the copy and line editors who polish the manuscript so expertly – without you this series wouldn't sparkle.

Grateful thanks also go to my agent, Sara Keane, for her sterling advice, professionalism and friendship. It means so much to me.

The wider Aria team and Head of Zeus are a truly awesome group of people and I can't thank you enough for your amazing support and encouragement.

To my wonderful husband, Lawrence – you truly are my rock!

There are so many family members and long-term friends who understand that my passion to write is all-consuming. They forgive me for the long silences and when we next catch up, it's as if I haven't been absent at all.

Publishing a new book means that there is an even longer list of people to thank for publicising it. The amazing kindness of my lovely author friends, readers and reviewers is truly humbling. You continue to delight, amaze and astound me with your generosity and support.

Wishing everyone peace, love and happiness.

Linn x